PRAISE FOR

THE GREENLAND BREACH

"Original and harrowing."

—*Cosmopolitan*

"Bernard Besson takes the eco-thriller to a whole new level. Masterfully paced and wondrously prescient, here is a cautionary tale where colorful characters battle both man and nature to save the planet from a combination of the two. Equal parts Clive Cussler and Michael Crichton, the story charges out of the gate and speeds in relentless fashion to a wholly satisfying finish."

—*Jon Land, bestselling author of the Caitlin Strong series*

"This is cousin to thoughtful works such as Buckell's *Arctic Rising*, but the narrative's tone and tendency toward grand spectacle resembles more lurid thrillers like *The Day After Tomorrow....* Besson constructs a complex plot and confidently portrays the grandiosity as it unfolds."

—*Publishers Weekly*

"For those who enjoy a rollercoaster of a ride with thrills galore, this book certainly delivers. For the James Bond fan, there are plenty of sophisticated gadgets, fiendishly complex puzzles and clever use of technology. If you look beneath the glossy, high-paced surface, there is a thought-provoking plea to re-examine the way we live and act today. Global warming is but one of the culprits in this story. Corporate and personal greed, national pride, inflated egos and lack of concern for the future of humanity are all equally to blame. Yet the author conveys this message without any preaching, simply by recounting an exciting adventure."

—*Crime Fiction Lover*

"Bernard Besson clearly doesn't do things by halves. Everything about *The Greenland Breach* is on a grand scale—global powers playing with global stakes, quite litera tial disaster on the grandest scale, th i that entertains while cautioning re awareness."

D1366337

Book Reviews

MORE PRAISE

"Suspense is omnipresent from beginning to end. The story navigates between climate change, subsequent natural disasters, corporate rivalries, murder, espionage, mysteries and love. Besson progressively weaves a web that entraps the readers. Each page make you want to turn the following one quicker to find out what happens next."

—*Culture et Plaisir par la lecture*

"This book is rather like one of these slightly more upmarket chocolates. It has a thick outer layer and something completely different as a filling.... It hits the sweet spot of enjoyment."

—*Thinking about books*

"A thrill ride that often felt too real to be fiction that is contained in the pages."

—*I am, Indeed Blog*

"*The Greenland Breach* was a heart-pounding adrenaline-filled thriller that I hated having to put down to eat and sleep. Right away, I felt myself being sucked into the story line.... It damn near took my breath away. I would recommend this book to fans of Clive Cussler, Michael Crichton and overall fans of thrillers that have a lot of action, adventure and laughs to balance of the seriousness of the story."

—*Turning the Pages*

"It was fascinating to read a story set on the background of global warming and cyber conflicts, with all the ugly intrigues and fights such a situation could easily lead to in a not too distant future.... If you feel bored in your little corner of the Earth and are eager for adventure, read this smart book now!"

—*Words and Peace*

"The prose is taut and fast-paced, as befits a thriller, and you can tell that Monsieur Besson really knows his stuff. Yet it has more poetry to it than some American thrillers I have recently read. The beauty and severity of Greenland is lovingly described, as is the community feel of the Montparnasse district in Paris, where the Fermatown posse work and live. In conclusion: buckle up tightly, you are in for a roller coaster of an exciting read."

—*Finding Time to Write*

The Greenland Breach

Bernard Besson

Translated from French by Julie Rose

LE FRENCH BOOK

First published in France as *Groenland* by Odile Jacob
©Odile Jacob, January 2011

English translation ©2013 Julie Rose
First published in English
by Le French Book, Inc., New York
www.lefrenchbook.com

Translated by Julie Rose
Copyediting by Amy Richards
Proofreading by Chris Gage
Cover designed by David Zampa

ISBNs:
Trade paperback: 978-1-939474-07-0
Hardcover: 978-1-939474-13-1
Kindle: 978-1-939474-94-0
Epub: 978-1-939474-95-7

The Daguerre
Village

1

SUNDAY

Lars Jensen felt the ground tremble beneath the snow. He straightened up and abandoned his position, petrified by what he was seeing to the west, toward Canada. The last phase of global warming had begun just as a big red helicopter flew past from the east. It doubtless belonged to Terre Noire, the Franco-Danish oil-and-gas company that was carrying out geological surveys.

From the rocky slopes of Haffner Bjerg, events were taking an unimaginable turn worthy of Dante. With a sound as ominous as the crack of doom, the Lauge Koch Kyst had begun to tear away from Greenland and plummet into Baffin Bay in the North Atlantic Ocean. A colossal breach a mile and a half deep was opening up in the middle of the island continent. The trench ran for miles, as if an invisible ax had just split the ice cap in two.

Terrified, Lars backed away, forgetting what he had come to the top of the world to do. He'd guessed that his presence on the slopes of Haffner Bjerg had something to do with the death of the Arctic. The advance wired from an anonymous account on the island of Jersey was every bit as incredible as the cataclysm under way.

A mist shot through with rainbows rose from the depths of the last ice age. Behind the iridescent wall, thousands of years of packed ice raked the granite surface and crashed into the sea, stirring up a gigantic tsunami. He pressed his hands to his ears to muffle the howling of Greenland as it began to die.

It took Lars awhile to get a grip. His hands were still shaking as the thunderous impact reached him. It was even more frightening than the ear-splitting sound. Greenland was plunging into Baffin Bay. In a few hours, the coasts of Canada and the United States would be flooded. He fell to his knees like a child, overcome by thoughts that had never before crossed his mind. An abyss was opening inside him, and it was just as frightening as the one in front of him. It wasn't until his fitful breathing slowed and his lungs stopped burning that he was able to get back to the tawdry reality of his own situation.

He lay down again on the hardpacked snow. With his eye glued to the sight of his rifle, he found the trail that the dogsled had taken from the Great Wound of the Wild Dog. That's where the team would emerge, heading for Josephine and the automated science base that sounded the great island's sick heart. The Terre Noire geologists were known for their punctuality, but at two thousand euros an hour, he would wait if he had to. Say what you like, the end of the world was good business.

PARIS, FOURTEENTH ARRONDISSEMENT, 18 RUE DEPARCIEUX, 11:30 A.M.

John Spencer Larivière put the phone down and shot Victoire a triumphant look. It was an expression she didn't like.

"What's got into you?" Victoire asked.

"North Land's offering me a hundred thousand euros for a mission. I've got a meeting tomorrow with Abraham Harper's wife, Geraldine."

"Where?"

"She'll let me know at the last minute."

"What kind of a job?"

"She didn't say."

"She's obviously going to ask you to investigate their European rivals, Terre Noire, Nicolas Lanier's outfit. I don't like it, John. Don't go looking for trouble. Don't forget you're French. Remember where you come from."

"Still, a hundred thousand euros..."

Victoire moved closer. Ever since John had set up his own business, he had agonized over not being able to measure up. They were in the red. She rarely saw him smile these days. She slipped her hand into his pants and confirmed what she'd already guessed. "That Canadian woman has an effect on you."

"She does not."

"Come here, you idiot."

They had met working in the government intelligence agency Hubert de Méricourt directed. Victoire and John wanted to have a baby, which was why they had quit together to start Fermatown, their own strategic- and criminal-analysis company. As the daughter of a Cambodian Khmer Rouge survivor and a French diplomat, Victoire bore a heavy legacy. After a spectacular nervous breakdown and a period of uncompromising psychoanalysis, getting pregnant had become her obsession. She wanted a son who would look like his father, a good-looking hunk, five feet eleven, with irresistible blue eyes and the blond mane of a movie star. John was a real man with simple ideas, a gentle giant who could massage her feet while getting his Cambodian and Cantonese hopelessly mixed up.

They left the media room and stepped into the space they called the confessional, where they settled into the welcoming arms of the black sofa. Their clothes soon lay where Fermatown's rare clients sat. John kneaded that supple body yet again and made Victoire's cheeks glow. She opened her eyes wide and encouraged him with her dancer's hips. They grabbed pleasure by the handful as though it were the last time. Or the first.

Putting aside their old wounds and disappointments, they made sweaty love, falling off the sofa and onto the teak floor. Now they were nothing more than two balls of rage. Watching as though he were outside himself, John pinned her delicate wrists to the floor and prepared his assault. Wildly, he thrust faster and faster, and, when the moment came, he grunted like an animal, shooting into this flesh that was torn, as he was, between two continents and two histories.

Out of breath, they slid next to each other. And then, holding hands and looking up at the ceiling, they started bickering again.

"With a hundred thousand euros, we could redo the kitchen and get new cars."

"A hundred thousand euros and a bullet in the head. Don't go there, John."

"I'll send Luc to Le Havre. That's where Terre Noire has its lab. I saw something on television. They sent one of their ships to inspect the lava that spewed into the ocean the last time Eyjafjallajökull erupted in Iceland. It wouldn't hurt to find out more."

"This is way beyond us. Everything about the North Pole reeks of ashes and disaster."

"I want to go there."

"You just want to prove to yourself that you can still stick your neck out and act like an idiot. You're worried about what your former colleagues think—all those people we wanted to get away from."

"I'm sick of sitting around reading CVs all day. I didn't start Fermatown to fact-check biographies and trawl through social networks looking for witnesses."

"Typical man. Too proud to ask the agency to pay us an hourly rate."

"You're starting to annoy me!"

John bounded to his feet and ran upstairs to the bathroom. Victoire was right, and that put him in a foul mood. Ever since Afghanistan, he had failed at everything. He couldn't even get her pregnant. He punched the railing of the staircase to the third floor. He had inherited this rambling four-story duplex and garden from an aunt. The property was situated between the Rue Déparcieux and the Rue Fermat, just outside the village on the Rue Daguerre.

This poisoned chalice of a gift had won Victoire over and tipped the scales in favor of her decision to leave the agency. John's aunt, Alicia Spencer, had been an eccentric American sculptor who had split her time between Montparnasse in Paris and Princeton, New Jersey. She had filled the lawns of Princeton with her creations, melted down and molded in the kiln that took up a whole room on the first floor. John had barely known her, but his aunt's presence could be felt on all four floors of this place, which was also Fermatown's headquarters. Pierre de Fermat, the mathematician who had given his name to the street, had helped baptize the firm John had started, which offered strategic advice and did criminal investigations. Unfortunately, there were a lot more unfinished sculptures and metal-cutting machines within Fermatown's walls than there were meaty investigations and consultations paid in full and on time. The sleepy old house was anxious for clients the same way a taxpayer yearned for a tax break. Victoire was not going to keep him from grabbing their first real job.

THE COMMAND BRIDGE OF THE BOUC-BEL-AIR, *6:50 A.M.*

Le Guévenec went to the screen and peered at it. It had been one disaster after another since they had left Le Havre. Surely this one would be the last. Terre Noire's geostationary satellite was filming the events live. The whole Lauge Koch Kyst crust had broken away from Greenland at 6:31 a.m. and had slid into the ocean, taking the village of Nugssuaq and its two hundred inhabitants with it. The ice had shattered into dozens of floes, each the size of a Paris arrondissement. And all that ice was driving a monstrous wall of water ahead of it.

Filmed from an altitude of twelve thousand feet, the *Bouc-Bel-Air* looked like a toy sitting in a puddle, but the camera picked up every detail. The two cages holding the bears saved from global warming were perfectly visible, as were the lifeboats and the yellow submersible attached to the rear deck.

The giant wave moved at an alarming speed. White spots in front of it caught the captain's eye. "What's that?"

"Icebergs, Captain."

"That big?"

"Yes."

Despite its powerful engines, the *Bouc-Bel-Air* could not escape the disaster. The shock wave was moving faster than the ship and would inevitably catch up to it. "How long before impact?" Le Guévenec asked in a controlled voice.

"Five minutes. Maybe six," the first mate replied.

He didn't have a lot of time to decide how they would die. The barometer, which had been stuck on good weather for hours, annoyed him, but he didn't let it show. Every shipwreck hid something incongruous, some overlooked detail nobody cared about.

Le Guévenec stroked his cheeks and thought about Isabelle. It didn't surprise him that he didn't feel anything. He was going to die as he had lived. Stupidly and without hate. Was he capable of feeling anything real? Even death didn't move him. What would he feel in the face of that horror? Was there anything worse than this indifference to everyone and everything? Le Guévenec didn't like himself much, and he wouldn't be sorry to go. Professional decency and a seafarer's exactness were his only reasons for deliberating. He made his decision.

"Port side, all the way!"

The captain of the Bouc-Bel-Air would face the wave head-on. The ship meant for scientific research groaned from top to bottom and in less than three minutes managed to point its bow at its destiny. Le Guévenec brought his binoculars to his eyes and stared death in the face. The mates around him were silent. Each sailor, pupils dilated and lips dry with fear, had his eyes fixed on the horizon. "It" finally appeared. Right in front of them.

"My God..."

An ocean above the ocean was hurtling toward them. Sharp crests like the peaks of the Alps shook convulsively between roiling chasms. The mass was driving mountains of ice. The monumental icebergs created by the cataclysm crashed against each other ahead of the massive wall of water.

The men on the bridge followed their captain's lead and attached their safety belts to the metal rails. An immense white pyramid, jagged with deadly edges, sailed past a few yards away on the port side before disappearing.

Day turned to night. The wail of the wounded ocean filled the crew with terror. The ship plunged bow-first into the valley of water that separated it from hell and kept going down. Then it steadied and straightened with an ominous sluggishness. Straight ahead, less than five hundred yards away, an enormous wave came at them like a combine harvester bearing down on a single stalk of wheat.

Terror set their bodies on fire and distorted their faces. The huge thing filled the world. It seemed to pick up speed. The water blew the windows and doors out and tore up everything that wasn't welded to the deck. Le Guévenec stopped thinking and felt himself swept away, with the boat attached to his belt, in a gigantic whirlpool of icy black mud. The descent into the underworld took a long time. The roiling water shook his body and made his limbs useless. He was nothing more than a dislocated thing at the bottom of an ice-cold vat.

Death tasted of salt. Standard for a seaman. But it wasn't exactly what he had imagined. Why all the dull, metallic sounds? Le Guévenec felt something move beneath him and found himself lying on the bridge of the Bouc-Bel-Air, chucking his guts up like a tuna on the deck of a trawler. The sea was full of debris and flowed around him like lava. He dragged himself toward the bulkhead, his hands gripping the safety rails, and managed to pull himself up.

The vessel had survived, but it was a mere shell of its former self. The barometer, still indicating good weather, was the only thing that seemed to be intact. The darkness suddenly lifted, and a blinding light lit up the heap of ruins. Le Guévenec could see the first mate's bare feet sticking out from under a gangway. The door was gone. The officer was no longer moving. Le Guévenec shook one of his legs and then examined himself. He was all there. The Bouc-Bel-Air was pitching on a calm sea. He snapped open the ring that held him to the rail and crawled toward the bare feet.

The first mate's head had hit the side of the gangway. Blood was running from his half-open mouth. No hope. Le Guévenec got up and started taking his clothes off. There was no one else on the bridge. The others had been swept away. His survival depended on finding dry clothes in the cabinet above his bed, and fast. He went downstairs to the lower deck. Dread took over, when, half-naked, he opened the door to his cabin.

Still in shock, he didn't immediately comprehend the drama that rushed at him. The boatswain was there, holding his severed forearm, which was oozing blood. Le Guévenec recognized the watch. He had seen it on the Spaniard's arm when he'd caught him trying to hide a box in the hold.

The boatswain, whose hair had suddenly gone white, stared at him in a way that no one had ever stared at him before. His inhuman cry matched that of the polar bear that had gotten out of its cage and hunted the man down. Le Guévenec was just in time to see the bear disappear, a big red stain on its fur. He grabbed the mutilated man, pulled him farther into the cabin, and locked the door.

He seized a cloth and handed it to the victim. Blood was spurting fitfully from the open wound. The pale white bone stuck out like a leek from the torn flesh. It took some cajoling to persuade the seaman to let go of his detached forearm and put it on the sink.

Le Guévenec removed his belt and tried to tie a tourniquet around the severed arm. But then, in the bathroom mirror, he saw the wounded man's back, and he almost vomited. The bear had literally boned the poor bastard, whose pink lungs looked like delicate sponges, still breathing on either side of his exposed spine, until they slowed and stopped. Le Guévenec passed his hand over the dying man's forehead, the same man who had betrayed his trust. "Everything's going to be all right."

He laid his body on the floor of the cabin and closed his eyes. Then he took out his cell phone. After several seconds, he reached Terre Noire's headquarters on the Champs-Èlysée and spoke with the chairman's personal secretary. "This is Le Guévenec, the captain of the *Bouc-Bel-Air*."

"You're still alive?"

"Tell Monsieur Lanier we're in distress."

"We're sending you help from Nuuk. Who's screaming like that?"

"A bear."

"How are Romain Brissac and the other scientists?"

"I'm going down now. There might be other survivors."

"What about the ice cores?"

"I'll worry about them later."

Le Guévenec hung up and dumped his wet rags before putting on his ceremonial uniform, the only dry clothes he could find in the waterproof cabinet. He slipped an oilskin over his fisherman's jersey, then wiped his feet and put on new boots. He cocked an ear before opening the door a crack, his heart beating fast. The bear had vanished, leaving behind a bloody trail diluted by seawater. He followed the tracks all the way to the command bridge. Blood had dripped over the helm and the navigational instruments, but the barometer was still stuck on good weather. The predator had taken one of the external staircases and gone back to the other bear. Le Guévenec saw them a few yards below him, going round and round on the bow. He looked up and saw a launch that had been cut in two by the tidal wave and rammed into a transmission mast on the poop deck. He gripped the hull and, with what little strength he had left in his arms, made a temporary barricade to keep the bears from climbing back up.

Next, he crawled to the stairs that led to the wardroom of the scientific mission that the *Bouc-Bel-Air* was to take back to France after its Greenland expedition. How many men had survived the tipping of the boat?

After an interminable descent into the icy depths, he managed to force open the door to the dining room. A flickering emergency lamp lit the room. Everything was in disarray. A man with a bandage on his forehead looked at him as though he were from another planet. Le Guévenec recognized him as the mission biologist, who doubled as a doctor. Unable to speak, the scientist pointed to the bodies of two men lying facedown on the floor. The large pool of blood and seawater left no doubt as to their condition.

"What about Brissac?" asked Le Guévenec.

The biologist turned his head toward a scientist in one of the metal chairs around the large table. Romain Brissac was staring at the two dead men. Le Guévenec went over to him. The Nobel Prize-winning chemist sensed his presence and looked up. "How did you do it?"

Le Guévenec did not understand the question, but he saw the blood running over the director of the scientific mission's hand, which he held close to his chest.

"You're hurt."

"It's nothing. Take me to the samples."

Brissac's mettle was as strong as the *Bouc-Bel-Air*'s tempered steel. He refused the captain's help and limped toward the gangway. Le Guévenec followed. The ice cores the ship was taking to France were the most precious cargo carried on the high seas since the invention of sailing. The two men went into the wrecked belly of the *Bouc-Bel-Air*. The refrigerated hold containing the samples was locked behind an armored door capable of resisting a rocket attack.

Brissac and Le Guévenec were the only ones who had the code needed to open the room, and each had only half of the code. Terre Noire didn't put all its eggs in one basket. The stakes in terms of potential energy were a million times higher than all the nuclear arms on the planet. Brissac and Le Guévenec entered their halves of the code. After a few troubled seconds, the door opened, and they anxiously stepped inside.

The flooding and the break in the main electrical circuit had set off the automated lighting system in the refrigerated hold. The blinding light contrasted starkly with the darkness that covered the rest of the *Bouc-Bel-Air*. Exhaling clouds of condensation, the two survivors advanced and found dozens of cylinders securely clamped to the walls. They leaned over the cylinders of ice, each a good ten inches in diameter. Recovered 7,710 to 7,720 feet below the surface of Greenland's ice sheet in the region of Avannaa, the samples contained the archives of the world's climate for the last hundred and fifty thousand years. Glaciologists had never before been able to go back much further than a hundred and twenty-thousand years.

"They're intact."

Le Guévenec turned to Brissac. The scientist was mesmerized by the find they had brought out of Greenland's depths. Right there in front of them, the collected ice held the secrets of the Eemian period, the holy grail of glaciologists and climatologists. Beginning a hundred and thirty-one thousand years ago, the Eemian period was characterized by a sudden warming of the planet that lasted fifteen thousand years. Hippopotamuses frolicked in the Rhine River valley. The water level was eighteen feet higher. Whole regions like the Paris Basin, the south of England, and Denmark were submerged. And then, suddenly, the Earth had reverted to ice before warming up again eight thousand years before Christ.

"You don't look so good."

Through the fog of his own breath, Le Guévenec could see the bluish tinge on the face and the dark circles under the eyes of the world's most famous and most controversial climatologist. Heart attack. Luckily, the *Bouc* was equipped with defibrillators.

"Where in God's name are they?"

PARIS, MONTPARNASSE, THE INDIANA CLUB, 12:30 P.M.

The patrons turned their heads toward the couple who had just swept through the door. Victoire was sporting a short tartan kilt and a pink shirt she'd bought at the Silk Road, a fashionable shop on the Rue Daguerre. Her dark eyes, laughing and intelligent, didn't know how to sulk. John, who was wearing white pants and had a navy-blue sweater draped over his shoulders, followed in her wake, displacing a mass of air in proportion to his bulk. The two were stunning and always aroused curiosity. Even fondness. Every Sunday at the same time, the founding members of Fermatown would come to the Indiana Club to play pool. Luc, the third partner, dressed in black, was sitting under a green light at the last table. Standing at his side, a sculpted young Adonis in tight jeans and a mauve polo shirt was staring intently at the colored balls.

The son of a technology whiz from Lyon, Luc had followed in his father's footsteps. After his father's business went bust and he'd died a tragic death, Luc had allowed Hubert de Méricourt to scoop him up. But Luc was uncomfortable in the official intelligence milieu because of his bisexuality and unconventional ideas. He asked for clearance to go somewhere else, where he could think and work outside the box.

Méricourt gave permission, and because he admired him, he put Little Luc, as he was called despite his six-foot-two height, in touch with a celebrity in the field—John. Luc and John met at Les Invalides, in the ground-floor office that was the lair of the head of France's shadow diplomacy.

"Little Luc," Méricourt had said, "let me introduce you to John Spencer Larivière, who's just back from Afghanistan, where he was a member of the ground intelligence team. He's like you. He wants a bit of fresh air. Team up with him. You won't regret it."

A little surprised, John didn't waste any time trying to figure out exactly what Méricourt's interest in this professional marriage might be. Luc flourished in John and Victoire's company, demonstrating outstanding talents.

Concentrating on his shot, Luc had stopped breathing. His cue slid between his fingers. The ball rolled straight toward one of the sides before changing direction and hitting another ball the same color, immediately propelling it into a corner pocket.

"Bravo."

"Not bad, huh?"

Luc tossed a lock of black hair out of his dark eyes and looked up at the two other members of Fermatown.

"I've got something to tell you," John whispered.

"Don't worry, he's German. He doesn't understand a word of French."

"Where'd you find him?"

"In Berlin, at a hackers conference. He's a totally inoffensive geek. Eh, Hermann, you're harmless, aren't you?"

The young German cracked an approving smile. There was no ambiguity about the fascination the visitor from across the Rhine felt for the tall, dark young man who was teaching him how to play pool. And a few other things. Victoire didn't let any of her annoyance at the unexpected presence of the stranger show, but she led Luc to the other side of the table so the guy could not overhear her whispering. Luc leaned in close.

"We've been sought out by Geraldine Harper, the head of North Land, Terre Noire's rival oil-and-gas prospectors. We came to talk to you about it. We don't know what she wants yet, but she's ready to put a lot of money on the table."

Luc raised an eyebrow and smiled. He moved farther away from the German and set up his shot. Fermatown ran like clockwork, but because of the financial crisis, clients were few and far between. Luc didn't want to return to the Boulevard de la Tour Maubourg and ask Méricourt for his old job back. "I know why Geraldine Harper called John," he said.

"Why?"

John and Victoire stared at their colleague in disbelief. Luc chalked his cue and raised it over the green baize. He aimed it at a corner of the large room and shouted to the bartender, "Sound, maestro!"

All three of them looked at the Indiana Club's plasma screen, where images of the latest global catastrophe were being relayed over and over again. There was footage of a ship drifting in a field of ice. In the United States and Canada, the East Coast was holding its breath, waiting for the wave to hit. No one had prepared for this, unlike the eruption of Eyjafjallajökull and the fires in Russia. Panic was spreading from one city to the next all along the Atlantic seaboard. Luc let John and Victoire immerse themselves in the situation and then added his own commentary. "It happened this morning, while you were so busy."

Victoire lowered her eyes. Luc made her laugh, but sometimes he disconcerted her. He was like her, blended, double-edged, not quite fitting in. His expression turned serious.

"The ship's red and black. Those are Terre Noire's colors. It's called the *Bouc-Bel-Air,* and it's probably going to sink. CNN reckons it was heading back to Greenland after prospecting in the Barents Sea. It seems that one of the people onboard is Romain Brissac, who won the Nobel Prize for chemistry and has some hard-hitting ideas about global warming." Luc took a breath and cut to the chase a little smugly. "I guess North Land would give anything to know what the *Bouc-Bel-Air* is carrying. That's what she's going to ask you."

"Little Luc, you're a genius!"

"How much is she offering?" Luc asked.

"A hundred thousand euros," John replied.

"You can ask for double that. The world's falling apart, and whatever the *Bouc-Bel-Air* has in its hold must be priceless."

"Victoire won't hear of it. She thinks it's a lousy deal. Terre Noire is a Franco-Danish company. She doesn't want us working for its rivals, the Canadians."

Luc studied Victoire. That sweet smile was like the surface of a lake, one whose depths he rarely saw. Despite the confidence she inspired in him, he still hadn't managed to figure her out.

"We didn't leave the agency to live on government pensions."

Victoire shrugged.

"Let's go and get some air."

Luc took leave of his German and joined the others outside on the Rue Froidevaux. They turned onto the Rue Fermat and walked past Number 9, one of the two entrances to Fermatown, and found themselves back in the village. On Sundays and holidays it was closed to cars from one end to the other. Passing La Bélière, the restaurant where Luc played piano on Wednesday nights, they waved to Colette and Krisna, who were posting the daily specials on the sidewalk. At the corner of the Rue Gassendi, John looked up hopefully at the building that housed the studios of Jean-Luc Miesch, the director of *Streamfield*, who had promised him a role. In her final years in Montparnasse, Alicia Spencer had redesigned the studio façade in a fanciful style that reminded him of the Sagrada Familia in Barcelona.

Flanked by Luc and Victoire, John walked in the middle of the road, freed of cars but cluttered with Velibs, Paris's popular rent-a-bikes. Geraldine Harper's industrial espionage mission for North Land and the hundred thousand euro advance rendered them speechless, puzzled, and suspicious. At the Rue Boulard, John was the first to break the silence. "She didn't exactly say it'd be espionage."

"Like that's the kind of thing you spell out on the phone," Victoire shot back, laughing.

"I'm going to buy some cheese, and then we'll go home. We've got work to do. We'll have lunch another time."

They stopped in front of the *fromager*. John had saved the cow sign one night, when some kids had set upon it. They were planning to put it in their truck and sell it to a collector. In three punches, Major John Spencer Larivière, fresh from the hills of Afghanistan, had KO'd the three hoods before allowing himself to be arrested by the local cops. Ever since this valiant exploit, the members of Fermatown were served first in the shops of the Daguerre village.

"And what would the lady and gentlemen like today?"

"Three small *chavignols*."

"I'll put a little bottle of chardonnay in with that, like the other day. On me."

"Thank you," John replied, avoiding Victoire's glare.

Believe it or not, John had discovered chardonnay in the American army canteens in the middle of Taliban country. He'd brought the habit back to Fermatown, much to Victoire's dismay. Her taste in wine was a tad more sophisticated.

AVANNAA, THE NORTH FACE OF HAFFNER BJERG, 8:50 A.M.

Lars Jensen stopped to study the wall of mist rising from Greenland's ripped insides. Looking through the scope of his rifle, he drew a bead on the strange green pyramid six hundred feet below that was supposed to lure the target. Since he had arrived, no one had come out of what looked like the entrance to a sort of man-made cave on the brink of the Great Wound of the Wild Dog. The structure brought to mind some sort of catheter sticking into the sick ice cap.

Large pools of water resembling man-made ponds stretched north from the foot of Haffner Bjerg. Dark moldy-looking splotches clung to the edges of the lakes. Neither the wind nor the cold could chase away the smell of putrefaction coming off these fermenting cesspools. Lars had had plenty of time to observe the phenomenon, protecting his nostrils with a mask he'd picked up during the last outbreak of bird flu.

The dark-green blotches were seething with tiny, nearly imperceptible bubbles. Greenland was rotting before his eyes. His cell phone rang and flashed the number they'd agreed on. Lars adjusted the angle of his scope to see the trail. A few minutes later, a dogsled appeared in his line of fire. He took a deep breath, wedged the butt of his rifle against his shoulder, and waited a few seconds. The driver raised his hand above the team of dogs and signaled for them to slow down.

Lars gently pressed the trigger with the index finger of his right hand. The shot left the barrel with a dull sound, and he felt the recoil against his shoulder. He took another breath. The Inuit had rolled backward. With one leg strapped in the sled, the poor man was being dragged along like a dislocated puppet.

Lars aimed at the passenger stretched out in his anorak. The second victim was still unaware of the drama unfolding. The next shot had a less spectacular effect. The man's head just rolled to the side. The third bullet followed immediately, more for form's sake than real necessity. Lars knew the first two hits were final.

The dogs surged ahead, then stopped outside the entrance to the pyramid. The barking ceased and was soon replaced by heart-rending wailing that rose all the way to Haffner Bjerg despite the gusting wind. Lars aimed at the leader of the pack, a magnificent animal, and fired. As it crumpled to the ground, he discharged ten more times.

After a three-hundred-and-sixty-degree survey, he fired up the snowmobile and left his shooting point. His employers were very specific about the next step in the plan. Straddling his vehicle, he raced down the slope and was at the scene in less than a minute. He approached the passenger he had just shot, lifted the man's hood, and removed his sunglasses with gloved hands. He took a photo of his victim and sent it to the e-mail address they had given him. He did the same with the Inuit.

In terms of cryptography and data protection, his client was at the top of his game. Nothing to fear on that front. What worried him was the completely unexpected nature of the circumstances, which no one had given him the lowdown on. He looked toward the west, still stunned by what he had seen. Columns of water and mist rose to an unimaginable height, blocking the horizon like an enormous wall. The men he had just killed knew the reasons behind these natural events. Lars would have liked to know, too.

Surprised by death, his victims looked tranquil. The nearly transparent blue eyes of the passenger were fixed on the sky. A frozen red stain branded his forehead, a forehead that looked intelligent. Too intelligent, no doubt. Lars envied them for leaving the planet before he did, and he told himself that he had done a good deed.

PARIS, 18 RUE DEPARCIEUX, 1:30 P.M.

John, Luc, and Victoire walked back to Fermatown via the Rue Deparcieux, which was parallel to the Rue Fermat. Surrounded by a garden visible from the sidewalk, the huge house usually cost a fortune to heat. But winter hadn't arrived this year. Global warming had saved Fermatown's finances.

The sun had set the neighborhood ablaze. Spring would be a scorcher. John told himself there had to be a way to accept Harper's offer. There was no point in resorting to espionage to find out what Terre Noire was hiding. Ninety percent of all corporate information was freely available to the public, especially in France. All you had to do was ask the right people the right questions and search the appropriate databases. As was his habit, John quickly glanced up and down the street before unlocking the garage door. They savored the semi-darkness of this space, where they parked the two cars and the two motorbikes that constituted Fermatown's fleet. He left Luc to close the door behind them and bent down to Caresse, the Persian house cat. "Come here, gorgeous," he said as he picked her up.

They took the spiral staircase up to the second floor. When they reached the big main room, Victoire asked the touch screen wall to light up and display the news channels. Hubert de Méricourt had asked Fermatown to test this latest technology before installing it in the agency's offices at Les Invalides. The prototype was nine feet high and six feet wide. The wall responded to fingerprint and voice command. It could show television channels, websites, newspapers, and documents from databases and had a host of apps.

Forgetting the cheese and wine, they stood glued to the screen. After inundating Baffin Island and the Labrador coast, the Greenland tsunami was heading for the mouth of the St. Lawrence River. Boston and New York were filled with scenes of panic. The most predictable of catastrophes was taking the world by surprise. Several Canadian ports had been submerged by a wave more than twelve feet high. The number of victims was still unknown, but a Quebec channel was talking about scores of deaths and extensive damage. Photos of two faces kept popping up on the news channels: the climatologist and Nobel Prize winner Romain Brissac and Loïc Le Guévenec, captain of the *Bouc-Bel-Air*.

"Shall we?" Luc asked.

"Go ahead."

Of the three of them, young Luc was the trailblazer, clearing their way by looking at problems from unexpected angles. More than a few times, John and Victoire had been impressed by Luc's unusual approach to situations that the cautious administrators at Les Invalides would never have thought of. In general, the administrators hated creativity. With a flick of his hand, Luc erased all the TV screens.

He brought up a mauve background. Like a croupier at a blackjack table, he fanned out the photos of Loïc Le Géuevenec and his ship, taken both before and after the catastrophe.

"Let's start with the captain. If we stick to the facts, we have a man who must know a hell of a lot about what's behind the disaster and the secrets of the North Pole. These are two subjects that would interest Mrs. Harper, since her husband runs North Land, the large rival oil-exploration company."

"The captain looks like a real fun guy."

Victoire approached one of the photos that Luc had just posted and pulled up some more pictures. The touch screen wall brought up several shots taken from public and private databases in the merchant navy.

"He's not very talkative, but he looks honest. If I had a dangerous and confidential mission, I'd give it to this Breton," Victoire said, studying Le Guévenec's face.

"You've always had a thing for sailors," John quipped.

"French marines pulled my mother out of the South China Sea. Le Guévenec looks to me as steadfast as a stone monument in a storm."

"We need to find out what he knows. This guy's the key," said Luc.

"If he's still alive," John replied.

Luc asked the wall for the latest images of the *Bouc-Bel-Air* and opened a window dedicated to news flashes. It quickly became apparent that the ship was listing but hadn't sunk. Luc selected a bright color from the bottom of the screen and moved a red arrow to another part of the screen, where he opened a site dedicated to Terre Noire. North Land's French rival often made the news in relation to earth sciences. He brought up satellite photos of Le Havre and asked for a display of the corporate profile, based on annual shareholder reports. The role played by the captain and his ship quickly became clear. The maritime branch of Terre Noire, whose headquarters were on the Champs-Élysées, employed Le Guévenec. Luc displayed the phone numbers and picked up one of the disposable cell phones that Fermatown kept in reserve for tricky operations.

"I'm calling Terre Noire."

"You're crazy!" Victoire cried.

"If we want to know what the *Bouc-Bel-Air*'s got in its bowels, we might as well ask the captain. Then we won't be going around in circles. John can make the recording and see if Harper's interested in the conversation. We're not going to spy on the guy. We're just going to talk to him, to comfort him."

John shook his head, but ever the good manager, he stood back. Luc amused and interested him. Victoire looked dubious.

"Let him be," he told her.

Luc switched to speakerphone and waited for someone to pick up. First he got a recorded message: "You've reached the offices of Terre Noire. A member of our staff will answer your call shortly."

Luc waited to get a human being on the line and when he did, he was both courteous and authoritative.

"Hello, could you please transfer me to your crisis team?"

"What are you talking about?" sputtered the woman on duty. "It's Sunday.

"I understand," Luc responded. "My call is urgent. Please put me through."

"Just a moment, I'll connect you to someone."

John and Victoire sighed in relief, and Luc motioned to them to be ready to take notes and pull up information on the screen.

"This is Claudine Després. Who's calling please?"

"This is Marc Racine. It's about the events in Greenland."

"Call back later. We're not giving out any information just now."

"I don't want to ask you anything. I'm calling with urgent information for Captain Le Guévenec."

The person on the other end of the line hesitated.

"What kind of information?" she asked in a shrill voice.

"Medical. His health depends on it. I'm his doctor, and I've just seen my patient's condition on television."

"Hold the line."

The three heard whispering brought on by Luc's request. Terre Noire's headquarters seemed to be in a shambles.

"What kind of medical information?"

"I'm his attending physician, and I'm bound by professional confidentiality. I've got a plane to catch in half an hour. Give me a number quickly where I can reach Captain Le Guévenec. He's in danger of dying."

The Fermatown trio was crowding around the phone in feverish anticipation. On the other side of the Seine, on the Champs-Élysées, another team, caught off guard, was attempting to make a decision in a hurry. After a few minutes, someone responded by giving the cell phone number of the *Bouc-Bel-Air's* skipper. Luc thanked him and started to breathe again.

He entered the number on the wall and made the call by tapping it twice. Then he pulled a web cam up, just in case Le Guévenec appeared.

"If he shows, *you're* the one who'll have to play doctor," Luc told John. "I'm too young. I've got no credibility."

John accepted the challenge and stepped up to the virtual window. Victoire planted her hands on her cheeks and listened to it ring. She couldn't believe what was happening. Those two were going to drive her nuts. How could a soldier like John let this kid lead him by the nose?

A face the color of cement appeared in the middle of the touch screen. The captain of the *Bouc-Bel-Air* seemed out of breath. John stood squarely in front of him.

"Who are you?" asked Le Guévenec.

"Marc Racine. I'm a doctor. Headquarters has permitted me to call you to offer remote medical and emotional monitoring. How are you feeling?"

"Bad, exhausted."

"What do you need?"

"To get back in touch with Nicolas Lanier as soon as possible. I have some extremely serious things to tell our chairman. It's unbelievable. Nobody can be bothered to get him for me!"

"We'll take care of it. What else can I do?" asked John.

Caught off guard, Loïc Le Guévenec stared at the man speaking to him.

"Reassure my wife, Isabelle. I still haven't had time to warn her. If *I* tell her everything's okay, she won't believe me. But if *you* tell her..."

"Could you give me her number?"

John chose another color and wrote the number the captain gave him on the wall.

"Be careful. Her nerves are more fragile than mine."

"Don't worry. We'll send someone to see her immediately."

"Thank you. Call me back later. I'm very busy."

The image of the captain vanished, along with his voice. The three members of Fermatown moved away from the wall, amazed by what they had accomplished. In less than ten minutes, they had gotten right in the middle of the action.

"Now what?" asked Victoire.

"Luc will call Isabelle Le Guévenec and try to find out what's eating her husband. If we can satisfy Geraldine Harper's curiosity, we collect the jackpot!" declared John.

"Drop it. You're acting like kids. You're nuts. This whole thing has smelled fishy from the beginning!" Victoire said, aggravated by the two men.

She felt like she was on the edge of an abyss, with two idiots in tow, about to leap into a trap set by either a jealous rival or a foreign secret service.

"Why would North Land suddenly take an interest in us? We're nothing on the geostrategic chessboard."

"That's precisely why: we won't arouse suspicion."

John put on his stubborn look, the one he had worn trudging up and down the hills of Afghanistan, she imagined.

AVANNAA, THE NORTH FACE OF HAFFNER BJERG, 9:50 A.M.

When his phone vibrated after he had sent the pictures of the two dead men, Lars knew his instincts were right. The mission wasn't over yet. Something told him it was as rotten as the ice cap's breath. The cataclysm had definitely changed the deal. His contact was bestowing another two hundred thousand euros on him for an extra job he already regretted accepting. Who said he was just a killing machine?

After making sure the money had been transferred to his account in the Channel Islands, he started the snowmobile and reluctantly sped downhill. The unbearable smell forced him to put a wool balaclava over his mask. He pulled up to the pyramid, which was made of plastic and reinforced with steel plates. An opening on one side served as the entrance to a tunnel that sank into the depths of the ice cap. He took a few steps into the milky light coming from the transparent walls. The tunnel was big enough for a large snowplow. He placed a hand on the wall of ice and continued inside. The sloping floor led to a bend. The light along the archway was green. He quickly saw why. Translucent algae were growing on the ice, clinging to the curved walls here and there. But most of it lay dead on the ground. The sight of all these dying plants made his skin crawl.

He kept going, past tall racks of long plastic tubes that contained ice. There were hundreds of tubes. Terre Noire was taking samples from the deepest part of the ice sheet to remove any doubt about the cooling and warming of the planet and the consequences. After passing the tubes, he found himself in front of a transparent cabinet six feet tall and twenty inches deep. Computer screens blinked behind fogged glass.

Electrical cords in all colors ran out of the cabinet, connecting it to both the floor and the roof. Measuring instruments that looked like seismographs sat cheek by jowl with tape recorders and supercomputers. All of this hardware was surely hooked up to Terre Noire's land and sea laboratories, which sounded Greenland's innards around the clock. On the seismograph, he found the exact time and path of the cataclysm. The graph paper wasn't big enough to register the violence of the shock. A few yards from the cabinet, a kind of turbine hummed softly, no doubt powering the whole system. The tunnel continued farther into the guts of the continent.

He found the box where they had said it would be and gently lifted the tarpaulin. The machine was in its slipcover, next to maintenance tools. Teams came here to read the instruments and hack away at the archway, which regularly buckled and warped. The tunnel was subject to immense pressure, judging by the outgrowths that poked like fingers up from the ground and down from the roof. Some had been sawn off. The walls exuded a sticky liquid like bleached blood. On either side, a thin trickle of water ran downward to the ice cap's wounded guts. He was walking inside a cadaver whose lymphatic fluid was draining into a horrific invisible orifice.

Although the hardest part remained to be done, Lars was relieved to get out of the tunnel. He went to the snowmobile and unfolded a clear plastic bodysuit that he put on over his clothes. Then he pulled the chain saw out of its cover. The motor started without a hitch. The two men and the eleven dogs spurted geysers of blood and flesh as he cut them up. The snow all around the sled turned scarlet. Lars suddenly remembered a wild chant he had sung on the beaches of Jutland. He started singing the first verse to loosen up a bit.

It took an hour to cut up the two men and the team of dogs. There was no one on the horizon. Once the work was done, Lars checked his cell phone to see if the information on his snowmobile's biometric radar was right. Throughout the operation, the system hadn't recorded any source of heat within a five-mile radius. No witness, utter solitude. After he burned the plastic bodysuit and tossed the saw into the flames, he started the snowmobile again and left the doomed slopes of Haffner Bjerg. Another mission was waiting for him in Nuuk.

BAFFIN BAY, THE ENGINE ROOM OF THE BOUC-BEL-AIR, *10:45 A.M.*

Le Guévenec felt relieved by the call from the doctor at Terre Noire headquarters. He had never been impressed with the firm's warmth or concern for his welfare. The planet had to go haywire, and the *Bouc* had to get practically shipwrecked for them to finally ask him how he was doing. He had a keen desire to kick the arses of the snooty little creeps of the Champs-Elysées.

Exhausted, Le Guévenec and his chief engineer returned to the turbine and tried once again to start the least-damaged engine. A clanking noise and acrid smoke signaled a return to life at last in the depths of the *Bouc-Bel-Air*. They wouldn't make record time, but at least they had enough power to glide along the coast to Nuuk.

Le Guévenec looked at the ladder that led to the upper decks and thought about the bears. The female had skinned the boatswain alive. The excited male had ripped the head off one of the surviving sailors with a swipe of his paw. Driven mad by the blood, the two animals were going round and round on the deck, barring the way to the armory, where there were guns capable of putting an end to the massacre. The noise of the engines finally covered their roaring. The *Bouc-Bel-Air* was moving again. The captain looked at his greasy, blackened hands and, for the first time since he'd been sailing, wiped them on his trousers. His ceremonial uniform. The pain in his hip, which had tormented him for several days, returned instantly.

Le Guévenec left the engine room, trying to put the pain out of his mind. Amid indescribable chaos, he made his way toward the front hold. The ship had been shaken like a cocktail, and water was streaming everywhere. The safety spotlights, hesitantly coming on again, dimly illuminated a scene of desolation. After a glance behind him, he opened the door and stepped into the hold.

A steel box marked with the Terre Noire logo had intrigued him. And he hadn't liked the Spaniard's look. He had suspected him from the day Christophe Maunay, the company's human resources manager, had sent him to replace the previous boatswain. Le Guévenec tucked the box under his arm and started climbing the ladder that led to the upper deck. After slipping on the rungs several times, he reached the hatch and lifted it to survey the situation. The way was still blocked. The two bears were coming and going from port side to starboard in an unending to and fro. A few feet away, the decapitated head stuck to the base of a launch was watching him with salt-reddened eyes. A black tongue hung out of the toothless mouth, which was now invaded by flies. Where did they come from?

He vomited violently without trying to stem the flow of bile that burned his mucous membranes. The main thing was not to pass out, not to fall to the bottom of the hold. He hung on and waited for nature to do its work without daring to look at the state of his uniform. After the final heave, he wiped his nose on his sleeve and slowly climbed down the ladder. Then he beetled along the internal gangways, hugging the walls. The hardest part was navigating the list with his debilitated back. His sciatica would soon be flaring, as well.

Now he had to find out how his passengers were doing. He crossed the dining room, which had been turned into a sick bay, and asked after the wounded lying on makeshift stretchers. The smell was unbearable. He greeted the expedition's biologist who, with the aid of an able-bodied sailor, was trying to get a bit of heat into this mausoleum. From the hold, they had brought up some gas canisters that had been spared by the tidal wave.

In the flickering light, Le Guévenec looked for Brissac, having saved the man from a heart attack with the defibrillator. He felt someone grab his arm. Looking down, he didn't recognize the expedition's scientific director at first. Brissac was lying on a cabinet that had been laid on the floor to serve as a makeshift pallet. The biologist and the sailor doing duty as a nurse had compensated for the incline of the ship by sliding volumes of the *Encyclopedia Britannica* under the cabinet. Leaning over his swollen face, Le Guévenec listened to the incoherent words coming from the man's cracked lips, something about algae and ice cores.

Le Guévenec thought he heard the name Isabelle. Like the captain and his wife, the Brissacs lived in Le Havre, Terre Noire's registered port, so Le Guévenec didn't give the scientist's mention of Isabelle's name much thought. All of a sudden, the man grabbed Le Guévenec's lapel.

"The South is heading north," Brissac said. "You understand, it's monstrous. It's the South's fault."

Le Guévenec nodded, although he had no idea what the man was talking about, and tried to be reassuring.

"We're going to look after you, Romain. We've asked for help."

Brissac looked at him and attempted to add a few words, but they wouldn't come out right. Le Guévenec made an effort to smile. He gently disengaged the hand that was clutching his pea jacket and took stock of the situation with the doctor. Three of the six members of the scientific mission were dead. Two, of which Brissac was one, were seriously impaired.

"If I've got it right, you're the only one who's okay."

"Yes."

Le Guévenec approached the expedition's botanist, who was sitting in a chair with one arm in a sling, his head covered in bandages.

"How do you feel?"

"I'll be fine, Captain. When do you expect the ship to go down?"

"We're not going down. You'll be evacuated."

Le Guévenec wanted to find something to say that did justice to the circumstances, but the words refused to come, as usual. He turned on his heels and walked away instead.

Dealing with the havoc and the injured and restoring the *Bouc-Bel-Air*'s nerve centers had worn him out. He retreated to his bunk, collapsed, and slept like a log until his cell phone woke him up. It was Nicolas Lanier, executive chairman of Terre Noire.

"I'm on board a helicopter. We'll touch down on the *Bouc-Bel-Air* in ten minutes. My presence must remain a secret. You'll be the only one on the platform to meet me."

"In any case, there aren't many of us left."

Le Guévenec had trouble taking in what he'd just heard. Lanier's arrival was even crazier and more improbable than the cataclysm he'd just been through. He suddenly thought of the two bears. The wild creatures were hemmed in on the foredeck between the prow and the central forecastle. No danger on that side.

"The platform aft is clear. The tidal wave swept everything away."

"I can hardly hear you."

"That'll be fine."

Le Guévenec looked at his suddenly mute phone. Where could this helicopter be coming from?

"That's all we need."

Nicolas Lanier was renowned for his rapid decision making. The young head of Terre Noire had been an enigma from the moment he took the job.

Le Guévenec's lower back was killing him as he left his cabin to go back to the platform, located aft, over the stern. He was greeted on the bridge by icy snow falling from an utterly cloudless sky. Around the *Bouc*, chunks of pack ice stretched as far as the eye could see, like fragments of a giant's broken dinner plate. Le Guévenec registered the jerking motion the ship was now making. The driveshaft of the propeller had to be hitting something in the bowels of the boat.

He climbed up the ladder that led to the platform, maintaining his grip on every rung with gloved hands. Once there, he discovered that the raging sea had swept everything away. There was absolutely nothing left.

He lifted his head when he heard the noise of rotor blades and spotted the Eurocopter. It was red and black, Terre Noire's signature colors. Le Guévenec signaled to the pilot and got out of the way.

The huge machine described a wide circle above the *Bouc* and then hovered in position over the drop zone. The engines revved and then dropped as the aircraft descended. Le Guévenec was nervous about its landing on the incline, but the pilot put his machine down as though he were planting a kiss on a swollen cheek. He cleverly pointed the nose of the copter at the pitched slope so that the two landing skids touched the bridge at the same time without tipping the machine over.

Le Guévenec appreciated the maneuver. Terre Noire was renowned for the skill of its pilots. And its sailors. He waited for the blades to stop rotating with a well-oiled hiss and stepped forward. The door slid open, and the sole passenger, his face hidden in the hood of a yellow oilskin, leaped to the ground.

"Hello, Captain."

Lanier, looking guarded and older than his age, shook his hand. The tall sandy-haired man aimed the piercing eyes of a Scandinavian warrior at Le Guévenec. Steering a strategic oil-exploration company between a world adrift and an uncertain future was as perilous as navigating between icebergs.

"I've reserved my first mate's cabin for you. It's free."

"Thank you."

Le Guévenec led Lanier along the bulwark, then through the leaning gangways of the *Bouc*. With the oilskin covering his head, the Terre Noire head officer looked like a dripping-wet yellow ghost. They didn't pass anyone. The first mate's cabin was next to the captain's.

Le Guévenec opened the door and, after a glance down the corridor, shut it behind them.

"We haven't had time to clean up."

"Doesn't matter."

"I'll get you a gas canister and a portable heater. There'll be a bit of hot water in an hour," he said.

"That'll be perfect."

"The shower should work."

The two men sat down on either side of a table and adjusted their bodies to the table's lean. Lanier unbuttoned his oilskin and scanned the room. The look on his face conveyed that he fully understood the cataclysm that the *Bouc* and its crew had been through.

"How's Brissac?" Lanier asked.

"Heart attack, fractures, delirium."

"Did he say anything about the ice cores?"

Le Guévenec made an effort to remember the climatologist's disjointed words. Lanier looked at him the way a shipwrecked man looked at the lifebuoy on top of the wave.

"What did he say?"

"'The South is heading north.' I didn't really know what he was trying to say."

"He said that? Are you sure?"

"Yes."

Terre Noire's chairman winced like a boxer taking a hit and shook his head. His curls framed a sweaty, rough-hewn face that was animated by a ferocious will. His gray-blue eyes took in every nook and cranny as if he were searching for something.

"Don't repeat that to anyone. Not to anyone, you hear me?"

"You can count on me."

"What about the Eemian samples?"

Le Guévenec realized he was alluding to the ice cores again.

"They're intact."

"Good. No one must know I'm here. I'm going to try to get some sleep. You should, too. You look beat."

"That's what I was about to do," Le Guévenec replied.

He left the cabin and went back to lie down. What he had just read in Lanier's eyes did not augur well. After the Lauge Koch Kyst catastrophe, the *Bouc-Bel-Air* would doubtless be the last ship to carry irrefutable proof of what had happened one hundred and thirty-one thousand years earlier and of what was happening to the planet at that very moment.

Luc reassured Isabelle Le Guévenec by phone, promising to call on her the next day. Then he went to the port and headed for the zone reserved for ore carriers. Terre Noire's ships docked in that part of the port and sometimes unloaded rocks and sediments taken from all over the globe. In the minds of many people, the Franco-Danish oil company was linked inextricably with the death of Greenland. And in the space of a few hours, one of its ships, the wounded *Bouc-Bel-Air*, had become the worldwide scapegoat for climate change.

You didn't need to be a rocket scientist to figure out that a spirit of vengeance drew the crowd that had gathered at this spot on a Sunday evening. The multicolored flags and balloons in the colors of innumerable eco-organizations were playing cat-and-mouse with the police amid tear gas and sirens.

The authorities were trying as hard as they could to keep people from climbing aboard the *Marcq-en-Barœul*, the *Bouc-Bel-Air*'s twin. Luc mingled with the demonstrators and curious bystanders, eavesdropping on conversations. Everyone was following the live coverage of the tidal wave arriving in New York and flooding Manhattan. The center of the Big Apple looked like a huge poster for a Hollywood sci-fi blockbuster. But this was real. The first floors of the island's skyscrapers were bathing in water, just like the Statue of Liberty, standing lonely and shrunken on the horizon. That image was going around the world and produced a horrible feeling of powerlessness in everyone who was watching. Something final had happened.

Because the alarm had been sounded in time, the tidal wave had cost no more than a few hundred lives. But scientists were debating among themselves about how the water would recede. No one could agree on whether the billions of tons of ice that had tumbled into the ocean would cause a permanent rise in the sea level. Theories clashed, as they had during the global financial crisis. Feeding the millions of displaced people was clearly going to be a second catastrophe, one that would be much more serious than the first. Luc put his phone in its sheath and watched what was going on around him. Whatever the end of the world might look like, Fermatown had at least been paid properly to figure out its mysteries. Geraldine Harper's call to John couldn't be explained outside the events taking shape.

A giant of a man who had climbed onto the roof of a van was haranguing the sailors guarding the *Marcq-en-Barœul*. His muscles bulging, the ponytailed eco-warrior was calling for Nicolas Lanier, the media-shy head of Terre Noire, to make an appearance. Luc moved closer to the red and black hull of the ship to size up the situation and home in on any undercover operators who might be hoping to go unnoticed. His instinct, always on the alert, told him that Fermatown was not the only firm on the prowl. Terre Noire knew too much not to be watched and dissected by all the intelligence agencies and private spy outfits on the planet.

He spotted a banner held up by the Northern Peoples Congress and, close by, exactly what he was looking for in the features of a sculpted blonde poured into a scarlet dress. The Valkyrie from the Northern Peoples had more Normandy locals around her than newly independent Greenlanders. She seemed to be verbally wagging her finger at the Terre Noire sailors, as if the melting of Greenland were their fault. The mob needed someone to blame. Luc elbowed his way over to her.

Wherever he was, Luc knew how to spot the sender and the receiver of coded information. Two-legged creatures communicated via preverbal ancestral codes. Looks and gestures had not changed an iota since the days when humans lived in caves. Whether it was around a board of directors' table or a fire where meat was being roasted on a spit, the nonverbal communication was the same. Luc knew instinctively that he had to bump into blondie if he wanted to find out more about Terre Noire.

He was less than ten yards away, when things turned nasty. Eco-warriors had just tossed grappling irons onto the rails of the *Marcq-en-Barœul* and were attacking the ship. Onlookers, meanwhile, were hurling projectiles at the sailors.

In response, the crew had turned two fire hoses on the assailants. The powerful jets of water sent the Northern Peoples packing. Red Dress found herself soaked from head to toe. Night was falling on Le Havre, and the air was chilly. Luc grabbed a flag abandoned on the ground and took advantage of the disarray. The god of war was offering him an opportunity that would not occur twice. The god of love wasn't far off, either. Eros and Thanatos.

He rushed toward the frozen-stiff siren and offered her the hospitality of his banner.

"You can't stand there like that!" he said.

Chilled to the bone, dripping wet, and abandoned by her fellow eco-warriors, the valiant blonde accepted the drape. Luc took her hand and dragged her off between two shipping containers on the wharf.

"I'll turn around. Get your clothes off."

Luc turned his eyes toward the battlefield and held the banner, to give her privacy. Wary, she took off her dress, wrapped herself in it, and thanked him.

"That looks even better than the dress."

"Really?" she answered with a Scandinavian accent.

She leaned over to wring out her thoroughly soaked hair.

"My motorcycle's only a hundred yards away," Luc said, aware that it was more like a mile. "I'll take you home."

She gave him a grateful look. Behind the two of them, the police were rushing to the aid of the sailors on the *Marcq-en-Barœul*. The Northern Peoples and their allies were losing the battle and scattering in all directions.

"Let's go."

He took her hand and led her toward the spot where he had parked his machine. Finally, it came within sight.

"Are you Swedish?"

"Danish."

"What are you doing in Le Havre?"

"I'm defending the interests of the Inuits of Greenland. I thought that was obvious. Is your motorcycle much farther?"

"There."

"It's a Harley-Davidson?"

"Yes. Hop on behind me, and hold on."

Through the thin material of the banner, Luc felt the Danish woman's shivering body pressed against his back. He fired up.

"I'm staying at the Mercure. My name's Connie."

"I'm Luc. Like the evangelist."

"You do have the look of an apostle."

Just listening to her Danish accent was worth the trip. Luc was already allowing himself to feel excited. The end of the world wasn't all bad. Twenty minutes later, they made a noteworthy entrance at the hotel. Holding her dress and underwear, Luc followed his red flag. Connie retrieved her magnetic card from the reception desk, smiling quite comfortably. She got into the first elevator and pressed the button for the top floor. Their eyes fixed on the elevator doors, they were no doubt thinking the same thing.

Five minutes later, Luc found himself in an expansive suite offering an unimpeded view of the port and its surroundings. In the distance, he recognized the lights of Honfleur and Trouville. Before she stepped into the shower, Connie opened the refrigerator and invited him to take whatever he liked from an array of alcoholic drinks. Defending the Northern Peoples looked like a nice little moneymaker. This was getting more intriguing by the minute.

Luc switched on the television and watched the news. In New York, the sea level had already dropped twenty inches. The damage seemed to be less serious than feared.

Connie emerged from the bathroom in a robe as white as the glaciers of the Arctic.

"Apart from playing Good Samaritan, what were you doing at the *Marcq-en-Barœul*?" she asked.

"I'm interested in Terre Noire and Nicolas Lanier, their executive chairman."

"No kidding!"

Luc saw in the eyes of the suddenly still Dane the sharp blade of a hunter. She continued drying her hair with the towel and sat down beside him on the sofa facing the plasma screen. The models in the commercials had nothing on her. She studied him as if he'd just landed from some exoplanet.

"And who do you work for?"

"For myself," Luc replied. "I publish articles on future-probe.com. I sell reports to the highest bidder. Photos, too. Information. Are you interested?"

The Dane scanned him with her lavender-blue eyes as though he might blow up in her face or bite. Luc could feel a vague danger. It was a sensation that could drive him wild. He was no longer involved in checking out dodgy CVs, but in disabling a geostrategic bomb, the kind of thing he'd always dreamed of. He had to watch his step and weigh every word.

"We could collaborate," he suggested.

"That's open for discussion," she said. "Drink what you like. I'll be back."

Half an hour later, she had transformed herself into a bombshell in a little black dress and white pearls. With a delicate yet deliberate move, she switched off the television and sat down next to him.

"What can you tell me about Terre Noire and its boss?"

Luc told himself he was right to have made the meeting with Le Guévenec's wife for eleven the following morning. The mysteries of the sailor lost at sea could wait till dawn. The night would be tiring but full.

"What exactly would you like to know, Connie?"

"Rasmussen. Connie Rasmussen."

"That rings a bell," Luc replied. He bit his lip, conscious of having made his first slip.

"I'm a practicing lawyer in Copenhagen. My Greenland clients have become independent, but they are still feeling their way. Power can't be improvised. It's a daily struggle."

Her smile became more professional, her demeanor less languorous.

"Since you're French and a journalist, I'd like to know about Nicolas Lanier's ties with the French intelligence service and the various ministries. I'd like the names of his contacts at Les Invalides, in particular. I'd like the same thing for Loïc Le Guévenec, the captain of the *Bouc-Bel-Air*. Which French intelligence agents are on board, and do any other powers have agents on that ship? Who's really paying them? Greenland's government doesn't want to be completely in the dark."

Luc told himself that he had his hand on a parcel bomb tied together with genuine pearls. Connie Rasmussen lacked neither means nor information. It was a volatile mix that could blow up in his face at the slightest slip.

"Is that all? You're not bashful about saying what you want."

"I'd like to know as much about North Land. But since you're French, I'm not in such a hurry."

"How much can you pay?"

"Whatever you're asking."

"A hundred thousand euros in cash," he replied, thinking back to what Geraldine Harper had promised John and trying to put up a credible front.

"Okay."

Connie Rasmussen hadn't batted an eye. He couldn't believe it and would have given a lot to see the faces of John and Victoire. He leaned back on the leather sofa. At that price, he was clearly walking into a nest of rattlesnakes.

"What you've asked for requires a real discussion. A proper exchange."

"Okay," said Connie Rasmussen. "But I'm dying of hunger."

"Shall we eat first?"

"An apostle. And a gentleman!"

THE COMMAND BRIDGE OF THE BOUC-BEL-AIR, *1:25 P.M.*

The ship was tilting three degrees to starboard and heading south at seven knots. The watch keeper, his head wrapped in a bandage, was trying to stay the course, with the aid of a sailor clutching the wheel, which was out of alignment. The transmission had been put rudely to the test. The ship was groaning as loudly as the bears on the bridge aft. A wind on the beam was whipping up the sea dangerously. Clouds were skimming the ocean at amazing speed. For the moment, at least, there was no way of evacuating the wounded by means of the helicopter that Nicolas Lanier had put down.

"Keep at it," Le Guévenec told them. "I'm going down to the cabin."

"Captain, who was that in the helicopter?"

"He's a guy the head office in Paris has sent to take stock of the damage and do an audit. It's the in thing at the moment."

Le Guévenec sensed he was doing a bad job of lying and fell back into the silence that suited him much better than management-speak. He met the sailor's skeptical eyes. No one challenged the skipper's word. Le Guévenec left the bridge and returned to the cabin. Five minutes later, he knocked on the door of the first mate's cabin.

Squeezed into a Terre Noire jersey that was too small for him, Nicolas Lanier questioned him immediately.

"What about Brissac?"

"Nothing's changed. Still delirious."

The Terre Noire CEO listened carefully as the captain dispassionately outlined the trials the ship, its mates, and its passengers were being put through. Le Guévenec, for his part, saw a young man who was aging quickly at the helm of the Champs-Elysées-based company. He had the weight of the company and its shareholders on his shoulders. With his fair hair and his grayish eyes, Lanier looked like a Viking. That resemblance troubled the tired brain of the captain as he attempted keep his balance by clinging to the table.

"I found this metal box that Rox Oa, the boatswain, hid in the hold with the cognac."

The two men looked at the heavy object painted in the company's colors. Nicolas grabbed it and put it at his feet.

"I'll hang onto it. Who knows about it?"

"Only you and me."

"What about your wife?"

"I never talk to Isabelle about my work."

"Good. Have you had any calls from the Champs-Elysées office?"

"Yes."

"Calls concerning me?"

"None."

"Good."

The discussion turned to the *Bouc-Bel-Air's* chances of survival and the time needed to get to Nuuk. Le Guévenec took his leave and returned to his cabin. Through the porthole, he saw how badly off-kilter the horizon line was. The ship was listing dangerously to the port side. He would keep it from sinking. Collapsed on his bunk, he stared at the damaged metal ceiling, aware that Lanier had crossed the oceans to retrieve the metal box and tend to the ice samples that the *Bouc* was taking back from Avannaa, the northernmost and most inhospitable region of the island continent.

He also thought of Isabelle, who was pretending to be waiting for him in their sad little apartment in Le Havre. It was the second time in less than twenty-four hours that someone had spoken her name to him. Never before in his twenty-year career had anyone uttered Isabelle's name on board the *Bouc-Bel-Air*.

He stroked his beard and told himself that Nicolas Lanier knew about Brissac and Isabelle. When he'd asked, "What about your wife?" he had read a sort of embarrassment in his eyes. Rumor had it that Lanier, too, had a secret life. Le Guévenec was ill-equipped for this world. No one had taught him about women. He preferred the sea.

2

MONDAY

Thanks to his earphone, John was listening to Victoire while looking at the latest news site photo of Geraldine Harper on his smartphone. Fermatown was putting a complete file together before he met her. He crossed the Place Vendôme without noticing the city's heat and humidity. Victoire had a gift for synthesis and clarity. A real Ecole Normale Supérieure graduate, thought John.

"Geraldine is Canadian. She brought to the marriage a fortune in Alberta oil sands and the technology that allows shale gas to be extracted at a competitive cost. She's the one who saved North Land from bankruptcy. Abraham, her husband, is American and twenty years older than she is. He has a reputation for being tough in business. Watch out. They're a pair of predators."

"Thanks."

John walked through the revolving door of the Ritz with a burning desire, despite everything, to keep his big chance from slipping away. A client like North Land wouldn't come within Fermatown's reach twice. He headed to the left with a decisive stride and entered the bar, which was populated with a few zealous Asian businessmen and a romantic couple who were letting themselves be lulled by a woman playing a harp. In the garden beyond the picture window, marble nudes were sweating in the tropical light, which, for days now, had made Paris feel like Bangkok.

On a discreetly placed television, a news show was covering the collapse of Greenland. John paid it no mind and smiled as he ordered a bottle of sparkling water. The bar, basking in the soft glow of brass, had a patina lent by generations of demanding clients rolling in dough.

"Ice?"

"Yes, please."

The bartender slid the glass along the zinc counter.

"Ice is going to be hard to come by, with what's happening at the North Pole."

John turned to the screen, where the topic was the polar bears on the *Bouc-Bel-Air*.

"That ship isn't going to help France's image," the bartender said. "Some people reckon it's the ship that caused the catastrophe in the first place."

"People will say anything," John replied. "A boat can't bring on the collapse of a continent all by itself," John replied.

"Yet that's what the Inuits are claiming. I don't understand why Terre Noire called its boat the *Bouc-Bel-Air*. Really, a name that means 'nice-looking goat.' Nothing like that to bring bad luck."

"True, some names are pretty fateful."

John agreed with everything the man said while watching the wreck crawling along, between chunks of Arctic ice. Geraldine Harper was going to ask him to look into Terre Noire. Be that as it may, he'd refuse to spy on a French firm, even for a hundred thousand euros. Fermatown would stay poor but would not betray its own country. Clean hands and head held high! Everything depended, though, on what you meant by spying. Part of him was ready to deal with the devil. It was time to get out of the fiscal rut.

Divided between the poles of his conscience, he swallowed a mouthful of water. In the mirror behind the bar, he spotted Geraldine Harper as she came in. With her black hair pulled back in a chignon at the nape of her neck, Madame Harper looked exactly like the photo in her company's last annual report. She was wearing pearls and a suit in North Land's colors, blue and white. The colors didn't soften her eyes, which had the penetrating look of an oil drill. She was walking toward a table in the middle of the room.

"I'm going to join that lady. The check's mine."

"I'll bring you your mineral water."

John crossed the immense stretch of wall-to-wall carpet and caught up with the woman, who had just taken a seat in one of the armchairs surrounding a table decorated with flowers. A card marked "reserved" had been placed next to the bouquet. He introduced himself and sat down. Geraldine Harper threw him a vague smile and gave herself a few seconds to scan the room. Abraham's wife was wearing her fifty-odd years well. Sure of herself, she turned to him with the kind of look a surgeon gives an open wound. John saw himself back on the slab after his accident.

"I'd been told you were a good-looking man, and that was no lie. Tell me about yourself, Major Spencer Larivière. Where did you get those looks of yours?"

"From my American ancestry."

"Now that's a good start," Geraldine Harper replied.

"I know you're the wife of Abraham, the head of North Land. Terre Noire is your main competitor. I have to tell you that as a Frenchman."

Disarmed by Geraldine's smile, he stopped dead.

"Monsieur Spencer Larivière, I haven't come to ask you to spy on your compatriots or betray your country. I know you wouldn't do that, not a man like you. Isn't that so?"

"Never."

"Let's not go overboard. Never say never. Especially not in your field."

She nodded at another table.

"I'd feel more comfortable under that painting over there."

John turned to look at the Flemish painting beneath a wall lamp. The rural landscape overlooked a round table. He followed her to it, turning over contradictory feelings. Geraldine Harper was acting like a professional: last-minute meeting, precautions to avoid any listening device that might be planted under a table. No point in playing the big shot. She knew what she was doing. He sat in an armchair and listened humbly. She'd mentioned his rank in the army and had to have a substantial file on him.

At the start of the climate upheaval, the Canadian Security Intelligence Service had come out from under the thumb of the CIA. The top of the world had become the future of humanity, and the Canadian service was now one of the most fearsome intelligence agencies on the planet. John suddenly realized that Geraldine and Abraham had to have their sources in Ottawa, as well as in Washington, and he tensed up.

"It was Abraham Harper, my husband, who advised me to meet you."

John raised his eyebrows. Never for a moment had he crossed paths with the founder of North Land.

"I know you don't know him, but he seems to know you. I'd go so far as to say that's he's not mistaken," Geraldine declared in a firm voice softened by the amused expression on her face.

How was he to interpret the sparkle that was lighting up the eyes of the queen of the oil sands of Alberta? The waiter put down the jasmine tea and the bottle of sparkling water and then disappeared, leaving them alone. The harp struck up a familiar tune.

"My husband and I hope you'll provide surveillance and protection for our daughter, Mary. She's studying geology at L'École des Mines in Paris."

John fell down to earth with a thud, like the helicopter he'd crashed when the Taliban hit it. The geostrategic mission he'd been expecting had been reduced to a babysitting job. He shrank in his armchair, humiliated, but not letting a hint of his feelings show. The pain flared around the skin grafts he had gotten after the crash. He took a long swig of sparkling water and felt his stomach turn again. Yet another illusion to pack away in the attic of the house between the Rue Deparcieux and the Rue Fermat.

"I'm sure you'll get on well with Mary when you see her. She's a delightful young woman. A bit capricious but adorable. The spitting image of her father."

"It's possible."

"We want someone for Mary who has not only competence in the field, but also an understanding of the power struggles among the governments of this world and multinational companies. Mary and her brother, Harold, are heirs to an empire. North Land has perfected technologies that will allow the mineral and oil resources of the North Pole and Greenland to be exploited. These innovations interest a lot of people. I think you follow the news and grasp the situation. We want to ensure our daughter's protection with a Frenchman who's capable and well-connected but has no ties to our rival, Terre Noire. We've checked."

John saw the steel in Geraldine's eyes. The situation he'd imagined had been turned on its head. North Land wasn't asking him to spy on Terre Noire, but to protect its heiress. The North American oil- and gas-exploration company was turning to him because he had no connection to Terre Noire. Unexpected, but damned effective. Who better than a former agent to protect a young student in Paris?

"Abraham was once a student at L'École des Mines himself, and our daughter dreamed of Paris. It goes without saying that the means you bring into play to ensure Mary's surveillance and protection will be reimbursed over and above the one hundred thousand euros that I mentioned. That's just an advance."

The sparkling water suddenly tasted like champagne. Geraldine Harper took a cell phone out of her handbag, along with a credit card, and placed them on the table between the water and the tea.

"This card will allow you to settle all expenses incurred, no matter what the sum. As for the phone..."

"Yes?"

"It will allow you to listen to all our daughter's conversations and familiarize yourself with her relationships. That way, you'll be able to sort the wheat from the chaff. Since we're asking you for surveillance, we might as well simplify things. My husband is a direct man, one who gets up at four in the morning and goes to bed at nine every night."

"I read that in the newspaper."

"He hardly ever eats out."

"I don't quite see the connection with the phone."

"I meant that Abraham's a practical man. If Mary is to be under surveillance, you might as well do it properly and thoroughly from the beginning."

"Meaning?"

"We wanted a Frenchman who knows Paris and has relationships within the French intelligence agency."

John felt the cold air of Canada descend on his shoulders. Fermatown clearly held no secrets for Geraldine Harper. He felt unmasked and exposed and had to make an effort to swallow his pride, which had already been seriously dented in Afghanistan.

"Aren't you worried that I might inform the agency about this surveillance?"

"Abraham thinks you'll be forced to talk to them about it. Actually, that seems to reassure him. Naturally, you'll do whatever you think you have to do. You're the boss."

Geraldine's look obviously contradicted what she'd just said. He was on the verge of dropping the whole thing and taking his leave. He was nothing but a mercenary and a go-between now. But he calmed down, thinking that, for the Harpers, Fermatown was, in essence, a private extension of Méricourt's agency, as it was being cunningly suggested that he inform them. He swallowed his pride and his flag and toyed with the phone Geraldine had just entrusted to him. He turned it over and read the number and the letters written on a sticky note.

"That's the code that will give you access to the different functions. I'll show you. It's not complicated."

Geraldine took the phone and ran her fingers over the keys.

"Thanks to the code, you'll find a whole host of applications, such as one that diverts all calls sent to and received by our daughter."

"I assume Mary doesn't know about this."

"Neither Mary nor her brother, Harold. This device, as you can imagine, was developed in cooperation with America's National Security Agency, where my husband has a number of contacts."

John nodded, as though this was all obvious.

"Harold is ten years older than his sister. You'll have to get used to the family. We've rented an apartment for Mary on the Boulevard Saint-Michel, just opposite L'École des Mines. That will make life easier for you. My dear John Spencer Larivière, do you agree to protect Mary?"

Geraldine Harper gave him a calculated warm and maternal look. The whole thing reeked of fraud and manipulation. A reasonable man would have fled.

"I agree."

"Bravo. There's just one little hitch."

"I thought there might be."

"My husband disappeared three days ago. We're very anxious. Mary's going to go look for him. I'd like you to meet her ASAP and help her find Abraham. The last time Mary had her father on the phone, the call came from the Great Wound of the Wild Dog."

"The Great Wound of the Wild Dog?"

"It's a geological phenomenon in the Avannaa region of north Greenland."

"Near the ice shelf that just fell into the ocean?"

"A few miles away."

"I sense I'll be getting frostbite."

"My husband was right. You're a well brought-up man, Monsieur Spencer Larivière. It goes without saying that Abraham's disappearance is totally confidential information that you must not reveal to anyone, not even to your agency friends."

"You can count on me."

"When people ask you what you're doing in Greenland, you're to say that you were hired to assess North Land's image up there. Your room's already booked at the Hans Egede, the best hotel in the country."

LE HAVRE, 11:30 A.M.

Isabelle Le Guévenec lived in a big, sad, functional apartment on the fifth floor of a building that had been rebuilt after World War II. Through the windows, Luc could see the cement curves of the Maison de la Culture, the city's community center, and hear the cry of the seagulls. His night at the Mercure with Connie Rasmussen had reconciled him to the frozen expanses of Greenland and the saga of the Vikings.

The Inuits' legal representative had talked to him about Erik the Red and other Danish conquerors when Greenland was a vast green prairie. Exhausted by his work obligations and stupefied by the Swedish *Flaggpunsch* liqueur, he had fallen into a deep slumber between the sheets and almost missed his meeting with the captain's wife. Since joining Fermatown, Luc was finding that there was much more to life than reading blue screens, role-playing, and gossiping on Facebook. Over the phone, John had congratulated him on the hundred thousand euros promised by Connie Rasmussen and asked him a multitude of questions about Greenland.

Luc turned toward Isabelle Le Guévenec, who was coming into the living room with drinks on a tray. She was dressed in a pencil skirt and a white blouse that showed off her voluminous bust. She didn't look forty-five, or truly anxious—more curious.

"You say Loïc's going to pull through?"

"Absolutely."

"What can I offer you?"

"Some mineral water. I've had a long night."

Luc added a bunch of ice cubes to his glass.

"It's really kind of you to come all this way. You couldn't say Terre Noire has actually spoiled us with their concern. Who do you work for at the Champs-Elysées office?"

"Employee health and safety," Luc replied carefully.

Isabelle Le Guévenec poured herself a slug of port and sat down on a leather sofa that looked new. It showed off her black eyes and chestnut-colored hair. Madame Le Guévenec looked taller than her husband, even though he'd never seen the man. It was a curious impression. The woman was obviously smart. He took the initiative before she could unmask the hoax with questions as orderly as the apartment.

"Did your husband express any particular fears before he left?"

"What fears are you thinking of?" she asked with a fake look of surprise.

"I'm thinking of Greenland, of course."

"Loïc knew, as everyone else did, that Greenland was on the brink of catastrophe. He got the order to go there just as he was leaving the Barents Sea and coming home to Le Havre."

"On Nicolas Lanier's orders?"

"I'm amazed you're not up to date."

"We really aren't kept abreast of day-to-day operations," Luc said. "Terre Noire doesn't like to disclose much about the company, even to its own employees. Actually, my department is more like a fifth wheel on the chariot."

"That hardly surprises me. Terre Noire's obsession with secrecy is really annoying."

"You're telling me!"

"Loïc is a real seaman. The ocean doesn't frighten him. Actually, I'm wondering what would frighten him."

Isabelle Le Guévenec crossed her legs again as she brought the glass of port to her lips. She put it down gently on a doily made of lace from Calais, where the Nord–Pas Mining Basin had just listed as a world heritage by UNESCO.

"It's not Greenland that worried Loïc, but Christophe Maunay, the new human resources manager. He's a graduate of L'École des Mines, the prestigious engineering school. He was posted to Gabon with Terre Noire before this. You know him, surely."

"Who doesn't!" Luc bluffed, telling himself she'd no doubt just seen through him.

"Christophe Maunay wanted Loïc to tell him exactly what the scientists on the *Bouc-Bel-Air* were doing."

"What's so odd about that?"

"That young man's predecessors had never asked for so many details about the geological surveys. Normally, those matters are confidential. The scientific research department and Romain Brissac handle them. But it appears that this Maunay is Nicolas Lanier's confidant. They're said to be very close."

"Why does that worry your husband?"

Isabelle Le Guévenec lowered her voice as if she feared being overheard by someone hiding in the background.

"Before collecting samples of ice in Greenland, the *Bouc-Bel-Air* was working with the *Jacob Smirnitskyi*, a Russian exploration ship, on the methane vents of the continental shelf off the coast of Siberia. So why's this little creep interfering in things that are no concern of his, I ask you."

"Methane vents?"

"I can see you need a chemistry refresher," Isabelle replied, moving in even closer. "Methane vents are forming all over the Arctic. As the atmosphere and ocean currents warm up, the permafrost and seabeds are releasing more and more methane. That gas is going to produce a greenhouse effect twenty times more powerful than carbon and speed up climate change. The thirty billion tons of CO_2 that rise into the atmosphere every year will be multiplied by a factor that's unknown but hair-raising."

"So?"

"Onboard the *Bouc-Bel-Air*, as on the *Jacob Smirnitskyi*, scientists have measured very precisely what's going to happen to us, and which corners of the world humanity will be able to survive in. They know all about it. This Christophe Maunay is meddling in something that's none of his business. There's something fishy about it. On the *Bouc*, it's Romain Brissac who's in charge of the Terre Noire team. Have you heard anything from him?"

Isabelle's face suddenly became agitated. She was wringing her hands. Luc's instincts told him that Madame Le Guévenec was not indifferent to Brissac's fate.

"I'm expecting to hear from him any moment now."

Isabelle gazed at the impeccably clean windows of her childless and husbandless apartment.

"What about the Norwegians in all of this?" Luc asked innocently.

"What do you mean, the Norwegians?"

"They were saying on television that the *Bouc-Bel-Air* had teamed up with the Norwegians."

"That's understandable, since the *Jacob Smirnitskyi* was entirely refitted in Tromso by Norway's sovereign wealth fund. Russia and Norway have signed an agreement on oil exploitation in the Barents Sea. You have to understand that right now, everyone's flocking to the North Pole. The disappearance of the ice shelf is going to free up sea routes for gas and oil companies. Gas and oil stir up greed. But there's more."

"There's more?"

"Terre Noire discovered an immense deposit of rare metals in Qaqortoq, in the south of Greenland. As a joke, Greenlanders call this the Banana Coast."

"You don't hear much about it in France."

"Strategic issues don't excite the French."

"It can't be easy extracting rare metals up there."

"You have to guess exactly where they are first."

"How's it done?"

"That's where Romain comes in."

"The Nobel Prize winner?"

"Yes, he and his team have developed Gaia, which is computer analysis software that lets us get a better handle on complex geological structures. Gaia has analyzed over a hundred years of mining operations all around the globe. The program doesn't always work, but it saves a lot of time. After the discovery of the Qaqortoq deposits, Gaia allowed Terre Noire to tell the Norwegians and the Russians what was under the North Pole and precisely where it was."

"So it's Terre Noire that facilitated the agreement between the Russians and the Norwegians?"

"They signed, thanks to us. That brought us enormous amounts of money, along with worldwide fame. We already had Romain, with his Nobel Prize. Now there's Gaia."

"I suppose our rivals would love to get their hands on Gaia."

"They'd do anything to buy or steal it from us, especially because they can't come up with a replica."

"Why?"

"Because Gaia isn't just a software program. It's the memory of all geological exploration in the world. Nicolas Lanier had a stroke of genius when he took the helm of Terre Noire."

"Oh?"

"Nicolas used the assets his predecessors had accumulated to buy up the archives and files of exploration expeditions all around the world that never got anywhere. Ironically, this data gave us a tremendous advantage. Gaia is based on the stuff our partners and rivals threw in the trash. Lanier also had his people interview all the engineers and prospectors who've been pensioned off by their respective companies. He realized that they have a wealth of experience that has a bearing on the future of the planet, Right now, we're quizzing the engineers and technicians who were handling the oil spill in the Gulf of Mexico. In the near future, we'll know how to avoid that kind of catastrophe. Nicolas calls it risk management."

"I haven't seen the chairman at the Champs-Elysées office much. I'm new, but everyone says he's a great guy."

"He's a good listener."

"A very rare quality."

Luc could feel Isabelle Le Guévenec warming up. The captain's wife seemed to have an even more strategic role in the company than her husband. Certainly more ambiguous, in any case. She stared at him with suspicion in her eyes.

"You're getting me to say quite a bit. Maybe that's part of the job of counseling women in distress. Am I a psychological risk?"

"We're very concerned about the welfare of Terre Noire wives. We're a family, you know. That's very clear from listening to you. We need to give meaning and a human dimension to what we do. That's how I see my mission."

Luc feared he'd overdone it but was immediately reassured. Isabelle Le Guévenec got off the sofa and sat down beside him. She placed a scented hand on his arm. Her milky skin and black eyebrows made her very appealing, and he felt a sudden surge of tenderness, mixed with strong attraction.

"I'm sure you haven't had lunch. You must be starving."

"I have to get back to Paris."

"Not before tasting Loïc's favorite dish."

After an exhausting night in the company of a Nordic Valkyrie, Luc felt himself go limp before the Calais lace and middle-class order that was crying out to be messed up, ever so gently. Of course, he'd Googled Isabelle on his cell phone before ringing her bell. The captain's wife, aided by Romain Brissac, presided over an association in Le Havre that was dedicated to the protection of wildlife. Luc suddenly remembered seeing a news clip about polar bears being onboard the *Bouc-Bel-Air*.

"I understand you're the head of a foundation sponsored by Terre Noire. Are you interested in bears?"

"Bears and other animals."

PARIS, METRO LINE 1, 11:55 A.M.

John got off at the Champs-Elysées-Clemenceau metro station and took Line 13 as far as Duroc. The man was still following him. He zoomed along various corridors to get to Line 10. The guy must have tailed him when he came out of the Ritz. It was the first time since he had gotten back from Afghanistan that he had experienced any real danger. This invigorated him. Forced into physical confrontation, he rediscovered the reflexes that he thought he'd lost in the musty setting of Les Invalides. He got into the subway car, pretending not to be interested in the man on his tail. Muscles tensed, he prepared himself for combat while scrutinizing faces. The theory mill was going full bore. He couldn't see Geraldine Harper being behind such a pointless and crude exercise. Fermatown held too few secrets for her. This man had something Nordic about him, and his bearing was paramilitary. A Russian or Scandinavian mercenary came to mind. Western firms working in Iraq and Afghanistan employed guys like this. Maybe a French rival of Fermatown had taken umbrage at his meeting with Geraldine. News traveled fast in the private intelligence market in France. A lot of people would like to work for North Land. A foreign agency could very well have commissioned some den of spies from Paris or Geneva. With the melting of the North Pole, strategic balances were going to be redefined. The spectrum of possibilities was immense.

Not knowing whether he had lost his tail, John got out at the Sèvres-Babylone station and headed for the Bon Marché grocery store. Fermatown was out of California chardonnay. He walked down the aisles of the store, waiting for Victoire to answer his call. He regretted sending Luc to investigate Terre Noire and Lanier. The escapade in Le Havre was now pointless. In front of the whiskeys, he checked the reflections. The man was standing between the freshly made pastas and the Italian hams.

John didn't like his style and could sense the cold, metallic menace in the killer's hand, out of sight under his jacket. He randomly chose a bottle with a tall neck that could serve as a handle. Effective for slashing someone's throat quickly and mercilessly. It was a nocturnal habit he'd left behind in the mountains of Central Asia. Here, he'd have to act in broad daylight among all the yuppies. Chaos in full view. Victoire wasn't picking up. A recovery operation always took time. He imagined her panic-stricken and anguished, getting the car ready in the garage, and he swore through his teeth. Under that serene appearance she'd inherited from her Cambodian ancestors, Victoire was a bundle of nerves and almost morbidly sensitive.

He regretted dragging her into this business and headed for the flower stand, where he chose the most extravagantly beautiful bunch— both to keep his enemy off balance and to seek forgiveness from Victoire if he managed to escape his pursuer unharmed. Stealing a glance at his stalker, he got the impression that there was a certain loosening between the shoulder blades. He didn't look as stiff. He imagined his hand was lighter on the grip. A foreigner in Paris, the man was there for a quick mission. Finally, Victoire called.

"Leave the grocery store and head for the intersection opposite the Hôtel Lutetia. I'm coming down the Boulevard Raspail."

John stared at the Bon Marché florist, who was winding a ribbon around the bouquet. The young woman's eyes met his, and she read there what others had detected before her. The man she was giving those flowers to had killed people. John picked up the change and left the frightened shop assistant.

He walked off, trying to avoid any reckless move. Passersby were stooped under their umbrellas in rain that was as hot as a monsoon. The asphalt gleamed in the headlights of the cars. He crossed the Rue de Sèvres, checking the shop windows to see how close the other man was. His grip on the neck of the bottle instinctively tightened. A taxi was parked on the pavement outside the Lutetia. He crossed and opened the door of the Mercedes.

"Good afternoon. Take me to La Motte-Picquet."

He slid into the seat and looked back down the Boulevard Raspail. Victoire was just arriving, a marvel of precision and cool-headedness. She was less than ten yards behind his taxi. He hugged the bouquet.

PARIS, SÈVRES-BABYLONE INTERSECTION, 12:15 P.M.

Per Sorenson was surprised by the reaction of his target, who had just dived into a taxi with his bouquet of flowers. He felt like John Spencer Larivière had just clocked him. Furious, he crossed the street and hailed the first taxi coming down the boulevard. He opened the door and shouted.

"Follow that Mercedes."

"A pal of yours?"

"Hmm."

Per Sorenson grabbed a laminated advertisement lying on the seat and nervously tossed it aside. The driver was a woman and Asian, to boot. She complied without making a fuss and wove her way through the traffic on the trail of the Mercedes. He suddenly noticed a big ball of white wool on the front seat.

"That's my cat."

"Hmm."

The Mercedes was turning onto the Rue de Varennes. Victoire slowed the car to make the turn. With a sinking heart, she saw the man give her a challenging look and pick up the advertisement again. Had he guessed the trap she'd just set? She gripped the steering wheel with sweaty hands and tried to make small talk, both to calm herself and to put the guy off-scent.

"My sister breeds Persians at a place in Beaumont. If you like, I can put you in touch with her. All you have to do is leave me your e-mail address."

"Hmm."

Stop dreaming, she told herself. You don't expect him to leave you his business card and his address on top of his fingerprints on the advertisement, do you? After the Rue de Varennes, the Mercedes ferrying John toward the fifteenth arrondissement went past the illuminated Invalides and took the road to La Motte-Picquet.

"Where's your pal going?" Victoire asked with a lump in her throat.

"Just follow."

The man spoke with a thick Nordic or Slavic accent. The Mercedes turned onto the Avenue de Suffren and then slowed and stopped at Number 77.

"Drive past, and let me out farther up the road."

Victoire did as she was told and dropped her client a hundred yards or so from the spot where John's taxi had stopped. She turned around, smiling, and announced the fare.

"Twelve euros, twenty centimes."

The passenger took out a twenty-euro note, and she immediately gave him his change.

"Sorry. It's the end of my shift, and I've only got loose change left."

"That's fine."

The man slipped his change into a pocket of his jacket and got out without saying another word. In her rearview mirror, Victoire saw him slowly approach Number 77. She took off again and turned right at the first intersection. Some two hundred yards down the street, she picked up John, who was waiting at the agreed-on spot in the shadow of an apartment building, an enormous bouquet in his hand.

Still in shock, they were silent for a good ten minutes as they drove toward the Seine.

"How do you feel?" John asked.

"Better now."

She parked their fake taxi behind a tourist bus, put on the hand brake, and leaned her head on his shoulder. He saw a tear welling in her eye. They sat like that for a long while.

"I don't want to lose you. Don't go. Luc rang me from Le Havre. He had a long talk with Isabelle Le Guévenec. We're about to be caught between two dangerous forces. The stakes are colossal. Don't go near Terre Noire."

"It's not what we thought. The Harpers are asking me to babysit their daughter. And to find her father."

"So why was that guy following you?"

"There must be something else. We have to figure out what it is."

"I'm scared."

"Too late now. We have to find out how the guy knew about the meeting, and why he followed me here."

He took her in his arms, eyeing the rearview mirror all the while. The bouquet reminded him of a smell he'd long ago forgotten. He, too, had skeletons in the closet.

ON BOARD THE BOUC-BEL-AIR, 8:30 A.M.

"Good morning, Captain. You look like you're in better shape today."

Le Guévenec nodded and thanked Lanier for sending someone to Le Havre to reassure his wife.

"It made her happy. I wanted you to know."

Lanier, balanced precariously in the middle of the cabin, looked at him with a stunned expression. The efficiency of his employee health and safety team was both welcome and suspicious. He'd check that out later. Le Guévenec was an unfathomable man who had been seasoned by the oceans. His wife and he had been of immense help to Terre Noire without realizing it. By becoming the mistress of the most celebrated climatologist on the planet, Isabelle Le Guévenec had boosted Romain Brissac's morale. Like most of the Brissacs, he had doubted himself. As for the Le Guévenec marriage, every union had to navigate unpredictable waters.

Transporting the Nobel laureate to the American military hospital in Thule in the far north of Greenland was a fresh source of anxiety. Lanier turned to his captain.

"Did you go through his pockets and check his bags?"

"Yes," Le Guévenec replied sharply.

"I'm sorry, but I'm suspicious of Americans. They've got a strategy regarding the transformation of the pole. They won't lose an opportunity like this. Romain mustn't take anything with him concerning the ice samples, the Qaqortoq ores, Gaia, or the data on the Barents Sea."

"I've checked. He's got nothing on him."

"They'll try to quiz him and get him to talk any way they can. The American military has its own intelligence and is hand-in-glove with the CIA and the NSA."

"We can't treat him on board."

"I understand that, Captain, but a hundred and thirty-one thousand years of climate change are going to take off with Brissac when he enters that American hospital. It makes me sick."

"That information isn't necessarily any safer on the *Bouc-Bel-Air*. Who was Rox Oa, the boatswain you sent me, working for? He's the one who loaded the cognac on board and hid the black box I gave you."

"We'll have to get to the bottom of that mystery," Lanier replied.

"Who's to say there aren't other hostile agents who've managed to sneak on board?"

The two men stood for a moment, with their hands in their pockets, gazing at the inclined floor. Each wondering what secrets the other was still hiding. Lanier was puzzled by the story about his employee health and safety department calling on Isabelle in Le Havre. It felt like one more oddity in the waking nightmare of the past week. A strong wave threw him off balance and brought him back to the present.

Le Guévenec's measured voice broke the silence. "Romain Brissac will be the first person to be put in the helicopter, just as you requested."

"You've done well, Loïc. Come back and see me when all the wounded have taken off."

That Lanier had used his first name didn't register with Le Guévenec. He left the cabin and headed toward the back of the ship. Because of the boat's tilting, his lower back was killing him. His hip was hurting, too. Gathering the wounded together had taken a lot of time. Romain Brissac had been a taciturn but attentive companion during the campaign in the Barents Sea and over the continental shelf of Siberia. Le Guévenec, the cuckold, surmised that Brissac wanted to be forgiven.

The botanist and three members of the crew whose injuries required hospitalization would follow Brissac. In just under two hours, the wounded from the *Bouc-Bel-Air* would be at the military hospital attached to the big American base in Thule. The Americans had offered to look after the victims even before Terre Noire's employee health and safety department had called him from Paris. Unbelievable!

Wracked with warring feelings, Le Guévenec made it back to the bridge just as the blades of the helicopter were starting to rotate. The strident noise of the turbines soon drowned out the roaring bears.

"They'll soon be in Thule," he told the few sailors at his side.

The watch officer nodded and put his hands over his ears to safeguard his hearing. The Eurocopter, with its nose up because of the list, rose in an infernal din. Thanks to the skill of the pilot and the power of the two engines, it managed to rise straight up in a perfect maneuver.

But when the helicopter was about sixty feet above the deck, a sailor next to Le Guévenec started shouting and waving his arms. The steel cable that had secured it to an air vent on the ship was stretched taut like the string of a bow. Before stupefied eyes, the Eurocopter was yanked out of its ascent. The pilot made a desperate attempt to escape the deadly trap by veering to the side, but he couldn't break the cable. The Eurocopter spun around on itself like a top, spitting black smoke. The rotation sped up in an terrifying ballet.

Le Guévenec watched as the pilot frantically tried to save the helicopter and its passengers. It was too late. The nose of the machine struck the platform violently, and the tail snapped in two. A thick cloud of black smoke enveloped the keelson and obstructed the skyline of drifting icebergs. Then there was an explosion, followed by an orange fireball.

Two sailors had just unhooked a fire hose. But the heat of the blaze forced them to remain at a distance, powerless. Someone had forgotten to untie the helicopter. Forgotten? Really?

In a measured voice that belied his feelings, Le Guévenec gave the crew his orders. His face was black with smoke, and he couldn't take his eyes off the blaze. Long minutes passed before he started toward the first mate's cabin to tell Lanier the tragic news about Romain Brissac. The head of Terre Noire stared at him for a long while and made him repeat all the details of the accident twice.

"Find the bastard who's killed Romain."

Paris, 18 rue Deparcieux, 10:10 p.m.

John helped set the table in the media room. Keeping his hands busy helped him think. The three of them were dining on the second floor, rather than in the kitchen, which was on the floor above. The two houses that Alicia Spencer had joined together to form a studio and exhibition rooms that were worthy of her genius didn't function well as a home. Seated in her armchair, Victoire, wearing a bolero and copper stress-relieving bracelets, was observing the two men in her life. John had the blond good looks of an actor who could have been a hero in a ninteen-forties French Foreign Legion movie. Luc had black eyes and dark hair, a lock of which curled over his forehead. He had an adolescent's face that was as pleasing to men as to women. Their almost identical height was the one thing they had in common. Victoire garnered smiles from onlookers whenever she strolled the streets of the Daguerre village with both of them at her side.

Luc stroked the Persian cat as he recounted his amorous adventures in Le Havre. The other two sat entranced.

"Connie Rasmussen and Isabelle Le Guévenec were both dying to spill the beans," he concluded. "I didn't have much trouble."

"Don't be so modest!"

John summed up the tailing episode and told Luc how he'd shaken off the man, thanks to Victoire and their rigged-up taxi.

"You were fantastic. He put his head in the lion's mouth the very minute he got in the car with you."

Ignoring John's compliment, Victoire raised her fork over the small round *chavignol* while John opened the chardonnay.

"That guy followed you from the Ritz because someone told him you were there. Who was in the know?"

The parquet floor creaked under John's two hundred pounds of muscle as he went over to the French windows to take in the nighttime scene. The neon lights of La Bélière lit up the corner of the Rue Deparcieux and the Rue Daguerre. A jazz tune was spilling out of the piano bar. He recognized the melodies of Théo, the musician who could single-handedly make the neighborhood come alive. But the atmosphere tonight was heavy. He owed it to himself to take things in hand again. In any case, the wine had been decanted, so to speak. It was too late to backtrack now. He was doomed to go through with it with his two cohorts at his side. He tried to be persuasive and reassuring as he reasoned out loud.

"Geraldine Harper wouldn't entrust her daughter's welfare to me and then put me down like a dog, especially not after giving me a company credit card and a phone to eavesdrop on Mary."

"She gave you a credit card and a cell phone so they'd be found on your corpse, and you'd be under suspicion," Victoire declared.

"For what? For being interested in the daughter with the mother's phone on me? You're wrong."

"John's right. There's something we're not getting," Luc said, making the cat purr.

Victoire, who was straightening up the table, interrupted the conversation and pointed to the touch wall. A signal had just appeared on one of the screens. The GPS system camouflaged in the euros she'd handed the man tailing John was indicating that he had reached the Rue de Richelieu in the second arrondissement.

"What the hell can he be doing there?" asked John.

"I don't see what there is on the Rue de Richelieu," Luc said.

Victoire zoomed in on the map of Paris. In a double click, she brought up the exact spot where the man was.

"He's at the Hôtel Louxor. Five stars."

"He's not on a fixed-term contract, our killer," John observed.

"I can't see Geraldine skimping on a killer's pay, considering what she'd give a babysitter," Luc said, trying to defuse the atmosphere.

"You'll pay for that," John shot back, glaring at him. "The Harpers head an internationally recognized firm. They're not going to take the risk of blowing us away at the very moment they're asking us to protect their heiress. That's absurd."

"What do we do?" Luc asked, nibbling tortilla chips.

John went back to studying the Rue Deparcieux. A bunch of kids were emerging from La Bélière. Nothing looked suspicious.

"Tomorrow morning, I'm going to call Mary Harper and arrange a meeting with François Guerot. We need to alert the agency, without telling them everything, obviously."

"You're going to warn the agency?" Luc asked.

"Yes. In any case, the Harpers predicted we would. I even wonder if that's why they chose us. Whether I take the assignment or turn it down, the guy who wanted to waste me will try again. This is the only way we can protect ourselves."

"And what if Mary goes to Greenland to look for her father at the Great Wound of the Wild Dog?" Victoire asked, looking at him with anguished eyes.

John smiled and went over to take her hand. Her fingers were extraordinarily supple and summed up her whole being. He took them between his hands and touched his forehead to hers.

"I'll go, too."

"Really?"

"If there's any danger, we need to identify it as quickly as possible. I know you understand me, my love."

John saw tears run down her face and fall onto her bolero. He knew she would withdraw. Victoire was capable of wrapping herself in silence for hours. Deciding to let her be, he took Geraldine Harper's phone out of his pocket. He punched in the code and began listening to Mary's conversations while Luc finished clearing the table. Student chatter of no interest. The last conversation was interesting, though. Mary had called her brother Harold in Montreal.

"Can you imagine. Mom has dumped a guardian angel on me. She wants me to be nice to him. One John Spencer Larivière, an ex-army major, a sort of warden. Can you believe it!"

"An American?"

"A Frenchman."

"Amazing. Have you heard anything about Dad?"

"Nothing. I called our subsidiary in Nuuk. No one's seen him. I'm worried. How are you?"

"I'll survive. The doctor says I'm making progress."

"Good. Okay, I'll leave you. Big hug."

"Ciao."

This intrusion made John uncomfortable. Mary's elder brother sounded fragile and sick. The voice gave it away. He used the speakerphone and played the conversation for his two associates. Victoire gave a feeble smile and reacted.

"If I get it right, you roam around with an NSA telephone specially made so that the Harpers can quietly spy on their family. It's lunacy. Who says that the phone won't be used by the NSA to know where you are at any time, like our coins in your killer's pocket."

"That's true," John replied. "Abraham Harper is on intimate terms with the NSA and no doubt the CIA. He'll know exactly what we're doing and if we're really protecting his daughter. In a way, that's reassuring."

Luc shook his head. Baffled, Victoire stared at John.

"If the Harpers' phone is bugged, the CIA already knows that you weren't blown away, and we've spotted the killer. They know that Luc slept with Greenland's lawyer and with the wife of the captain of the

Bouc-Bel-Air. And they suspect we're about to put the agency in the loop. The whole thing's crazy! Who are we really working for?"

"You're right," John said. "There's a hitch somewhere. Who says that the killer really wanted to kill me, anyway?"

"You're annoying me. I'm going up to bed." Victoire gave her long black hair a toss and headed toward the stairs.

Luc, peeling one of the pears that he bought on Sunday mornings at La Bonne Ménagère on the Rue Daguerre, spoke in a low voice.

"Do you really think he didn't intend to kill you?"

As a former military officer, John had no illusions about the true intentions of his tail.

"No, I said that to reassure Victoire. It's too late to backtrack now. We have to know where this mercenary comes from and find out who he works for and how he was told about my meeting with Geraldine. Have you cleaned up recently?"

Luc regularly checked Fermatown's walls and furniture for any surreptitiously planted listening devices. All the computers and cell phones in use or ready for use were regularly neutralized and wiped clean. To do this, he had the latest Chinese counterespionage technologies available on the Internet and in the shops of the main Paris Chinatown. The technologies were the ultimate in cybersecurity and dirt cheap there.

"I swept everything last week. Your mobile's clean. Did you give your number to anyone between last Thursday and today?"

"No, Geraldine Harper called me on the landline listed on our website."

"So, the leak doesn't come from her. I've just thought of something."

"What?"

"North Land is big in Greenland, same as Terre Noire. Lanier's firm, thanks to Brissac and his software program, is going to play a considerable role."

"You think Terre Noire might have a grudge against us?"

"I don't know. I looked at Nicolas Lanier's biography. There's hardly anything in it. We know almost nothing about his private life or his career. He heads Terre Noire, thanks to the shares his mother left him in her will. There are hardly any photos of him. All we know is that he taught in Copenhagen and Oslo. The guy who followed you looked Scandinavian."

"You don't seriously think that Terre Noire would have me taken out because I'm protecting the heiress of its rival!"

"No, but for something that we don't know about. And Terre Noire is every bit as Danish as it is French. Who really directs the firm?"

"Check with your conquests in Le Havre. We need tip-offs. They're becoming vitally important."

"I'll bait the lawyer," Luc said. "I'm going upstairs to do an article for future-probe.com on the sister ships."

"The sister ships?"

"I learned that the *Bouc-Bel-Air* and the *Marcq-en-Barœul* are twin ships," Luc said. "That's a good start for an article on the wife of a seaman and a legal advocate for the Far North. Moreover, I have the feeling that they're both playing a role in events we don't know anything about. They both have strong personalities. I'm going to paint a pretty picture of them on future-probe.com. If we don't get a few secrets after that, I'll go and become a whirling dervish in Alaska."

"Good," John said. "I'm going upstairs to tinker with my laptop. I've got an idea I think you'll like. I'll come and see you shortly."

"You know you can come any time."

"Cretin."

John laughed as he went up the stairs that led to the studio adjoining the workout room. He chose a laptop that looked right for what he had in mind. A well-crafted Toshiba, ordinary but solid. He plugged in the USB flash drive. An Israeli engineer in Haifa's Silicon Valley had given it to him in exchange for a microscopic Russian GPS tagging device that couldn't be detected in seaports or airports. After plugging in the flash drive, he found his digital bomb camouflaged in a file on the Museum of Celtic Civilization in Mount Beuvray. He launched the application. A few minutes later, the dialogue box confirmed that the installation of Boomerang had been successful.

The risk of starting up Boomerang was not negligible. But if it went well, the outcome would largely compensate for his stress. Danger, no matter what they said, excited him. Those waiting for him around the bend wouldn't see him looming up behind them.

NUUK INTERNATIONAL AIRPORT, 6 P.M.

Lars Jensen looked out the window at the slice of coast to the north of Nuuk. In less than a fortnight, the white part had receded another few miles. The jet had taken a bit more than three hours to get from the American base at Thule to the capital. The plane was filled to bursting. He thought back to the work he had done on the slopes of Haffner Bjerg and once again gave up trying to understand why his employer had asked him to saw up the victims, especially the dogs. Lars loved animals.

He looked once more at the photo of his next victim, who was expected to arrive in two days. According to his employer, John Spencer Larivière was a French agent working undercover in a sort of private-investigation firm on the Left Bank of the Seine. Unlike the Haffner Bjerg targets, Spencer Larivière was a professional, an opponent who was his match. One last time, Lars went over the file on the former military officer and government intelligence agent. JSL, as the Americans had nicknamed him, had served in Somalia and Afghanistan. He had become a sort of legend after slitting the throats of two Taliban soldiers who were threatening to stone to death two nurses accused of blasphemy. He had been badly injured when an unidentified group shot down his helicopter, and he had spent several months recuperating at Les Invalides before leaving public service.

Lars Jensen thought back to his own stay in Bagdad in the service of American firms that paid him handsomely to do the dirty work the United States Army didn't want to take care of. That's where he'd met Omar Al Selim, who later introduced him to his current employer. Lars carefully reread the reports that Spencer Larivière had sent his superiors after each mission. In the showdown to come, the slightest detail could make a difference.

The Frenchman had reactions and obsessions that were uniquely his. Every man in combat took advantage of the surroundings and the weather in his own way. It was useful to be able to read the enemy's thoughts. Lars then looked at the photos of the two people likely to accompany him. Luc Masseron and Victoire Augagneur didn't look dangerous. Per Sorenson, in Paris, would take care of them. Nevertheless, he dived into their files before fastening his seat belt for the landing and giving the flight attendant a smile.

The Greenland Airways A320 skidded along the runway and came to a stop outside Terminal 2, which the Chinese had completed just hours before starting construction on Terminal 3. Nuuk was spreading outward faster than global warming. He grabbed his travel bag from the overhead bin and, being careful not to jostle anyone, took his place among fellow passengers impatiently waiting to disembark and tread the soil of Greenland.

"Have a good stay in Nuuk."

"Thank you. Lunch was excellent."

"We hope to see you again soon."

Lars Jensen retrieved his suitcase from the carousel and went through customs without a hitch. He then headed to the car-rental agency, where a car had been booked for him under one of his assumed names. He left the airport and soon found himself on a road too narrow for the traffic. In spite of global warming, Greenland's *nouveaux riches* were rolling along in arrogant and polluting Chinese SUVs.

When he got to a rocky ridge, he turned off toward a wasteland cluttered with bulldozers. The sky hanging over Nuuk was incredibly blue and unperturbed. There was no hint of the catastrophe that had just unfolded a few hundred miles to the north. Lars pulled out the map of the town and a pair of binoculars to observe his future hunting grounds.

He began by observing the port, which was choked with a multi-colored armada that was heading into the fjord. He then studied the office block that housed the North Land headquarters. The Canadian-American company owned the top two floors and overlooked the town from a balcony. Lars then spotted the more modest building housing the Terre Noire offices. The firm had two ground-floor rooms in the building. He took in the strategic buildings linked to his mission, starting with the Katuaq, the cultural and political center of Greenland, then the Conference Hall of the Northern Peoples, two hundred and twenty yards away, and last, the Hans Egede Hotel, a pearl of well-heeled tourism that saw all the ministers on the planet in quest of climate legitimacy pass through its doors.

He swung his binoculars toward the fjord, which was clogged with drifting chunks of ice. The quaint wooden houses staggered over the two banks evoked images of fishing and kayaking. He easily spotted the house that belonged to North Land. Another quarter turn of the binoculars, and there was the mountain, looming over the town with its black peak shaped like a rhinoceros horn.

3

TUESDAY

As he walked along the Rue Deparcieux, John was trying to figure out who would have it in for him. He had changed course several times and taken one of his anti-surveillance shortcuts between the boulevard and the Avenue de l'Observatoire. No trace of his tail. According to the rigged coins, he was still in his room at the Hôtel Louxor. In a bad mood, John strode through the gate of L'École des Mines. Mary Harper had arranged to meet him in the cafeteria. Good at remembering faces and endowed with an uncommon memory for voices, John would have no trouble recognizing her, even if she were disguised as a polar bear. The sound of Mary's voice on her mother's phone was burned forever on his biological hard drive. He had an excellent ear—thanks to a childhood divided between two continents—and a certain skill in languages. He might not speak them fluently, but he understood Arabic, Pashto, and even Farsi.

The old Latin Quarter building was a cauldron of feverish students and third worlders. White sheets pinned to the walls displayed the message "Miners Stick Together" in big red letters. John weaved his way through the crowds milling in the halls, trying to respond to inquisitive eyes with a smile. His muscular build and rugged looks, appropriate for a physical fitness advertisement, were out of place in this setting, which was filled with skinny kids in tight jeans and short skirts.

"Where's the cafeteria?"

He had to go on a charm offensive before a student in blue and green pointed to the second floor. Taking two steps at a time, he reached the top of the stairs and found the cafeteria. Mary Harper had her mother's determined forehead but lighter and noticeably more insolent eyes. He was going to be earning his hundred thousand euros! They acknowledged each other amid the hubbub, but some students bumped into them just as he was holding out his hand to shake Mary's. He took advantage of the moment to slip a one-euro coin into the young woman's canvas shoulder bag. He figured he'd put his tags in place right away.

"It wasn't the best idea to meet among your comrades. They might not appreciate it."

"Why?"

"A bodyguard for the North Land heiress. You can't say that it makes for solidarity with the rest of the student body."

"I was told you were good-looking, but you're also an idiot!"

John restrained himself from giving the cheeky brat a slap, surrounded as she was by her giggling girlfriends. He paused for a moment, staring at her black T-shirt, which was emblazoned with the image of a polar bear.

"Could we find a quiet corner somewhere?"

A few seconds later, John was sitting opposite the last of the Harpers. With her elbows on the table and her hands on either side of her face, she stared at him. Her skin looked lighter than in the photos. Her blue eyes and thick eyebrows reminded him of Abraham Harper. Under the makeup, John saw genuine wildness. According to Luc, who'd poked his nose into North Land's database, with a little help from some hackers, Geraldine Harper's ancestors were hunting bears in the Canadian Rockies at the beginning of the nineteenth century. They were lone brutes who had built an empire in fur and wood in Hudson Bay before turning to the extraction of bitumen from the tar sands. Nothing could be less green or more polluting.

"My mother chose you so I'd sleep with you, but there's no chance of that!" she said, murdering a Canadian accent that didn't suit her at all.

"Listen, Mary, we could start off on another note."

"What did she tell you?"

"That it was your father who had the idea of contacting me to ensure your protection here in Paris while you're studying. It seems you excite envy. I'm just repeating what your mother told me. That's why I called you early this morning."

Mary looked put out.

"I hope you didn't believe her."

"Who?"

"My mother."

"I shouldn't have?"

"You sound incredibly naïve, despite your conspiratorial act."

John pulled out one of his cards. He had to raise his voice because the loudspeakers were calling students to a general assembly in the Eiffel lecture hall.

"Here's my number in case there's a problem. Don't hesitate to call me."

Mary Harper threw a disgusted glance at the little card, as though it were an over-ripe camembert.

"It's odd, your name. What are you, really?"

"Spencer is my mother's name, and Larivière is my father's."

"I see now why my father chose you."

John thought the remark was interesting.

"Fermatown, what is this shit?"

"It's my bread and butter."

"It's dumb, whatever it is. Farm Town. You live on a farm on the Rue Deparcieux, in the middle of Montparnasse?"

John clenched his jaw and focused on the mission.

"Have you noticed anyone or anything suspicious around you lately?"

"I'm sometimes followed by boys."

"That doesn't surprise me. Nothing more sinister?"

Mary Harper got up, slipped the card into a back pocket of her jeans, and turned toward the door. The announcement was emptying the cafeteria.

"Nothing worth noting. Do your job, and leave me alone," she finally replied, walking away.

John swallowed hard. This little bitch of a kid had humiliated him. It was no easy feat, earning a living this way. He finished his coffee and got up to pay the bill. In the corridor, older heads were mingling with the mob of students. Intrigued, he let himself be swept into the throng.

The spectacle he found in the lecture hall was worth the detour. A polar bear projected as a hologram above the platform was gazing at the crowd with sad eyes. Everyone was staring at the screen next to the bear. It was a televised press conference, and a woman in her fifties was quickly explaining the events that were unfolding. It looked like the press conference was taking place outside a convention center. Patches of snow gave John the impression that it might be in Greenland, maybe Nuuk, the capital of the newly independent state.

Laura Al-lee-Ah, whose name had just been displayed, was bemoaning the plight of the bears, the victims of global warming. The news report drew to a close to a round of applause. John recognized Mary's black hair and denim jacket close to the platform. The *Bouc-Bel-Air* was featured in the second report. After a few sequences on the drifting of the Terre Noire ship in the middle of the smashed ice sheet, the camera zoomed over the estuary of the Seine and swooped down toward the sedimentation ponds of Sandouville. John had to move back to let a new group through. The school kids of the Latin

Quarter were rushing in to the siren call of the North Pole and the endangered polar bear.

The sound suddenly cut out. A student armed with a mike climbed up to the platform, replacing the commentary of the journalist, who'd apparently sold out to the multinationals. "What you see here is the homeport of the *Bouc-Bel-Air*. The boat in view now is the *Marcq-en-Barœul*. It's the exact replica of the other ship."

Hostile cries erupted from the rows of seats.

"This is where Terre Noire carries out the analysis of the soils and geological strata that its ships collect from all over the planet. With the complicity of the French and Danish governments, they're opening Greenland up to all its predators!"

Whistles shot out from the crowd. The following live coverage showed a crowd outside Terre Noire's Champs-Elysées headquarters. A young man speaking under a Northern Peoples Congress banner condemned the experiments being conducted in the sedimentation ponds. Those around him were nodding. All of a sudden, John recognized the silhouette, then the face, of the man who'd followed him the day before. Same hard look, same gray bomber jacket. The phantom evaporated almost as soon as it appeared.

John left the lecture hall and found a less congested corridor to call Victoire and ask her to view the footage on CNN.

"The guy that followed me is on the Champs-Elysées."

"Yes, he left his room. We're keeping track of him. I'll keep you posted."

Back in the lecture hall, John saw that Mary had disappeared. That wasn't surprising. Without getting flustered, he retraced his steps to the Boulevard Saint-Michel. The idea of taking a bit of initiative again gave him some comfort. The sky over Paris was as luminous as the sky over Greenland. He crossed the street and sat down outside a café where he could see both the school entrance and the door of the apartment block opposite it. The Harpers had rented an apartment for their offspring in this building.

"A *grand crème* and two croissants."

A few minutes later, he grabbed Geraldine's phone and checked it. Mary's last call was again to her brother.

"It's getting crazy here because of the melting ice cap and the *Bouc-Bel-Air* business. Everyone's coming down on Terre Noire. I'm amazed we haven't been attacked yet. But I sense it won't be long. I'm leaving tomorrow for Greenland to look for Dad. How are you?"

"The doctor reckons I'm making progress."

Mary Harper paused for a few seconds, which moved John.

"What about your guardian angel?" Harold asked.

"Gorgeous as a god. Dumb as they come. He's probably crouched under one of my windows now. Dad was the one who chose him."

"Why him?" Harold asked in a tired, depressed voice.

John picked up the sister's embarrassed silence.

"He must also suit Geraldine. You know what she's like."

"Take a photo of him. I'm tired, little sister. I'm going to hang up."

John's identity and physique had become an issue in the very bosom of the Harper family, where no one was telling anyone everything. It made him feel uneasy. He stopped listening in and glanced around. That little bitch was capable of pulling out a camera and filming him for her own amusement. Everything looked normal, but it had become suffocatingly steamy. Now disturbing black clouds were hanging over the Jardin du Luxembourg. He was beginning to sweat.

"Mademoiselle, do I look dumb?" he asked the waitress, who had come over to see if he needed anything else.

"Not at all. You remind me of my philosophy lecturer."

John almost blushed. It was rare for anyone to take him for an intellectual.

"Really?"

"I assure you."

When the waitress had gone, he checked on Mary Harper's phone calls again. After she'd talked to her brother, she had called a number in Burgundy that she'd also called the day before, without success. Using his personal phone, he sent Victoire the number and asked her to find out whose it was.

John left the waitress a tip befitting her compliment and headed back to Fermatown. While he was crossing the Boulevard Montparnasse, he received Victoire's call.

"The man who followed you yesterday is in a café on the Champs-Elysées."

"Which one?"

"The Deauville. It's opposite Terre Noire headquarters."

"Send Luc."

On the way home, John stopped at a *boulangerie* and bought a box of *calissons d'Aix*, the almond-shaped marzipan sweets made in Aix-en-Provence.

"Is it a gift?"

"Yes."

Paris, 18 Rue Déparcieux, noon

Back at Fermatown, John announced that Mary was planning to go to Greenland.

"I can still refuse."

Victoire gave him a bored look as she smoothed her long black hair. He loved her enough to guess the contradictory feelings that were keeping her awake at night.

"I've looked at the accounts. We have no money coming in next month."

"So we need the money from North Land."

John put the *calissons* on the table. Victoire understood that the present was not for her but for someone in Greenland. She had a talent for guesswork and making it known without saying a thing. Yet again, he felt he'd been seen through and forgiven without a word being exchanged.

"You're not going to land in Nuuk with nothing but Geraldine Harper's cell phone and a credit card in the name of North Land, are you? It reeks of a trap."

"You're right. I'll take precautions. That's why I bought this..."

"Sh!"

Victoire put her index finger over her lips. She didn't want their conversation to be caught by a listening device. Luc swept the place regularly, but there could always be a spy drone somewhere. John smiled and kissed her fingers.

The opening notes of the *Eroica Symphony*, Beethoven's Third, filled the media room. That was Luc calling from his stakeout on the Champs-Elysées. Victoire grabbed one of the cell phones.

"Well?"

"The Rue de Richelieu killer is talking to a guy he's just met. I'm sending you the photo."

"Got it."

John and Victoire turned as one of the screens opened on the touch wall. Wearing a bomber jacket, the guy who'd tailed John was sitting with a young man in a tie and a dark suit. The man was wearing glasses with black rectangular frames. It was the perfect getup of a busy, self-important executive. Victoire called up the identification software that John had gotten from the logistics department at Les Invalides.

"Bingo! Got it!"

Christophe Maunay appeared on the Terre Noire website with his e-mail address, his direct line, and his title: manager of human resources. A closed face and razor-thin lips. He looked like a clam.

"Pinched little rat face of an informer. Madame Le Guévenec wasn't spinning Luc a story. This guy's Lanier's protégé, the one who grills the scientists about what they've discovered in the Barents Sea."

"What's a Terre Noire exec doing with a killer?"

The Franco-Danish company had wasted no time reacting. Victoire called Luc to give him the identity of the man in the business suit.

"Can you record them?"

"They're talking very softly, and there's music. What's more, there's a demonstration outside Terre Noire. But I'll take advantage of that and try to slip a coin in Maunay's pocket."

As Victoire continued to monitor the unusual tête-à-tête, John went upstairs to pour himself a cup of coffee in the kitchen. Through the window, he saw that the forsythias were in bloom in the garden that opened onto Number 9 on the Rue Fermat. Spring was really early this year. The three little balls that he intended to take to Greenland were bathing before him in a Nevers earthenware dish filled with alcohol. The meeting between his killer and someone from Terre Noire had left him stunned. Why would the protection of the North Land heiress bother Lanier and his HR man? He had almost turned down a hundred thousand euros so as not to spy on a French company, yet Terre Noire had had him followed, probably even before he'd met Geraldine Harper. There was more to this than protecting that kid. He felt manipulated and disarmed.

But he was determined to force the hand of fate and get Fermatown out of the poverty rut, even if that meant battling the Scandinavian killers employed by a French firm! In the fog of what looked like war, he'd use weapons his adversaries, no matter who they were, could never match. It was make-or-break time. He went upstairs to take a shower and phone Patrick, Fermatown's official physician.

"I need you."

"When?"

"Straightaway."

"Do you have the material?"

"Yes."

"The Rue Sarrette. Be there at three o'clock."

Back in the media room, John found Victoire in front of a map of Greenland. A few red dots flagged places with bizarre names. Every other one ended in the letter q.

"Weird, all these q's. Where's the Great Wound of the Wild Dog?"

"Somewhere over here."

Victoire pointed to an area hatched in red. It was the size of a French *département*. A tiny piece of the island continent had been touched by a mysterious illness. Actually, it was a gaping wound.

"It should be around here."

"It's weird. No one talks about it. Nothing online or in the newspapers. You'd think it was a black hole. What the hell can Abraham Harper be doing up there?"

"His job. It's not a place you go for pleasure. I can't see you wandering around up there, John. You'll get lost," Victoire said, visibly troubled by the immensity of the problem.

"Would you be unhappy if I ended up in an ice block?"

"Don't be an idiot."

John planted a kiss on the nape of her porcelain neck.

"I've made arrangements to meet Patrick, and I'll be seeing Guerot shortly. I have to tell the agency. Any news from the Champs-Élysées?" he asked.

"Nothing new on the Terre Noire front. On the North Land front, Mary Harper has left her apartment. She's on the Rue de Richelieu right now."

"Don't tell me she's going to join the man in the bomber jacket! Not her, too?"

The notion that both oil-exploration companies were having him followed by the same Viking with the herring head was too much for his brain to handle.

"We'll know soon enough. Luc is following the guy. You told me you were going to take precautions."

"Find me the address of North Land's subsidiary in Nuuk. I'm going to send them an urgent parcel."

"What have you dreamed up now?"

John wrapped his arms around her and whispered in her ear, the ear of the little girl she had never been.

"The Harpers may well want to fuck me over for some reason that escapes me, but we'll soon see who fucks whom. That's why I bought the *calissons*. If there's a gorgon in the snows of Greenland, I'll cut its head off with my confectionary."

BAFFIN BAY, 8:05 A.M.

Pursued by bloodthirsty bears, Le Guévenec woke up screaming like one of the damned. With both hands gripping the bunk, he steadied his breathing as his memories of the events arranged themselves in his mind.

After washing his hands and face in the thin trickle of warm water that was all the *Bouc-Bel-Air*'s boiler was able to produce, he checked the ship's list. The inclination was no worse. Lanier's unexpected arrival and the way he'd taken hold of the steel box obsessed him as much as the helicopter catastrophe. He found a change of clothes in the closet and left his cabin to join the platform aft. The sight of the helicopter seized him with terror. Frozen by the violent drop in temperature, the machine looked like a charred scorpion with a broken back. At the bottom of the wreckage, a black hand pointed toward the sky. Perhaps it was the hand of Romain Brissac, his wife's lover. Le Guévenec turned away and grabbed his phone.

"Bring a tarpaulin to the deck aft, and cover up this coffin for me."

Chilled to the marrow, he headed toward the passenger deck and passed the scientific team's cabins. With the aid of his master key, he opened Romain Brissac's cabin. Everything was topsy-turvy, thanks to the tidal wave. He wouldn't be able to find the slightest clue here. Everything was soaked and scattered over the floor. He was about to leave when a stench of rot that was different from the stench on the rest of the ship made him turn toward the refrigerator. He thought of the blackened hand sticking out from the guts of the helicopter and had a sense of foreboding. What atrocity was he going to stumble upon now?

He walked over hesitantly and then quickly opened the door. A mass of tangled algae fell at his feet in a greenish and gelatinous glob. The organic matter looked to be alive and was moving almost imperceptibly. A noxious gas immediately seized him. Covering his mouth and nose with his arm, he retreated from the cabin and headed to the first mate's cabin to tell Lanier what he had just found. The Terre Noire leader listened attentively and asked him to come closer. Lanier then sniffed his clothes, which were still impregnated with the gut-wrenching odor.

"Those are algae that have been genetically modified to live on the ice by feeding on methane emissions."

"Why?"

"To block the sunlight and stop the melting, but especially to stop up the wells," Lanier replied.

"What wells?"

"The wells of methane that are springing up from the decomposing permafrost under the ice cap. We're seeing the same phenomenon at the bottom of the Arctic Ocean. Unfortunately, the algae haven't worked."

Le Guévenec nodded. Something Brissac said as he lay on his stretcher obsessed him.

"Before he died, Brissac said that the South was heading north. I didn't quite get it."

"He actually said that?"

"Yes."

Lanier leaned right to counterbalance the tilt of the ship and ran his hand over his red beard. Le Guévenec unconsciously did the same. The head of Terre Noire looked agitated. He stared at the captain of the *Bouc* and began talking in a low voice.

"We know that during the last ice age, temperatures in Greenland veered sharply, going up and then down by twenty-five degrees Fahrenheit in the space of a few decades. Studies in Greenland over the last several years have led to the discovery of what's called a bipolar seesaw. The energy necessary for these variations has to come from somewhere. In this thermal shift, as the Arctic warms, the Antarctic cools. That's what Brissac was trying to say before he died."

"That's incredible."

"But true. We've known about these extreme changes for a long time. The mechanism stems from shifts in the atmospheric flow, which actually occur from one year to the next. It can also arise during the planet's hot periods, like the Eemian some one hundred and thirty thousand years ago. We're seeing something similar right now. Brissac's initial analyses are consistent with that. It's fantastic. And it's terrifying."

"How is it possible?"

"The Earth's axis and orbit around the sun shift, and because of that, some regions of the planet get more exposure to the sun, while other parts get less."

With his fist above the leaning table, Lanier imitated the change in the planet's axis. "At the end of the Eemian, about one hundred and fifteen thousand years ago, the Earth entered an ice age from which it emerged some ten thousand years ago, once again because of a change in the planet's rotational and orbital parameters."

"Are they sure about that?"

"Yes. The Eemian lasted sixteen thousand years. If we find out how it started, we'll know how we're going to live in the sixteen thousand years to come."

"If I understand you correctly, CO_2 emissions and the other ways we're polluting the planet count for nothing in what's going to happen to us."

"Several factors enter into the equation, but larger phenomena are driving things. The Earth has no interest in assigning guilt, as Brissac would have told you."

Le Guévenec shook his head, thinking of Isabelle and her Nobel Prize lover. Guilt seemed to be irrelevant for them, as well.

"And where's all this going?"

"Climatic upheaval that may happen very fast."

"The end of humanity."

"Yes, but not because of the climate."

"Then what?"

"Because of our inability to govern a new planet together. The most fatal inclination isn't the Earth's. It's the one that makes us lean toward an outdated economic and political model. But I'd really like to sleep now, Captain."

"I'll leave you to it."

Paris, Sarrette Clinic, 3 p.m.

Staring at the opaque-glass window set ablaze by sunlight from the Rue Sarrette, John let his doctor examine the grafts. Patrick had done this regularly since John's return from Afghanistan.

"What do you think?" John asked, averting his eyes from the scarred flesh on the right side of his body.

"Looks like it's holding," Patrick responded. "I'm still impressed. Can you feel my fingers?"

"No."

John had been stitched up with the frozen skin of a Taliban soldier shot down not far from Special Forces headquarters. Then he had been flown to France for treatment in the special burn unit at the Hôpital Saint-Louis, which was renowned for reconstructive surgery. After a spell in the Val-de-Grâce, a French military hospital, he had returned to Les Invalides to push a pen before leaving the government.

"You think I can go to Greenland?"

"Yes."

John put his clothes on again and settled into the chair used for minor surgical procedures. The telephone vibrated in his pocket.

"Excuse me, but business is picking up again."

Victoire was calling from Fermatown.

"The man in the bomber jacket has returned to his hotel on the Rue de Richelieu. Mary Harper is nearby on the same street. She's visiting an exhibition of paintings at Greenland House. For the moment, they haven't met."

"That's surprising."

"I'm looking into Christophe Maunay. The guy graduated from L'École des Mines five years ago and joined Terre Noire. He was sent to Libreville in Gabon, but it looks like he must have quickly been sent back to France."

"Why?"

"I have no idea. Something happened there. In fact, Terre Noire began its expansion into Africa well before it got interested in the poles. Maunay takes care of the nonscientific personnel on the exploration ships. We're being had somewhere."

"How do you mean?"

"Geraldine Harper promised you that we wouldn't investigate Terre Noire, but that's exactly what we're doing."

"I have to give it some thought. I'll call you back later. Patrick's here's with me. He sends his love."

John turned off his phone and tried to relax before the procedure. Fermatown was being dragged into a peculiar whirlwind. One of Terre Noire's executives had just met up with the man who'd tailed him from the Ritz. This same executive had studied at L'École des Mines. They were caught between Terre Noire and North Land—between the devil and the deep blue sea. He thought of the captain of the Bouc-Bel-Air, who was getting quite a bit of attention from the media and whose wife Luc had seduced too easily. He felt bad about that and thought back to fighting in the Afghan mountains. Over there, everything happened out in the open. You could see the enemy. But then, of course, there were the land mines that maimed people on both sides.

"Worries?" asked Patrick.

"I take off tomorrow."

"Does your trip involve the ship that is accused of damaging the ice shelf?"

"In my business, you never know what you're really dealing with."

Patrick nodded and, with the aid of tweezers, picked up the three tiny steel balls on the tray and examined them closely.

"I assume you have your reasons, and they're inside these little balls."

"Right. They have to rub against each other nonstop to generate energy."

The doctor put the balls back on the tray. He picked up a syringe and pricked John's right earlobe.

"Just giving you some local anesthetic."

Five minutes later, he began his work with an ear-piercing gun.

"Avoid swimming pools and chlorinated water."

"Yes, boss!"

"How's Victoire?"

"Not good. If you could, stop at the house and reassure her."

"I'll show her the pictures I took during our Greenland cruise last summer. That way, she can see where you're going. We visited glaciers that were melting into the Ilulissat Fjord on the coast of Baffin Bay. It was impressive. There were thousands of people there. That's where I met the Chinese guys who gave me this stuff."

Patrick handed John a little pot of blue cream. The pot was decorated with Chinese characters and a fire-breathing dragon.

"Dab this on your grafts once a month. It regenerates the dermis and keeps the evil spirits away,"

"Thank you."

John got another call from Victoire as he left the clinic.

"Luc paid a visit to Mary's apartment. He opened her computer and found confirmation that she's taking a flight to Copenhagen tomorrow, then going on to Nuuk on Air Greenland. The plane is booked solid because of everything that's going on up there. But with a bit of luck, at least one passenger won't show up."

Victoire, at Luc's request, had hacked into hotel and airline booking systems to see if she could find any last-minute cancellations.

"Did Mary Harper meet up with the killer from the Ritz?"

"They're in the same neighborhood, but they haven't connected. Not yet, anyway. I'm trying to figure it out. Did the procedure go okay?"

"Yes," John replied, looking at his reflection in the mirror of the *boulangerie* across the street from the clinic.

"Can't wait to see it!"

"Patrick gave me some Chinese ointment, and he wants to tell you about his trip to Greenland."

John took in the silence at the other end of the call. Victoire didn't like Patrick's style. He was attractive, but for some reason, the surgeon bugged her. With Victoire, nothing was ever simple.

MAINE-MONTPARNASSE BOWLING ALLEY, 6:20 P.M.

John ended his tenth frame with a strike and sat down at an unoccupied table illuminated by a Coca-Cola sign. He felt the admiring glances of the adolescent girls in the lane next to his. The piercing, meanwhile, was bothering him, and he fiddled with the three steel balls that Patrick had inserted without asking even one indiscreet question.

As usual, François Guerot, his handler at the agency, had arranged to meet him in an unlikely place. Since he had opened Fermatown, John had met the man a dozen times and had never detected the tiniest security team accompanying him. Either he was blind or Guerot had complete confidence in him. It didn't occur to John that Guerot didn't want any witnesses. Once again, John scrutinized the place, but nothing looked remotely like a support team—unless Guerot was employing schoolgirls these days. And maybe he was. The government was always looking for ways to save money.

Deputy Director Guerot headed security-clearance investigations. After the global financial crisis and the rise of ethics committees, the agency at Les Invalides headed by Hubert de Méricourt had instituted more rigorous background checks on staff and prospective employees. But it was too much even for the agency to handle, and so it relied on private subcontractors such as Fermatown.

Fermatown, which reported to Guerot, drew the bulk of its cash from this contract work, which consisted of confirming the accuracy of employee and prospective-employee résumés. It wasn't the kind of money that Asian and African firms were making in more intelligence-rich places where good information sold at a premium. In France, private intelligence was just barely above suspicion, and regularly subjected to bad press. The revenue stream provided by Guerot helped pay the bills. But Fermatown needed more than this contract work to flourish, and it couldn't afford to pass up a client like North Land.

There he is, John said to himself, spotting the low-key blazer and grim mouth of the deputy director. According to Victoire, who was fond of him, Guerot wasn't interested in women. He liked literature and passed for an intellectual, which wasn't an asset in the world of Les Invalides. For the past few years, Guerot had despaired of making it up the greasy pole to inspector general. No doubt he'd forgotten to join the right Masonic lodge, or he'd unwittingly stepped on someone's toes.

Guerot sat down with a grimace. His tiny gray eyes had just spotted the three steel balls. Shouts from a group a few lanes down greeted a strike. Real life continued around them. John smiled.

"You asked to see me," Guerot whispered.

"I need your help."

"I'm listening."

The deputy director's countenance didn't give John much hope. He decided to prioritize what was most important.

"I'm still waiting for you to pay me for checking the sixty CVs you gave me three months ago. Times are tough."

"I'll see what I can do. It's hard for everybody. You wanted to talk to me about something else?"

"Fermatown has gotten a security contract for Mary Harper."

"Mary Harper?"

"The daughter of Geraldine and Abraham Harper, the North Land bosses. You know who I'm talking about?"

"I see."

The smooth, impassive face of the once-youngest and soon-to-be-oldest deputy director at the agency went from milky white to ash gray. Paranoid as he was, he seemed shocked at this turn of events. John was almost moved. Guerot paid badly, but from time to time, he came up with the money urgently needed to keep Fermatown going.

"Why you?" he asked, looking dumbfounded.

John felt that the moment was right to hammer the message home. He leaned in. "Fermatown is starting to have a reputation. I told myself it was only right to warn you."

"You've done the right thing," Guerot replied with an air of resignation.

"I'm most likely leaving for Greenland," John confided, not mentioning the disappearance of Abraham Harper at the Great Wound of the Wild Dog.

"Oh."

"Mary Harper's going to Nuuk. I just thought I'd let you know."

Guerot stared at John as if he were from another planet. John told himself he'd just ventured into a murky and dangerous area—a very dangerous area, judging by the expression on his handler's face.

"Do you think she'll be interested in the *Bouc-Bel-Air*?" Guerot asked anxiously.

John knew he was walking in a minefield, just as he had so many times in Afghanistan. It seemed that the agency and Terre Noire were connected in some way. This was a scenario he dreaded the most. It was crucial now to avoid lying and say as little as possible.

"Geraldine Harper has hired me to provide security for her daughter. She hasn't asked me to do anything in regard to the *Bouc-Bel-Air* or Terre Noire."

"For the moment."

"There is something else, though," John continued.

"Of course."

"After my meeting with Geraldine Harper at the Ritz, some guy tailed me. He was most likely from Scandinavia or the Baltic region. Victoire's worried, and we'd like some discreet security at Fermatown."

Guerot's eyes widened.

"Are you still at 18 Rue Deparcieux, near the Rue Daguerre?"

"Yes."

"Tomorrow I'll have an envelope dropped off with all the money we owe you. I'll send some surveillance. You can reassure Victoire."

John remembered that Guerot had a soft spot for his beautiful, exotic wife.

"Thank you," John responded, keeping quiet about the means at his disposal for identifying his shadow.

There was no point in humiliating Guerot.

"This may surprise you," Guerot said, "but in exchange for our protection, I'd like you to look into the *Bouc-Bel-Air* and what Terre Noire's doing in Greenland."

John drew a long breath. Guerot was asking him to investigate Terre Noire. It was the exact opposite of what he had foreseen. The situation was becoming unbelievable.

"I thought you'd seize the opportunity to find out more about North Land."

"One doesn't exclude the other. If Terre Noire's in trouble, France needs to know."

"What sort of trouble?" John asked, thinking of the meeting on the Champs-Elysées between the mercenary and Terre Noire's HR manager, Christophe Maunay. It would be hard to tell Guerot about that without giving away Fermatown's secrets.

"The Geological Survey of Canada has just published a new atlas of the Arctic. According to the Canadians, the geological extension of their continental shelf authorizes them to claim just about all the resources in the subsoil. France registered a protest with the UN. We've urged Terre Noire to come up with countermeasures. Romain Brissac, the Nobel in chemistry, and Lanier have developed software that saves a lot of time in assessing resources. We're watching very closely."

"I follow you."

"Abraham Harper is American, but Geraldine is Canadian and owns three-quarters of the tar sands on the planet. She's the one keeping North Land going. Her daughter has dual Canadian-American nationality. She's studying in France. Until now, everything was going nicely for France in the Far North," Guerot concluded.

He looked angry. John tried to be reassuring.

"You know you can count on us."

"I'll send the Canadian committee's report this evening. It's been published, and you can take it with you. Try not to get lost on the ice cap. These days, it tends to shift."

John rubbed the balls in his right earlobe.

"I only half trust my distress beacon, and I don't think I can count on Greenland authorities to help me if I get into any trouble up there. These balls will allow you to localize me wherever I happen to be."

Guerot looked at the three little objects in disgust and held his hand out for the card on which John had written the frequencies that would allow the agency to track him.

"So, you're also asking us to provide security in Greenland."

"I've become your agent abroad, no?"

"Right," Guerot replied with a fake smile that revealed a well-maintained set of teeth.

"Obviously, all that will entail expenses. Greenland-bound planes are packed, and the hotels are full to the rafters. Because of the *Bouc-Bel-Air*, the media have flocked to the Far North."

"I suppose North Land's paying you to ensure little Mary's security."

"Yes, but not to spy on them or on Terre Noire."

"We've been very interested in Nicolas Lanier since he allowed the Russians and the Norwegians to collaborate, based on research into the subsoil of the Arctic Ocean. We wouldn't want anything nasty to happen to him. But there's a more awkward issue."

"I was waiting for it," John replied.

Guerot was on the verge of confessing a secret that was tearing at his guts. John suddenly sensed that he was in a strong position. He didn't let it show and made himself as small as possible, despite his javelin-thrower build.

"The Chinese, as you know, own ninety-five percent of the seventeen chemical elements that constitute what we call rare earths. Among them is praseodymium, which goes into very resistant alloys used in the manufacture of airplane engines. It's also used in the production of radar equipment and electronics, such as cell phones and those balls in your earlobes."

John instinctively brought his hand to the three spheres that were making his earlobe itch. Guerot continued.

"In the region of Qaqortoq, in the south of the island, there's a fabulous deposit of rare earths that could undermine Chinese supremacy in the sector. Every country on the planet is interested in it. Well, it's Gaia, a French software program invented by Terre Noire, that can point to where and at what depth praseodymium, rubidium, lanthanum, and other treasures can be found."

John felt that Guerot was going to make another revelation, but the deputy director held back. Terre Noire's relationship with the agency wasn't exactly transparent. This was to be expected in the current time of global warming.

"I'll do my best to keep you informed."

"In the envelope you get tomorrow, there'll be a substantial advance. The sum will astound you, if I say so myself."

"It will be put to good use."

"But I'd still like to see your expense account when you return. We don't have the means of all these multinationals."

"Cross my heart and hope to die."

ON BOARD THE BOUC-BEL-AIR, 2:35 P.M.

Shut away in his cabin, Le Guévenec pulled the map of Greenland out of a drawer and taped it to one of the walls. With a ballpoint pen, he marked the position of the *Bouc* when the helicopter had landed and drew a large circle around it.

Nicolas Lanier could have flown from the western part of Greenland just as easily as the east coast of Canada. But could he have taken off from another ship? The only vessel in the helicopter's range was a Danish ore carrier, the *Copenhagen*, which was also equipped with a landing platform.

Lanier had given him no explanation. And there were more pressing matters on their minds at the time. Where did he come from? Le Guévenec carefully folded the map and slipped it back in the drawer. He thought again of the metal box and the boatswain. He decided to lance the abscess. He left his cabin and went back on deck. Then he took out his cell phone and called Terre Noire headquarters on the Champs-Elysées.

"Who's calling?"

"Le Guévenec, captain of the *Bouc-Bel-Air*. You remember me?"

Anxious whispering greeted the call from the Far North.

"Hello, can you hear me?"

"I'll put you through to the vice president."

Le Guévenec recognized the voice of Terre Noire's second in command. He was clearly embarrassed, but courteous.

"I'd like the file on Rox Oa, the boatswain you sent me from Le Havre just before we left."

Le Guévenec felt the man hesitate. The former French ambassador whom Nicolas Lanier had entrusted with routine business responded with polished confidence, giving the impression of having solved the problem.

"I'll ask Maunay to get back to you pronto. I want you to know that the entire company is behind you, Loïc. Don't hesitate to call me if you need anything."

"Thank you."

Le Guévenec hung up with a feeling of unease. The seaman's death and Lanier's bizarre attitude disturbed him as much as the death of Brissac and the other people on the helicopter. Two minutes later, the phone vibrated in his pocket.

"Christophe Maunay here. The vice president asked me to call you."

"I'd like to get hold of the file on Rox Oa, the boatswain who was killed by the bears on the *Bouc*."

More embarrassed silence.

"I'm at the Champs-Elysées office right now. We've got a crisis meeting and a demonstration under our windows. It would be better if you asked Monsieur Lanier directly for the file."

"I'm asking you!"

"I know, Captain, but it's just..."

"Just what?" Le Guévenec shot back, riled.

"Monsieur Lanier downloaded it and asked me not to give it to anyone else. You see?"

"Yes, I see."

Le Guévenec hung up and headed back to the bridge, wondering what was going on. From the Barents Sea on, a heavy silence had replaced the bonhomie at mealtimes. The collaboration with the Russians and Norwegians had given way to long and painful conversations among the scientists from the three countries. As the captain, he hadn't meddled, but he had felt the tensions rise. The atmosphere had deteriorated after the long stopover in Narsaq. The mission, back on board after taking the soundings in Qaqortoq, was no longer enlivened by a spirit of camaraderie. Nobody smiled at the table anymore, despite the excellent food. Only Lanier could understand the nature of the stakes that had darkened the climate on the *Bouc-Bel-Air*. His presence on board was proof of that.

Le Guévenec went back over his conversation with the HR manager. What was there between the chairman of Terre Noire and Rox Oa? He thought about the black box that he'd returned to Lanier. What was in it? The sky above the shattered ice shelf looked sick. The watchman was miraculously managing to navigate through debris as sharp as razors caused by the global warming. The roaring of the bears reminded him that the nightmare was ongoing. Or maybe it was just beginning.

Sitting next to Victoire, Luc was listening to the news. John had returned with more than the three little balls in his earlobe. He'd brought back a revenue stream. Money would finally rain down on Fermatown. Farewell, stakeouts at fifty euros an hour, sleazy cybercafes, nights spent leaping from one anonymizer to the next, stolen minutes sorting through the wastepaper bins of the future ethics directors of tired old companies. Holding a knife above his second pear, Luc gazed at John the way a baby gazed at his mother.

"We're in business."

"When I think about how you didn't want to spy on Terre Noire, and now, it's France that's asking you to," Victoire said, looking somber.

"They trust us," John responded. "That's all."

"They don't trust anyone. They're up against something that's too big for them, just as we are. Did you tell him about the killer?"

"Yes. They're going to put surveillance in place around the house."

"They ought to protect us in Greenland, as well as in Paris!"

"Any developments here while I was gone?" John asked.

In one precise move, Victoire took the knife out of Luc's hand and declared that he had things to say. The ex-hacker cultivated weird tastes that ranged from gothic music to underground gatherings in the catacombs of the fourteenth arrondissement. John had intervened more than once to smooth over a sticky situation. The Internet pirate gave his plate one last glance and got to his feet.

Brilliant in everything he did, the tall dark man in sneakers, as Colette, the woman who ran La Bélière called him, sometimes had trouble keeping work and play separate. John had sniffed traces of coke more than once on his clothing. But if the company Luc kept wasn't always savory, it was thanks to him that Fermatown could get in all over the web and even beyond. Luc's stormy eyes finally lit up.

"Mary Harper spent part of the day at Greenland House, Rue de Richelieu. She talked to artists at an exhibition of paintings by Laura Al-lee-Ah."

"That's the woman I saw on television this morning at L'École des Mines," John said. "She paints bears."

"Bears are her favorite subject. She also makes seals and seagulls out of wrought iron. A bit repetitive, but nice work. There's something poignant in the way those creatures look at you. It sends shivers down your spine. So, she's one strange woman I'd like to meet. She's supposed to be coming to Paris soon."

"And Mary?" John asked.

"She didn't hook up with your shadow, who was three hundred and thirty yards away in the Hôtel Louxor. I checked in person. I'm positive."

"It's still a strange coincidence, though."

"Mary Harper went back home. Right now, she's packing her bags in the apartment that Daddy and Mommy rent for her. The Dane is still in his room at the Louxor. No physical contact."

"You said the Dane?"

"I asked one of our friends in Lyon to give Interpol the fingerprints on the laminated ad that Victoire put in the backseat of the taxi. We also have his DNA and the photos taken at that meeting on the Champs-Elysées."

"Can't do any better than that. So?"

Luc moved to the touch wall and whistled the three opening notes of one of the voice-recognition programs. Photos of the man in the gray bomber jacket appeared on one of the screens, front-on and in profile, first in black and white and then in color. He had the menacing face of a mercenary trained for combat. A wild animal.

"Per Sorenson was born in Copenhagen, Denmark."

"Interesting."

"According to Interpol, he was a sergeant in the Danish army, but he was thrown out for mental cruelty and homophobia. He then sold his services to a private British army. He fought as a mercenary in Somalia and Iraq, but he quit a few months ago. They don't know who he's working for now."

"Fascinating."

"He was seen a month ago in Oslo, Norway, in the company of a Spaniard going by the name of Rox Oa, who is wanted in Denmark for identity fraud. He supposedly faked a diploma as a boatswain in the merchant marine."

"So what?" Victoire quizzed.

"There are strange things going on between Terre Noire, the Norwegians, and the Russians. The Danes and the Spanish are all we need," Luc replied.

"What about Christophe Maunay, Terre Noire's HR guy?" John asked.

"I managed to slip him one of our coins, taking advantage of the pushing and shoving outside the Champs-Elysées headquarters. He went back to his office and has just returned to his home on the Rue de Bourgogne, near the National Assembly. To sum up: for the moment, we know only that a Danish mercenary is tailing you in Paris. He reports to Nicolas Lanier's HR man. He must know you're in contact with North Land and believe that you're working for the Canadians. Lanier's having you followed. Logical, no?"

"But why? He's in contact with the agency. If he needs to know something about us, all he has to do is ask Méricourt or Guerot," John said.

"And why is the latter asking you to gather information on Lanier?" Luc wanted to know.

It was all too confusing. John felt caught between Terre Noire and the agency, two monsters with dubious connections. He went to the window and scanned the Rue Deparcieux as though expecting to see the Dane or the director of human resources at Terre Noire.

"You see, we've had our noses to the grindstone while you were off getting your ear pierced," Luc said, reaching for another pear.

"What about your article on the *Bouc-Bel-Air*?" John asked.

"I've just given Victoire the draft. She liked it. She's a woman, too."

"I'd noticed," John responded sarcastically.

Victoire gave her opinion, pushing the fruit bowl out of Luc's reach. "Luc has written a fabulous article for the website. I've hardly corrected a thing. He's done a vivid and realistic portrait of Connie Rasmussen and Isabelle Le Guévenec. He's made them really sympathetic. You feel like you want to meet them and find out more about them."

"They're certainly subjects he's delved into."

Victoire didn't respond to John's comment and simply continued. "I think we'll get some instructive reactions on future-probe.com and the social networks. Those two women are fabulous entrées into the world of Terre Noire and North Land."

"It'll create buzz. All we'll have to do then is set our nets and collect the information," Luc said, slicing away the bruised parts from his pear.

John agreed. A fan of open-source software, he had confirmed numerous times that most secrets all over the planet were available if you asked the right people the right questions at the right time. The site they'd created to attract bees to the honey of critiques and unusual points of view was a wonderful tool. All you had to do was read and listen. With its analysis software, Fermatown was equipped to map the invisible colleges and networks of leading experts who could answer questions on any subject whatsoever. There was no need to blast through safes or climb over walls, as spies had in the good old days.

"We're just finalizing the article now," Victoire said. "We'll draw to future-probe.com all the people interested in the *Bouc-Bel-Air,* Greenland, Brissac, and the bears. People are crazy for climate theories. A lot of them have family and friends working for North Land and Terre Noire. I'd be very surprised if we didn't find someone we've already come across."

"I don't doubt it," John said, a bit envious of Victoire's gift for weaving connections between people and distant events. He himself wasn't capable of inventing original stuff.

"Did you identify the number Mary Harper called several times in the Morvan without getting anyone on the other end?" John asked in a gruffer tone than he would have liked.

"Yes," Luc answered. "It corresponds to a chalet in the village of Dun-les-Places. The middle of nowhere. We'll have to do some digging, there, too."

"I'm going up to get my bags ready. My flight's at dawn."

John took the stairs up to the kitchen. He got a yogurt from the fridge and a banana, which he put on the table and looked at without enthusiasm. The idea of leaving Victoire in Paris was tearing at his guts and taking away his appetite. Since the crash that had nearly cost him his life in Afghanistan, he'd become slightly paranoid. He observed the lights of the Rue Fermat through the kitchen window and tried to spot the surveillance team charged with protecting Fermatown in his absence. He didn't notice anything in particular and sighed before going upstairs to the studio.

John got out the laptop that he intended to take to Greenland. He turned it on and checked for the presence of the little monster that was supposed to leap at the enemy's throat. Something rubbing against his leg made him jump. He was ready for combat.

"What are you doing here?"

He gathered Caresse in his arms.

"If you take care of them, I'll bring you back some fish."

4

WEDNESDAY

John looked at his watch before he stepped on the moving sidewalk that connected Terminals 1 and 2. He had twenty minutes to make his connection. Even with Luc's help, Victoire hadn't succeeded in finding him a seat by surreptitiously canceling someone else's reservation. Their little Internet tricks didn't always work. Lady Luck had smiled on him, though. The drama in Greenland meant that airlines were changing their schedules and adding flights. He was able to get a flight in an ordinary and legal way on Greenland Airways, the new company operated by Greenland's government.

Kastrup Airport in Copenhagen was crawling with reporters who had arrived to interview passengers going to and coming from the great island. A cold milky light was coming through the cement archways. A blond woman wearing a red and mauve suit was answering the questions of a phalanx of journalists bristling with mikes. On the mezzanine, two bronze sirens watched the spectacle. John looked up, searching for Mary Harper. Although Victoire had confirmed his take-off time on an Icelandair flight an hour earlier, he was feeling anxious. With the Harpers, a person clearly had to be ready for anything.

Two young women coming toward him on the moving walkway stared at him, giggling before they melted away. He was scratching his ear, as the balls were itchy. He crossed the concourse in the direction of Gate 18. The hostess checked his passport and his boarding pass.

"Seat 19C, sir."

"Thank you."

He stowed his bag in the overhead compartment and took his window seat, which was too narrow. Who would occupy seats 19A and 19B? Less than a minute later, the blond woman in the red and mauve suit arrived to claim the seat next to him. She was no little vixen in lamé and high heels, but a sturdy-looking athletic creature with an ace serve. Gallantly, he offered to help her with her bags and got a shock. One of Luc's conquests from Le Havre, whose photo accompanied the future-probe.com article, would be traveling beside him. Lady Luck was overdoing it.

"I saw you in the airport with the press. Are you an actress?"

"Connie Rasmussen," she said in perfect English, gazing at him with the smile of a praying mantis.

John held his breath while remaining cool, calm, and collected. His seat had been reserved in the name of Spencer Larivière, a consultant with North Land. It would not be too hard for someone, even one new to the game, to recognize him as an intelligence agent. Per Sorenson had missed in Paris, but this Danish bombshell would no doubt want to finish the job. Maybe midflight, he told himself, not daring to imagine Victoire's face if she saw him sitting next to this Nordic beauty. Victoire scarcely ever showed it, but she was the jealous type.

"My name's John Spencer Larivière."

"American?"

"French. You're not too disappointed, I hope."

"On the contrary, I'm delighted to be flying with you. People are talking a lot about the French right now in Greenland. Does your trip have anything to do with this famous boat that's the talk of the town?"

"No way," he replied, trying to lie as naturally as he could.

"Tourism, then?" she asked, all lipstick, in her delicious Danish accent.

John smiled too. He was dealing with high-density neurons wrapped in gorgeous musculature. Luc must have spent a much nicer night than he'd owned up to on his return from Le Havre. What was she looking for, provoking him so brazenly?

"I work for North Land," he said completely naturally. "What about you?"

"I defend the interests of the Inuits, the people you call Eskimos. I'm a lawyer in Copenhagen. I work for the Northern Peoples Congress, the NGO that represents Inuits living in Russian, American, Canadian, Norwegian, and Danish territories. I travel to Nuuk regularly."

John thought of Victoire, who had warned him about unexpected pleasant encounters of this sort. "Watch out. Don't get the wool pulled over your eyes by the first spook who turns up," she had told him.

"What about you? Are you interested in the ship?" he asked.

"Among other things."

They buckled their seat belts at the same time and continued their conversation once the plane was flying over the waters of the Baltic.

"What exactly is your job at North Land?" Connie Rasmussen threw out, just a tad too innocently.

It would be stupid to feed her nonsense, especially because she had to be fairly close to the young Greenland state's intelligence operations. The game was beginning—a close contest.

"I'm supposed to meet one of the North Land teams in Nuuk," he said.

"So you'll be working in our country?"

That "in our country" sounded strange. It definitely indicated the Danish woman's close ties to the new authorities. Was this some kind of warning?

"I'm responsible for assessing North Land's image. I need to know how the company works out in the field, especially at this time in a place that's so strategic. I'll be checking into how well we're handling the current developments in Greenland and how well we're anticipating future developments."

"That's quite smart."

"What about you and the Inuits?"

"Greenland has become an independent country. People have rights, which I represent. I also defend the fauna and threatened species, notably the bears. Those animals are an integral part of the history and mythology of the Far North."

"And beyond those creatures, how do you become a lawyer for the Northern Peoples?"

"Does that really interest you?"

"Yes."

"It's a long story."

"We've got all the time in the world."

THE BRIDGE OF THE BOUC-BEL-AIR, 7:15 A.M.

Le Guévenec let his binoculars fall back on his chest and gave instructions to the watch officer. The boat was lurching among the icebergs like a wounded animal. Despite the laborious efforts made in the engine room, which was now a swimming pool, they hadn't been able to restart the second engine. With its grotesque shroud tethered to the stern, the ship was cleaving the waters beneath the screeching seagulls and in the company of the bellowing bears.

Part of the night had been devoted to interrogating the surviving crew and passengers on their schedule between the helicopter's landing and the aborted takeoff. Le Guévenec had questioned everyone in a calm, even manner. As in the days of sailing ships, he had scrupulously noted the answers in the log, starting a new page for every man—this ship had no women on board. Both the captain and the survivors had tried their best to ignore the cold and the stench from the flooded holds as they detailed their individual schedules.

Le Guévenec brought his binoculars to his eyes again and looked southward.

The officer of the watch addressed him. "We've received a call from the *Copenhagen*. Their skipper wants to know if we need anything."

"Give him the list of wounded in order of priority, and ask him if he has a medical team."

"He wants to know if representatives of the Northern Peoples Congress can come aboard to check on the bears."

The request clearly shocked and offended Le Guévenec. In response, the officer replied, "Their lawyer, a certain Rasmussen, says we risk being reported for illegally harboring threatened animals."

"The *Copenhagen* is a Danish ore carrier. I didn't know the Congress had chartered it."

"There's a lot we don't know, Captain."

Le Guévenec left the bridge, aware of the truthfulness of that remark. He pretended to be heading for his cabin but instead stopped in the kitchen to pick up mineral water and canned food for Nicolas Lanier. The more time that elapsed, the more he was convinced that Lanier had good reasons to be hiding. He found the Terre Noire boss stretched out on the bunk. Le Guévenec put the water and canned food on the table. "Thanks, that's good of you."

"I wasn't going to let you die of hunger."

Le Guévenec told him about the *Copenhagen*'s approach and went through the interrogations he had conducted.

"I'm sure that Rox Oa has corrupted my crew and that there's a traitor on board. One of the sailors sabotaged the takeoff of the helicopter and caused the death of Romain Brissac."

Lanier sat up on the bunk. He was silent for a good while before fixing his eyes on the captain of the *Bouc*. The look on Lanier's face seemed to say it all: Brissac's death probably isn't bothering you all that much. Might you be the one who made sure the helicopter was still tethered?

Le Guévenec held his boss's gaze.

"Do you have a phone on board that's never been used?" Lanier asked.

"Yes," Le Guévenec replied.

"Get it for me. But first, let's have a bite to eat. I'm starving."

PARIS, 18 RUE DEPARCIEUX, 11:30 A.M.

Victoire jumped when she heard the doorbell ring. She went to the little salon on the second floor that served as a reception area for clients and checked her makeup in the mirror behind the bar. She waited for the bell to ring two more times before going downstairs. The night had been short and alarming. John's absence made her feel ragged. His plane was probably skirting around Iceland to avoid the cloud of ash given off by a volcano that had awakened at the wrong moment. She could already see him stuck at the other end of the world.

"Coming!"

She reached the ground floor of the old studio, which had been turned into the garage that housed Fermatown's two cars and two motorcycles. Although Fermatown had a street entrance, some visitors came in this way. Unbolting the door took Victoire more effort than usual. The expressionless face and razor-thin lips of François Guerot greeted her.

"I'm so glad to see you."

"Me too," Victoire replied, inviting the deputy director to come in.

She shut the door and went to the stairs ahead of Guerot.

"From the street, you wouldn't think this place was so big."

"On this floor there's the garage, along with a forge and a kiln, which, for some reason, are listed as historical monuments. We are not allowed to touch them."

"I see," Guerot said, giving the place a once-over.

"Lots of visitors are intrigued by this place," Victoire said. "You're in an old printer's shop that was turned into a sculpture studio, art school, and exhibition hall by Alicia Spencer, John's aunt, his mother's elder sister."

"The American."

Guerot had always suspected John of having divided loyalties, and he was not alone.

"Alicia Spencer bought this house and later the one at 9 Rue Fermat. Then she connected the two buildings on all the floors. That's what makes the whole thing look so quirky."

"It has a lot of charm," Guerot said. "You feel like you're between two centuries."

"Exactly," Victoire replied, wondering what the deputy director's remark meant before she went on with her running commentary.

"It's anything but functional. The floors of the two structures don't match up perfectly, and there are extra steps everywhere. Shall we go up?"

Guerot followed Victoire to the second floor and admired the touch wall in the media room. The vertical plane looked like the screen of an immense computer on standby. A revolving solar system occupied the center of the wall and served as a screen saver. The extraordinary effect gave a visitor the sensation of traveling aboard a spacecraft.

"I see you're superbly equipped. Better than we are!"

"But thanks to you," she joked.

Victoire took the visitor into the confessional and offered him a seat.

"Would you like something to drink?"

"No, thank you."

Guerot, who was wearing a dated blazer, dropped into the red leather armchair. Victoire watched as he plucked off one of Caresse's hairs and let it float to the floor.

"I hope you're not allergic to cats," she said.

"Not at all," he replied, removing another hair from the sleeve of his jacket. Victoire pretended not to notice and also sat down.

"Has John arrived safely in Greenland?"

"He's still on the plane."

"It's good that you were able to get him a seat," Guerot said. "It couldn't have been easy."

"No," she replied, not wanting to go into the methods that Guerot would not have condoned. Anyway, they hadn't worked.

"I get the feeling that this business is very important to you," Guerot said, sounding overly solicitous. "Am I right?" He seemed uncomfortable.

"That's true," Victoire replied.

"May I ask you a few small questions?"

"Of course."

"How did Madame Harper make contact with you?"

"She phoned."

"Of course. But why you? Why Fermatown?"

"I don't know. You're better equipped than we are to get that answer."

Guerot gently drummed the tips of his fingers together. He appeared to be giving something serious thought. Victoire watched as he took an envelope—a fat one—out of his blazer.

"Here's the twenty thousand euros we owe you and an advance of forty thousand to investigate Terre Noire and North Land in Greenland."

Victoire almost fell off her chair. Fermatown had never had so much money at one time. What misfortunes would follow?

"Here."

She stood and took the envelope and then discreetly put it down on the marble console table.

"You can count it," Guerot said, sounding virtuous.

"We've always trusted you," she lied with a contrived smile.

"Does John have any news concerning Nicolas Lanier?"

"I'm waiting for a report. What do you want to know, exactly?"

"We'd like to know what contact he has with the Northern Peoples Congress in Nuuk. When does he see them? What do they say to each other? Why was the *Bouc-Bel-Air* rerouted to Greenland? What was its course when the catastrophe struck?"

"Okay."

"We'd especially like to know if Nicolas Lanier has had or will have contact in Greenland with the Chinese or the Americans."

"So you think he's in Greenland?"

Guerot pressed his fingertips together again and gave Victoire an earnest look. "We have reason to believe he is."

"I guess John's assignment to keep an eye on Abraham Harper's daughter has come at just the right time," Victoire said innocently. "Fate sure is a great provider, isn't it?"

Guerot's countenance clearly indicated that fate had nothing to do with it. The deputy director had his little family secrets, too. Victoire decided it was pointless to get this functionary to disclose more than he wanted to after he had just dropped forty thousand euros in their laps. The money was enough to live on comfortably for a while. The technology needed for digital skullduggery cost a fortune. Now they could make some much-needed improvements, and they could finally pay the vet.

"Are you sure you don't want anything to drink?"

"No, thank you. Where will John be staying?"

"At the Hotel Egede. I think he even gave you..."

Victoire brought her fingers to her ear to wordlessly indicate what she meant to convey. Guerot looked annoyed. His reply slipped through his lips like bad coins spit out by a vending machine.

"We won't use his ear unless it's urgent. For reasons of security, we need to draw as little attention to him as possible. On that score, you need to sign a receipt for me. I have to be accountable, like everyone else."

"Certainly, Monsieur Guerot."

"You can call me François. We've worked together long enough. John confided his anxieties to me concerning a Scandinavian man who seems to have tailed him. How did he manage to shake this mercenary off?"

"John used one of his shortcuts."

"Where?"

"La Motte-Piquet."

"He didn't give me that detail. That's a shame."

Victoire picked up a reproach in the deputy director's tone. Guerot had a love-hate relationship with John that was pretty classic in the closed world of espionage. Guerot was eager for some measure of success. He had spent too much time fighting with his colleagues over crumbs of stale bread. Guerot's division hadn't arrested a spy of any caliber in more than ten years.

"I'm going to have your house watched. You've also got an entrance on the Rue Fermat, haven't you?"

"Yes, at Number 9."

Guerot asked for more information concerning Luc and Victoire's comings and goings and let Victoire escort him to the door.

She knew how to stroke the ego of this closet homosexual. "I wonder what we'd do without you, François."

He looked at her and smiled vaguely as he shook her hand.

"Don't leave the house without letting me know. Don't take any risks. I'm watching over you."

"Thank you."

Back in the media room, Victoire received a call from Luc. She told him about her conversation with Guerot and let him know that the agency believed the head of Terre Noire was in Greenland at that very moment.

"Guerot wants to know everything about him. He seems stressed out."

"Are you sitting down?" Luc interrupted.

"Yes."

"Christophe Maunay is on a Trans Oceanic plane that took off from Le Bourget airport an hour ago."

"Where's he going?"

"I just got the flight plan. He's going to Nuuk!"

"Warn John. Where's Sorenson?"

"Still in his hotel. He's not moving. It's crazy."

Victoire turned toward the touch wall to track the two planes. John's plane had a comfortable lead.

GREENLAND AIRWAYS FLIGHT 860

John came out of his catnap and opened his eyes. Although he had not wanted to drop his guard, the soft drone of the Airbus had put him to sleep. He also felt slightly chilled and disoriented. Beside him, Connie Rasmussen was staring at her computer screen.

"I suppose you're also interested in the image of your rival, Terre Noire?"

"Obviously," John replied.

The lawyer slipped the computer onto her neighbor's knees. Still not quite awake, John read the article Luc Martinet had just published on future-probe.com. Under the headline "Sister Ships," the freelance journalist had recounted the interwoven sagas of two ships and two women who, indirectly, found themselves at the center of the global catastrophe. Connie Rasmussen and Isabelle Le Guévenec, according to him, were the mysterious heroines of a world in distress. Victoire and Luc had masterfully laid out the facts and issues.

All the internauts interested in Greenland's woes were rushing to future-probe.com. John recognized two or three phrases that could only be Victoire's creation. Her skill with words was inimitable. John savored his team's work. He pretended to be reading the article for the first time, along with Connie Rasmussen.

"It's well written. The portrayal seems very true to life. Who is this guy?" John asked innocently.

"He's Luc Martinet, from future-probe.com. He interviewed me during a press briefing in La Havre. A bit cheeky, but a good journalist."

John looked the Dane in the eye to see if she was mocking him. As far as he could tell, she hadn't yet made the connection between her neighbor and Luc Martinet. Incredible. He felt confident again but knew he had to be on guard.

"This guy seems to know a lot. I didn't realize you were a descendant of the great Knud Rasmussen, the founder of Thule. Now I know why you're so interested in the Inuits."

"My grandfather had an Inuit grandmother. What Martinet says is accurate."

"I'll make a note of the site," he said, pulling out his latest smartphone.

John could check the response to the article. Connie Rasmussen seemed to be touched by the unexpected qualities the online reporter had sensed in her. But the plane was losing altitude. The flight attendant announced that they were about to land in Greenland. Connie's eyes were on the ceiling. Perhaps she was thinking about the house in Nuuk that her grandfather had grown up in. The journalist had described it so beautifully without ever having set foot in it.

"So you're a Viking with Inuit blood. Now I know why you inspire such confidence."

"You're insinuating that it's thanks to my connections that I managed to reserve the two seats next to you?"

"Maybe," John replied diplomatically.

"I'll tell you everything. When you booked the flight, we made the connection with the room reserved in Nuuk under North Land's name. Then I used my sources to make sure to get a seat next to you, and for the other one to be kept free. North Land and Terre Noire are strategic partners that don't always tell us what they've found in our subsoil. When we can have a relaxed discussion with a representative from either company, we jump at the chance."

"I understand. All's fair in love and war. So you feel just as much a Greenlander as a Dane."

"Erik the Red was a Viking of Danish origin. He lived in Iceland. After murdering one of his enemies, he fled the island and discovered Greenland. That was in 982 AD, near Qaqortoq, where your company would like to know what Terre Noire has discovered."

"Of course," John said, pretending to be in the loop.

"Back in Iceland, Erik the Red told everyone that he had found a vast green land."

"There was no ice?"

"A lot less than today. The Vikings set themselves up in Greenland, which became Groneland in Danish. They were the first inhabitants. There were no Inuits then. There were just about four thousand men and women, most of whom raised sheep along the fjords between Qaqortoq and Ilulissat, on the southwest coast of the island. They built churches and farms. They traded seal skins and walrus tusks for wood and iron from Europe. The Vikings lived there for four centuries. Then they vanished."

"Why?" John asked, picking up a certain emotion in Connie Rasmussen's voice.

"Because of a sudden temperature drop. From 1300 onward, the green land became increasingly ice-covered. The Inuits of the Far North of Canada and the ice shelf moved down the coast. They had adapted to climate change. The Danes arrived in the seventeenth century."

"Your ancestors."

"Yes. Now Greenland calls itself Kalaallit Nunaat."

"And you regret that?"

"I don't regret anything. But we'd like to know what lies ahead. We Greenlanders know that our future is written in the past, nearly eighty-four hundred feet below us. That's the depth at which the ice cap registered the events that occurred a hundred and thirty-one thousand years ago, during an episode of climate change that may well have looked a lot like the current one. It's people like you who hold the keys to our future. We absolutely have to have such information. Maybe you've talked to Madame Harper about all this?"

"Not really."

"If you do have any information or theories concerning the climate phenomena under way and the consequences, we'd be very grateful if you'd tell us. We'd also compensate you at a rate commensurate with the stakes, if you know what I mean."

John assimilated the proposal, which was obviously on par with the one Luc had benefitted from in Le Havre. The Dane was greedy for information.

"I'll certainly think about it."

"It would make your stay more pleasant."

John caught the light in Connie Rasmussen's eyes. It implied that a lack of cooperation on his part could make his trip rather painful.

"Do you mean that my visit to Greenland could become unpleasant?"

"I believe we understand each other."

The flight attendant announced that they were about to land in Greenland. John and Connie Rasmussen buckled their seat belts and tried to relax, having said what they had to say to each other.

NUUK INTERNATIONAL AIRPORT, 7:05 A.M.

The Airbus landed on the runway and added the blue and orange of Kalaallit Nunaat to the colors of the other planes. John helped the descendant of the great Rasmussen get her bag from the overhead compartment and followed her to the exit. The legal advocate for the Northern Peoples looked like she would be just as much at home in a courtroom as on the ice cap. Their intimacy hadn't gone as far as owning up to the real reasons for their trip, but a few ambiguous smiles were food for thought. They said good-bye to the flight crew and walked together toward the baggage carousels.

"Which hotel are you staying at?" John asked.

"The Seamen's Home. Have a nice stay at the Hans Egede. North Land hasn't skimped on you. It's obvious the Harpers really value their image."

The bags from the Copenhagen–Nuuk flight appeared one after the other on the carousel before being whisked away by their owners. Soon, the only passengers left were a middle-aged couple and John. The pair spotted their suitcases, grabbed them, and disappeared. John found himself alone, staring stupidly at the belt, which eventually stopped. Trouble wasn't long in coming.

Two men in uniform asked him in impeccable English if he was, indeed, Monsieur John Spencer Larivière, a French citizen working on behalf of North Land."

"That's me."

"Could you follow us?"

"I'm waiting for my suitcase."

"It's at customs."

John thought he could see Connie Rasmussen's silhouette behind the succession of glass partitions letting in the light of the Far North. The bitch!

He followed the two customs officers, and, after passing through a corridor plastered with posters glorifying local cottage industries, he found himself in a big room that reminded him of an autopsy suite. Two women who were built like elephant seals and appeared to be Asian were picking through his things, which were spread over a long table. It was more than enough to make him regret the trip. One of the gloved women was still holding the box cutter with which his suitcase had been torn to shreds. The new state of Greenland wasn't fooling around with customs formalities.

He responded to instructions by placing his carry-on bag next to the shredded suitcase. Razors, underpants, *eau de cologne,* socks, pajamas, and other items were shamelessly manhandled. The computer had disappeared. He met the cold, empty eyes of the customs officer.

"Empty your pockets."

He hesitated for a moment and then placed his keys, his wallet, his phone, his nail cutters, and the little plastic pig good-luck charm that had accompanied him everywhere for years in a metal box. One of the women picked up the box and vanished behind a door, where other members of the welcoming committee had to be toiling. She returned five minutes later and planted herself in front of him. She was empty-handed.

"Take your clothes off."

"I beg your pardon?"

The woman who had one more stripe on her shoulders than her neighbor repeated the order in a bureaucratic tone. John turned to the two giants barring his exit. They upheld the verdict with a nod. A heap of habeas corpus stories, along with human rights and political considerations, went through his mind. Incendiary letters of protest, a call to the Quai d'Orsay, the French foreign office in Paris, press conferences, etc. Meanwhile, he could only comply.

John removed his jacket and shirt, his shoes and socks, and finally his trousers. He was standing in his underpants in front of the Far

North's female wardens. When they saw the state of his arm and the scars that spread out from his groin and his hip, the two women regarded him differently. The two men, too. John looked like a caramelized store mannequin restored with a soldering iron. Impressive. The head customs official lowered his voice and spoke in a tone tinged with respect.

"The underpants too."

He obliged while the two snowshoes who'd welcomed him looked on. Horrors: one of the jailor women was now arming herself with a translucent surgical glove.

"Turn and face the wall."

John did so, looking behind him.

"Look straight ahead and step forward. Put your hands above the line."

A red line ran from left to right six feet above the floor. John moved forward and raised his hands.

"Put your hands against the wall. Spread your legs."

Scenes of unbelievable violence with blood everywhere flashed through his mind. He pulled himself together by telling himself that there was a price to pay if he wanted to achieve his ends. A sort of prerequisite. He got into position and thought he smelled someone's herring breath at his back. Powerful hands unceremoniously spread his buttocks. He clenched his jaw. An inquisitive and enterprising finger foraged around inside his anus. Deep inside.

"Relax."

Another hand examined the balls in his pierced ear, making them roll against each other. John felt like he might vomit. He broke into a cold sweat as he envisioned surgery. The hand disappeared, and the finger slowly withdrew. That witch Connie Rasmussen had to be having fun behind one of the windows!

"You can get dressed."

Red with shame and anger, he put his clothes back on, taking his time. He pretended to be examining his scattered things and noted that the carry-on bag had been gone over from top to bottom.

"Where's my computer?"

"It's in the hands of the police intelligence service," the snowshoe replied with a triumphant smile.

"I want it back."

"These gentlemen will accompany you when you've put your things away."

The two reception hostesses disappeared behind a door, and John was alone with the two men.

Ten minutes later, he was following them to the next stop in the program. John was invited to sit at a table behind which a Viking in civvies was quietly putting together the scattered pieces of his cell phone. The computer, apparently undamaged, had no doubt undergone an examination every bit as careful. The functionary opened a drawer and pulled out the yellow wallet that Victoire had given him. He spread out all the credit and loyalty cards that trailed along with him wherever he went.

"Is there anything missing?"

John resisted the temptation to answer yes and invent some complication that would cause a cascade of problems for the bureaucrat, but he restrained himself. In any case, he would destroy all his luggage and contents to spare himself the presence of a listening device or microchip that would allow him to be located on the ground. All things considered, things weren't going too badly. He took his time examining each object and concluded that nothing had been lost or taken.

"We're obliged to perform thorough checks because of terrorism."

"I noticed. But why me?"

"We do random checks. You were just unlucky. What have you come to Greenland for?"

Despite appearances, John was in control of the situation. His plan was a hair's breadth from succeeding despite the ambush—or rather thanks to the ambush—they had just set for him. He calmly replied:

"I've come to assess the way North Land is handling itself in regard to your compatriots and your wildlife. France is very committed to human rights, and our president is an animal lover."

He wished Victoire and Luc could see the police officer's face. He gathered his things, signed the discharge slip, and headed for the exit with mixed feelings. Using the circumstances to his own advantage, something he had always preached at Fermatown, had gone from theory to practice. This evening, he would know if he had pulled it off. He passed a succession of windows that looked out on black mountains flattened by one ice age after another before reaching his meeting spot at the airport.

A short Inuit man, stocky as a forklift and dressed in a red wool pullover, was holding a placard with the name "John Spencer Larivière" written on it. It couldn't have been less discreet. Above the rolled neck of his pullover, the Greenlander held high a round head covered with black hair. John walked up to the man and shook his hand. The man took off his sunglasses and looked at John as though he were an extraterrestrial. North Land's spin doctor read a reverential fear, mingled with mistrust, in those ink-black eyes. Despite his nugget size, the Inuit appeared to have formidable physical strength.

"I work for Madame Geraldine Harper. I was waiting for you."

"Thanks for coming to get me and for waiting."

"I'll take you to North Land headquarters."

John followed his chauffeur to a Mercedes SUV in a parking lot that was full to bursting. The sharp, dry cold felt less penetrating than in his fantasies. The Far North looked like a worksite at a winter resort. He put his bag and the tin container offered by customs as a replacement for his suitcase in the boot before climbing in beside his guide. The SUV skirted around the airport on a road that was being rebuilt. Bulldozers and a cohort of Asians in yellow anoraks were bustling about on the berms. The Chinese were pouring money into Greenland, John recalled. After blowing the horn a few times, the driver took them above a rectangular peninsula hacked out by a sea strewn with chunks of ice. The dark soil was striped with splotches of white. On the left, a narrow harbor was cluttered with boats, both big and small. At the far end, ten- to fifteen-story apartment buildings were intermixed with modern office buildings. Broad avenues curved like racetracks led to stilt houses that were painted bright reds, yellows, and greens

They crossed an intersection in the middle of which a pole indicated the time zones in various capitals of the world. John calculated that on the Rue Deparcieux, it would be almost one o'clock. Victoire would be making her noodles and broccoli, while Luc would be following the killer with his coins.

After leaving the port on their left, John and his driver came to one of the buildings they had seen from the distance. The agile Inuit parked the SUV and helped him with his bags.

Once in the hallway, John realized that he had forgotten his sunglasses. You always forget something, he said to himself.

"Mademoiselle Mary Harper has already arrived."

John nodded and wondered which of them—Connie Rasmussen or Mary Harper—had fed him to customs and Greenland intelligence. He dived with the Inuit into the most luxurious elevator he had ever set foot in. It had impeccable carpeting and walls inlaid with precious woods. The hallway on the top floor was similarly crafted. His chauffeur pressed the bell, and a young Inuit woman opened the door. John said hello and followed her into a salon with dark wood paneling. The view of the bay was stunning. A door opened, and Mary Harper appeared before him.

"My mother warned me that you'd arrived and told me to be nice. Would you like something to drink?"

"Not just now. Have you had any news of your father?"

"None. Mom told me your *calissons d'Aix* contain her latest instructions. I didn't really get it, but I suppose the box that's just arrived from Paris is for you?"

"Yes."

Mary Harper signaled to the young secretary, who went to get the parcel he had addressed to Geraldine Harper at North Land's Nuuk branch. John took the package and examined it closely. It did not look as though anyone had opened it.

"I need a private moment. Is there somewhere quiet here?"

Mary nodded to the young woman, who led John to a spiral staircase. A minute later, he was alone on the roof, safe, in principle, from any listening device or camera. Examined in the daylight, the parcel didn't appear to have been tampered with, judging by the inconspicuous marks where the lid went over the box. He opened it and found the North Land credit card and Geraldine's cell phone. He had been cautious enough to keep them out of the reach of Greenland customs and the beautiful Connie Rasmussen.

He had told Geraldine Harper that he would send the parcel, and she had given instructions to her daughter. Then she had left a voice message on the phone that she'd given him at the Ritz.

"If you're listening to me, that means you've arrived. Be patient with Mary. She's not comfortable with herself at the moment. Go and look for Abraham. I fear the worst. Qaalasoq will guide you."

John turned the phone off and looked around. To the west, the waters of Baffin Bay stretched as far as the eye could see and were filled with small icebergs that looked like ice cubes taken out of a fridge. It was quite a spectacle, but he didn't have time for that now. He went back down to the apartment and offered Mary the *calissons*.

"Who is Qaalasoq?"

"He is."

Mary Harper indicated the chauffeur who had picked him up after customs. The Inuit bowed as confirmation.

"We're taking off tomorrow for Qaanaq in the north of Greenland, 1,243 miles from here. From there we'll go on to Avannaa and the Wound of the Wild Dog."

"You'll be coming with us?" John asked the heiress to Canada's tar sands.

"You'll go ahead with Qaalasoq," Mary replied. "We'll catch up with you. Tonight, there's a meeting at the Katuaq. We'll be discussing your French friends from Terre Noire and the *Bouc-Bel-Air*. Maybe those are subjects that interest you?"

Either this girl was the devil in person for having guessed Guerot's request, or Hubert de Méricourt's agency was leaking all over the place.

"The Katuaq?"

"That's the Nuuk cultural center. There's a gallery exhibit on the polar bears. It might interest you. But of most importance is a meeting of the Northern Peoples Congress. Everyone's talking about the catastrophe. If people see you with me, that'll give credence to the idea that you really have come to Nuuk to size up North Land's image. It will give you a sort of cover. After all, you need to be taken seriously. Officially, that's what you're here for, right?"

Mary looked him up and down, but he kept his cool.

"So it seems," he said.

"Where are you sleeping tonight?"

John let out a breath and remembered the mother's instructions.

"At the Hans Egede."

Looking emotional, Mary Harper grabbed the canvas bag that she had been lugging around at the L'École des Mines and left the room. Her father's disappearance was doubtless affecting her. John went over to a map of Greenland that covered one of the walls. Most of the surface area was covered in white, verging on brown. It was green along the coastline. The geographers had visualized the effects of global warming perfectly. Red spots along the seafronts indicated villages and towns. Qaalasoq commented on the black dots that had letters and numbers.

"Those are North Land and Terre Noire facilities along the Great Wound. That's where we're going tomorrow," he said, pointing his finger northward. "Before that, we'll have to get you equipped."

"Speaking of equipment, I need new clothes."

"I'll take you to the shopping center."

NUUK, KNUD RASMUSSEN HOUSE-MUSEUM, 8:10 A.M.

Connie had been stirred to the very depths of her being by Luc Martinet's article. Did the wild and adventurous temperament of her forefather really flow in her veins, as her French lover of a night had written so beautifully? As inconspicuously as she could, considering all the visitors who were there with her, she examined the many faces of her forefather, who was both a Greenlander and a Dane, an expedition leader, an administrator, and a peerless ethnologist. The adventurers of the early twentieth century, when the world was fresh and safe, still aroused admiration. More and more tourists visited the old dwelling that, after Knud, had been the residence of the vice-bishop of Greenland, Mathias Storch, Greenland's first novelist.

It all made for a curious mix that lately had taken on a singular resonance. She hadn't been back in this house for years. Connie went over the photos and portraits and recognized her somewhat prominent nose, as well as the engaging intensity of her eyes. The thick, sensual lips had crossed a century and half. Of course, Knud had black hair like the Inuits. A nice shade.

She went down to the second floor, telling herself that history was knocking on the family door once more. How could she tell what was true and what was not true in this whole business? On the ground floor, she went into what was once the vice-bishop's office and recognized the pagan tupilaks and other monsters of Greenland's legends that had haunted the young Knud's nights and those of her own childhood. With a decisive gesture, she punched in the number of the good-looking kid she had a more than agreeable memory of.

"*Bonjour*, Luc. It's Connie. Remember me?"

"You're unforgettable. Where are you?"

"In Greenland. I read your article on the plane. It's fantastic. I had no idea that you knew so many things about me. Your style's extraordinary. What are you up to with Nicolas Lanier, who heads up Terre Noire?"

"I'm scratching around, Connie. I'm scratching around like a bear on ice."

"I've got a lead that might help both of us."

"I'm listening."

"On the flight between Copenhagen and Nuuk, I met a guy who claims he's checking out North Land's image up here. Be a sweetheart, and see if you can find out more about this playboy. His name's John Spencer Larivière. He's the kind of pretentious brute French intelligence uses to carry out its dirty campaigns behind the European community's back. You know the type?"

"Perfectly. I've already come across scum like that."

"While I've got you, I'd love it if you could give me Isabelle Le Guévenec's number. You made me into a sort of twin sister, but I hardly know the woman. It could help us understand what's happening on the *Bouc-Bel-Air*. After what you wrote about her, a reader really wants to know her. You've got talent, Little Luc. I'm impressed."

Connie jotted Isabelle Le Guévenec's phone number on one of the house-museum's business cards.

"Please don't talk to her about me," Luc asked.

"Don't worry. I can behave myself."

After a few seconds of silence, Luc spoke again. "I've got a favor to ask you in turn, Connie. Is there anyone in Greenland or Copenhagen who uses the services of a Per Sorensen? He's a Dane who apparently had a career in a private army in the Middle East. He's a sort of mercenary of the same ilk as the guy you came across on the plane."

"How do you spell his name?"

Connie held her breath and kept her cool. She wrote the name below Isabelle Le Guévenec's phone number and promised to look into him. The young Frenchman was making swift progress, dangerous progress.

"What role does he play, this Sorensen of yours?"

"The role of a killer."

She began to sweat.

"I promise I'll call you back, Little Luc."

She ended the call and felt a wave of heat flooding the nape of her neck despite the cold wind coming down from the pole. How could Luc have tracked down Per Sorensen? Her meeting in the shopping mall was waiting for her. The clock was ticking. The weather forecast for Baffin Bay was uncertain. Just like her mission.

NUUK SHOPPING MALL, 8:45 A.M.

Inspired by what was done best in Montreal and Stockholm, the underground shopping mall in Nuuk, built in less than a year by the Chinese, had become one of the premiere attractions of the Arctic. All the innovations spawned by climate change were first exhibited in Nuuk: clothing, food, botany adapted to the melting permafrost, snowmobiles, kit homes, chain saws for ice, unbreakable photovoltaic cells, electric cars from Korea, miniwaste stations, etc. The Northern Peoples came to do their shopping here. As a result, the heliport sitting on top of its six levels of retail was the scene of endless comings-and-goings.

Furious over what he had been forced to submit to in customs, John had asked Connie Rasmussen to meet him at the shopping mall for an explanation. The thought that Luc had enjoyed her favors only added to his fury. The ease with which his associate got men and women into his bed left him gobsmacked—and shamefully envious.

Suddenly he saw the blond mane and the red and mauve ensemble of the Copenhagen-Nuuk flight heading in his direction. Flattered all the same that she had accepted his invitation so quickly, he put down the boxer shorts he was examining and confronted the lavender eyes.

The Congress lawyer had armed herself with a smile fit to melt what remained of the pack ice on the planet.

"I didn't think you'd come."

"Why not?"

John told her about the search in customs and his interrogation by the police. Connie listened attentively, drinking in every word. John felt that she was genuinely shocked—or a peerless actress.

"You think it's me who set that up?"

"You're a Dane and a Greenlander. You made it clear that my stay could become unpleasant if I didn't sound your ice cap fast enough."

"Not that quickly, all the same."

"You were the only person who knew I was in Nuuk to look after North Land's interests."

"Everyone in Nuuk knows what you're up to, starting with Mary Harper. You don't really think you can travel incognito when you've come to see the Harpers, do you?"

"I hardly think they'd set up one of their collaborators."

"Don't go by appearances. Troubled waters may well run under the ice. It isn't just the ice cap that's melting. Alliances are changing at a startling speed, even in families."

"You mean all is not cozy in the bosom of the Harper tribe?"

Connie didn't answer and picked up the boxer shorts.

"Don't tell me you wear these monstrosities?"

"Don't change the subject."

She pushed her hair back with a sweeping gesture and added in a low voice, "I'm told you're taking off soon for Qaanaq. What are you going to do up there? It's a revolting place."

"I see you're well-informed. You didn't answer my question about the Harpers."

"Are you sure you told me your real reasons for coming here? I'm having a hard time believing that you're here to polish North Land's image."

"What do you know?"

"Abraham and Geraldine Harper have access whenever they want it to your government and the best intelligence agencies in France. Your story doesn't stack up. You're here for something else, but I don't want to pry into your little secrets, especially after what you've been through. Heroes can be such fragile creatures."

Connie held up the red crab-print boxers.

"Sexy."

"The boxer shorts or me?"

"Both!"

John felt the Danish woman's breath on his neck and the pressure on his arm. The bitch had seen through him. He wanted to know the real reasons behind her visit, too.

"You should remove your earring. It doesn't suit you at all. You look like a polar bear with a Louis Vuitton bag."

John took it on the chin, telling himself she wasn't entirely wrong.

"If you come back in one piece from Avannaa, I'll tell you some amazing things about the life the Harpers lead. But you'll have to be nice to me and tell me what's under the ice over in Qaqortoq. It's vital that we know. You won't regret it, either. Right now, I have to leave you."

"Where are you going?"

Connie picked up a size XL men's T-shirt that displayed a map of Greenland. She held it in front of herself.

"How do you think I look in this?"

"Superb!"

Connie pointed at Baffin Bay a few miles off the west coast.

"That's where I'm going," she declared.

"You'll find yourself in the water surrounded by icebergs!"

"Like the *Bouc-Bel-Air*."

John weighed her words.

"What do you mean? You think you can get on the ship?"

Connie gave him a knowing smile.

"I'm going to see if your compatriots are behaving themselves with our bears. Don't forget, I'm the lawyer for the Congress."

"How are you planning to get there?"

Connie pointed heavenward.

"In a helicopter, of course. Didn't you know Greenland has fifteen percent of the world's helicopters?"

"No, I didn't know."

They walked to the checkout together and said good-bye. As she was walking away, Connie turned around, as if something had suddenly come to mind, and asked, "Do you know a Per Sorensen?"

John thought he had misheard her when she mentioned the name of the man who had tried to kill him on the Boulevard Raspail.

"Who is this guy?" he asked, trying to stay calm.

"What's in the holds of the *Bouc-Bel-Air*?" she replied.

Then she tossed him an enigmatic smile before disappearing behind the shelves, carrying the T-shirt. Bitch twice over, he told himself.

Le Guévenec stuck wax plugs in his ears to silence the ceaseless clamor of the bears, which had almost killed yet another sailor. He reviewed the schedule of one of his men, Sylvain Velot. According to witnesses, he was the only sailor who was not at his post just before the Terre Noire Eurocopter was sabotaged. What's more, he had boarded the ship in Bergen, Norway, just before the Barents Sea campaign. Le Guévenec checked the information in the log and read what the first mate had noted: "Sylvain Velot, recruited in Bergen as a replacement for Hu Yuanyuan, disembarked owing to diarrhea. Approved by Rox Oa, the boatswain, with Christophe Maunay, HR manager."

Le Guévenec left his cabin and made his way to the bridge. He found the number of the Norwegian hospital in Bergen without any trouble and got a nurse who agreed to talk to him.

"I'm calling about Hu Yuanyuan, a Chinese sailor you treated three months ago. I'd like to know what happened to him when he got to the hospital."

"Who are you?"

"Loïc Le Guévenec, captain of the *Bouc-Bel-Air*, the French scientific exploration ship he worked on."

"You haven't heard?"

"Heard what?"

"Your sailor had to have his stomach pumped after ingesting tainted food. It was food poisoning. I'm surprised you're calling back. Someone from your ship already inquired."

"Who?"

"Wait, I should have written his name somewhere."

Despite the currents of cold air that were sweeping over the devastated bridge, Le Guévenec's hands were hot and sweaty. He tightened his grip on the phone to keep it from slipping. One minute later, the Norwegian nurse was on the phone again, sounding so clear, she could have been in the next room.

"It was Rox Oa, your boatswain."

Le Guévenec blanched. For the first time, something important had happened on his ship and he didn't know about it. Rox Oa had not informed him, and the first mate hadn't either. He felt like Greenland was falling on his head for the second time. Resuming the conversation was an effort.

"Where is Hu Yuanyuan?"

"What? You don't know that, either?"

"What?"

"Your sailor died an hour after he left hospital. He was hit by a truck. We alerted your boatswain, who told us he would handle the arrangements with Terre Noire. I thought you knew."

"I didn't. Thank you."

Le Guévenec hung up and felt a weight as heavy as the ice cap on his shoulders. The *Bouc-Bel-Air* had been docked for a week before setting sail for the Barents Sea. Rox Oa had gotten rid of Hu Yuanyuan so that he could get Sylvain Velot, an accomplice, on board. After the seaman's death, Velot had continued working, sabotaging the helicopter that was to take Romain Brissac to Thule. The *Bouc* had turned into a nest of vipers without his knowing it.

The first shot made him jump, and the second one felt like a punch between his shoulder blades.

"What's going on?"

"The bears, Captain! A sailor has just shot them!"

Le Guévenec went to the shattered windows and surveyed the disaster. What remained of the crew was applauding the man who had just gunned down the two wild creatures.

"Who did this?"

"Sylvain Velot. Ship to starboard, Captain!"

Le Guévenec turned his head and brought his binoculars to his face.

The *Copenhagen* was emerging from a blanket of fog and coming straight at them.

18, RUE DEPARCIEUX, 12:30 P.M.

Carrying a bowl of Chinese noodles, Victoire went into the media room. "Aren't you eating?" she asked.

"I'm not hungry," Luc replied, looking drawn.

Standing at the touch wall, he was juggling databases and putting together the report he planned to send John when they established contact again. The first paragraph was dedicated to Christophe Maunay.

"What have you found?"

"He began his career in a Terre Noire branch in Libreville in Gabon as soon as he graduated. He stayed there for five years, but what he did isn't clear. Then he came to Le Havre to take charge of seafaring personnel before being named HR manager at the Champs-Elysées headquarters."

"What happened?" Victoire was listening attentively.

"I don't know, but there's a file on him at the Quai d'Orsay. That's very odd."

"What's in it?"

"The office has a new security system to protect its data. I haven't been able to crack it yet. I need to go out now."

"Why?" Victoire asked, not daring to admit how scared she was of being on her own.

"Per Sorensen is on the move."

Luc pointed to a map of Paris on the wall. The Dane had just left his hotel and gone to the Saint-James on the Rue de Rivoli. With the aid of the geolocalization software, he zoomed in on the building.

"It looks as luxurious as his hotel."

"He's been there ten minutes. I'm going to have a look."

"Be careful."

"The Saint-James is one of the most exclusive clubs in Paris. This guy must have a meeting there with a major player. We need to know who..."

"Who what?" Victoire asked, her eyes filled with apprehension.

Luc caught himself in time. He had come to love this woman.

"Who's trying to throw a spanner in our works."

"Take a gun."

"Don't worry. He won't recognize me."

Victoire sighed as she watched Luc go to his room. Luc had once put on heels and a flattering designer dress to go out on a job with John. It disturbed her. A rival, she had thought. Luc was capable of anything.

"You're not going to change into a bimbo all the same!" she shouted up the stairs.

"The Saint-James is very strict about unaccompanied women. I'll get myself chucked out the door."

Smiling, Victoire shook her head and dipped her chopsticks into the bowl. On the wall, the weather report displayed a temperature of thirty-six degrees Fahrenheit and dry sunny weather in Nuuk and on the west coast of Greenland.

Victoire walked over to the touch wall and examined the portraits of North Land Chairman Abraham Harper. Abraham's rough-hewn face resembled that of Lincoln, another force of nature. And his hands were like a lumberjack's. The years that Victoire scrolled through on the touch wall took nothing away from the man's determined look. But his eyes became increasingly somber, as though something was darkening the soul of this predator, who had bought out all his rivals— all except Terre Noire.

Informal photos of Abraham and Geraldine Harper were hard to come by. At least you could say they were discreet. There were only a few snapshots that showed the couple at charity auctions and international gatherings. Victoire knew all too well that the real bosses of the planet shunned sequins and cameras, but there was something else about the Harpers that she could not put her finger on.

Victoire searched through the accounts and spreadsheets for an explanation of the couple's reclusiveness. She found nothing. The more North Land prospered, the more the Harpers seemed to make themselves scarce on the world stage. It was surprising and, frankly, a bit weird.

Victoire moved back until she reached the media room's big table, and suddenly, she got it. The gradual retreat of the Harpers from international life coincided with the slow and then total disappearance of their son, Harold, from family portraits. She went back to the rare photos of the young man and enlarged them. The immense sadness she read in the teenager's eyes corresponded with the father's. Mary Harper was four years old in the last photo. Harold, her elder by ten years, was sitting on a bench, tennis racket in hand, outside the entrance to a club. It was one photo too many, a lie to be spread by the company's communications department. The young man's limbs betrayed a weakness that ruled out any game of tennis.

Something intimate and tragic was added to the crumbling Arctic stakes. John would not be long finding out what. Victoire thought about the man she loved and how he was perhaps not the best equipped to explore the human soul and family secrets. She abandoned the idea of alerting him so as not to upset him. What would she have said, anyway? What was in Harold Harper's sad gaze as he held a racket without conviction in the shade of a blooming lilac tree?

Nuuk, 10:40 A.M.

Pulling along his new luggage, John emerged from the Nuuk shopping mall. Behind his dark glasses, he spotted the SUV in blue and white North Land colors waiting in the parking lot. Hardly discreet. His arrival in Nuuk hadn't gone unnoticed. Why, for God's sake, had the Harpers chosen him? What obscure role was he playing in this showdown? What monster was lurking under Greenland's ice fields? Dressed in his red pullover, the Inuit got out of the car and came to help him in silence. This man, with his fixed smile, moved with a precision and an economy that were impressive.

"Can we go?" he asked John.

"Yes, let's go."

Qaalasoq had been driving on a heavily rutted road for half an hour when he stopped in front of a blue wooden house built on stilts above a fjord. The Inuit got out of the SUV and began taking the luggage to the front steps.

"You're better off here than at the Hans Egede. This house belongs to North Land. It's where we put up our distinguished guests. Madame Harper is eager for you to accept. She insisted."

Surprised at these instructions disguised as an invitation, John ran an anxious eye over the surroundings. Icy air blew over the black waters and rocks shattered by successive freezes and thaws. He spotted a few neighboring houses built on stilts, like this one.

"Yet you booked a room for me at the Hans Egede."

"You're better off here. It will be less conspicuous. We're leaving early tomorrow for Avannaa. Would you like me to take you to the Katuaq for the conference?"

John thought back to Mary Harper's remark about the events affecting the *Bouc-Bel-Air* and the undermining of Terre Noire. Guerot was waiting in Paris for his report. North Land's image was linked to that of its rival, Terre Noire. His mission consisted of protecting the Harper heiress. Something broken in the voice of Harold, her elder brother, told him that Mary would one day be the real boss. Why, then, deprive himself of the opportunity to find out a bit more? At the price he was being paid, he could make the effort to go to a fashionable gathering and dip his fingers into the *petits-fours*.

"I'd like that."

Qaalasoq's face cracked a wan smile. John sensed that the Harpers had assigned him their most trusted man in the Far North. The Inuit opened the door, and they found themselves in a hall that smelled of beeswax. Everything was impeccably clean. The house had a second floor and could accommodate a large family. There was a salon on the right and another salon on the left. That one held a grand piano. The place was filled with mahogany furniture and exuded a retro chic. Victoire and Luc would have loved it, especially Victoire, whose tastes were pretty traditional.

"The bedrooms and bathroom are upstairs."

John looked toward the steps, which were protected by a red wool runner. As he was about to go up, his gaze was drawn to an object on the marble console table. It was staring at him with asymmetrical white eyes in a huge smashed skull. Curled over its four legs, the figurine was scarcely ten inches high, yet it exuded malice. It was half beast, half Frankenstein's monster.

"What's that?"

"It's a tupilaq. In the Inuit culture, that is a monster made of dead human and animal parts. Some shamans collect bones and frozen flesh scattered in the snow. They then mark out a magical place where they can commune with the dark forces. They chant and dance around the debris they've gathered to breathe life into the monster."

Qaalasoq ran his fingers over the monster's vertebrae, as though he were caressing a pet.

"Naturally, it's just a legend."

"Of course," John replied, convinced that the man was lying.

"Stone tupilaqs like this one are a local craft. Each monster is unique. This one is for you. It's a welcome gift."

"Who's offering it to me?"

"You have to take it first, and we'll only find out later who really gave it to you."

"And if I don't?"

"You won't be able to carry out your mission."

"Are you serious?"

John didn't need to wait for the answer to know that Qaalasoq wasn't joking. He took the object from him and studied the monster's wild-eyed gaze. He thought of Victoire and the chain of events that had led him here. Who had really offered him this surreal mission in the Far North? He thought of the Harpers, as well as Guerot and Connie Rasmussen, who was also ready to pay dearly for information. Who was he working for?

"You may well be right. We'll only find out later who really gave it to me."

"You are a wise man, Monsieur Spencer Larivière."

"Call me John."

"And me, Qaalasoq. The full name. Don't shorten me with a diminutive. That would bring us both bad luck. I don't want to be cut up like the tupilaq before I rejoin my people."

"Yes, Qaalasoq," John replied, looking into the Inuit's bottomless eyes.

The guest room upstairs had a view of the fjord and was worthy of a Viking prince. Nothing was lacking in the ensuite bathroom, either. Qaalasoq turned on the tap to run a bath.

"Rest. I'll come and get you shortly."

When his guide had gone, John inspected the premises from the ground floor to the attic, looking for anything suspicious. He was amazed to be able to go anywhere without a hint of trouble. He went outside and walked under his house on stilts. Then he retraced his steps and went back inside. In the hall, the tupilaq was staring at him with animus. Sports bag in hand, John turned around and went back outside.

The closest house was a hundred yards or so south in the direction of Nuuk. He walked along a path that headed north and hugged the fjord for a quarter of a mile before finding a rock that could shelter him from the wind. After looking all around, he opened his bag and took out the computer that the customs officers and the intelligence services had had all the time in the world to take apart. The screen lit up as usual. He immediately checked to see if Boomerang, the program he introduced at Fermatown, had suffered any damage during the customs search.

The dialog window displayed the rectangular box with the rounded corners. But there was no bright color filling it in. It was desperately pale and empty. A cold sweat made him feel like he was dipping into the fjord, like one of the seagulls that were everywhere. He had taken his clothes off and been sodomized for nothing. He pressed the F9 key again and saw a thin streak of blue appear at the far left of the rectangle. His lungs filled as the little blue light turned into a vertical line and then slowly into a brushstroke.

"Come on."

The blue light gradually filled the whole space.

"Victoire!"

Rarely had he said her name, French for victory, so jubilantly. Fermatown hadn't yet won the war, but it had just won a battle. The software had been invented by an Israeli whose computer had been subjected to customs checks at various airports. John remembered what Isser Sarfaty had told him during the swap they had made in Tel Aviv. "If customs searches your computer, you can get the upper hand. They'll download your data with a USB key, and you can contaminate them with a kind of Trojan Horse. They won't see a thing, since your version of Boomerang splits up and comes back together again when those officials translate French into the country's language."

The dialog window suddenly changed color and displayed a French text signed by Luc, who was driving Boomerang from Fermatown.

"I've gotten into the Greenland security database. There's a report on your search in customs."

"What do they say?" John wrote.

"Don't know yet. Here's the latest news from Paris: Per Sorensen, your killer, took off for the Saint-James, where he met someone by the pool. They had a drink."

"Who did he meet?"

"Don't know, but Christophe Maunay has taken a plane to Nuuk. He will, of course, try to find you and warn Lanier. Guerot thinks he's somewhere in Greenland."

John immediately knew what needed to be done.

"Track Maunay, and let me know when he's getting close. Connie Rasmussen asked me if I knew Per Sorensen. How does she know about him, and why did she grill me?"

"Don't worry—I asked her to look into Sorensen. She's gathering information. That's to be expected. She's just doing her job."

John appreciated the irony of the situation and felt reassured.

"Your article scored a bull's-eye. She likes your style. She's going to board the *Bouc-Bel-Air*. I feel sorry for the captain. She wants leads on the global-warming samples that are stashed in the ship's holds."

"She wants to know the scientific markers of the next warming event. The whole planet's waiting for that after what's happened. I'm going to sound out Isabelle Le Guévenec."

"*You little bastard!*" John wrote in italics. Then he shut down the computer, more determined than ever to return blow for blow. It's just you and me now, North Pole, he thought.

On board the Bouc-Bel-Air, *11:30 A.M.*

The *Copenhagen's* first boarding attempt was a failure. Low in the water, the Danish ore carrier could not throw its grappling irons onto the *Bouc-Bel-Air*, a problem further complicated by the French ship's list.

Le Guévenec had warned Lanier that a certain Connie Rasmussen, who was defending the interests of the Northern Peoples Congress, wanted to board. Lanier advised him to cooperate so they could evacuate the wounded. This seemed reasonable to Le Guévenec. Lanier had also given him the metal box and asked him to find a better hiding place. The head of Terre Noire was preparing for a search by the Congress people if and when things got ugly.

Returning from the depths of the *Bouc*, where he had just hidden the box, Le Guévenec opened the door with his passkey and resumed the conversation that had been interrupted.

"What's in that box?"

The head of Terre Noire studied his captain's exhausted face.

"Trouble. If the police were to find it, they'd sink Terre Noire once and for all."

"Why not destroy it then?"

"Because it's the only proof I have that will allow me to bring down the network that's out to get us."

A fierce hatred flashed in Lanier's eyes. Le Guévenec found himself carried back centuries to red oceans filled with bloodthirsty brutes and seafaring monsters.

"What's the risk for the ship?"

"It's in no danger."

Le Guévenec let out a long sigh. Lanier looked like a warlord. Was his conscience clear?

"I'm going to tell you something you won't like, Captain. But it's my duty."

"After what I've been through…"

"The guy who went to Le Havre to reassure your wife was not one of our people."

"Who is he then?"

"An imposter. He's part of the network that's out to get us. We're going to take him out."

"What about Rox Oa, the boatswain?"

"Also a spy. I know now that you're not involved in all that. Your wife should get out of harm's way. Isabelle's in danger."

"You think they can put pressure on me through her?"

"They'll try. That guy's going to go back and see her again. But we'll trap him."

Le Guévenec couldn't help thinking that Isabelle seemed to appreciate the man's visit, whoever he was. Isabelle had no trouble appreciating other men. He ran to the bathroom and vomited into the frozen toilet water. Emptied and contrite, he reemerged.

"Pardon me. I don't feel well."

"Loïc, I have to talk to your wife."

"I understand."

Le Guévenec knew that Lanier was aware of the pitiful state of his marriage. There was nothing for him to do but let Lanier get on with it. He would look after the *Bouc-Bel-Air* while the Viking looked after his wife. But it was time to move on to something else.

"There's a second traitor on board. I was about to talk to you about it when the *Copenhagen* loomed up out of the mist. I believe that Sylvain Velot sabotaged the Eurocopter and murdered Brissac."

Lanier frowned and shook his head. His beard, which was as dirty as his hair, made him look like a pirate.

"Go up and negotiate with this Connie Rasmussen. Anyway, we no longer have a choice."

NUUK FJORD, 12:30 P.M.

Back inside the blue house, John searched for a place to hide his computer. Everything in this abode was sleek and open. No trapdoors, no hidey-holes. Certainly, it was nothing like Fermatown, where everything was jumbled over different levels. Yet, the Harpers' hospitality seemed to hide something icy and bleak.

He decided to go with the flow and left his computer in plain sight—next to a bottle of milk on the kitchen table. For now, at least, out in the open seemed to be the best hiding place. He listened carefully to Mary Harper's latest conversations and learned nothing in particular, except that North Land's heiress knew a lot of people involved in defending wildlife. He thought he recognized the grating accent of the animal lover Laura Al-lee-Ah warning Mary, "The Frenchmen on the *Bouc-Bel-Air* have killed a pair. They'll pay for it!"

"That's terrible. I'll see you at the Katuaq," the heiress had replied.

John thought about the Harpers. What did they really want from him? He told himself that they wouldn't take the risk of having him killed in their own house. And anyway, why have him killed when he hadn't yet served any purpose? But what purpose?

The tupilaq's scary gaze prompted him to go back upstairs, where he stared out the window, scanning the area. A few minutes later, he spotted Qaalasoq's SUV trundling over the potholes. The Inuit was maneuvering with the skill of a rally driver. He parked in front of the house and rang the doorbell. John went down and ushered his guide inside.

"Any news of Abraham Harper?"

Qaalasoq's face clouded over, and he paused for a moment, gazing at the tupilaq. That creature was like an evil magnet.

"No news."

"It's been four days since he vanished in the North. Can a person survive up there?"

"Sometimes."

"Why hasn't he given any sign of his whereabouts? His wife and kids are worried. His colleagues, too, I assume. You can't leave a major enterprise like North Land in such uncertainty."

"Of course not."

John folded his arms. He still could not figure out what they wanted him to do.

"And despite all the means at North Land's disposal, you need me?"

"Yes," replied the short man, whose skin had been weathered by the icy air. He motioned John to follow him out to the car.

John had been in Greenland for only a few hours. Yet the blinding light and the black mountains looked strangely familiar to him. It was as if he had been there before. John hopped into the front passenger seat and waited. Qaalasoq went around the SUV and hoisted himself into the driver's seat.

"Open the glove compartment."

John found an envelope with the blue and white North Land insignia. It proudly bore the word "recyclable." The check inside the envelope was signed by Geraldine Harper and had several zeros—four John counted, with an eight in front of them: eighty thousand euros. Nuuk suddenly looked a lot nicer.

"How's Geraldine Harper?" he asked.

"She's worried about her husband. You'll see in the note. You'll meet her daughter again at the museum, with the entire scientific community of the Arctic."

"Have you been working for North Land long?"

"Forty years."

Qaalasoq stared at the badly rutted road with a distant smile on his face. John carefully tucked the check into his wallet and did a quick calculation before turning toward his chauffeur.

"But how old are you?"

"Seventy-two."

"No way!"

Nuuk, 1:30 p.m.

The Katuaq cultural center was more than a match for the multipurpose museums of European and American capitals. Its undulating façade and slanting windows seemed to defy the law of gravity and sliced the light into triangular mirror-like forms. It was breathtaking.

"The Chinese took over construction after the initial Icelandic builder was ruined by Bernie Madoff and went bankrupt. They demolished the old building and finished the new one in less than a year. Now people call it the Great Wall of Greenland."

John couldn't get over it. Qaalasoq had just spoken three whole sentences.

"You work with the Chinese a lot."

"Greenland excites greed. They're buying deserts still covered in ice to be the first to cultivate the permafrost when it melts. Humanity will be moving to the Poles."

John nodded. He was amazed by the affluence of the crowd milling around the building—and by the steep downward pitch of the access ramp that took them into the bowels of the Katuaq. Qaalasoq found a place in the vast parking lot and guided John to an elevator big enough to hold thirty people. The size was fortunate, because they soon found themselves squashed in a crowd of colorfully dressed Inuits and others who had raced from the far reaches of the globe to be in Greenland for the end of the world.

The lobby was also crowded. Sundry groups were waiting to register and get badges that would allow them to gain entry to the great lecture hall and the conference rooms where experts were answering the delegates' questions. Illuminated panels advertised the schedule of workshops and seminars.

"Follow me."

John followed Qaalasoq to a ticket office staffed by two hostesses in navy blue who reminded him of the customs officers at the airport. But the hostesses were nicer. Qaalasoq clearly enjoyed privileges. Duly badged, they walked into the vast lecture hall, and John felt like he was back at L'École des Mines in Paris. Two thousand people were here to witness the drama in impressive silence.

Pictured on the screen was the *Bouc-Bel-Air,* listing badly as it sailed through a sea choked with debris. Pictured beside it was the ore-and-oil ship that sported the logo of the Northern Peoples Congress. It was slicing a more pronounced route through the ice-filled sea.

A drone equipped with a camera was flying over the Terre Noire ship. It zoomed in on the *Bouc-Bel-Air* and provoked the wrath of the audience by showing the bloody cadavers of the two bears on the foredeck. John scanned the crowd of scientists, journalists, businessmen, and ecologists. A small sampling of informed humanity.

"Come," said Qaalasoq.

They left the semi-darkness of the lecture hall through a side door and crossed a vast teak-paneled mezzanine. On the left, triangular windows opened to the sky. On the right, doors led to seminar rooms. Qaalasoq pushed one of them open. They found themselves at the foot of a platform, where an expert was commenting on sketches displayed on a screen. A hundred or so people were crowded into the room. Some of them were sitting on the floor, as all of the seats had been claimed.

Qaalasoq whispered in John's ear, "Arvid Moller is North Land's scientific director in Greenland. He's like Romain Brissac for us."

The speaker heard the whispering and turned toward the two intruders who had dared to enter the room in the middle of his talk. When he recognized Qaalasoq, his expression became a lot friendlier.

John concluded that the Harpers' man had much more influence than his unkempt looks led outsiders to believe. Someone in the audience raised a hand and asked a question.

"If I understand you correctly, the catastrophe at Lauge Koch Kyst was caused by seepage."

"Yes, and you're about to understand even better," Arvid Moller replied.

North Land's scientific director brought up a picture of a white mass sitting on black granite soil. Blue lines linked sheets of surface water to a thin layer that divided the ice cap from Greenland's bedrock.

"As you can see, lakes are forming at the surface of the ice cap as a result of global warming. Water is seeping as far down as ten thousand feet, where the granite surface lies, forming a layer of liquid that separates the ice cap from its support. Consequently, the ice cap is no longer stationary and can slide. That's what happened at Lauge Koch Kyst."

John looked around him. The room was hanging onto Arvid Moller's every word. Someone else raised a hand and asked a question.

"Could the Great Wound of the Wild Dog phenomenon in Avannaa produce an even greater catastrophe?"

"That's what North Land is studying," Moller replied, casting an eye briefly at Qaalasoq.

A young woman asked, "Are you in touch with the French teams from Terre Noire in regard to this?"

"They also have bases along the edges of the Great Wound. We're in constant contact with the French. Obviously," Arvid Moller added in a diplomatic tone, "we're all working together to save the planet."

"What was the *Bouc-Bel-Air* doing off the coast of LKK?"

"You'd have to ask them that. I think it was coming back from an expedition in the Barents Sea. Neither the French nor the Danish alerted us to their presence."

"Isn't that odd?"

The scientist gave Qaalasoq a brief glance. John detected an almost-imperceptible nod on the part of the Inuit beside him.

"Yes, you could say that," Arvid Moller replied, looking embarrassed. "We would have preferred being notified. We could have shared data. North Land has never hidden the results of its research."

"They say Terre Noire has discovered rare earths in Qaqortoq. Is that true?"

"It's a rumor," Arvid Moller replied.

A Chinese man asked to speak.

"Isn't it bizarre that a European exploration company like Terre Noire is so involved in prospecting on your island, yet is withholding information?"

"It's not our island, sir. North Land is a Canadian-American company. We've been invited here. As for withholding information, I can't speak for Terre Noire, but that's not North Land's style. All of our discoveries are featured on our website."

Arvid Moller glanced at Qaalasoq, who approved with a movement of his eyelids.

"Terre Noire, at any rate, is only one of our competitors. I might remind you that it's not a French company but a Franco-Danish company, which in Greenland is an important distinction. Don't forget that Denmark was the tutelary power of this island for four centuries—and even longer if we go back to the Vikings in the ninth century, well before the Inuits arrived in the South. Danes represent more than twenty percent of the population. So the bonds with Copenhagen remain very strong."

John thought again of Connie Rasmussen, whose ties with the island were, indeed, more apparent than the exact nature of her mission. But his own mission wasn't exactly clear either.

It was a Norwegian scientist's turn to ask a question.

"How do you explain why Greenland's prime minister and energy commission chose North Land for the offshore oil wells? The Norwegian oil-and-gas companies that have engineered many wells in the North Sea were shocked by the choice."

"The Greenland Energy Commission chose us because North Land acquired real expertise in oil-well drilling after the catastrophe in the Gulf of Mexico. We've filed various patents for a bandage, Patchflex, that's designed to reinforce offshore wells. This product employs complex polymerization technologies. We were proud of winning the contract over the Norwegians and the Danes with their know-how."

John was forced to abandon the power struggles in the Far North when his phone displayed an urgent alert from Luc. He quietly left the room and crossed the vast mezzanine to an isolated spot near a window, where he could talk to Luc in privacy.

"What's happening?"

Luc sounded angry.

"I've just had a Norwegian academic on the phone from Oslo. He read the article on Connie Rasmussen and Isabelle Le Guévenec on future-probe.com. He sounds furious and wants to speak to the editorial director. He says he's got some serious things to tell you."

John read the Norwegian's name and noted the number. He thanked Luc and dug out a different cell phone from his pocket.

"May I speak to Monsieur Olsen?"

"Speaking."

"My name's Florent de la Salle. I'm the editorial director of future-probe.com. One of my writers told me you called."

The man sounded about thirty and spoke with a heavy accent. "I really like what you write on your site. It is second only to Loïc Tribot la Spière's articles on the Centre d'Etude et de Prospective Stratégique website. Only the French can analyze strategic stakes with such precision. The others don't have the same feel for issues or the same ability to summarize what is happening."

Looking out at Baffin Bay, choked with the remains of Greenland, John wondered what nasty surprise this compliment was paving the way for. Over time, he had learned how to decipher the most vicious undercurrents in academic jargon. That closed world sometimes cooked up hate worthy of the Aztecs.

"I'm told you have something you'd like to say about an article on the Lauge Koch Kyst catastrophe."

"Your writer, Monsieur Luc Martinet, presents Connie Rasmussen as a lawyer concerned with the defense of the bears and the precious resources of Greenland. You paint a magnificent portrait of her, and you correctly mention her descendance from the great Knud Rasmussen, of whom there are a lot of things one could say, too. I believe your site has let itself be hoodwinked."

"Are you a scientist?"

"I'm a sociologist. I teach at the University of Oslo."

"Why do you say we've been duped?"

"Because I've had the opportunity to meet Madame Connie Rasmussen twice, when she was going by her husband's name, a Mister Larsen, at gatherings not exactly devoted to the defense of bears and Inuits, contrary to what she's told your colleague."

"What kinds of gatherings?"

"Ones at Club 88 in Copenhagen—rallies for neo-Nazi activists who sprang up around the Dansk Folkparti. I really wanted to let you know, because future-probe.com is considered to be on the far left. That's what surprised me. If you'd like, I could send you an article I published recently on the decline of political life in Denmark. It has photos of Mrs. Rasmussen."

"Thank you. How far do these gatherings go back?"

"Five years. Club 88 was shut down by the Danish authorities."

"Thank you for this information. We'll read your article with great interest. I'll talk to the editorial committee about publishing it, with your permission."

"You've got it. I'll send the photos to your writer. He'll be enlightened."

John couldn't believe it. He called Luc.

"You didn't tell me future-probe.com was considered far left!"

"I forgot."

"It's pretty incredible, all the same! We'll have to talk about it. Meanwhile, your Norwegian accuses Connie Rasmussen of being a neo-Nazi militant."

"A minority of Danes aren't happy with the economic consequences of Greenland's independence. But from that to being a Nazi? I've got to go. I'm trailing your tail."

As he hung up, John pictured the mercenary who had followed him after the meeting at the Ritz. The notion that Connie Rasmussen was acting on behalf of Danish nationalists gave the events a new wrinkle. He returned to the seminar to look over the shoulders of the powers playing poker on the top of the world and tried to read the cards they were holding.

PARIS, INDIANA CLUB, AVENUE DU MAINE, 5 P.M.

Luc geolocalized Per Sorensen's position on his cell phone. The Dane had gone back to his hotel after his little interlude at the Saint-James. There was no danger for the moment. The Indiana Club in Montparnasse was starting to fill. Luc lifted his head and looked at the man sitting opposite him in front of a soda and a paper cup full of popcorn.

Aimé Toussaint was a beautiful and muscular black lifeguard at the Club Interallié, not far from the Saint-James. They had met briefly but intensely a year earlier at a symposium on Web 3.0.

"I remembered that you worked on the Rue du Faubourg-Saint-Honoré," Luc said, raising his glass of soda water.

"It's nice that you remembered me."

"Do you know your colleagues at the Saint-James?"

"A few. Why?"

Aimé looked intrigued. Luc pulled a photo of Per Sorensen out of his pocket and slid it across the table.

"Don't tell me you're chasing a guy with a mug like that?" He laughed.

Luc reflected before he reacted.

"This guy was at the bar of the Saint-James swimming pool a few hours ago. He met someone."

"So?"

"I'd like to know if your pals over there know who that someone is. You lifeguards must see each other from time to time."

"What are you insinuating?"

"I need to know more about that rendezvous."

"This is an affair of the heart, isn't it? You're jealous."

"No, a nasty story. Name your price."

Aimé rolled his eyes and brought his pectorals into play. "Two thousand euros in cash. I'll incur expenses."

Luc took a thousand euros out of his jacket.

"An advance," he said.

The lifeguard grabbed the bills. Smiling, he rubbed them between his fingers. The two men parted as quickly as they had met.

Luc went down the stairs at the Gaîté metro station and caught the subway to the first arrondissement. The Rue de Richelieu started at the Comédie Française and was one of the narrowest streets in Paris. He passed the Hôtel Louxor, where the rigged coins indicated that Per Sorensen was in, and continued toward the Greenland House, which had become a media attraction in Paris. A mixed crowd of French and Inuits had left off contemplating Laura Al-lee-Ah's bears and other critters to watch events unfold on a plasma screen. Luc recognized several journalists greedy for commentary. He walked over to an Inuit and, looking perfectly innocent, asked him, "Laura Al-lee-Ah stays at the Louxor when she's in Paris, doesn't she?"

The Inuit, eyes riveted on the *Bouc-Bel-Air,* answered without even turning his head.

"She stays with her husband, of course!"

Luc was completely thrown. That Laura Al-lee-Ah, the conscience of the Arctic, could have a husband in Paris seemed so incredible, his usual quick wit deserted him. Everybody was following Greenland's death throes. He left the Greenland House and headed for the Louxor. The terrace of the cafe opposite the hotel was an excellent observation point.

He punched in Connie Rasmussen's number to confirm that Laura Al-lee-Ah had a husband in Paris, but he got her voice mail. "I can't answer the phone right now, but leave your number, and I'll get back to you as soon as possible." Then he ordered coffee and stirred it slowly as he took stock of the situation. Mary Harper, daughter of Abraham and Geraldine, had an apartment in Paris at L'École des Mines. The North Land heiress hung out at the Greenland House. Laura Al-lee-Ah, the high priestess of the Arctic, had a mysterious husband in Paris. Just opposite him, a Danish killer was waiting for instructions in his hotel room. Greenland, the promised land for energy traders and rare-earth prospectors, had been Danish only a few months earlier.

ON BOARD THE BOUC-BEL-AIR, 2:30 P.M.

Anchored side-by-side, the *Bouc-Bel-Air* and the *Copenhagen* were now separated by only a few yards. The sea was calmer and would allow them to do the swap. Armed with his bullhorn, Le Guévenec repeated orders, and the maneuver got under way. The *Bouc's* wounded could be transferred to the Danish ore ship, thanks to steel grappling irons slung between the two hulls. Strapped into bearing chairs, the survivors were ready to pass slowly from one vessel to the other.

In exchange for the assistance given to the wounded, a delegation from the Northern Peoples Congress had been authorized to board the *Bouc* to examine the two bears shot dead by a Frenchman, as well as the holds.

"Get ready for the maneuver!"

The sailors on both ships cautiously put the winches and pulleys into action. The slightest mistake could cause people suspended twenty feet above the icy waters to tumble into the sea. Survival couldn't be guaranteed beyond a minute. The *Copenhagen* had put an inflatable rubber dinghy in the sea to fish out any unlucky people, but a gust of wind could crush the vessel at any moment by jamming the two ships together.

Someone in a red oilskin was picked up and helped out of the harness by the sailors on the *Bouc*. The human figure walked clumsily across the listing deck to the staircase that led to the bridge. From the *Copenhagen*, a cameraman from the Northern Peoples Congress was filming the scene. Underneath the oilskin, Le Guévenec discovered a blue-eyed Nordic woman. She removed her hood and released a mane as golden as the sun.

"I'm Connie Rasmussen. I'm a lawyer practicing in Copenhagen and Nuuk and the union rep for the Northern Peoples Congress."

Le Guévenec identified himself. The old sea dog realized that he was facing a fresh storm, and it could well be worse than the previous one.

"Can you take me to the victims?"

"What victims?"

"The bears, of course!"

Le Guévenec nodded. The lawyer welcomed her Inuit bodyguard and followed Le Guévenec to the scene of the crime. She leaned over the cadavers of the two bears laid out in a pool of frozen blood. She almost slipped and was caught by the captain of the *Bouc-Bel-Air* under the eye of the camera filming live for the whole world. Le Guévenec saw an inappropriate gleam in the Danish woman's eyes. She didn't seem too upset by the fate of the two wild creatures. Another one who's playacting, he said to himself, thinking of his wife, who was pretending to be languishing in Le Havre. According to management at the Champs-Elysées office, Isabelle was doing a lot for Terre Noire's image. Whose image was this Danish woman concerned with?

Barricaded in his cabin, Nicolas Lanier finally got in contact with Isabelle Le Guévenec.

"Bonjour Isabelle, it's Nicolas. I want to confirm that Loïc is in good health and is behaving like a hero."

"That doesn't surprise me. He's made for it."

"On Monday morning, you received a visit from one of our employees."

"A charming young man. He gave me news and reassured me. You know Loïc isn't the talkative type."

"Did this young man give you a phone number?"

"No."

"Can you describe him?"

"Tall and dark and very sexy. He had velvety eyes and curly black hair. Well, I mean he was very sympathetic. I said so to Loïc."

"Did you notice any particular marks?"

Nicolas noted a silence, followed by a tone of insincere surprise.

"No, why are you asking me?"

"The young man is not a Terre Noire employee. He's an imposter working for our enemies."

"What enemies?"

"Isabelle, you're running a real risk. You must get out of your apartment. I'll call you back and tell you where you should go. We absolutely must identify this character. Think. Did you notice anything? Your life is in danger."

Another silence. Nicolas wondered if he had lost the call. From their base in Thule, the American technicians working for the NSA would be recording every phone call and every conversation in the Arctic. They would be transmitting the data to CIA headquarters at Langley. Greenland had become the priority to end all priorities, ahead of Afghanistan and Pakistan.

"Hello?"

Isabelle Le Guévenec spoke once more.

"We talked about Christophe Maunay and the methane vents discovered during the expedition with the Russians. He seemed to know Maunay well."

"Did he ask you about Romain?"

"No. He didn't talk about the research on tax systems, either."

"Don't say another word, Isabelle!"

Lanier felt his muscles tense. Romain Brissac had also been supervising the teams charged with testing the tools for measuring emissions of greenhouse gases such as methane. The whole tax system of the postindustrial era and the new international financial system could well rest on standards developed by the Terre Noire teams.

Without intending or wanting to, the Franco-Danish company was about to play a role as world regulator. In Le Havre, they had invented a slide rule that allowed the health of the planet, the world's gross domestic product, and people's happiness to be measured in the same equation. Thanks to a handful of Fields Medal winners and Abel laureates in mathematics, the coming economic model would be inscribed in the balance sheets of the Champs-Elysées company. No one had really sought it, but the out-of-whack state of the climate had largely contributed to this.

"Isabelle, we're faced with an imposter, a mercenary without scruples. I need something that'll help the investigators we're going to set on him to keep you safe."

"I know he's called Luc and that he has a butterfly."

"A butterfly tie?"

"No, a tattoo."

"Where?"

She hesitated. "On his stomach. Low down."

"Many thanks, Isabelle."

Lanier sensed that he wouldn't get any more out of her and ended the conversation. He waited for the captain to return, again observing the tilt of the walls that were invisibly closing in on him, crushing his lower back. How could the crew hold out in this torture chamber? The door opened, and he saw the anxious look on the skipper's face.

"Did you reach Isabelle?" Le Guévenec asked.

"She's worried about you. She said some very nice things."

"Oh, really. What about that guy?"

"She described him, but the meeting was too short. I advised her to leave the house. And up there, how's it going?"

"We've transferred our wounded. I took Connie Rasmussen to the bears. She wants to know who gave the order to shoot them. I told her it was one of my sailors trying to defend himself. A case of legitimate self-defense."

"Did she believe you?"

"No, I think she's here to give us the *coup de grâce*," Le Guévenec answered.

"She won't need to try too hard, the way we're going."

John found himself on the top floor of the Katuaq in a vast circular room whose windows offered a three hundred and sixty-degree view of the capital of Greenland. A throng of delegates and curious on-lookers were wandering about, looking at the paintings and sculptures of polar art paintings and sculptures. He followed Qaalasoq through the groups and came upon a circle of devotees surrounding Laura Al-lee-Ah, the queen of the white bears, who was telling the tragic story of what the species was going through. John recognized her gravelly voice. She was clearly an ex-smoker.

Wearing a white wool shirt with red laces over a finely embroidered low-cut dress, Laura Al-lee-Ah was a glowingly energetic woman in her sixties. Her round face, skin browned by the great outdoors, and almond eyes spoke for all the Inuits. The female symbol of independence who was also called the "mother of the bears" stopped talking when Mary Harper bent down and whispered something in her ear. Laura Al-lee-Ah turned toward John. And the custodian of native wildlife was as sweet as pie.

"My friends, we have the great fortune to have with us tonight John Spencer Larivière, who, despite his name, is French. This gentleman is working for North Land in Nuuk. He may well have some things to tell us about the *Bouc-Bel-Air* and the assassins who've just executed the bears."

John felt a forest of hostile eyes on him, as though he were the incarnation of evil, a sort of monster, like the tupilaq "offered" by the Harper family in the blue house above the fjord. Mary was looking at him intently, as though he held a primordial truth about the unfortunate ship and its crew.

"I'm afraid I'll have to disappoint you. I have no information regarding the ship or its crew."

Laura-Al-lee-Ah's voice rang out like an accusation. "But you're working for North Land, Terre Noire's rival. I thought you would know everything."

John explained that he had known his Canadian boss for only a few days. He was in Greenland to look into North Land's image. He wanted to size up the situation thoroughly before he returned to Europe to defend his new employer's colors. The smirks and raised eyebrows told him that no one was buying his story. He did not believe it himself. How could he convince them? Laura Al-lee-Ah seemed to be enjoying herself but came to his rescue.

"I'm going to borrow our guest, with Mary Harper's permission. Okay, Mary?"

The last of the Harper line agreed in a way that spoke volumes about Laura Al-lee-Ah's authority and her pivotal role in the life of Greenland. John had to give this woman her due. Geraldine's substantial check was not the only thing at stake. Death was on the prowl around him. He needed to learn fast if he was to survive. Every smile, every *petit-four* could hide a land mine, as in Afghanistan.

"I see you're the person everyone's talking about."

Laura Al-lee-Ah dragged him beyond her circle of accomplices and squeezed his arm tighter.

"Say what you're really thinking, Monsieur Spencer—I'm at the heart of the scheming. Greenland's sick, but it invites every kind of ambition. We're in danger of dying rich. It's true I'm very close to the new government."

John nodded and let himself be led by Laura to one of the glass shard-like windows. The spectacle on the other side was awe inspiring. The cry of the seagulls and the sounds of the city reached them through an open door. They stepped outside and found themselves on a teak deck.

"What happened to you at customs?" Laura had adopted a complicit air.

"I can't say I was struck by the warmth of my welcome. I'm wondering if Connie Rasmussen pointed me out to the customs officials and your police."

"What makes you say that?" Laura asked, sounding genuinely surprised.

"She was the only person on the plane who knew the purpose of my trip."

"She's lucky," the Greenlander said with a smirk. "I'd also like to know the real reason you're here."

Laura Al-lee-Ah's piercing eyes flew over the immense expanse of sky over Nuuk. John, with a wealth of hand-to-hand combat experience behind him, was convinced that the Inuit's nostrils were quivering at the approach of danger. There was something animal-like and primitive about the woman. He himself felt a strange apprehension.

"What are you going to do in Qaanaaq?" Laura demanded.

"Visit North Land's facilities to get an idea of the way they work and how they deal with the Inuits."

"Was it Mary who assigned you Qaalasoq as a guide?"

"You know him?" John asked.

"His clan is part of the Harpers' inner circle. You're being spoiled. Why isn't Abraham Harper in Nuuk?"

"Was he supposed to be?"

"Every time the Congress gets together, he honors us with his presence," Laura Al-lee-Ah replied. "He was supposed to be here this evening, and you're leaving tomorrow with Qaalasoq for Avannaa. Don't you find that a bit odd?"

"There are so many odd things in your beautiful country. Just like in Paris, come to think of it. I'm sure that you'll soon have a show there."

Laura took her eyes off the invisible mystery hovering over the town and swiveled to face him.

"Thank you for your interest in my painting, but there's nothing odd about it. I regularly show in Paris—at the Greenland House."

"On the Rue de Richelieu?"

"The very same. Thanks to Geraldine and Abraham Harper and the North Land Group. They've supported me for years. The fact that they prospect our subsoils doesn't mean they're not the sort of people you'd want to associate with. Independence has taught us to see things differently."

"You sound like you're promoting North Land," John said.

"Why are the French so obtuse? You think you're so superior. But others have their dignity and their feelings, too. You don't measure the consequences of your acts, especially abroad. You kill two bears on board that boat. With two shots, you've just lost the support of all the Northern People. Your image wasn't all that brilliant to start with; now it's going to be appalling. Terre Noire can get out of Greenland. You've lost."

"You forget that I work for North Land, not Terre Noire."

"Are you so sure?"

John didn't appreciate the two sharp blades that pierced through to his soul. The Taliban in their mountains suddenly seemed like Boy Scouts on a hike. He did not answer.

Like his neighbor, he suddenly looked at the sky. Something was happening, but he could not say exactly what it was. The most buried part of his brain noticed an anomaly. His instinct for war woke reflexes buried deep in his genes. Where was the danger? He spun around with his hand on the weapon he had not carried since leaving the service.

"Listen!"

"I can't hear a thing."

"Exactly. The seagulls have stopped crying, and the dogs aren't barking anymore."

Now everyone on the teak deck of the Katuaq was looking at the sky. The birds had vanished. An oppressive silence had fallen over the town from the black mountain, whose pinnacle looked as if it had been crushed by some gigantic anvil. Engines and conversations had stopped. Nothing moved, save for the indescribable heart-wrenching terror squeezing the air out of deflated lungs.

HOTEL HANS EGEDE, NUUK, 4:30 P.M.

Christophe Maunay had the taxi drop him off at the hotel and found himself trapped in a crowd of people who were all looking at the sky. Like everyone else, the Terre Noire manager looked up, trying to discern what was demanding everyone's attention. There was an unsettling silence. Already worried about the turn of events that had forced him to leave the Champs-Elysées office for Nuuk, he realized something unnatural was taking place here, too.

"What's happening?" he asked a passerby frozen to the spot next to him.

"You'd think time was standing still. Nothing's working anymore. It happened fifteen minutes ago. It's extraordinary. Where've you come from?"

"Paris."

Maunay stared at the man with the deeply lined face and realized that he had heard the guy's Danish accent somewhere before. He was probably a bodyguard for some surveillance or security firm. He thought of Per Sorensen, the mercenary he had met with. He was dangerous, but they wanted him to work with him. Since Greenland's independence, the Danish were back with a vengeance, to say nothing of the Russians and the Norwegians who were lying in ambush.

Someone raised a hand and pointed to a bird in the air. The seagulls were finally rushing in from everywhere and screeching again. Normal conversations took up where they had left off. Maunay grabbed his suitcase and looked for the man he had just been talking to. Gone. Too bad.

At the desk, he confirmed that the room that had become available was still reserved for him.

"Yes, Monsieur Maunay. Someone canceled just before your secretary called us. You're in luck. There will be a surcharge."

"No problem."

"You're from Terre Noire, aren't you?"

"Right."

"Have you come about the ship?"

"Yes."

"I hope you have a nice stay. Your room is on the top floor. It's totally soundproof because of the seagulls and all the noise from the port. Here's your key card."

"Thanks."

When he got to the top floor, he slid the card in the door and walked into a room as vast as a presidential suite. He went to the windows and scanned the horizon. Far away to the north, frightening columns of vapor were rising in the sky like giant towers. The *Bouc-Bel-Air* had to be under them. Perhaps it had even gone down with all its remaining hands.

He turned around to get a better look at his room. He noticed the enormous bouquet on the coffee table, along with a business card. Something was written on it in blue ink. He read it and almost felt sick: "The *calissons d'Aix* have arrived. Please forgive me. Mary Harper." Thinking hard, he turned the business card bearing the blue and white North Land logo every which way and then collapsed on the bed. He picked up the room phone and called the concierge.

"Christophe Maunay here. The client who had to cancel their reservation received a parcel that's still in the room. Who was it?"

"Could I put you on hold for a minute?"

Ever since the *Bouc-Bel-Air* had left for Greenland, events had been moving at a disconcerting speed. Maunay felt as though he had reached the end of his tether.

"Hello, Monsieur Maunay?"

"I'm listening."

"The room was reserved by North Land for one of its executives. A gentleman phoned to cancel. Quite a funny coincidence, isn't it?"

"Who was the client?"

"Monsieur John Spencer Larivière. Do you know him?"

"No."

Maunay hung up and put his head between his clammy hands. Who was this John Spencer Larivière, and why hadn't the Terre Noire intelligence guy ever mentioned him? Why had he canceled his reservation? Maunay switched on the television and came across a picture of the *Bouc-Bel-Air* alongside a Danish ore ship commissioned by the Northern Peoples Congress. The two vessels seemed to be riveted together. The blood drained from his face. The tarpaulin-covered carcass of the helicopter that had crashed on the deck ruled out any possibility of landing on the *Bouc-Bel-Air*. To reach the ship, he would have to use a smaller craft, at the risk of being hit by a new tidal wave.

Absolutely nothing was going as planned. Having been subjected to an outrageous search at Nuuk customs by two harpies in uniform, he could no longer trust his cell phone. Terre Noire was being targeted from all sides. He caught sight of the computer on the mahogany desk and sent an e-mail to his secretary at the Champs-Elysées office: "Ask you-know-who what we've got on John Spencer Larivière, and what he's doing in Greenland. He's working for North Land." Back at the plasma screen, he found the round face of an Inuit woman being interviewed on the terrace of a big building in Nuuk.

"Laura Al-lee-Ah, you're not only an artist, but you also represent Greenland at the Northern Peoples Congress. Just a short while ago, our island experienced a moment of terror, from Qaanaq in the north to Qaaqortoq in the south. What happened?"

"We don't know yet, but our scientists are gathering information. I can tell you that the phenomenon affected the whole country."

"We've heard you're about to join the *Bouc-Bel-Air* to question the captain of the French ship. Is that true?"

"I'm waiting for authorization to board from the Greenland Parliament. This ship is in our territorial waters. We already have a vessel on the spot, and I've asked Connie Rasmussen, our legal advocate, to board the ship."

Maunay massaged his eyes and told himself that the only way to board the *Bouc* was to join the Congress flotilla that was gathering off the coast of Greenland's capital. He grabbed the phone that connected him to the concierge desk again.

"Could you get me the headquarters of the Northern Peoples Congress?"

NUUK, NORTHERN PEOPLES CONGRESS HEADQUARTERS, 5 P.M.

John quickly realized that Congress headquarters were the Arctic's center of gravity. Greenland's elected representatives mixed there with the Inuits from Canada, the Lapps from Scandinavia, and the delegations that had come from Alaska and Siberia. The top of the world had given itself an appointment with the most northern NGO on the planet.

Famished but watchful like a hawk, he rose from a sofa that was as streamlined as a kayak. Laura Al-lee-Ah entered the room, flanked by Arvid Moller, whose conference he had listened to so closely. From Paris, Luc had warned him that Christophe Maunay had arrived at the Hans Egede Hotel. The man who had met with Per Sorensen was getting dangerously close.

Laura Al-lee-Ah granted John a curt nod before addressing the guests.

"My friends, you're about to be the first to hear an explanation," Laura said. "We finally know what occurred a short while ago. Why did animals and birds all over the continent observe twenty minutes of silence? Arvid Moller from North Land is about to deliver the frightening answer."

A silence fell over the room, as heavy as the one before. Arvid Moller looked stricken. The way he stood, like a slain but upright giant, made the expression on his face all the more disquieting. He was a strong man who had been confronted with the unthinkable.

"I would have greatly appreciated the opinion of my French colleague, Romain Brissac, before revealing what we've measured," Moller said. "But I've just learned of his tragic death on board a Terre Noire helicopter that was attempting a takeoff from the *Bouc-Bel-Air*. The death of the Nobel laureate leaves a huge vacuum. It is unfortunately on par with what I'm about to tell you."

John felt questioning eyes on him, as if he knew anything about the demise of the eminent climatologist who was one of the most influential personalities at Terre Noire. He just folded his arms and listened like everybody else. Arvid Moller delivered the verdict.

"The animals and birds fell silent because just a little while ago Greenland rose two and a half feet above the Earth's crust."

John exchanged disbelieving looks with his neighbors. Everyone looked petrified, even without knowing the full scope of what had happened.

"This phenomenon has troubling causes and consequences. When the Lauge Koch Kyst crust broke off into Baffin Bay, it lightened the weight bearing down on our island. But that mass was not enough to cause this."

"So, why did we rise?" someone asked.

"For the same reason that Lauge Koch Kyst slipped into the bay. The ice cap is melting from below. The lakes formed by global warming are carving out channels that are carrying the water down to the rock surface."

"Do you mean that the whole ice cap of Greenland is in danger of falling away?"

"Yes, with consequences a lot more terrible than those provoked by LKK."

"Are you going to tell the press?"

"I wish I had Romain Brissac beside me. I can't say anymore at this point."

A voice rose. "You can't leave us without an answer! The situation's far too serious. What should we do? Run?"

The audience murmured in agreement, and questions erupted on all sides.

Arvid Moller tried to restore calm by putting the danger of an imminent catastrophe into perspective. He used the word "fragmentation" instead of "separation," but the harm had been done. Everyone had the images in their heads of the tsunami pounding the American coastline. John moved to one of the tables. A little bite to eat before the end of the world couldn't hurt. For him, the threat was called Christophe Maunay, and he feared that peril was imminent.

John was about to sample one of the regional dishes when Laura Al-lee-Ah approached him and blocked the way.

"You are going to grant me the pleasure of learning a bit more about Terre Noire, aren't you?" she asked.

"If you insist," John replied.

"I've got something to tell you."

John managed to plant his fork in some salmon. Laura allowed him only one mouthful before she went on.

"A certain Christophe Maunay, who's checked into the Hans Egede Hotel, wants to see me right away. I want to know why. You're a Frenchman. It shouldn't be too hard to find out."

John gave himself a few seconds of thought before replying.

"Do you know him?" Laura insisted.

"No. Never met him."

"Really? You don't seem to know very much. One wonders why North Land's paying you so well!"

"So do I."

She moved away just as he was about to ask her who her husband was and what he was doing in Paris. Maunay's presence, however, was forcing him to deal with first things first. John made his way to a table dedicated to the finest delicacies of Greenland. The variety of dishes surpassed anything he had seen before. He chose a plate of shrimp with translucent fantails.

"The crustaceans are back."

He turned around and found Mary Harper.

"What do you mean?"

"It seems that the new direction of the Gulf Stream has brought the halibut and shrimp back to us."

John hated talking with his mouth full.

"Hmm."

"How did you like my flowers? I hope I didn't annoy you. For a man like you, it's dopey to get flowers, isn't it?"

"Not at all," John replied, trying to chew unobtrusively and thinking about Christophe Maunay. Why was she going on and on about flowers? The girl really was capricious and unpredictable.

"Have you heard from your father?"

"We're very anxious. My mother's worried sick. She thinks he's dead."

"Are people curious about his absence?"

"Everyone's calling. Even the US ambassador in Nuuk."

John remembered the latest update Victoire had sent to help him understand the diplomatic game that the great powers were playing in Greenland.

"I was told that before he was named ambassador here, he was posted to Japan."

"That's right."

"The world changes fast," John replied, helping himself to more shrimp.

The revelations about Connie Rasmussen from the future-probe. com reader sprang to mind. He took advantage to sound Mary.

"North Land benefits from a good image with Laura Al-lee-Ah and the Inuit community. This Connie Rasmussen seems particularly effective. She'll destroy Terre Noire's reputation by keeping those two bears in the spotlight. Do you know her well?"

"Connie's an amazing lawyer."

John bit his tongue between two pink nuggets and advanced cautiously.

"What did she do before defending the Inuits?"

"I think she was a lawyer in Copenhagen."

"How was she hired?"

"You'd have to ask Laura Al-lee-Ah. The Greenland government doesn't really share its secrets with us. We don't play politics."

John nearly choked and reached for some Scandinavian sauce that reminded him of a pleasant stay in Stockholm.

"For a firm that doesn't play politics, you're doing pretty well with the locals when it comes to image. At any rate, that Connie Rasmussen seems to know you quite well."

"What makes you say that?"

"She's convinced that my image mission is bogus and that I'm here for something else. Are you sure your phone calls aren't leaking?"

"I forgot you were a cop."

The tone wasn't aggressive, and John took it in stride. Through his earbud, he received a message from Luc, who was following the Terre Noire manager step by step. The situation was becoming urgent.

"Excuse me."

"Where are you rushing off to like that?" Mary asked.

"I've got to get ready for tomorrow."

"I've changed my mind."

"About what?" John asked.

"I've decided to go north with you. I could talk to you about Connie in a more out-of-the-way place."

"Really?"

"My mother's paying you to protect me. But I'll be protecting you. And you'll owe us."

"Is that so?"

"Don't look at me like that!"

"It's nice you're going with me. See you tomorrow."

"I'll stop by the Hans Egede tonight," she shot back.

"Right," he said, stepping up the pace.

He suddenly wheeled around. Mary Harper didn't know he'd be sleeping elsewhere tonight. The North Land heiress had not been kept in the loop about the change of plan.

PARIS, 18 RUE DEPARCIEUX, 9:30 P.M.

Victoire came into the media room with a soft cloth in hand.

"You haven't seen Caresse, have you?"

"No."

"She's hiding again. She doesn't want me to clean her eyes."

Luc was in front of the touch wall, mesmerized by a series of photos. Victoire promptly realized that the kid had stumbled on something troubling.

"What have you found? You look petrified."

"The Norwegian who complained about the way future-probe.com presented Connie just sent us a report on her former activities."

Victoire took a closer look at one of the shots and paled. She would never forget the face of the man who had come to kill John.

"That's him?"

"That's Per Sorensen. Here, he's having dinner at Club 88 with Connie Rasmussen and some other people of ill repute."

"I recognize him all too well. How long ago was this?"

"Five years ago, before Connie became Laura Al-lee-Ah's legal adviser."

Victoire and Luc couldn't get over it. The lawyer for the Northern Peoples Congress was raising her glass with several militants, one of whom was the Scandinavian mercenary who had nearly killed John.

"Send John the photos."

"Done. He's going to try to bump into Maunay down at the port."

Luc and Victoire shifted their attention from the lawyer to her Greenland employer. Photos capturing the artistic and political life of Laura Al-lee-Ah filled the best-read magazines on the newsstands. Luc summed up his research.

"She shows in Oslo, Copenhagen, and the United States. In Paris, she exhibits in a third-rate gallery on the Rue de Richelieu. I'm trying to identify all the people who've been photographed with her over the years, but I still haven't found him. Not a trace."

"Who are you looking for?"

"Her husband! She has a husband in Paris, but I can't find a single Al-lee-Ah in France. I have to go back to the Rue de Richelieu."

"What about the Dane?"

"Still in his room. Looks like he's waiting for instructions, no doubt from the man he met in the bar at the Saint-James."

"Maybe he's watching the Greenlanders?"

"I don't think so. You can't see the Greenland House from the hotel. I'm sure Mary Harper didn't meet the Dane. The coins don't lie."

Victoire put the cloth on the table, along with the lotion she used to clean the Persian cat's eyes.

"Hey, the boss is sending us something."

Luc launched the decryption process. The small symbols on the screen began to dance. Then they turned into letters and, finally, words. The system invented by Jean-Claude Possin, the last French Fields medal winner, was inviolable, because it didn't have an algorithm. It provided protection from any wiretapping or Trojan Horse dreamed up by official intelligence services, including the one Fermatown had sprung from. The Chinese were the only ones who believed in the mathematician's semantic engineering. They had bought up Possin's firm for a phenomenal sum."

"Tell me precisely where Maunay is," John relayed from Greenland.

Luc displayed the echo returned by the coin still in the pocket of the Terre Noire manager. He brought up an enlargement of the town before typing his answer.

"He's left the Hans Egede. He's outside the harbor master's office on the port five hundred and fifty yards away from you, facing south."

"Thank you."

The dialog window was erased. Puzzled, Luc and Victoire were left staring at the wall. Then Victoire's phone vibrated. She answered it and recognized the voice of Guerot, the security-clearance boss and deputy director.

"François here. I'd like to see you. What would you say to meeting me at the bowling alley at Montparnasse in an hour?"

"I'll be there," Victoire replied.

Luc went from one geolocalization to the next and got interested in the Dane again at the Hôtel Louxor.

"The coins say he's still on the Rue de Richelieu. Go to the bowling alley. I'll cover you."

"You're going out armed?" asked Victoire.

"If anything happens to you, John will put my ass in a sling."

"In your dreams."

On board the Bouc-Bel-Air, 7:15 p.m.

Seated opposite the sailor in the captain's dining room, Connie Rasmussen questioned Sylvain Velot a second time.

"Who gave you the order to shoot the bears?"

"No one."

"Don't try to cover for Le Guévenec. You're in Greenland territorial waters, and, therefore, the justice system in this country will handle the matter. You have nothing to fear from the French authorities. Unlike Paris, we have no political police here. You will benefit from habeas corpus. You can even make me your acting lawyer."

"You guarantee me legal protection?"

"Yes."

Connie was getting closer to her goal. She needed to act with the greatest possible care. The slightest false move could cost her her life.

"You really represent the interests of the Congress?" asked Velot.

"I'm authorized to conduct a preliminary investigation in the name of the president, Laura Al-lee-Ah."

The name of the woman who embodied the conscience of the Arctic seemed to have an effect on the French sailor. Velot looked around and seemed reassured by the bodyguard, a stocky Inuit hewn out of granite, a somber brute.

"I got the order to kill the two bears, both the male and the female, from Captain Le Guévenec himself."

"Who procured the weapon for you?"

"Le Guévenec."

Connie Rasmussen pulled a tape recorder from the canvas bag she had brought with her and asked the sailor to repeat word for word what he had just said. Sylvain Velot did so.

"How long have you been on board the *Bouc-Bel-Air*?"

"Since I embarked in Norway three months ago."

"Who recruited you?"

"I was sent to Norway by the Terre Noire human resources department, headed by Christophe Maunay. A man who had become ill on the ship had to be replaced. He was a Chinese man, I think."

"Have you been involved in other crimes in Norway?"

Sylvain Velot looked shocked at the question and answered no.

"Are there any other things you'd like to talk to me about?"

"I need to show you the hold. The *Bouc-Bel-Air*'s involved in trafficking alcohol behind Greenland's back. I also reckon there are drugs in the black box."

Connie switched off the recorder and walked out of the room, trying to compensate for the tilt of the deck. Using the wall to steady herself, she took the gangway and arrived at the command bridge. Le Guévenec turned around and did his best to mask his feelings about her intrusion.

"Captain, I'd like to visit your ship's forward hold."

"I have to get permission from Paris first. Please wait for me on the bridge."

Le Guévenec pretended to be going back to his cabin and went to Lanier's instead. He wasted no time.

"She wants to visit the forward hold. Velot must have told her about the bottles of cognac floating around down there. What'll we do?"

Curled up in a ball, the Terre Noire chief was holding his phone tight in his fist.

"Take her there and tell her the truth. We don't have a choice."

"She'll never believe me."

"What did Velot tell her?"

"I don't know."

"Expect the worst, Captain."

"That's all I've done since we left the Barents Sea."

Back on the bridge, Le Guévenec told Connie Rasmussen that he had spoken to headquarters and was authorized to show her the forward hold. Terre Noire had nothing to hide. Connie Rasmussen entrusted her witness to her bodyguard and followed hot on the captain's heels. They were soon descending into the stinking bowels of the ship. Le Guévenec was gallant enough to keep Connie Rasmussen from slipping on the rungs of the ladder. Together, they surveyed the disaster. Hundreds of bottles of cognac were floating in a mixture of seawater and fuel oil.

"Where do these bottles come from?"

"The boatswain loaded them at Le Havre. Without my authorization."

"The one who attacked one of the bears?"

"The one who was killed by the female."

"Who were the bottles for?"

"I have no idea."

"You can't not know the havoc alcohol has wreaked in Greenland. For a squeaky-clean company, this doesn't look good. When word gets out, Terre Noire won't be able to set foot on the continent again."

"It's a setup to foul our image."

"If I were in your shoes, I'd talk to Nicolas Lanier about it immediately. I can't get hold of him. You wouldn't know where he is, by any chance?"

Le Guévenec was a bad liar. He looked down and replied that he was in touch with a Terre Noire administrator. After everything he had gone through, this female presence disturbed him. The Danish woman would rip the reputation of his ship to shreds. Women were not his strong suit. He felt himself flagging.

"Do you know a John Spencer Larivière, who's just arrived in Greenland to shore up North Land's image?"

The strategic stakes of the situation were not Le Guévenec's strong suit, either. Cornered between his boss and this Valkyrie, he felt dirty and stupid. "The name doesn't ring a bell," he said.

"You should take an interest in him. I'd let Nicolas Lanier know the guy's in Greenland. I'm sure he's working against your interests."

"He can get in line!"

Le Guévenec studied the healthy-looking Northern Peoples lawyer. "And you? Who are you working for?" he asked.

"For the truth, Captain," Connie answered, clearly relishing her power.

"Don't you mock me. You knew perfectly well there was cognac. Your ship turned up a few minutes after Velot killed the bears. The whole thing's been carefully orchestrated to sully our reputation and advance North Land's interests. Velot's working for you or for someone connected to you. There you have it, the truth!"

For a Frenchman, the captain of the *Bouc-Bel-Air* is almost well informed, Connie Rasmussen told herself.

"One truth can hide others, Captain. I'm cold."

"Me too."

John headed toward the harbormaster's office, wondering what on earth he could say to Terre Noire's HR manager. There was no way he could tell him the truth. Guided by Luc's voice, he eventually found Christophe Maunay in the middle of a milling crowd.

"I see him."

"I'll leave you to it," said Luc. "I'm going out with Victoire. Guerot's arranged a meeting with her at the bowling alley."

"Twice in the same place? He musn't be feeling well."

John had no trouble spotting the black-framed glasses of the HR manager. He seemed lost in the crowd, which was rushing toward a trawler bearing a huge Northern Peoples Congress flag. Inuits sitting behind a table were vetting candidates for boarding. The *Narvik* was connected to land by a narrow gangplank. John elbowed his way through and reached Maunay just as he was asking for permission to board.

"I'm a Terre Noire board member, and I must get to the *Bouc-Bel-Air*. I'm on a humanitarian mission. My name is Christophe Maunay. You can check."

Maunay feverishly searched his pockets for his passport, which he held out to the Inuit. The man turned the pages and, without realizing that he was reading it upside down, handed it back to its owner.

"This document is not standard."

"It's an official document of the French Republic."

"That may be, but you won't be getting on board."

"There are injured people on the *Bouc-Bel-Air*. I have to get to them. They've suffered a workplace accident, and I'm responsible for them as manager of the company's human resources department."

"They've been picked up by the *Copenhagen*. You have no business in our territorial waters."

John leaped at the opportunity to make contact with Maunay.

"Don't tell me you don't have any more room. I'm French, too. I know your president."

"Who are you?"

"John Spencer Larivière. I work for North Land."

A blast of the ship's horn, signaling imminent departure, set off a burst of applause. The Inuits left their table and walked over to the gangplank without paying any further attention to the two Frenchmen. The mob was becoming hostile. An old hand at handling hostiles eager for a lynching, John suggested to his neighbor that they beat a retreat and go have drinks at the Hans Egede. Maunay agreed.

They walked for a good while without saying a word. Christophe Maunay seemed in the grip of dark thoughts.

"Shit of a country," he finally said.

"You're telling me!"

The palpable tension around them diminished the closer they got to the Hans Egede.

"You know the hotel?" Maunay asked.

"I was supposed to spend the night there, but North Land booked me a room somewhere else," John replied. "Shall we have a drink?"

"Gladly. Those assholes have made me thirsty."

John was sizing up his adversary. The man he had imagined as the merciless manager in Nicolas Lanier's *cabinet noir* looked more like a stressed-out executive on the verge of a nervous breakdown. There was no point in bringing out the knives or squeezing the man's larynx at the edge of a ravine like some vulgar Taliban. He would get him at the table, on the tablecloth, in civilized French fashion. But that did not keep him from being wary. He looked for shadows in the windows and studied the people they passed along the way. No one seemed to be holding anything threatening. No car slowed down and accelerated in suspicious fashion. There were no tense faces, other than that of the man walking at his side. Greenland was full of surprises.

MONTPARNASSE BOWLING ALLEY, 11:50 P.M.

Victoire didn't have to wait long. François Guerot, wearing his usual blazer, looked concerned. He glanced at the bowlers and the customers sitting at a table.

"Thank you for coming."

"Not at all, François."

"Let's not stay here. Let's walk, if you don't mind."

Victoire rose from her chair and followed Guerot to the other side of the Avenue du Maine and then to the Rue de la Gaîté. They walked past the restaurants and mingled in the crowd spilling from the theaters.

"How's John's trip going?"

"Very well, except for one small detail."

"Go on."

Victoire told Guerot about the humiliating body search John had been subjected to. The deputy director seemed keenly interested in the story, especially the scandalous details that Victoire, sly creature that she was, conjured up.

"They must have seized the Geological Survey of Canada report you sent him. He had it hidden in a copy of Saint Simon's memoirs."

The gaunt-faced Guerot stared intently at the ground as he walked, his hands at his back.

"Does he know who ordered the customs search?"

"He thinks it was Connie Rasmussen. She's very close to Laura Al-lee-Ah, the Greenland Congress representative."

Guerot stopped and turned to her, intently processing the information. "Are you sure?"

"In these kinds of circumstances, you're never sure of anything. This Connie had a long conversation with John on the plane before they landed in Nuuk. We're wondering how she fits in."

Victoire did not tell him that the same Connie had spent a night with Luc in Le Havre and was once a neo-Nazi militant. There was no point in laying it on too thick.

"Ask John for a full report on this lawyer. We need to know everything she's doing up there."

"Done. Why did you want to see me?"

Guerot cast a swift glance behind them as they were passing the Théâtre de la Gaîté and the Backstage. Victoire dragged Guerot inside the restaurant.

"There are always tables free at the back."

Victoire smiled at the waitress, whom she knew well and who lost no time moving them safely away from indiscreet ears. Guerot, his eyes darting, seemed nervous. They sat down facing each other.

"Tell me what's eating you, François."

"I'd like John to track down Christophe Maunay."

Victoire felt a chill run down her spine. She slowed her breathing as she pretended to focus on the menu, which she knew by heart. Neither she nor Luc had alerted the agency to the existence of Christophe Maunay. They would have had to reveal the existence of the rigged coins, and Fermatown jealously guarded its secrets.

"Who's he?" she asked indifferently.

"He's Terre Noire's HR manager in Paris, Lanier's trusted sidekick. He's left France, and we've lost all trace of him in Greenland."

"You were following him?"

Guerot didn't answer, but Victoire guessed that the agency had followed him for a long time.

"We'd like John to find out what he's doing in Nuuk. We don't trust Maunay. We'd like to know what he's cooking up. Who is he meeting in Nuuk? Where is he staying? What are his plans?"

"I'll pass on your requests to John and keep you posted."

Guerot promised an additional advance, without mentioning the actual amount, and left the Backstage in a hurry. Victoire tried to get her thoughts in order. Not easy.

Back at Fermatown, she sent John an encrypted message and sat down at the touch screen wall. Guerot had interrupted her investigation of Abraham Harper and his wife, Geraldine.

The head of North Land had amassed his fortune from the tar sands of Alberta. The extraction, cleaning, and production of the petroleum alternative consumed astronomical quantities of water and released incredible amounts of the greenhouse gas. North Land, which diligently groomed an image of environmental consciousness, derived its power from the most polluting of oil-producing industries. The most unbelievable part of it was that no news organizations appeared to be interested in this contradiction. The silence that surrounded North Land's activities was deafening. It was another mystery surrounding the mysterious Harper couple and their progeny.

Victoire studied the patriarch's features once again. The more she looked at Abraham Harper, the more she saw a predator, a man fiercely determined to dominate. The figure of Abraham Harper gradually faded, replaced by a brute ready to do anything to dominate the planet. His disappearance somewhere in the north of Greenland suited the character perfectly, and it wouldn't be the first time he had suspiciously disappeared. Abraham Harper was a chairman only when it suited him.

She jumped when she heard the doorbell. Who would be disturbing her at this hour? She ran to the window. Patrick Soutine, the doctor from the Rue Sarrette, was standing at the door. She went downstairs and found herself face-to-face with the man who had followed John's medical regimen ever since his return from Afghanistan.

Victoire had always felt uncomfortable around the doctor. What nerve, coming around at night when John was away. Soutine had a reputation as a dermatologist who liked a bit of skin. She cracked the door open, quite determined not to let him in.

"What's going on?" she asked in a firm voice that made it clear she wasn't playing ball.

"I'm so sorry to be here so late, but I'm between operations at Léopold-Bellan Hospital. As you were close by, I told myself that it was now or never."

"Now or never for what?" Victoire asked.

"To leave this with you."

Patrick handed her a USB key.

"What is it?"

"A report on Nuuk and our trip down the fjords where the glaciers are melting. I promised John that I'd give it to you as soon as possible. He seemed pretty keen to have it."

Victoire took the USB key and thanked him coldly.

"Have you heard from John?"

"He's fine. Thank you."

Patrick Soutine spun on his heels and left as swiftly as he had come, vanishing into the Rue Daguerre. Victoire went back upstairs to the media room. She plugged the key into the touch wall's port and pointed a finger at the OPEN button. She stopped just as she was about to press it. That story about operating at night at Léopold-Bellan sounded weird. She didn't like that pretentious macho creep. He made her skin crawl.

HANS EGEDE HOTEL, 8:50 P.M.

Slouched in a sofa at the bar of the hotel, John couldn't believe his ears.

"So just like that, those two bitches stripped you naked at customs and shoved a finger up your ass?"

"Yes," replied Christophe Maunay.

"Well, me too!"

"No way!"

The ice was broken and the conversation lubricated with several shots of Greenland whiskey. Nothing could fortify the feeling of Gallic camaraderie in the Arctic Circle better than a salacious story.

"The fat one was the biggest bitch. The one with a zit on her forehead."

"The other one wasn't bad either. She made sure she got an eyeful."

On the way to the dining room, they each recounted their interrogation in the minutest detail, comparing the questions, which were exactly the same.

"They go on and on about their bears and their precious climate," Maunay said. "And then they act like Nazis with us! They asked me a whole bunch of questions about Terre Noire and my positions in Gabon and Paris. And they wanted to know all about my private life."

"Same with me."

"Christ, it's us who are sounding their subsoil to see if there's any gas. And it's those slobs plowing around in snowshoes with their oil-tycoon pals who are cashing in on it. I've had enough of their politically correct bullshit and their hypocrisy. They're ten times richer than us. Terre Noire worked that out for them. With their rare earths and shale gas reserves, all Greenlanders could retire at thirty-two and draw pensions equal to ninety percent of their pay. Add their welfare payments, and everybody except foreigners could get a hundred percent."

The HR manager was letting it rip. Information was pouring out like coins from a slot machine. All John had to do was listen. It wasn't the time to ask Maunay what he was doing on the Champs-Elysées with the Dane. He decided to wait. But considering the looks they were getting from all around, John figured the French were going to get themselves a bad reputation again.

They were down to their last oyster when Christophe turned a shell over on his plate and asked with a jeering look, "So, the *calissons d'Aix* arrived safely, did they?"

John felt like he had been punched in the gut. How could the other guy know the ruse he'd used to keep the customs people from finding the cell phone and the credit card Geraldine Harper had given him?

"You know about them?"

"I see you've caught Mary Harper's eye. What amazing luck you've got," Maunay said, grinning.

"What are you talking about?" John asked, looking as dumbfounded as he could.

Maunay pulled the calling card from Mary Harper out of his pocket.

"I found this in the room that was booked for you. It was next to a bouquet of flowers. You were supposed to be sleeping in my bed!"

"Christ, that's right. How incredible," John replied, relieved.

"Don't you find that weird?" asked Maunay, who had switched to chardonnay.

"Yes, it is quite a coincidence."

John remembered that Mary did not know about his change of address. Qaalasoq had forgotten to tell her that he was staying in the blue house above the fjord. The Inuit was playing a funny game. He recalled what Connie Rasmussen had said about the Harpers and their secrets.

"You did the right thing, showing me the card," John joked. "She could be knocking on your door tonight."

Christophe Maunay's bloodshot eyes widened. The HR manager of Terre Noire was warming up.

"You mean to say she might hop into my bed?"

"No, mine!" John replied, surprising himself with this notion. It was risqué, to say the least.

"You think the heiress wants to sleep with you?" Maunay said. "Can you imagine what that could mean?"

"I'm just trying to get my head around it," said John, who was also enjoying the chardonnay.

"You ought to be screaming for joy instead of putting on a long face like that. Anyone looking at you would think the ice shelf had fallen on your head."

John was still having flashes of lucidity. The devil was in the details. This story about the reservation being canceled at the last minute by Qaalasoq and Geraldine was too much to believe. It was when it came time to settle the bill that the ice shelf really fell on him.

"John," Maunay said, slurring his words. "I'm ready to come work with you at North Land."

"What are you saying?"

"I'm quitting Terre Noire and coming over to your company. I'll bring you some unbelievable shit. Everyone says you're the one in charge of their image. In fact, everyone knows you're their headhunter, and you handle their investigations. It's the kind of thing that my firm doesn't know how to do."

Maunay had stopped drinking and was staring hard at John.

"Why do you want to quit Terre Noire?" John asked.

"I can't do it anymore. Lanier's going to make me pay for what happened on the *Bouc-Bel-Air*."

"Why would he do that? It's not your fault," John said.

"It's a long story, but I can't stay at Terre Noire any longer. I know too much."

Maunay dropped his gaze and fell silent.

"Like what?" John asked.

"I can't tell you right now, but if you manage to persuade Mary Harper to hire me, North Land won't regret it, believe me. It's an incredible stroke of luck that I ran into the Harpers' right-hand man. It's a sign," Maunay said, suddenly relaxed.

Things were not unfolding the way John had expected. He thought of Victoire and the pressure Guerot was putting on them to find out what Maunay was up to. The man who was planning to have him murdered in Paris with the help of a Dane was now begging him for a job at North Land! The time to hook the fish had come!

"What are you offering us?"

"I'd bring new possibilities for farming the permafrost for a thousand years to come. Thanks to Terre Noire, the Russians and Norwegians are twenty years ahead of the Canadians and Americans. I've got the results of all our experiments on the flora and fauna in Russia. The frozen lands of Siberia and Greenland are about to become habitable. I'm offering to tell you how. For North Land, it would be Eldorado. Every government in the world would be eating from the palm of your hand. You'd have completely untouched land and instructions on how to use it, a manual for the new world. You're going to make money you've never dreamed of."

"I thought you'd be showing us gas or oil," John said, pretending to be disappointed.

"I'll bring you something a lot better than an outmoded model," Maunay replied, upping the ante. "I'll give you the twenty-first century and beyond. For that, I need a Canadian passport and a new identity. I can't live in France any longer. I'm asking for political asylum in Canada."

"Is it that dangerous in Paris?" John asked.

"People are dead. Others are going to die. I'll bring you things that are even more shocking. You'll be amazed. I can't say anymore until I'm Canadian. Otherwise, I'll get a bullet in the head."

"What did you come here to do?"

"I came to see Lanier, but I've changed my mind."

"Why?"

"Because I ran into you. For me, this is an unhoped-for stroke of luck. You're my life preserver."

John nodded. Never could he have imagined, when he saw Maunay at the harbormaster's office, that the conversation could take such a turn. He could not pass up such an opportunity to find out more.

"I'm leaving Nuuk in the morning for Qaanaq. Meet me at the airport before takeoff. I'll introduce you to someone who might be able to help you. She'll give you a phone number and an address."

"Who is it?"

"Mary Harper."

"You're taking her with you to Qaanaq?"

"Yes. You might well get a chance to see her tonight, in which case you can explain everything to her privately."

Maunay was on cloud nine and en route to a radiant future far from the Champs-Elysées. John felt torn between Guerot's demands and the loyalty he owed his client. Taking the hour and the state of his neurons into account, he decided to leave major decisions to the next day.

The waitress came and whispered something in his ear.

"There's a gentleman..."

John turned and saw Qaalasoq's dark eyes staring at them.

"My treat," he said.

He took out his North Land credit card.

"No, mine," Maunay said, flashing his platinum Terre Noire card. John let him pay.

"See you tomorrow at the airport," he said to Maunay.

"Without fail."

The Inuit, as quiet as stone, took him back to the North Land SUV. Reeling from the alcohol and Maunay's revelations, John let himself be driven through a night unlike any other he had ever known. The deadly traps of the war on terror seemed downright transparent compared with those of the economic war. The thought of returning to the house above the fjord was disquieting. And, at his side, Qaalasoq was as unnerving as the mutilated mountain above Nuuk.

NUUK FJORD, 9:15 P.M.

Lars Jensen looked in the sight of his rifle and visualized the distance that separated him from the blue house above the fjord. The Dane had waxed his gun with shoe polish to stop any reflection in the bright moonlight, which could give him away. He stroked the cover of the Chinese ice saw that he had bought at the shopping mall in Nuuk and set it down next to the firing point. North Land's private house where John Spencer Larivière was staying was less than a hundred yards away. For some reason, in Paris, Per Sorensen had failed to get the target. He would have fun correcting that mistake.

NORTH LAND'S PRIVATE RESIDENCE, 10:30 P.M.

Qaalasoq stopped the car in front of the blue house and turned to John.
"I'll come and get you at seven tomorrow morning to take you to the airport."
John almost asked him why he hadn't informed Mary Harper of his change of address, but his instinct told him to be quiet. For his part, nothing obliged him to tell Qaalasoq anything about the conversation with Maunay. Besides, Qaalasoq hadn't asked. Maybe there was a listening device somewhere.
"Good night."
John got out of the SUV and went into the house. He locked the door and found himself face-to-face with the tupilaq. The horrible assemblage of body parts was staring at him, backlit by a completely pointless lamp. The bright icy night seeped in everywhere. There were no shutters or curtains on the windows. He headed to the kitchen and found his computer. In a few seconds, he re-established connections with Fermatown and sent Victoire a message: "Christophe Maunay is staying at the Hans Egede in the room originally booked for me. He wants to pack up and leave Terre Noire and come over to North

Land. Never imagined Laura Al-lee-Ah could have a husband in Paris. Haven't had time to broach the subject with her. Mary Harper is going to tell me Connie Rasmussen's secrets up in the Far North. We're taking off tomorrow—in theory."

He then activated the intruder program on his phone, so he could use it to get inside the local police in the far reaches of the icy north, if needed. John read the report Luc had sent: "Greenland intelligence is interested in you and Christophe Maunay. They've searched your computer and his and analyzed all the data. They're wondering what both of you have come to Nuuk to do. Watch your credit card: they've traced your purchases at the mall. They have a complete list of your gear. You forgot to get sunscreen and socks. But you bought a screwdriver. They're wondering why."

John saw himself at the checkout, paying for his purchases after his conversation with Connie Rasmussen. She had tricked him again!

He mused while admiring the incredible light setting the fjord ablaze. He told himself that Geraldine Harper, by giving him a credit card, had also made it easy for Greenland's spooks to track him every step of the way. The ties between North Land and the local authorities were pretty damned tight. The Canadian-American oil-and-gas company wasn't content just to sponsor bears and shrimp. Geraldine Harper and her daughter had the means to finance the new state's bumbling intelligence agency. A good investment. He stopped admiring the fjord. It was not wise to let his silhouette stand out against the backlit window. He went back to his phone.

Luc had sent him another message: "They're looking for Nicolas Lanier. They don't understand how both the head of such an important firm and the Nobel laureate Romain Brissac could have disappeared at the same time. I get the impression that they have an informer in Le Havre and another in Paris. Someone is following you closely, but I haven't managed to identify who it is. All the names are encoded. They fear something serious. Back soon. Victoire sends her love, and Caresse is getting fat. Your Persian is depressed and wants you home."

John smiled. He might not know what the hell he was doing in Greenland, but he at least had a family in Paris whose silences he understood without needing to rack his brain. He missed Luc and Victoire and realized that he wanted very much to be back in the Daguerre village. He poured himself a glass of milk, which, after the whiskey and the chardonnay, tasted funny. He quietly moved to a window again and gazed at the fjord, which looked as forlorn as he felt. Suddenly, he felt a wave of fear. The man who had tried to kill him in Paris was probably not alone. To take his mind off that disturbing idea, he picked up the phone Geraldine Harper had given him and listened to Mary's conversations. The heiress had clashed with her mother.

"I'm leaving tomorrow for Qaanaq with Spencer Larivière."

"You are not."

"I'm going to see him tonight at the Hans Egede to tell him the truth."

"No, you won't!"

Geraldine Harper seemed to lose her control. At last, an interesting development.

"You can't stop me," Mary declared. "We have to stop sending the poor guy off on a wild goose chase with this trumped-up story. He's not as stupid as that."

"I forbid you to go. Anyway, he's not at the hotel."

"How come?"

"None of your business."

Furious, Mary Harper had hung up. The other conversations were of no interest. He turned out the light and went to the window. The three balls he had had Patrick graft onto his earlobe were irritating him as much as the little secrets of the Harpers. The more headway he made, the less he understood the game people were playing with each other. It was time to go to bed.

He went upstairs, but instead of getting into bed, he pulled out his sleeping bag, picked up the screwdriver he had bought, and went downstairs. He spread the sleeping bag on the floor, right behind the door. Moonlight lit up the atrocious face of the tupilaq. Suddenly, he had the feeling that something in the house had been moved. Or maybe it was something outside. He went through all the photos of the interior he had taken on his phone when he arrived. Nothing was different. Yet when he had gotten back from Nuuk, there was a blip, which the excessive alcohol had erased. He wound back his film of events but found nothing. He turned out the lights. With a screwdriver in his fist, he lay down and slept like a log by the door.

NUUK FJORD, 11 P.M.

Lars Jensen saw the lights go out in the blue house and gave himself a few minutes to still his breathing before the attack. He could have shot the target from the position he was in, with a nine-out-of-ten chance of scoring a bull's-eye. But there was a one-in-ten chance of missing. It was an unacceptable risk. He liked the idea of an ending that matched what he had done on Haffner Bjerg. While the target was ambling about Nuuk harbor with the HR manager of Terre Noire, he had filled one of the barrels under the blue house on stilts with gasoline.

On the plane, Lars Jensen had memorized the files about John Spencer Larivière, including his medical record from Saint-Louis Hospital provided by his employer. He knew the man never slept in his bed when he was on a mission, but behind the front door instead. It was one of those things you learn in special forces training. The Frenchman had no reason to change his ways in Greenland, even if he had moved into the private sector.

Lars Jensen loaded special ammunition into the firing chamber. The first incendiary cartridge would set the floor on fire in a few seconds. That would flush the wolf out of the woods. The second would blow Spencer Larivière's head off as the house went up in flames. He would finish things off with the ice saw, slicing into matter that was still alive, though caramelized. He crept toward the house.

Just as he was about to go into action, his cell phone vibrated. He pulled it out and looked at the screen. He was being diverted to a more urgent task.

5

THURSDAY

John awoke with a start and, in his mind's eye, saw the scene clearly. One of the barrels under the house had been moved. He leaped out of his sleeping bag and raced outside, screwdriver in hand. The sky was a transparent gray. He rapped the barrel and smelled the gasoline. The traces on the ground were unequivocal. Someone had set a trap for him. It had failed. He was wondering if he would make it to Qaanaq. What could he do in that hole of a place anyway? The whole thing was just a pretext to get him here and kill him. Why? How was he more useful dead than alive?

When he spotted the North Land SUV at the end of the road, he went back inside to gather his things. The climate could warm up all it liked, but he could still catch pneumonia. Mary Harper and Qaalasoq were waiting for him in the hall when he came back down the stairs. The ambience had never been so gloomy.

The North Land heiress had to be angry with the Inuit for not telling her where he was. Certainly, Mary had to be feeling foolish after winding up in Christophe Maunay's room. The Terre Noire HR manager had probably confessed his reasons for his next act of betrayal. And no doubt, he had gotten some bad news.

"Is your luggage ready?" asked Qaalasoq.

"I just have to pack my sleeping bag," John said.

The Inuit looked down and realized that the Frenchman had spent the night on the floor. Qaalasoq kept a granite-like silence, and Mary Harper was sulking. He picked up his suitcase and was about to step outside when Qaalasoq stopped him in his tracks. The Inuit was pointing to the tupilaq.

"You take it with you," he said.

John thought he had misunderstood, but the faces of the two visitors confirmed that he had heard correctly. He went to the little beast and picked it up.

"You want me to lug this abomination all the way to the North Pole?"

"Yes."

"But it weighs a couple of pounds at least. Do we need the extra weight?"

"Two pounds is nothing."

The urge to chuck it on the ground and smash it to smithereens was strong, but John thought of Victoire and Luc. He would play the buffoon right to the end. It had become his way of loving them.

"Take it, for heaven's sake," Mary Harper whispered.

With her sullen look and downcast eyes, he felt sorry for her. He slipped the obnoxious critter into the leather suitcase he had bought at the shopping mall, thanks to the mother's credit card, and turned to the daughter.

"What's happened?" he asked. "You look terrible."

"You'll understand when you get in the car. Come on."

John descended the front steps and caught Qaalasoq glancing at the space under the house where someone had moved the barrel that was supposed to turn him into barbecued meat. The expedition to the Far North looked like it would be painful.

18 RUE DEPARCIEUX, 10:10 A.M.

Victoire put her coffee down on the table and went to the window to check the entry to 9 Rue Fermat and do some hard thinking. John's absence was distracting her, and because of that, she also felt an urgent need to pay attention. The motionless presence of Per Sorensen at his hotel obsessed her.

"It'll all work out. Don't worry," Luc said, combing Caresse's fur and diligently untangling the Persian's knots.

"I've told you not to brush her in the kitchen. Her hairs are even in the fridge!"

"It's the only place she'll let herself be brushed. And anyway, it relaxes me."

Victoire shrugged and looked down at the street. She wouldn't hear from John during the flight from Nuuk to Qaanaq. The sudden rising of Greenland was all over the news, and it alarmed her. For the first time, humanity was measuring the physical effects of global warming on the Earth's crust. According to a Chinese scientist, this geological event had imperceptibly altered the Earth's orbit, causing global warming to speed up. The climate was having an effect on the trajectory of the planet, which was, in turn, affecting atmospheric phenomena. A vicious cycle.

For indigenous people, man was a parasite that the planet would end up vomiting out. Global warming was a fever secreting antibodies designed to repel the aggressor. In the Cambodia of her childhood, the elders used to speak of the planets as living people with bodies and souls. Victoire regretted her contempt for legends. The elders were right. The Earth was sick with a deadly virus that had mutated two million years earlier and was walking around on two legs. A monster.

"Don't worry," Luc murmured as he walked over. "John's pulled through much tougher missions."

"It's not the mission itself that worries me. It's the context. Nothing's clear. I can feel death stalking. I sense huge confrontations coming on. I think we're more involved than we imagine. And I don't know why. It's making me sick."

Luc put the cat down on the tile floor.

"I can hear an alert."

They left the kitchen and went down to the second floor. The touch wall was displaying photos from Greenland that immediately dragged them into hell. It looked like someone had taken an ax to a corpse. Body parts were arranged over the bed and other furniture in what appeared to be a fairly luxurious hotel suite. A scalped head with its eyes gouged out had pride of place on a table next to a bouquet of flowers. The software fanned the shots out, one after the other, in a rainbow over the touch wall. One of them showed a business card beside the head and the message "The *calissons d'Aix* have arrived. Please forgive me, Mary Harper."

Victoire screamed like a madwoman and took her head in her hands. Luc, paralyzed by the methodical butchery, tried to stop the parade of photos but could not. The photos captured the severed calves and thighs, placed with care on chairs and a bureau. Detached arms had been laid on a windowsill. And the macabre scene went on from there.

Trapped between the hell on the wall and the wailing at his back, Luc felt like he was losing it. He forced himself to keep his eyes open, and he took in the nude torso, which was propped in an out-of-place crib. The penis had been cut off, leaving a hideous wound.

The author of this vile bit of staging had arranged the corpse as though he worshipped some bloodthirsty divinity. Each part had been carefully washed and made ready for some monstrous act of reassembly. The penis finally turned up in the bathtub. The sight of the remnant of flesh, placed between the legs of a plastic baby doll, was beyond unthinkable.

"Who is it?" screamed Victoire. "Please, tell me it's not John."

"I don't know," Luc said, trying to breathe.

Victoire, unable to look at the screen any longer, ran from the room. Her shrieking filled the house. Luc went back to the photo of the torso and enlarged it. He studied the abdomen and went back to the thigh, which he carefully inspected. Then he shouted, "It's not him!"

He went up the stairs, two steps at a time, and took Victoire's hand as she stood sobbing. He forced her to go back downstairs and look at the wall.

"See. There are no scars."

Victoire moved closer to see for herself and then collapsed on the floor.

"What is this horror?" she groaned, relieved that John had been spared but still appalled. "What's happened?"

Why, Luc wondered, had their information system just opened the doors of this abominable cold room for them?

"Our intruder program has captured Greenland's intelligence and police photos. We're getting all the documents related to this crime that they have in their possession. Thanks to Boomerang, we have access to files being read at this moment by Greenland security officials who are interested in John. The program read Mary Harper's name on the business card and alerted us while we were in the kitchen. It's brilliant."

"It's awful. How can you say something like that?"

Luc took Victoire in his arms.

"Everything's going to work out fine. Calm down. John's alive."

Nuuk road, 6:35 a.m.

Sitting in the back of the SUV, John put the newspaper down. He had been reading about an especially brutal murder. The victim, Christophe Maunay, a French executive with Terre Noire, had been killed and carved up in a soundproof suite on the top floor of the Hans Egede. It was the suite he was supposed to be in. There was just one photo with the story. John looked at it closely and recognized the red frieze on the wall at customs.

Maunay had been photographed upon his arrival in Nuuk, just as he himself had been. The press was getting its information from the very heart of Greenland security. He shivered and felt his muscles tighten. Cold determination took over the place in his skull reserved for combat, and something furious rose inside him. He turned to the somber North Land heiress, who was sitting beside him.

"What do they call a ritual slaying in this country?"

"I've got no idea," Mary Harper replied.

Qaalasoq emerged from his silence while overtaking a truckload of Chinese workers. "We don't use the expression 'ritual slaying' up here. It's Western. It comes from your part of the world, that business. The people from around here would never dare."

John put the paper on his knees and turned to Mary.

"I met Christophe Maunay last night. He wanted to leave Terre Noire and join North Land. He said he had serious things to reveal to you. Did he?"

"No."

"You never met Maunay?"

"Never," Mary replied.

The young woman opened her eyes wide, questioning what he was trying to get at. John was looking for logical explanations.

"You didn't go the hotel last night?"

"No, I phoned ahead, and they told me your room was taken by someone from Terre Noire. I was disappointed. Who are you really working for, Monsieur Spencer Larivière?"

"I'm not the one who decided I'd spend the night above the fjord in that house. I'm amazed you weren't informed."

Mary Harper hunched her shoulders and seemed to be in the grip of a painful thought. John pursued his line of reasoning.

"Christophe Maunay was murdered last night at the Hans Egede, in the room your mother reserved for me. I'm wondering if I should thank you or if I should be worried."

Gripping the wheel, Qaalasoq was not missing a word. Mary Harper seemed completely thrown. John added, "In any case, thank you for the flowers and the kind note. Pity that someone else got them."

Mary Harper turned to him and asked in an anxious voice, "What was Maunay getting at when he said there were serious things he wanted to reveal to us?"

"I have no idea. He offered to bring you the results of Terre Noire's research in the Barents Sea and Siberia. He wanted to reveal something shocking to your mother in exchange for a new identity and a Canadian passport. I suggested that he meet you this morning at the airport."

"Was he killed so he couldn't meet me?"

"Maybe. And that would mean that hanging around you worries some people."

Mary Harper ignored the implication and looked back at the road. Qaalasoq's presence no doubt was keeping her from speaking. Once they were on the plane, John would find a way to pick up the conversation. The car went around a bend and pulled up to a barrier blocking access to the airport. Qaalasoq held out a laminated card, and the guard opened the gate. They drove for about five hundred yards and found themselves facing the brand new airport. They loaded their bags onto trolleys and headed to the departure lounge for domestic flights.

The three of them presented themselves at the company counter and took their place in the line of passengers departing for Thule. Air Greenland Flight 76 linked Nuuk to the airport of the big American base charged with watching the top of the world. Washington was falling over itself with goodwill toward the new Greenland administration, now that the island had gained independence and opened sea routes around the pole. Thule had become the most important military base in the northern hemisphere. John noted that his two travel buddies were as quiet as mice. You could have cut the atmosphere between the daughter and the mother's right-hand man with a knife. He prepared himself for a particularly bumpy ride.

They had just gotten their boarding passes when two uniformed officers and a man in civilian dress approached them. John sensed that he was about to wind up in an interrogation room again. No doubt, the alcohol-laced evening with Christophe Maunay had drawn attention to him. He was actually one of the last witnesses to have seen the victim alive.

The plainclothes cop stopped in front of Mary Harper. John recognized him. He was an officer who had questioned him at customs.

"Miss Mary Harper?"

"That's me."

"Follow me, please."

Mary Harper picked up her suitcase and followed without protest, as if the arrest was a release, a way of getting out of flying to Thule. Maybe it was staged. John raced after her, but the officer intervened.

"Mary," he shouted. "I'm coming with you."

She looked at him with tears in her eyes. "Votre place est dans le Grand Nord. Il n'y a que vous qui puissiez découvrir qui est derrière tout ça. Partez, je vous en supplie," she said, begging him to go to the Far North and find out who was behind everything, using French so the Greenlanders wouldn't understand. "Go, please!"

The police officers firmly ordered him to stay where he was. Disconcerted by what Mary had just said, he just stood there like an idiot. When he turned around, Qaalasoq was as white as the ice sheet.

"What is this farce?"

"Do what she says."

Qaalasoq understood French perfectly. Did Mary Harper know that? Regardless, he was going to rip the veil off this affair and get at the truth.

Seated by the window, John stopped gazing at the scattered fragments of the ice shelf and turned toward the cabin. Qaalsoq's eyes were closed. The Inuit hadn't said a word since takeoff. The seat that Mary Harper would have occupied was between them, and John couldn't stop thinking about her. The Harpers' daughter had let herself be arrested without making a fuss and had begged him to fly to the Far North. Qaalasoq hadn't flinched or uttered a word of protest.

"Why didn't you say anything when Mary got arrested?"

Qaalasoq opened an eye.

"Because there was no point."

"Why didn't they take me? There's something fishy going on. I was in the Hans Egede with Christophe Maunay. He was found in the room meant for me, which you canceled to take me to the fjord house. Why am I free?"

"I don't know, but we'll soon find out. Abraham and Geraldine Harper hired you for that reason."

"You mean the Harpers offered me this contract to find out why I wasn't arrested by the Greenland police at the same time as their daughter?"

"Among other things."

A number of passengers had begun to move around in the cabin, which was irritating the buttoned-up flight attendants in orange and white uniforms, the colors of the new nation. The captain's voice rang out. "I must ask passengers to stay in their seats. We'll soon be banking and flying over the *Bouc-Bel-Air* at low altitude. You'll be able to take all the photos you like without having to change seats."

The Airbus began its descent toward the sea and came closer to the black waters of Baffin Bay. After a minute, the plane pivoted to the right, and John could see the red and black hull of the *Bouc-Bel-Air* and, beside it, the *Copenhagen*. The two ships were heading south.

"Did you know that Connie Rasmussen is probably on board the *Bouc-Bel-Air*?" John watched for Qaalasoq's reaction.

"I know," Qaalasoq replied without looking at him.

"Before getting himself killed, Christophe Maunay was also thinking about getting on the ship. But your compatriots wouldn't let him board the *Narvik* to reach the *Bouc-Bel-Air*. Maunay identified himself as a high-up Terre Noire official. He may have died as a result."

Qaalasoq listened intently and then leaned over the empty seat. His black eyes shone with savage intelligence. A true hunter, John thought.

"If I've got this right, only after he was refused permission to board the *Narvik* did he propose going over to North Land," the Intuit said, suddenly talkative.

"Yes," John answered, looking his neighbor straight in the eye.

"What happened that evening while you were with him?"

"Ah, well, we talked."

"You have uncommon powers of persuasion, Monsieur Spencer Larivière."

"Except that I didn't try to recruit him," John replied.

Qaalasoq smiled. John looked back at Baffin Bay and thought about all that he had been through since his arrival. He had been credited with playing a central role that went way beyond protecting Mary Harper. He discreetly took out his cell phone and looked at what Fermatown had sent him. The remains of Christophe Maunay nearly made him gag. Ritual slayings might have been unheard of before, but there was definitely a monster haunting the place now. He deleted the images and cleared his mind by gazing at the ocean. Qaalasoq, to his right, had gone to sleep and was snoring away like a seal.

On board the BOUC-BEL-AIR, *8:30 A.M.*

Le Guévenec used his mug of coffee to warm his hands as he quizzed Lanier in the first mate's cabin.

"What do you think?"

Lanier read the last paragraph again and put down the article that had been downloaded on one of the *Bouc*'s computers that was still working. Le Guévenec had jury-rigged a printer to copy the article.

The Terre Noire chief was deeply troubled by the slaying and mutilation of Christophe Maunay.

"I'm the one who summoned him to explain how the boatswain and Sylvain Velot got on this ship. I had him sent up from France to account for the treachery of those two men. And doubtless his own."

Despite his suspicions about the HR manager, Le Guévenec was floored. Lanier went on. "Christophe Maunay was killed by people who didn't want the three of us to have a conversation in this cabin. Even if he'd set foot on the boat, I'm not sure he'd have made it this far alive. Maunay knew too much. We're in trouble, Loïc."

"I'd figured that much out."

Nicolas Lanier turned his gaze to one of the portholes. Another plane was circling overhead. Helicopters and planes of all kinds had been filming the side-by-side ships for hours. The *Bouc*, a victim and protagonist of the disaster, had turned into the freak with two heads. Another fleet led by the *Narvik* was sailing toward them. The situation was about to become untenable in the face of demands for transparency from the Congress and the international community.

Le Guévenec interrupted Lanier's thoughts.

"Connie Rasmussen told me about a certain John Spencer Larivière, who's some sort of image consultant for North Land. As such, he could do further harm to our own image. What should we make of him?"

Lanier looked distraught. "Why did she tell you that?" Lanier asked.

The way Lanier was looking at him gave Le Guévenec the feeling that he was talking to a third person in the cabin. Le Guévenec almost looked around to see if someone else had come in.

Le Guévenec wondered if his boss wasn't starting to crack up. That's all the expedition needed. He transferred his weight to his other leg to ease the pain in his hip, which was becoming more severe. The list, meanwhile, was compressing his lower back.

"How long are you planning to stay shut up in here?" Le Guévenec asked.

"Until the truth comes out."

"What truth?"

"There's an alliance that's out to get us. I want to know who's behind it."

Le Guévenec looked aghast. "The crew's beginning to ask questions about your presence in this cabin. They saw a passenger disembark from a helicopter, and they know someone's here. Tongues are starting to wag. In Paris, reporters are asking about your absence. The vice president won't be able to fend off the questions much longer."

"He's a diplomat. He's in the habit of lying. That's what I pay him to do. Don't feel sorry for that bureaucrat—he earns more than you do. And that's a mistake I'm going to correct. If I come out of this cruise alive, I'll fix that, I tell you."

"I won't mind if you do."

"What's Connie Rasmussen saying?"

"She asked me who the anonymous passenger was. Velot, the guy who killed the two bears, must have told her some bullshit. Now she says she wants humanity to finally know what happened on board the *Bouc-Bel-Air.*

Nicolas Lanier looked appalled. But then the distress morphed into a giggling fit. He's sinking into madness, just as my ship is threatening to sink into the sea, Le Guévenec thought. After a moment, Lanier apologized and composed himself, wiping the saliva off his beard.

"Give her some kind of answer, but be careful. We can't have the Congress on our backs. The whole planet is watching us. And look at the state we're in, Loïc!"

Lanier stretched out his arms to call attention to their decrepit faces and shipwrecked clothes. He burst out laughing. And now the reserved captain joined him. He belly laughed so hard, his hip felt like it was about to buckle. The world was going mad. And so were they. Their laughter rattled the walls, unsettling the remaining able-bodied men on the *Bouc*.

AIR GREENLAND FLIGHT 76, 9:45 A.M.

John could feel the plane losing altitude and came out of his half-sleep. Qaalasoq had moved into the empty seat between them.

"We're flying over the Great Wound of the Wild Dog," the Inuit said.

John saw a vast white expanse studded with pools and little lakes. Greenish filaments that looked like gelatin joined the blue lakes here and there.

"What's that?"

"That's the algae your French friends invented to keep the ice cap from sliding into the ocean. It's from Brittany, it seems. But it didn't work. You'll soon see for yourself."

The plane banked to the left and headed northeast. John registered shock—which was shared by all the passengers on Flight 76—as they flew over the Lauge Koch Kyst site. The breach was stunning. Directly beneath them stretched an expanse of black granite as vast as a French province. Like some moon blackened by a blowtorch, the surface was lacerated with cracks and crevices. Chunks of trapped ice and strewn boulders showed how violent the separation had been. The bleakness exceeded anything of the kind that the planet had ever come up with.

"Do you know what the locals call this new space?"

"Terre Noire," John replied. The answer seemed so obvious: Black Land.

He sensed amazement mixed with respect in the look the Inuit gave him.

"You can divine names. That's a good sign for what comes next."

"It wasn't hard."

"Don't be modest."

John accepted the compliment, worrisome as it was. Fifteen minutes later, they were flying over bristling ice fields that looked like daggers hurled chaotically on top of each other. Rivers and inland seas were

choked with drift ice from the dislodged Lauge Koch Kyst, now separated from the continent. A deathly silence pervaded the cabin. The
plane headed north.

They touched down on the runway of the brand-new civilian airport, built at a distance from the military base. Thule, the mythical
city of the Northern kings, was letting the United States eavesdrop
nonstop on everything in the sky and at the bottom of the ocean.

Before getting out of his seat, Qaalasoq turned to John. "After
World War II, the Americans drove us from this land, with the complicity of the Danes," he said. "We were forced to move to Qaanaq."

"I hope the Americans are paying you a decent rent."

"It's like drawing blood from a stone. But ever since the government
let them know that the Chinese are offering us double, things have been
getting better."

John said nothing and took his place among the disembarking
passengers. As he stepped out of the plane and started down the steps,
he took in the American, Danish, and Greenland flags flapping and
crackling above the spanking-new terminal. Once inside, they walked
down a corridor and retrieved their bags without any trouble.

Then two men in uniform approached John.

"Are you John Spencer Larivière of North Land?"

"Yes."

"Please follow us."

Qaalasoq stood between them but was abruptly put in his place.

"We'll call you. Stay here."

Offended, he stiffened but obeyed.

As John walked toward a sliding door, he mentally prepared himself for a fresh striptease and another round of interrogation. He was
invited to sit at a table in front of two officers, one in American uniform and the other in Greenland uniform. He immediately thought
of Geraldine's phone and the NSA's big ears. Thanks to him, the
Americans knew all about Mary Harper's conversations and the details of his mission.

The Greenland customs man spoke first.

"We'd like to question you about the murder of Christophe Maunay,
a French citizen and HR manager of the company Terre Noire."

John slumped, expecting the worst.

"You had reserved the room that was finally taken by Monsieur
Maunay. Don't you find that strange? Terre Noire and North Land in
the same room?"

John sensed that the American was on high alert, and he wanted him to show his cards first. Experience had taught John to wait for questions before replying.

"Did you want to leave North Land and join Terre Noire?" the American officer asked. "After all, you're French. It would be understandable. Maybe you wanted to go back home?"

This is the dizzy limit, John told himself, thinking of Christophe Maunay's proposal to join North Land. Did it look like it was actually the other way around—that he wanted to leave North Land for Terre Noire?

"I've never considered leaving North Land and joining Terre Noire."

The man in US Air Force uniform opened the file in front of him.

"I see you have dual nationality—French and American. Spencer is your mother's name, isn't it?"

"I was born in Paris, but I spent my childhood in Princeton, New Jersey."

John told himself that, yet again, he was going to have to clarify his origins. For years, he had been forced to explain himself to military and administrative officials in both countries. How could he make this Yankee bureaucrat believe that it was Maunay who wanted to betray his firm?

"Yet you did reserve the room."

"North Land reserved it. Not me."

"We'll check. You had a long conversation with the victim last night at the Hans Egede."

"I did."

"What did you talk about?"

"Global warming and the new diseases it could lead to."

"Have there been any exchanges between your two companies on the subject?"

"We spoke only in very general terms. We're not scientists, and, for my part, I don't have access to technical dossiers."

"Where were you last night between midnight and three in the morning?"

"In a house that belongs to North Land," John replied in a calm, confident voice.

"Is there a witness who can confirm that?"

"Qaalasoq, the man with me."

The American scribbled a few words in his notebook and let his Greenland colleague take his turn.

"Mary Harper is in custody in Nuuk and is also being questioned. She claims that the business card that she used to thank the sender for the *calissons d'Aix* was meant for you. Is that true?"

"That's right."

"Why did she have flowers delivered to you? For a man, that's odd."

"Out of sympathy, I assume," John replied without smiling. "It's something people do in France. We send each other flowers and plants for our balconies. The bees are fleeing the countryside because of pesticides and taking refuge in Paris. Mary Harper has an apartment on the Boulevard Saint-Michel, just opposite the beehives in the Luxembourg Gardens."

"What is there between you and Miss Harper?" the Greenlander asked.

John knew he was on slippery ground and gave himself a few seconds to think. The American looked tense. John saw him glance at the three steel balls in his earlobe. The two civil servants no doubt knew more than they were letting on. Who was working for whom in this business? Rival governments were sometimes forced to become temporary allies. John had seen this more than once.

"There's nothing between me and Mary Harper."

"Yet she writes on the business card that she hopes you'll forgive her. What did she do that needed forgiving?" the Greenlander asked.

"She might have thought that her behavior was a little chilly, which would explain the flowers at the Hans Egede," John said.

"Because normally your relationship is warmer?"

"No."

"Where did you meet?"

"In Paris."

"What are you doing in Greenland, Monsieur Spencer Larivière?"

His face was expressionless.

John repeated word for word what he had told the customs officers in Nuuk.

"Do you belong to Greenpeace?"

"No."

"What's your religion?"

"Catholic."

"Do you intend to commit acts of terrorism against the United States in Greenland?"

"No."

"You have nothing else to declare?"

"No."

The two men walked out of the room and left him on his own, without even a glass of water. Minutes passed. The dumb story about the flowers made him think of Victoire and how much he loved her. The door suddenly opened, and the two uniforms came in.

"You can't leave Greenland without advising the police. Is that clear?"

"Yes."

"Tell the man with you to come in here."

John rose and left the interview room. He had dodged the land mines—for now, at least—and he was starting to earn his fee.

PARIS, HÔTEL LOUXOR, RUE DE RICHELIEU, 3:30 P.M.

Per Sorensen left the hotel, holding his red-and-black-wrapped package with great care. Ever since he had failed to execute John Spencer Larivière outside the Hôtel Lutetia, he had been confined to his hotel room, waiting for new instructions. The meeting in the bar at the Saint-James' swimming pool with the person who ordered the hit had brought clarity.

He avoided walking in front of the Greenland House, which, since the catastrophe, had seen endless comings and goings of journalists and politicians desperate for news on global warming. There was something he didn't get, in any case, in the choice of hotels. Why had his employer picked a place so exposed? He reached the taxi stand and took a seat in the back of a Mercedes.

"The Eiffel Tower. But drive slowly. I'll pay whatever it costs."

Per Sorensen put his money where his mouth was and dropped a one-hundred-euro note on the front seat. The car pulled out slowly. On the radio, there was nothing but talk of Greenland.

"It's terrible, what's happening up there."

"Yes, dreadful."

Per Sorensen couldn't stop himself from smiling. Inside. The muscles of his face weren't fit for that kind of exercise.

PARIS, 18 RUE DEPARCIEUX, 3:35 P.M.

Standing in front of the touch wall, Victoire and Luc were trying to figure out how the others could have gotten wind of John's meeting at the Ritz with Geraldine Harper. No hypothesis was satisfactory.

"Apart from us, no one knew about Geraldine's phone call," Victoire said.

"Yet Per Sorensen was in place before John arrived," Luc replied.

"So the leak came from Geraldine or her daughter. And they were in Paris that day."

Luc brought up photos and the latest information they had gleaned about the two women.

"I can't believe it's the mother," he said. "And I can't imagine it's the daughter, either. Why would they kill a man they're paying to protect them? I can't see them murdering the Terre Noire guy, either, even if he was a rival. It doesn't stack up."

Victoire was thinking.

"Let's expand the circle of nearest and dearest who might have been aware of the meeting at the Ritz."

"Abraham Harper had to be in the know," Luc said. "That guy seems ready for anything. He's eliminated practically all of his rivals."

"He'd already disappeared in Greenland when the meeting took place," Victoire responded.

"Yes, but before disappearing, he'd authorized Fermatown to protect his daughter," Luc said. "So he knew his wife was about to meet John at the Ritz."

"Still, he doesn't have a serious motive," Victoire said. "Why order a hit on John when he's never been involved with Greenland or North Land before in his life?"

They were going around in circles. Luc went on. "What if Abraham Harper mentioned the meeting to someone who deliberately or accidentally betrayed him?"

Victoire was good at the game of Go and was able to apply the strategy to situations beyond the board game.

"Yes, I think we're getting closer to the truth."

She tried to imagine Abraham Harper at the Great Wound of the Wild Dog. Talk about a sinister name. The truth probably lay there. She was sure of it, even. She pointed at the northern part of the great island.

"This is where Abraham was betrayed by someone he was talking to."

"Or by someone who heard something about the meeting at the Ritz."

Luc had obtained photos of the region around Lauge Koch Kyst, which had just broken away from Greenland. In a few hours, John and Abraham Harper would be face-to-face at the Great Wound of the Wild Dog. While they were thinking about this encounter in Greenland, a touch wall alert brought them back to Paris.

"Per Sorensen just left his hotel."

"He's probably gone to hook up with his contact at the Saint-James again."

"I'm outta here."

When Luc had gone, Victoire buried herself in news accounts, looking for a clue. The Harpers rarely appeared in public. Victoire brought up what few photos she could find. The couple was sometimes in the company of their daughter, Mary. It was a long while before she found something of interest. It was on a Canadian newspaper's website: "Among those attending the ceremony at the Oslo Opera House honoring Jean-Claude Possin, the latest Abel Prize winner for mathematics, were Abraham Harper of North Land and Romain Brissac, the Nobel laureate for chemistry, of Terre Noire." A few minutes later, the visual recognition software allowed her to complete the list of those who were at the ceremony, based on numerous photos available on blogs and websites around the world. Victoire started. The woman sitting next to Romain Brissac at the opera house was none other than Isabelle Le Guévenec.

She went up to the kitchen to make herself some tea before going on with her investigation. Maybe she had a lead. Then she decided to make coffee instead and allow herself a slice of cake. Just one slice.

PARIS, CHAMPS DE MARS ESPLANADE, 4:10 P.M.

Per Sorensen got out of the taxi and merged into the crowd milling under the Eiffel Tower. He spotted a group of Chinese tourists getting ready to join the line at the southwest pillar. A young woman stuffing souvenirs into a canvas bag drew his attention. The ideal carrier. He moved closer to start up a conversation and deftly slipped the euro coins that had betrayed him into her bag. Spencer Larivière had obviously spotted him and somehow slipped him the coins fitted with transmitter microchips. He'd been had like a beginner.

His employer, whom he'd met at the Saint-James swimming pool, had seen him at the hotel to explain the new instructions. Now he had the upper hand. He gripped the chain saw in its cover, flagged a taxi and asked to be taken to the Rue Froidevaux. There, he would find a modern apartment building facing Montparnasse Cemetery. According to the map, the building ran between the Rue Fermat and the Rue Deparcieux. It overlooked the smaller houses on those streets, where his targets lived. He could gain access to the roofs and would not be seen.

John saw Qaalasoq's stocky figure finally emerge from the interrogation room. The Inuit's face was devoid of all expression. The guy was a muscle-bound taciturn enigma. John was sure that he had given them a run for their money, unless he was in on a *mise-en-scène* aimed at getting John to swallow a new chapter of this Arctic soap opera.

"They kept you a long time," John said.

"They wouldn't believe that I was the one who made the reservation at the Hans Egede and then canceled it. And yet it's the truth," Qaalasoq said with a sly smile.

"If you say so," John replied.

Qaalasoq seemed ready to talk.

"They didn't believe that you spent the night in the blue house at the fjord, either. It took me awhile to convince them."

"How did you do that?"

"I don't know."

"What do you mean, you don't know?"

John was trying to discern any lie in what Qaalasoq was saying. He tried to look affable, almost uninterested.

"I called Geraldine Harper," Qaalasoq said. "She spoke to them and gave them proof that you weren't lying."

"What proof?"

"I don't know, but the American whispered something in the other one's ear. You didn't tell me everything about your relationship with Geraldine Harper. There are things I know nothing about that I'd like to learn before I die."

John very nearly lost his cool. He was being attacked for hiding things from a bunch who had been taking him for a ride from day one in Paris.

"I get the impression it's you, not me, who hasn't been disclosing everything."

John picked up his bags. He followed Qaalasoq to the other end of the airport and out to the helicopter that served the neighboring villages. Fifteen minutes later, they were buckling their seat belts aboard a Sikorski in North Land colors. The machine rose quickly and headed toward Qaanaq sixty miles north, at the far end of the old hunting grounds of the polar Eskimos, as they were called at the beginning of the twentieth century.

As they flew, Qaalasoq drew John's attention to a patch of ground.

"That's where an American atomic bomber crashed on January 21, 1968. It took years to persuade the Air Force to clean up the area and more years on top of that to get precise information about what happened. The former Danish government did nothing. The place is cursed. We've been driven away. We've been radiated. We've been polluted. We've been turned into alcoholics, and we've been drugged. Now we're about to be looted."

"Yet you work for North Land," John said. "This helicopter, the fjord house—all of it belongs to a Canadian-American company."

"North Land doesn't exploit Greenland directly. Abraham Harper drills the ground to find out what's under it, but after that, it's the mining companies and the agricultural developers that step in. The Chinese have already bought up over twelve thousand square miles of land that's still frozen. They're storing up the land to pay for the retirement of future generations."

Qaalasoq had never let himself go as much as he was now. But the infernal racket of the rotor arms was bringing back bad memories for John. Ever since his crash in a tribal area of Afghanistan, John had loathed helicopters. The memory of the accident was inscribed in the grafted skin on his body. Whenever he got emotional, the grafts would swell and could turn blue. The pain was bearable, but the feeling of being an assemblage undermined his morale. He suddenly realized that the tupilaq in his bag, like him, was made of bits and pieces. The similarity scared John. Did the Harpers have access to his medical files? Nothing would be spared him in this crusade.

Qaalasoq interrupted his thoughts and raised his voice above the noise of the chopper.

"Here, no one can hear what I'm saying. I can talk freely."

"It's about time! Tell me frankly what I'm being used for."

"Abraham Harper is counting on you to find out what's really going on."

John felt humiliated by this unscrupulous oligarch who had chosen him according to criteria that were obscure, to say the least. He had become no more than a gadget on the economic warfare shelf, disposable, just like the Danish killer he had escaped from in Paris. He would die in combat without knowing why.

"I've never seen your Abraham Harper."

"I can't believe that," Qaalasoq replied.

"And yet it's the truth."

"But I'm sure that you're going to help us," said the Inuit, who seemed sincere.

John shook his head, conveying that he was having a hard time understanding anything that was going on. They were alone in the cabin of the helicopter, which smelled of motor oil and burned scrap metal. It was time this ended, one way or another.

"How long before we reach Qaanaq?"

"Twenty minutes."

PARIS, 18 RUE DEPARCIEUX, 5:05 P.M.

Victoire was at the touch wall, looking for information regarding the Harper couple's relationship with their daughter, Mary, as well as Geraldine's relationship with Abraham. News stories hinted that Geraldine and Abraham had differences of opinion. Victoire sensed that family dynamics had something to do with John's mission. And now the daughter's protection and the father's disappearance in some remote hole in the Far North were taking on a whole new light. Had Fermatown been pulled into a family squabble? Harper versus Harper? Or, more seriously, was it Canada versus the United States? The warming of the pole and the opening up of new sea routes were turning Canada into one of the giants of the twenty-first century. Victoire paused for a few minutes and drew up a list of key words: Geraldine Harper – tar sands – technologies – Canada – United States – patents – oil – gas.

Fermatown's semantic analysis program brought up several documents and posted them before her eyes. One of them was a report published on the website of the Centre d'Etude et de Prospective Stratégique, the CEPS. The French NGO involved in long-term planning and economic forecasting shed a harsh light on the geostrategic context into which they were being propelled like a moraine pushed along by a glacier. North Land started off mining Alberta's oil sands, but then invested in hydraulic fracturing, or fracking, to extract shale gas. The company had made great strides using extraction systems that required massive volumes of water, according to the report written by Tribot la Spière.

To release the gas trapped in rock, North Land injected water mixed with sand and chemicals into boreholes at very high pressure. Once the rock was fractured, the sand filtered in, the injected water was pumped out, and the gas rose to the surface, facilitated by microscopic vents in the sand that allowed it to come up naturally.

The chemicals used included agents designed to improve the yield and keep the gas in suspension, along with anti-microbials to prevent the proliferation of organisms at bore level and acids to dissolve certain materials.

North Land closely guarded the exact composition of the mix. The patents belonged to a small research consultancy. Geraldine Harper owned fifty-one percent of the consultancy, and the state of Alberta owned the other forty-nine percent. For several years, United States authorities had been discreetly pressing for a merger of the consultancy and North Land Holding. The United States, via Abraham Harper, owned forty-three percent of the holding company's capital. It was rumored that Geraldine Harper didn't intend to go along with the merger, which meant that the Canadian government would have greater bargaining power in relation to the United States in Greenland.

Victoire brought up the map attached to the report, which showed the areas in Greenland where shale gas extraction looked conceivable. Canada did seem to have a strong presence. This could explain the close ties between the Harper women and Laura Al-lee-Ah. These three women perfectly embodied the Canada-Greenland axis. With a bit of chutzpah and a dose of cynicism, you could even see Abraham Harper's disappearance as a weakening of America's position. The logic was irrefutable.

Too good to be true, Victoire said to herself.

Victoire looked at her watch. John would soon be landing in Qaanaq. She pictured him on board the helicopter, reliving the accident that had nearly cost him his life in Afghanistan. John would go to any lengths to match his father's fearlessness. John Larivière, the father, was a high-mountain guide who had vanished in the Andes when his son was only two years old. John, the son, relished rock climbing, whether it was in Fontainebleau or the American Southwest. He did it to commune with his father, but he seldom talked about it with Victoire, because she had her own ghosts. Her Cambodian mother had escaped from the Khmer Rouges, but died without ever having spoken about her ordeal. Luc, who hung out in the Montparnasse catacombs, had once called John and Victoire "memory levelers." Their medicine cabinets held the same anti-depressants. In establishing Fermatown, John and Victoire had discovered the lightness of being and a certain nonchalance, thanks to Luc. The big kid was almost like a son. Where was he, anyway?

She moved back to the big oak table that occupied the middle of the media room. Per Sorensen's portrait stood out from the others. He had a sinister mug. Why hadn't Luc called?

She felt something rub against her ankle and found Caresse. The Persian raised her head and meowed. Victoire bent down to pick her up. Suddenly, she spotted a shadow on the wall, cast by the sun coming in from the windows along the Rue Fermat.

Someone had forced entry into their home through the roof and was coming downstairs to the second floor. In a nanosecond, Victoire realized that any attempt to flee would fail. The man was about to surge up in front of her. There was only one place to hide in this big room. She hoisted herself under the top of the oak table. Pressing her hands and feet against the apron that ran all the way around under the table, she watched as the sneakers went right by her and stopped at the touch wall.

Per Sorensen got a shock when he saw his portrait on the wall amid people he had never laid eyes on. He placed a finger on the photo, and more pictures came up. He saw himself in the back of the taxi that had taken him to the Sèvres-Babylone–La Motte-Picquet intersection. The man who hired him had not been spinning tall tales. He then looked for the portrait of his boss and could not find it. The enemy did not know who his employer was. That was good, but he had no time to lose.

Per Sorensen turned around and saw a steaming cup on the table. He gently put the chain saw on the table and thought. When he had passed through the workout room on the fourth floor, where one of the skylights was open because of the heat, he had not seen any equipment that could be used to make fake euro coins. The taxi had to be in the garage that opened onto Number 18, Rue Deparcieux.

Victoire's muscles were burning and would soon give out. The man had probably spotted her hot coffee, which betrayed her presence. He had just put down something heavy above her head. She could feel the sweat running from her scalp and her armpits. The first drop fell on the tile floor, making a quiet plop that sounded deafening to her. Terrified, she pressed against the wooden rim like one of the damned, regretting that she had not confronted the invader when she was still in full possession of her faculties. It was a dreadful strategic error. In a few seconds, she would be nothing but an exhausted and vulnerable rag doll. Drops were falling, one after the other. Plop, plop.

Fascinated by his image on the wall, Per Sorensen registered the sound of something dripping. It made him think of leaking water in the basement. He grabbed his chain saw and headed for the stairs that went down to the garage.

Paris, The Eiffel Tower, 5:45 p.m.

Luc stared at the tourists on the second-story platform of the Eiffel Tower. None of them resembled Per Sorensen, not even remotely. He checked the manual receiver indicating the presence of five coins less than ten yards away and walked toward a young Chinese woman who was captivated by sight of the Arc de Triomphe. Rarely had he felt so stupid. Per Sorensen had hoodwinked them. Terrified, he raced toward the elevators. They had just been cordoned off, thanks to a bomb scare.

PARIS, 18 RUE DEPARCIEUX, 5:50 P.M.

Bent over, Victoire was catching her breath and wiping away the sweat stinging her eyes. She took off her shoes and crossed the tile floor to the hall. The stranger had gone down to the garage. She put a toe on the first step and crept down, trying not to hear the heartbeats that were turning her rib cage into a Bronx drum.

Like an idiot, she had forgotten, after parking her taxi, to reactivate their system devised to trap burglars. Security tarps, approved by the European Commission and certified ISO 28000 by Orca Security, were all the rage in home security circles, especially with owners of vacation houses. They were popular among wealthy Chinese who had lavish seaside retreats. Fermatown had purchased one for its primary residence. Victoire thought she might be able to reach the manual controls on the wall halfway up the stairs.

In the garage, Per Sorensen looked over the fake taxi that had snared him outside the Hôtel Lutetia. He pictured the woman at the wheel. Then he remembered touching the laminated ad extolling the merits of Persian cats. It had mentioned a breeder in Beaumont.

Not only had the bitch made him look like a fucking idiot, she also had lifted his fingerprints and no doubt a bundle of epithelial cells. Now they probably had his DNA too. On top of being the source of a lot of frigging hassles, these French guys were diabolical. He put the chain saw on the floor and examined the interior of the locked car. No doubt about it. A white cat on the laminated advertisement taunted him from behind the window, waiting to snatch the fingerprints of other unwitting passengers in the fake taxi.

"The bitch!" he muttered.

A noise like the squeal of a bat made him lift his head. Before he knew what was happening, he grabbed his chain saw. Too late to escape. A mass dropped from the ceiling, enclosing him in sticky, smelly darkness.

Victoire's jaw dropped in shock. She had never seen anything like it in her life. The tarpaulin, attracted by the heat source, had fallen from the ceiling and tightly wrapped itself around the stranger. The intelligent fabric spread an anaesthetizing solution over the skin that was designed to minimize the captive's stress and keep him hydrated. Injections of vitamins and glucose made up for the lack of food. The European Commission had stipulated that any captive had to be able to survive under the sheet for forty-eight hours. France had demanded even more survival time, and regulations required biological sensors and a system to alert the nearest police station and ambulance service.

Victoire's vague feeling of guilt turned to out-and-out terror when she heard a motor whining inside the tarpaulin, shaking the cement floor under her bare feet. The teeth of the chain saw chomped through the fabric, spitting fibers and droplets of moisture. A hideous steel tongue was slicing the tarp in two. Per Sorensen's crazed eyes appeared in the shadow of the ruptured husk.

The killer pointed his power tool at her. Like an insect that had escaped from a honey pot, he dashed after her, laughing. Incorrectly dosed tarpaulins could induce fits of euphoria.

Unable to get to the garage door, Victoire raced up the stairs, hoping to reach the top-floor workout room before her pursuer. Even doped with vitamins and rehydrated with organic substances, the killer would be hard-pressed to catch her. She got there first, leaping atop the pommel horse and gripping the edge of the skylight the man had gotten in through. In a matter of seconds, she was on the roof.

He arrived, yelling over the roar of the chain saw, which he threw to the floor. He climbed onto the pommel horse and started to hoist himself through the skylight. Precariously balanced on the burning roof tiles, Victoire knew she couldn't get far in bare feet. She gave up the notion of fleeing and swapped fear for rage. She would face the bastard. The hideous snout emerged from the workout room. She skirted the square skylight and slammed it on her would-be executioner. The glass broke over Per Sorensen's skull, causing blood to gush. He swore, calling her a filthy Chinese. Doubly wrong and very insulting. She grabbed the skylight's rusty frame and managed to yank it out of the casing. Per Sorensen, blinded by his blood, didn't realize what was happening.

Using what remained of the metal and the shards of glass stuck to it, Victoire started hacking at her pursuer's neck. Blood spurted everywhere. With a rage only she and her Cambodian forebears could understand, she kept hacking away at anything jutting out and bleeding. She stopped only when she could no longer breathe. By the time she had caught her breath, Per Sorensen's head, severed from his torso, had rolled into the gutter and lay staring up at the sky. The chain saw, abandoned while it was still going, had finished the job. Human pulp, mixed with pieces of green tarpaulin, awaited her below. Hellish housework, she thought. Lucky John couldn't see it.

Luc burst into the house, exhausted after racing back from the Eiffel Tower. He ran up the first flight of stairs and saw her coming down with a blood-covered chain saw in her hand and dragging long blood-soaked tatters of some kind of material behind her. David had just killed Goliath.

"Victoire?"

"Victoire!"

ON THE BRIDGE OF THE BOUC-BEL-AIR, *12:10 P.M.*

Le Guévenec gave up gazing at the coast of Greenland. A catastrophe even more enormous than the first was gathering momentum under the mantle of ice. What they had gone through was just a warning, the first act in the demise of the northern hemisphere. The ice cap had been destabilized by the collapse of Lauge Koch Kyst and was greatly weakened. A wall up to sixty-five hundred feet high in places and stretching for thousands of miles could crash into the ocean at any moment.

In his spare time, Lanier had taught at L'École des Mines in Paris and Beijing. He had been very clear. "Picture the Alps dropping into the water!" Depending on whether it tipped to the east or to the west, the ice cap would, according to the software on board the *Bouc*, produce a tidal wave that would reach as far as Western Europe or the East Coast of the United States.

The nations that had spawned the industrial age were at risk of being swept away by the consequences of their own inventions. That was assuming that the planet's most developed nations were the cause of this disaster. Brissac had had his doubts, but the outcome would be the same, regardless of who bore responsibility. Le Guévenec thought of his apartment in Le Havre and saw the ocean covering the town and Isabelle with it. He would still have to phone home, all the same, before the end of the world.

He put down his binoculars. A more immediate danger awaited him. Connie Rasmussen was also watching the horizon.

"I'm ready," she said.

"Do you have your gloves?" Le Guévenec asked.

"Yes."

"Let's go."

The Dane followed the captain—the sole master on board, apart from God—and went down to the lower deck and into a maze of tilting gangways cluttered with detritus of all kinds. Since she had boarded the *Bouc,* she had come to appreciate the virtues of this straightforward, thickset man, unjustly suspected of being responsible for the world's woes. Le Guévenec had had the bad luck of being in the wrong place at the wrong time. She was starting to have powerful and troubling feelings for him. Thanks to Luc Martinet, it would not be long before she knew more about this honorable survivor of another age.

They went down another ladder and wound up in the main galley. Two men balanced in front of a stove that was still working were preparing some steaming grub, with victuals supplied by the *Copenhagen.* They saluted the captain.

"We put the boatswain's body in the cold-storage locker."

"Not very hygienic," Connie Rasmussen pointed out.

Le Guévenec almost said something nasty but remembered Lanier's instructions. This woman was the legal conscience of the Arctic. He opened the hatch and stepped aside to let a glacial mist escape. Le Guévenec removed the sheet covering the seaman's body. Dressed in his uniform, Rox Oa was on his back, his color livid and his eyes registering the horror he had witnessed before dying. Connie turned her head away.

"Help me," the captain asked.

Using an iron bar, Le Guévenec attempted to peel the corpse off the frozen metal table. Finally, it came loose with a sinister cracking sound. Le Guévenec turned the corpse over and held it firmly to keep it from falling off the table because of the ship's incline. Connie Rasmussen examined the seriously mauled back. Under the exposed vertebrae, she could see the man's lungs. The boatswain had clearly been a victim of the bears.

"The male or the female?" Connie asked.

"The female," Le Guévenec replied, giving her a nasty look, full of meaning.

"May I?"

The lawyer took off her gloves and pulled a small camera out of her anorak to photograph the victim's back.

"Where did he come from?"

"Terre Noire's HR manager sent him to me."

"The one who was murdered in the Hans Egede last night?"

"Yes."

"It seems he wanted to board the *Bouc.* Do you know why?"

"Make yourself useful, and give me a hand," was all that Le Guévenec was willing to say.

Connie Rasmussen put her camera away and helped the captain turn the corpse back over. They were leaving the cold room when a dull thud made them turn around. The corpse had fallen off the table.

"Leave him. He won't be going anywhere."

Le Guévenec closed the hatch once more and went back along the gangway. Connie Rasmussen followed, bracing her arms against the wall to avoid falling.

"You didn't answer my question about Christophe Maunay. Why did he want to board the ship?"

"I have nothing more to say," Le Guévenec answered sharply.

Back in the cabin the captain had assigned to her, Connie called Laura Al-lee-Ah.

"Hello, the bears did, in fact, kill the boatswain."

"Are you sure?"

"Absolutely."

"Why did Christophe Maunay want to board the ship?"

"I don't have the answer yet," Connie Rasmussen replied.

"There's a rumor in Nuuk that the clandestine passenger on board the *Bouc-Bel-Air* is none other than Nicolas Lanier. I need to know."

"I'm looking into it, Laura."

Connie ended the call. She gazed at the *Copenhagen* through the porthole. The Danish ore carrier had moved away a little after the transfer of the wounded. She had never played a game with stakes this high before. The "coincidence" that had placed this ship in her path would not occur twice. She waited another few minutes and observed the poop deck. The searchlight went on and off a few times. Connie had learned Morse code when she was barely five on a beach in Jutland, where the Rasmussens had a country home less than sixty miles from the Danish capital.

If everything went well, in a few hours she would be back in control—on the condition that she knew which side John Spencer Larivière was playing on. What was a guy built for hunting bears doing in this game of poker? Why had Geraldine Harper decided to launch him onto the ice shelf at the risk of wrecking everything? There had to be compelling reasons for getting him involved in the already complicated playoff for the Far North. Geraldine and North Land had to have some idea in the back of their minds that she had yet to fathom. She thought again about the captain and about Luc Martinet. Really, the French caused trouble wherever they went.

QAANAQ, 12:50 P.M.

John smelled the kennels well before he laid eyes on Qaanaq. Huts yellowed with urine extended on both sides of an empty lot covered with snow. There were dogs everywhere and a few human figures hunched over in the wind. Around these solitary figures were parked snowplows. The wind barely covered the barking from behind the wire fencing. The Bleak Pole.

The snowmobile stopped outside a building that was bigger than the others. A battered sign in Danish was nailed above the door. This was nothing like the opulence of the American Thule.

"The Rasmussen Hotel," Qaalasoq yelled, getting off the snowmobile. "Magnificent!"

John managed to extricate himself from the synthetic furs Qaalasoq had thrown over him before they set out. He stretched his badly jarred back. The Far North no longer fooled around with bear skins, now that the bear was an endangered species and a god in peril. He dragged his leather bag up the steps and entered the building. The silence hit him first. Then the heat and the alcohol. In the vast smoky room, a few Inuits and Greenlanders stared at them before returning to their beer and the television, where scientists gathered in Nuuk were offering their analyses. The atmosphere was as light as a sandbag in front of a trench.

Qaalasoq spoke to the Inuit woman who presided over the destiny of the Rasmussen, "Tooky, let me introduce you to John Spencer Larivière. He's French, but he works for North Land."

"They're all crooks, anyway. They're poisoning us now, after having irradiated us. The French are no better than the rest of them. Let their ghosts wander over the ice for millions of moons. What would you like to drink?"

"I don't drink anymore."

"That so? I forgot, with all that's going on. The dogs barked all night. They say the moon's getting closer."

"It may well be."

"What are you doing here with the Frog?"

"He wants to visit the Great Wound of the Wild Dog."

Tooky looked at John as though he were tainted meat to be thrown in the garbage.

"They destroy the planet. Then they come and measure the damage. They call that responsible tourism. Responsible, my ass!"

The sound of smashing bottles made heads turn. John saw that one of the Inuits, dead drunk, had slid to the floor, knocking over the whole lineup of Corona bottles that he had just downed. Judging by the stares,

John's presence wasn't appreciated. Qaalasoq whispered in impeccable French, "Don't look at them. Otherwise, they'll have your hide."

John followed the advice and concentrated on the television screen. The television was showing images of New York. Fifth Avenue was now no more than an enormous mudslide traversed by a long line of bulldozers. The secretary general of the United Nations and a spokesman for the G20 announced the umpteenth world conference on global warming. This one would take place in Oslo. John recognized the glass façade of the Opera House, where the last-ditch meeting was to take place in less than a week. The disappearance of Lauge Koch Kyst had quickly elevated the conscience of the planet. Shouting shot through the smoky room, immediately followed by the noise of breaking plates and chairs being overturned. Two Inuits were plowing into a third, who was armed with a broken bottle. Qaalasoq took a key hanging from a hook. He pulled John behind the bar and then to a door that opened onto a hallway. A series of bungalows was connected to the back of the Rasmussen Hotel.

"What's going on?"

"He's a Red who misses the days of the Danish. The Blues want to polish him off. They may well kill him."

"The Blues? The Reds? What are you talking about?"

"The Blues support the Norwegians and the Icelanders."

"Explain it to me."

"The Wall Street crash ruined Iceland. A lot of people from Reykjavik and Isafjordur came here looking for work. There were also a lot of Norwegians."

"What about you? Are you a Red or a Blue?"

"I'm from the Wild Dog clan, a son of the land of Ellesmere, unjustly claimed by Canada. I'm fighting for all the peoples of the Arctic."

"So, you're on the side of the Northern Peoples Congress and Laura Al-lee-Ah?"

The Inuit didn't reply and slid the key in the lock. He opened the door and introduced John to his new abode.

"I advise you to rest here and await my return. Tokmingwah will bring you a piece of seal. You should get some sleep and put on a bit of fat. You're going to need it."

"What about Abraham Harper?"

"I'm about to find out the latest. I couldn't broach the subject with you near me."

"It must embarrass you, lugging a Frenchman around," John said with a halfhearted smile.

"A lot less since Paris has taken issue with Ottawa over the continental shelf around Saint Pierre and Miquelon. We may be primitive alcoholics and smokers, but that doesn't stop us from being well-informed."

"I bet you've had access to my computer, thanks to your little pals at the airport. Where'd you learn French?"

"In Paris, at the Greenland House. You know it?"

John reeled with the blow and didn't answer. Qaalasoq disappeared, and he was left alone in a room that had a small shower and a sort of storage room, where he put his bag. A window with small square panes looked out over the sea, which was choked with ice chunks as big as dolmens.

He took out his computer and established contact with Luc, only to learn that the Per Sorensen case had been "dealt with once and for all." In Nuuk, Mary Harper's interrogation had ended happily with her release. John was alarmed, though, by an internal message sent to the Greenland police demanding clarification of his "relationship" with Mary. On board the *Bouc-Bel-Air* Connie Rasmussen was looking into the death of the *Bouc-Bel-Air's* boatswain, and she had informed Luc that Nicolas Lanier was hiding on the ship. She was urging him to publish the news on future-probe.com. John answered, using the keyboard.

"Why?"

"She wants to draw attention to how silent the heads of both companies have been. She thinks they should enlighten the world concerning what's in store for the planet, since they seem to be playing a pivotal role. She also thinks that Maunay's murder is directly linked to Lanier's disappearance. She's wondering who this intriguing John Spencer Larivière is. Furthermore, she'd like info on Le Guévenec and wants me to get his wife to talk."

John turned toward the flat, misty horizon that stretched beyond the windows of the Hotel Rasmussen. The line between the sky and the ocean looked as blurry as the one that separated information from disinformation. All these people were pursuing objectives he couldn't quite decode. The fact that Lanier and Harper were nowhere to be seen was a legitimate concern. The Danish woman was right to raise the issue. Why were these two men lying so low? Was the situation that catastrophic? John bent over his keyboard once more.

"Why doesn't she turn to her pals in the Northern Peoples Congress? She doesn't need us."

"She's got a crush on me," Luc replied from his cell phone.

"It's not normal for her to rely on a freelance journalist she hardly knows to pass on information of that caliber," John wrote. "Get her to talk. She's trying to use us. I wonder if she didn't see through you."

"I don't think so. We had a really nice night. She knows we're on the same page, and that excites her. She confessed that she'd never met a real French investigative journalist who was willing to dig into the strategic and financial stakes in Greenland."

"She's flattering you. Don't fall for it. Take the lead again. How's Victoire doing now that the Per Sorenson problem has been solved?"

"She'd doing well. Don't worry about the consequences. We're on it." John ended the encrypted connection and moved from the written word to the spoken word, using his babysitter phone.

The most interesting call was the one Mary Harper had made to Laura Al-lee-Ah to thank her for her intervention. The artist and Congress president had put pressure on the police to let Mary go. The most frightening bit was Laura's reply to a question about the meaning of Christophe Maunay's ritual slaying.

"They're saying the body was cut up. What does that mean?" Mary had asked.

"It's a pagan rite that originated in the lands of Ellesmere," Laura answered. "Whoever did it wants the victim to turn into a tupilaq, that is, a monster made up of human and animal flesh, a cursed creature doomed to wander over the ice and snow looking for victims to carve up in turn."

"So it's an Inuit who killed Nicolas Lanier's HR guy?" Mary asked.

"Maybe."

Several seconds of silence followed. Laura Al-lee-Ah resumed the conversation. "Where's John Spencer Larivière, the guy who's supposed to be looking after your image?"

"In Qaanaq with Qaalasoq."

"Come over to the house this evening. We need to talk."

John listened to the recording again. Then he took the horrible tupilaq out of his bag and listened to the recording once more. Laura Al-lee-Ah gave the impression of believing what she had said. Surprisingly, Mary Harper also seemed to swallow the fable. Qaalasoq came from the land of Ellesmere, like all the Inuits since the Middle Ages, John reflected. And his badly healed wounds made him a sort of tupilaq. He was about to wander over the snow-covered ice. Who was it that he was looking for? And for whom?

Luc had incredible trouble getting into the Hôtel Louxor's database. The establishment had such outdated digital architecture that the hypersophisticated intruder tools invented to circumvent the most elaborate defenses gave up, baffled by the absence of any serious security. He had to dumb down his tools. Unbelievable.

He walked into the hotel lobby with one of Victoire's handbags and remembered with a knowing smile the object of his visit. The woman's clothes he was wearing and the carefully applied makeup won over the night porter. Victoire had phoned the hotel reception desk a few moments before to pave the way.

"I've come to see Monsieur Per Sorensen."

"Good evening, Madame. Room 212. The elevator is to your right."

"Thank you."

Luc fluttered his eyelashes at the young man, who ran an appreciative eye over his slender form. Flattered, Luc made it to the elevator without twisting an ankle in Victoire's heels. He gave his skirt a little swish as he got in.

The room Per Sorensen had booked was at the end of the corridor. He stuck a biometric sensor behind one of the console tables that served as decor. Then he placed a microcamera on the back wall, which would display on the screen of his watch any nuisance that might turn up.

Luc took the magnetic key found on the dead Dane and opened the door. After a few seconds of silence, he took off his shoes and circled the room. It was a luxurious room with a marble bathroom and a teak closet. The window overlooked an interior courtyard.

There had to be some connection, though, between the hotel and the Greenland House. It was bugging him that he had not found it yet. He thought back to Laura Al-lee-Ah's husband, whom he also hadn't managed to identify. Nothing on Google. No trace on the social networks. No response to the thousands of requests launched on the web. An incredible black hole. He would ask Connie Rasmussen who this mysterious husband was. Per Sorensen's attack had caught them off guard and slowed things down. He went through the night table and then looked under the bed, thinking of all the visitors who had stayed in this room with its retro wallpaper.

Maybe he was not a magician, which he had dreamed of being when he was little, but thanks to John and Victoire, life was never boring. These days, it had even taken an operatic turn. He thought of the opera house in Oslo, which had no doubt hosted the fleeting love

affair of Isabelle Le Guévenec and Romain Brissac. It was yet another
lead that he hadn't had time to explore. He couldn't do everything.

After examining the sheets and the carpet, he concentrated on the
closet. He photographed the clothes so that he could put everything
back in place before leaving. Per Sorensen might have had a mistress
or a male lover who would try to find him. It was hard to get neater
than this guy. Luc started with the suits. The Dane wore the great cou-
turiers. Paris, Oslo, Copenhagen. All that was missing was Greenland.
Wearing latex gloves, Luc went through the pockets systematically
without finding anything, apart from a cloakroom ticket from the
Saint-James.

He went on to the shirts and then the underwear, which was neatly
stacked on the closet's mahogany shelves. He found a few stylish ties,
but for the most part, the Viking didn't go in for anything fancy.

After that, he attacked the armoire, and that's where he found what
he was looking for. Per Sorensen's notebook computer was a current
model. He booted it up and plugged in the USB key containing the
scan-and-save program for encrypted files. The hard disk didn't contain much, apart from some images in a file named "vacations." He
opened this without any trouble and went from one surprise to another.

The first series of photos showed a beach filmed from a boat.
Behind the beach were houses and a skyline densely planted with wind
turbines. Then the photographer had gotten interested in a cottage
with white walls and red shutters. He zoomed in to show the details
and then the silhouette of a woman. Luc recognized the woman. He
was looking at a report devoted entirely to Connie Rasmussen. Why
had Per Sorensen spied on her when he already knew her from the
neo-Nazi club? John had taught Luc not to jump to hasty conclusions.
Nothing could lie like a photo.

Qaanaq, Hotel Rasmussen, 4:05 p.m.

The sound of someone knocking woke John, who had nodded off. He
jumped off the bed and cautiously approached the door, asking who
was there. Qaalasoq identified himself, and John let him in. The Inuit
looked vexed but began with good news.

"Mary Harper was released."

"They didn't really think she'd killed her rival's HR guy, did they?"
John said, shrugging.

"Greenland's independence is very recent," Qaalasoq answered.
"Justice is still in its infancy."

"So I gathered."

Qaalasoq went over to the tupilaq and picked it up gently, as though it were a tiny baby.

"I see you've taken it out."

"I thought a little fresh air would do it some good. You really think this little atrocity is going to help us?"

"In cutting Christophe Maunay's body up with a chain saw, they were trying to turn him into a tupilaq. For us Greenlanders, it's a message," Qaalasoq said, looking dark.

John thought of his meeting with Maunay and felt the anger rising over all the two-faced bastards in Greenland with hidden agendas. He remembered that Qaalasoq had learned French in Paris. The choice of Fermatown by the Harper clan was apparently motivated by something other than what John had thought. And where was all this taking him? Victoire and Luc had just risked their lives for him. His feelings of guilt were very unpleasant.

According to Victoire, who had called him on the encrypted phone, the relationship between Geraldine and Abraham Harper was not clear. On several occasions, the couple had not shown up together at official festivities. John promised himself that he would bring it up with Qaalasoq.

"Where are we going now?" John asked Qaalasoq.

"To see a friend. Put it back in your bag," the Inuit replied, handing him the tupilaq.

He told John to follow. They went into the corridor, and then crossed the big room full of Greenlanders, who were still riveted to the television. John thought he had to be dreaming when he saw a slot machine. He had not noticed it when he arrived. Tooky, the cantankerous boss, let them pass through without saying a word. John found himself on the windy front steps, facing a pack of dogs that reeked of urine.

"The man we're going to see doesn't like snowmobiles," Qaalasoq said. "You'll sit in the sled. I'll drive."

John released a cloud of condensation and went down the steps. He inspected the eleven wild and smelly dogs in the team. They were nothing like the lapdogs of Daguerre village. He got in the sled and pulled the cover up to his chin. One brief command and a crack of the whip threw him backward. The few dilapidated houses of Qaanaq disappeared on either side of what looked like the main road. In the pale light, the riotous dogs attacked a huge hill at the top of which John felt like he could reach out and touch the sky.

After that, they descended on a broad trail bordered with snowplows and abandoned vehicles and left Qaanaq behind. The sled was heading for a horizon of shimmering ice fields interrupted by black mountains that looked like chopped-off pyramids. He read a half-erased number on a sign pointing to the Humboldt Gletsjer. Qaalasoq was yelling to urge the dogs on. The trail rose without slowing the team. On the contrary, the tougher the slope, the harder the dogs mushed on.

After an hour, they reached the edge of a plateau, beyond which an immense field of fissured ice stretched. Now the mountains looked bigger. Between each dark mass a white tongue ran down toward the frozen plane that was spread at their feet. Qaalasoq asked his passenger to climb off the sled.

John got off the sled and wordlessly questioned his guide. They were alone in the middle of nowhere. The other man could give the dogs a command and abandon him to die of cold and hunger.

"The house is over there."

Qaalasoq pointed to a passage between two snowdrifts. John had missed it, the brilliance of the snow having blurred his vision. A well-wrapped shadow, hunched against the wind, was heading toward them.

"That's Navarana, Sakaeunnguaq's wife. They'll be putting us up for the night. She'll look after the dogs and see to our bags."

John greeted a pair of mischievous eyes hidden under a fur of an indeterminate color. He followed Qaalasoq between the snowdrifts and came to a space occupied by two huts identical in size that reminded him of the houses of Qaanaq. A satellite dish indicated that the hermits living here were not cut off from the rest of the world. Qaalasoq climbed the steps and knocked on the door, which was promptly opened. They were welcomed by a wave of heat and a man who was elderly but apparently robust. He invited them to sit on fur pelts draped on seats around a rug with a circle of white wool in the middle. Animal skins, harpoons, and hunting weapons, all smelling of rancid oil and seal meat, were hanging on the walls. On a table, a computer in sleep mode gave the room a totally out-of-place blue tinge.

"John, this is Sakaeunnguaq, who lives here with his wife, Navarana."

John bowed his head respectfully. The wrinkled seal hunter had almond eyes that sparkled with intelligence. He stared at John with amused curiosity. The Inuit must have been between sixty and seventy years old. He was taller and thinner than the average Inuit. He radiated wisdom and a kind of nonchalance that was not devoid of nobility.

"You can call me Saké—everyone else does," he said in perfect English before pulling a bottle and two china cups from his fur. He filled the cups halfway.

John took the appearance of the bottle as a sign. He saw himself back in the Bon Marché grocery store a few days earlier, buying the same brand of whiskey to cut his possible stalker's throat.

"Here's to you."

"Cheers."

John observed the local custom and emptied his cup with the same enthusiasm as the man offering him hospitality.

"Who do you think will win the Tour de France this year?"

Saké's question left John speechless for a few seconds. His notion of the Nordic shaman huddled in an igloo had just taken a hit.

"I have no idea."

Qaalasoq told John that that Saké had correctly predicted the winner of every Tour de France for the past twenty years.

"Then you know a lot more than I do," John replied politely. "Do you also pick trifectas?"

The two Inuits burst out laughing. Then Qaalasoq became serious again.

"Saké will take us to the Great Wound of the Wild Dog tomorrow to look for Abraham Harper."

"You know where he is?" John asked.

"No," Saké replied. "I've never seen him, and I have no connection to him, unlike you. I don't know what's happened and don't believe for a second all the stories about geological exploration that my friend Qaalasoq is wallowing in. But I can take you wherever you tell me to."

Saké emptied his cup and looked at this Frenchman who had crossed the ocean and all of Greenland to get to him. John wondered what planet he had landed on and said, "I'm way behind you when it comes to knowing where Abraham Harper is. I'm no shaman."

Saké smiled.

"But you are—you just don't know it. Hold your hand over the rug."

John did as he was told and held out his right hand. Saké pulled seven greasy knucklebones from the fur he had been sitting on and put them in John's hand.

"Throw them on the circle."

John, hovering over an unfamiliar world, felt stupid.

"Don't be scared. Throw them."

Annoyed, he threw the knucklebones on the circle of wool. Two of them rolled out of the circumference and lined up, one behind the other. Saké leaned over and observed them for a long time. Then he looked up at his guest and declared, "You've already encountered two murders in the case you're handling."

John realized the man opposite him was right. Saké had visualized Victoire killing her pursuer. He also had seen the butchered body of the HR manager in the hotel room intended for him. There were effectively two corpses in this case, one in Paris and one in Nuuk.

"For the moment, we know about only one," replied Qaalasoq, who had no idea of the events that had unfolded at Fermatown.

"There is another one," John said with an unintentionally mysterious air.

"Who?" asked Qaalasoq.

"I can't tell you just yet."

It was his turn now to keep secrets. The two Inuits looked at the Frenchman with respect. Outside, the dogs had fallen silent. The wind was blowing through the wooden ceiling planks. Saké picked up the two knucklebones that had gone outside the circle and contemplated the five others that had stayed inside the circle. John took his cue from the Inuits. Something inside him was a loosening up. Sensations and smells buried since childhood were floating back to the surface. He felt his stomach unknot and remembered the words of some Eastern sage, "Things don't change. Change your way of seeing them. That is all you need to do." He understood that now.

"The five that are in the circle are the deaths in the helicopter on the *Bouc-Bel-Air*," John declared with a conviction that surprised him.

"Accident or murder?" asked Saké.

"Murder," John replied, persuaded that he knew the truth.

"You see it's not witchcraft, becoming a shaman," Saké joked, filling their cups again.

PARIS, 18 RUE DEPARCIEUX, 11:55 P.M.

Still in shock after committing her first murder, Victoire did not really hear what Luc was saying. Beheading Per Sorensen had brought about a radical change in her. In vanquishing her enemy, she had risen up for her victimized Cambodian family. An overwhelming feeling of release had dissolved the shame of not having been there when they died. Victoire could finally breathe.

"I killed him with my own hands," she said, displaying her bandages. "Do you realize? It's appalling!"

"You looked murder in the face," Luc said. "It's no longer an abstraction. It's your enemy's corpse, and it smells good. The guy got what he had coming."

"But I enjoyed it!" Victoire cried.

"I damn well hope so. After all you've suffered, you should take it as a gift. You needed to go through this. You made a sacrifice on your family's altar. You're amazing."

"But the body. All the same..."

"I'll take care of it. Think about something else."

Victoire smiled.

"Thank you."

Luc took her to the touch wall.

"I want to show you something that'll surprise you. Look what I found on Sorensen's computer."

With his index finger, he brought up the series of photos. The strange landscape looked like something out of a Discovery Channel show on alternative energy. A house appeared at closer and closer range. And Victoire recognized Connie Rasmussen.

"That guy was one step ahead of us all the way. Who was telling him about our comings and goings?"

Luc sped up the photos. The shots of Connie Rasmussen on the North Sea coast were soon followed by photos of the legal advocate at various cocktail parties. The photographer had tailed his subject everywhere. Why?

"You should have gotten him to talk," Luc joked.

"I'd like to have seen you do it!" she shot back.

She recognized the interior of the Oslo Opera House, having seen shots of it on the websites she had consulted. Connie Rasmussen, flute of champagne in hand, was talking to Romain Brissac.

"She knows all the big names in the Arctic," Victoire said.

"She's a lawyer and a union rep. That's what she's paid for."

"Go back," Victoire demanded. "There's a guy I've seen somewhere."

Luc spread the photos over the touch wall again. Victoire asked him to stop on a shot of Connie Rasmussen talking to a good-looking man with a magnificent white mane.

"That's him."

"Who is it?" asked Luc.

"His name's Thor Johannsen, and he is a director of Arctoil, the Norwegian North Sea oil company that finances the Abel Prize. The Norwegians created the award because there's no Nobel Prize in mathematics."

"Why not?" asked Luc.

"Because the woman Alfred Nobel was in love with chose a celebrated mathematician over him. Since then, math wizards have been frowned upon in Stockholm."

Luc didn't spend a day with John and Victoire without learning something. His real family was here, between the walls of the Rue Fermat and the Rue Deparcieux, streets named after two other mathematicians whose discoveries Victoire had told him about—and he had promptly forgotten. He shuddered at the thought of what could have happened if she hadn't had the presence of mind to confront the killer at the right place and at the right time. Her courage and humility impressed him.

He selected all the photos showing the lovely Rasmussen conversing with Thor Johannsen, the Norwegian oil man. The Danish woman was clearly making eyes at the old rake.

"Second-biggest market capitalization on the European stock exchange," Victoire said, unable to keep herself from smirking. "Your girlfriend doesn't waste her time."

In the following photos, Connie Rasmussen was having breakfast outside a café with the same man. This time, the Eiffel Tower replaced the wind turbines of Jutland and the mirrors of the Oslo Opera House. Luc stepped back to get some perspective.

"A Danish killer who spends his time photographing a Danish lawyer he met in a neo-Nazi club who's chasing after a Norwegian oil magnate—what's that?"

"A bad business," Victoire replied, looking at her bandaged hands. "But go on. It's just starting to get interesting."

Luc obliged and continued. He blushed when he saw the port of Le Havre and the red and black hull of the *Marcq-en-Barœul*.

"I can see you!" cried Victoire.

He was transfixed by the photos. In one, he was rescuing Connie Rasmussen from the eco-warrior demonstration. Other shots showed him at the hotel and then outside Isabelle Le Guévenec's apartment building.

Victoire flinched. "He didn't let you out of his sight."

"He must have been in the building opposite us. He shot my interlude with Isabelle."

"Go on."

They stepped back when they found the entrance to 9 Rue Fermat and the entrance to 18 Rue Deparcieux in the next shots.

"He reconnoitered before he came here," Victoire said. "He avoided the street so the security officers wouldn't spot him. Who gave him our address? Look! He climbed onto the roof and photographed the skylight! Go back."

Luc went back to a shot of the entrance to 9 Rue Fermat. A city garbage truck was in the photo.

"He photographed the house last Friday, I think," cried Victoire. "That's when they pick up the garbage."

Luc held his breath and made a quick calculation.

"That means he identified us three days before John met Geraldine Harper at the Ritz. How did they know we'd get the job of protecting Mary three days before it happened?"

"Because there was a leak or a betrayal."

Victoire brought her injured hands to her forehead. New photos appeared.

"That's John!"

She saw John outside the Ritz in the Place Vendôme.

"Last photo," said Luc. This showed John carrying a bouquet.

"That's the bouquet he bought me at the Bon Marché to throw the Dane off," Victoire explained.

Luc and Victoire stood there for a long while without reacting. What they saw on the wall frightened them. A few notes rose up from La Belière. But the Daguerre village suddenly felt far away—very far away. Luc tried to sum up what they knew, which was not a lot. Victoire remembered that they had a corpse on their hands. They couldn't call the police. John didn't want them to. He had told them by encrypted message.

"I haven't got the strength to go up and look for his head on the roof," Victoire said. "How are we going to get rid of the body?"

"Victoire, don't worry about it. I'll take care of it," Luc said. "I've got an idea. You get some rest."

ON BOARD THE BOUC-BEL-AIR, 7:30 P.M.

Connie Rasmussen allowed her Inuit bodyguard to open the cabin door. Sylvain Velot, the man who had murdered the two bears, wanted to see her. She discreetly turned on the tiny recorder that would assist her when the time came to write her report. The French sailor waited until they were alone.

"I know now that I can trust you," Velot said. "I've got something important to tell you."

"I'm listening," Connie replied.

"Nicolas Lanier, the head of Terre Noire, is on board the Bouc-Bel-Air. In the first mate's cabin."

Velot watched for her reaction.

"That's incredible! I've just been talking to several members of the crew. They don't seem to be in the loop. When the Terre Noire

Eurocopter landed, no one got a good look at the passenger. The pilot didn't tell anyone, and then he died in the crash. How do you know it's Lanier?"

The sailor let a few seconds pass. Then he lowered his voice as if he risked being overheard. "I received information from you know who. I have a mission to carry out. You're here to help me, aren't you?"

Connie nodded and refrained from questioning him any further. Simple astonishment or any hint of reluctance could turn her into a tupilaq.

"How can I be useful to you, Sylvain?" she asked in a honey-coated voice.

The sailor didn't hesitate for a second. "I need to get into the boat-swain's cabin, but Le Guévenec has the keys. You're the only one who can help me."

"What do you want to do in the cabin?"

"Retrieve something."

Connie gave him a conspiratorial smile. "I'll see what I can do."

And she left the cabin, using the walls for support. Once on the bridge, she pulled out her cell phone and went over the latest news bulletins. No one was saying anything yet about Lanier being on the *Bouc-Bel-Air*. She called Luc Martinet in Paris.

"Hi, Luc, it's Connie. I wanted to hear your voice."

"Really? I'm flattered. How's it going in Greenland?"

"As well as possible. Luc, I have some information that might interest you."

"I'm listening."

"I can confirm that Lanier is actually on board. You can run with the story without fear. Don't hesitate."

"You're brilliant, Connie!" he exclaimed. "Speaking of which, you wouldn't happen to know a certain Thor Johannsen, would you? He's a Norwegian in North Sea oil."

Connie reeled. This two-bit journalist was moving way too fast. A red alert went off in her brain. She calmed her breathing and replied as naturally as she could. "He's one of the big boys in Arctoil, the Norwegian oil company."

"Do they have interests in Greenland?"

"They have interests everywhere, my dear Luc."

Connie cut him off, saying the captain wanted to speak with her. Then she speed-dialed Laura Al-lee-Ah's number.

"Hello, Connie, I was waiting for your call. Did you see the seaman?"

"He's just spoken to me. I suppose..."

"It's fine. Do what he tells you."

"What's going on?" Connie asked in as calm a voice as possible.

"I'll call you back," Laura Al-lee-Ah replied sharply and ended the call.

Connie stared at her cell phone. Ever since she'd met Thor Johannsen, Laura's husband, her relationship with the muse of the North Pole had become strained. A shadow had come between the two women. Connie felt absolutely no attraction to the oil magnate or his money. Only Denmark's interests mattered to her. It was hard to tell Laura Al-lee-Ah that.

She retraced her steps, musing on the way she would proceed when the time came. The best thing to do right now was to let things take their course. She headed for the captain's cabin, again bracing herself against the wall. Le Guévenec unbolted his door and grumbled when he saw her.

"What do you want from me now?"

"I need the key to the boatswain's cabin."

"And why's that?"

"I have to take photos of where he lived for my report. You can come with me, if you'd like."

"I don't have time," Le Guévenec said. "We've just learned something awful."

The captain seemed extremely agitated. He retrieved the key from his cabin.

"Here."

Connie thanked him and looked at the door of the first mate's cabin, where Lanier was holed up.

A few minutes later, Le Guévenec left his cabin and climbed up to the bridge, where they'd just learned of a second catastrophe. The *Narvik* and the flotilla that had been chartered by the Congress had been swept off the coast of Aappilattoq by a huge swell that was washing icebergs along with it. The sudden collapse of one of the biggest glaciers in Greenland was now barring their way to Nuuk.

"We've received several SOS calls," the watch officer said.

"Steer a course for the *Narvik* and its escort," the captain commanded.

As a man of honor, Le Guévenec couldn't imagine for a second abandoning the *Narvik* to the icy waters of Baffin Bay. The *Bouc* would go at its own pace, but it would not shirk its duty. Despite or because of what he'd just been through, he was beginning to understand these Greenlanders, victims of a civilization that they hadn't chosen. He, too, was starting to wonder how any of this made sense. Weird ideas that would never have crossed his mind before this cruise were germinating inside his brain like so many poisonous, intoxicating, flowers.

"Raise the Breton flag!"

"Yes, Captain."

HUMBOLDT GLETSJER, 10:05 P.M.

While John and the two men were enjoying their meal, Saké's wife, Navarana, came and went between the kennel and the house. When she was finished tending to the dogs, she joined them, taking off her anorak and revealing the body of a young woman. Her embroidered wool dress was short and tight enough to inflame any man's imagination. She smiled at the three men and went over to the computer.

"Saké has a gorgeous wife, doesn't he?" Qaalasoq said.

"But I don't lend her to anyone," the old man replied. "You shouldn't believe all you hear about those you call Eskimos."

The three men laughed. John felt it was time to take his leave and let Qaalasoq escort him to the other house. A strawberry-colored cloud lit up the night with sublime clarity. The field of ice looked like a carpet of diamonds. In the distance, the topless black pyramids blocked the horizon. The dogs were yelping in the kennel, and John's boots made a crunching sound on the luminous snow as he made his way.

"But I *had* heard that the Inuits lent their wives," John said when they reached their destination.

"Certain hunter clans used to—in very specific circumstances," Qaalasoq answered.

The Inuit opened the door and showed John the place intended for him. The nocturnal brightness lit up a bed and a table. A washbasin and a doorless toilet completed the accommodations.

"It's rustic, but you're a soldier, right?"

How did Qaalasoq know about his military past? John found his luggage tidily stowed and saw that Navarana had carefully made up the bed.

"I'll be sleeping on the other side of the hall," Qaalasoq said. "I'll wake you."

Once he was on his own, John took out his computer and acquainted himself with the latest news. Luc had sent him the photos discovered on Per Sorensen's computer. John reeled when he saw that the killer had been on their tail for some time. Luc wrote, "Connie Rasmussen is asking me to publish the attached article confirming that Nicolas Lanier is on the *Bouc-Bel-Air*. The article's ready, but I'll wait for the green light from you before doing anything with it. I don't trust Connie. I'm wondering what she's after."

John read the article that Luc had written. It was mainly about the Lauge Koch Kyst catastrophe. The role of the ship was mentioned in passing, and the presence of the Terre Noire head was just touched on. "Nicolas Lanier boarded the ship following the news of a helicopter crash that killed five crew members of the crew and the scientific mission, including Romain Brissac." The mainstream media would definitely pick up the information. And the news would ignite a powder keg when readers joined the dots between Lanier's disappearance from the public spotlight and the simultaneous disappearance of Abraham Harper, the other great man of geological prospecting.

John then went on to read the Greenland police and intelligence reports and nearly fell over when he saw the memorandum sent to the Greenland government:

Suspicious activities—John Spencer Larivière

Report NK 2089—FR USA

Mary Harper, heiress of the Canadian-American company North Land, founded by Abraham and Geraldine Harper, was seduced in Paris by John Spencer Larivière and has since become his mistress. This former soldier in the French Army was obliged to leave the intelligence agency directed by Hubert de Méricourt at Les Invalides for unknown reasons. The agent is pursuing a goal that is believed to be linked to differences that pit France against Canada in relation to the continental shelf off Saint Pierre and Miquelon. Spencer Larivière is in possession of the Canada Geological Survey report. Considering this agent's dual French and American citizenship, it is reasonable to assume that he is hiding ties to the CIA. We know that Abraham Harper, an American, also has close ties to the CIA. Spencer Larivière has been seen on several occasions with Geraldine Harper, a Canadian and the mother of Mary Harper. Spencer Larivière has also seduced Geraldine Harper. In addition, he is implicated in the murder of Christophe Maunay, a French citizen, from the company Terre Noire, North Land's rival. Spencer Larivière is currently under very close surveillance in the province of Avannaa, and he is considered a threat to Greenland's sovereignty.

How could anyone write such lies? John was flabbergasted. So that was the sort of stuff the Greenland intelligence agency was serving up for government leaders: impressions sprinkled with the malicious slander and ulterior motives of bureaucrats eager to shine for the top brass. The great island was getting off to a bad start. Once his anger had subsided, he told himself that all intelligence agencies did this, including the one he had left.

He stopped reading to listen to Mary's phone conversations. None of it was of any interest. But then he heard something disturbing. Laura Al-lee-Ah was talking about him.

"You didn't tell me that the Frenchman had left to look for your father up at the Great Wound of the Wild Dog."

"I thought Geraldine was keeping you up to date."

"Since independence, your mother's been snubbing me. It's the last straw."

"She doesn't want to look like she's influencing you. You've become an influential politician. We don't want to embarrass you."

"In any event, you could have asked the Nuuk police to help you find your father instead of calling on a French mercenary. It seems he doesn't have much of a reputation. And tongues are starting to wag about the two of you. They're even saying he's got his eye on your mother."

"We thought about calling on the police here, but Mom doesn't trust the Danes. They've still got a lot of influence in the administration. You ought to know."

Mary Harper was obviously alluding to Connie Rasmussen. John noted Laura Al-lee-Ah's silence.

"Where's your father?"

"We have no idea," Mary answered.

"How long ago did he vanish?"

"A week ago. His last call was from the Great Wound."

"I'll step in and see that he's found. Get your mother to call me."

"I'll get on her right away."

After her conversation with Laura Al-lee-Ah, Mary had once again called a number in the Morvan backwater. Incredible. She had let it ring for a long time and called again five minutes later without an answer. John went back to the computer and asked Luc to find out what he could. They had not given this mystery the priority it deserved. What obscure role could this rather austere and little-known part of France be playing in the planet-spanning tragedy?

"Check on the spot right away. Something's going on in Burgundy."

John left his room, crossed the hall, and nudged the partly open door. Qaalasoq looked up from his sleeping bag.

"Could you ask Geraldine Harper if she'd issue a statement confirming that Nicolas Lanier is on board the *Bouc-Bel-Air*?"

"He's alive?" Qaalasoq asked, looking stunned.

"Yes," John replied. "Does that surprise you or sadden you?"

"I don't know yet."

"Luckily, you're paying me well. Otherwise, I'd be asking myself questions."

Qaalasoq seemed dazed by the efficiency of "the French mercenary." John went back to bed, convinced that Geraldine and Abraham Harper would soon be commenting on the discovery of Nicolas Lanier on the *Bouc-Bel-Air*. He didn't know why, but he was sure. I'm turning into a shaman, he told himself, half-convinced.

ON BOARD THE *BOUC-BEL-AIR*, 11 P.M.

Connie Rasmussen stood at Le Guévenec's side on the bridge, watching the *Copenhagen* sail away. A milky night hung over the black ocean waters. Le Guévenec had called the captain of the other ship to inform him of his change of course. It was his duty to rescue any ship in distress. The *Bouc-Bel-Air* was about to find itself alone again. Connie had taken the news like a punch in the gut. The sudden collapse of the Upernavik Gletsjer into Baffin Bay and the dispersal of the *Narvik* flotilla were forcing her to change her plans.

"When will we be there?"

"Tomorrow, during the day. Maybe around noon."

Clutching the key to the boatswain's cabin in her pocket, Connie looked at the iron man. She reluctantly left the bridge. Returning to Sylvain Velot, she put on a dismayed look.

"Do you have the key?" the sailor asked.

"Le Guévenec was about to give it to me when we received an SOS from the *Narvik*. He sent me packing. He's very worked up. It seems a new piece of Greenland has just broken away."

"I know. I absolutely have to have that key."

"I'll try again."

6

FRIDAY

Victoire was wringing her bandaged hands. Why hadn't Luc come back? She would never forget Per Sorensen's gory, grimacing head. Luc had pried it out of the gutter and shoved it into a garbage bag, along with the rest of the body. It would take quite a few storms to remove the traces on Fermatown's roof tiles.

John's absence was becoming unbearable. What she'd just read about him in the Greenland intelligence archives had outraged her. Those people made it up as they went along, constructing a surreal scenario based on appearances.

Paralyzed and alone in the garage, she once again checked their house-cleaning efforts in the flickering florescent light. They could wash and scrub all they liked for weeks on end. There would always be a trace of blood somewhere. She heard a scraping sound. Luc was finally home.

"Where'd you put the body?"

"With Sartre and Beauvoir," Luc replied. "No one will go looking there."

"How'd you manage to lift the marble slab?" Victoire asked, astounded.

"With jacks from the studio. No one saw me."

Familiar with Montparnasse Cemetery, thanks to his excursions into the catacombs, Luc even had a duplicate key to the gate on the Rue Froidevaux side. For him, getting in and out of the cemetery was child's play.

"John sent a message," she said. "He says you can publish the article."

"Good. Then I'll be able to call Connie to find out why she's so keen on the world knowing that Lanier's on the *Bouc*."

"I'd wager she doesn't have the best interests of Lanier or Terre Noire at heart," Victoire said. "John also wants you to go to the Morvan and identify the chalet Mary Harper keeps calling."

"I know, but I can't leave you alone in your state. Doesn't he realize what you've been through?"

"No, you should go to the Morvan. You'll be doing a better job of protecting me by finding out what's going on there. I called Guerot—without telling him about Sorensen, obviously. I told him I was frightened. He promised to send additional security."

Luc knew that insisting on staying with Victoire was pointless, so he went upstairs to his room.

"I'm going to sleep for a bit before I go."

Just then his phone started ringing. He recognized Connie Rasmussen's voice trying to make itself heard above the noise of the *Bouc-Bel-Air*'s engines.

"Good evening, Luc. I hope I'm not disturbing you."

"Not at all."

"What about my article on Lanier?" Connie asked.

The time had come to find out why the Danish woman wanted it to be published. Luc made himself sound warm but insistent.

"It'll be online in less than five minutes. Why are you so keen for the world to know that the head of Terre Noire is on the *Bouc-Bel-Air*?"

"Because I find it totally shocking that the two chief executives who are in the best position to let us know what's going to happen are apparently in hiding and aren't saying a word. Don't *you* find that shocking?"

"I agree," replied Luc, who didn't believe a word of what she'd just said.

Connie Rasmussen might well be gearing up to pull a dirty one on Terre Noire, but her argument was irrefutable. Who were the good guys and the bad guys in this ecological disaster? Victoire, by his side, looked puzzled.

"How do you assess the potential damage if the experts are nowhere to be found? We need all the experts, both the researchers and the heads of these companies."

"I see."

"Lanier and Harper have to come out in the open and answer the planet's questions," Connie continued.

"You're right, Connie."

"Have you heard anything about pretty boy?"

Luc hesitated for an instant and cast an apologetic glance at Victoire.

"Do you mean Spencer Larivière?"

Victoire frowned.

"Yes, the creep who hit on me on the plane," Connie replied. "That guy's unbearably arrogant. He says he's an image consultant for North Land. I don't believe a word of it."

"I have some well-placed contacts, and I'm conducting a discreet investigation," Luc answered cautiously.

"I've learned that he heads some Paris outfit called Fermatown, a more or less disreputable outfit that's into shady ops," Connie said. "I can't figure out what he's up to. He's also implicated in the murder of a Terre Noire exec. And there are rumors that he's chasing after Geraldine Harper. What on earth can Mary Harper be doing with a peacock like that?"

"I have no idea, Connie. I'm asking myself the same question."

"The Harpers know everyone there is to know in Paris," Connie went on. "They don't need this clown. Unless..."

She didn't finish her sentence.

"Unless what?" Luc pressed.

"Unless there's something that stinks. Whatever the case, I remember our night in Le Havre. We'll have to get back to that as soon as I'm in Paris. I'm still all excited. What do you say, Luc?" she asked, as smooth as gravy.

Victoire, who'd heard everything, shot him a look. He was reminded of his teacher at Croix-Rousse primary school in Lyon, who would glare at him the same way when he misbehaved on the playground.

Luc cleared his throat, turned down the volume on the speakerphone, and walked away to avoid further humiliation. He knew what Victoire was thinking: So, two women in the same port.

ON BOARD THE BOUC-BEL-AIR, 2:15 P.M.

Connie Rasmussen walked along the gangways that led to the boatswain's cabin. She had to ram her shoulder against the door to get it to open. The shock of the tidal wave had affected everything on the ship. Half of the doors no longer shut, and the other half were hard to open. Much of the equipment either didn't work or worked tentatively. But no one was in a fit state to fix anything anymore. Connie shut the door of the cabin as best she could. She didn't want to be spotted going through the former boatswain's things. Why had Sylvain Velot asked her for the key to the cabin, she wondered, opening one drawer after another. No doubt he had been told to retrieve any compromising objects.

Reflecting, Connie looked under the bunk. She could see things better now. Before killing the bears at the opportune moment to destroy

Terre Noire's image, Velot had been recruited by the boatswain on the instructions of Christophe Maunay, the Terre Noire manager who had been chopped to bits at the Hans Egede. The three men had been part of the same team. She had to act fast. The *Bouc-Bel-Air* had been tampered with behind the back of its captain, a decent guy a thousand leagues from the intrigues of the Far North. He was a character straight out of Jules Verne, the French writer who had captured her imagination as a little girl and colored the sorry beaches of Jutland.

She opened the closets and threw their contents on the floor. She went through the pockets of all the clothes before taking a breather and rubbing her lower back. The boatswain had a workbench, and she examined every drawer. She found nothing and was becoming increasingly fearful. At any moment, someone could burst in. In the bathroom, she inspected the washbasin, the cabinets, and the shower— nothing suspicious. She went back to the bed. The seaman hadn't left anything even slightly embarrassing, either in the mattress or under the bunk. She stood motionless in the middle of the cabin, trying to think. Had Le Guévenec cleaned up? Back in front of the metal closet, she tossed the underwear around and slid her hand into the boots and shoes. Nothing.

All that remained were a dozen pairs of socks, which she desperately started picking through. She felt something hard in a red wool sock. She stuck her hand in the sock and pulled out a Smith & Wesson, fitted with six cartridges, and a new smartphone. That's what Sylvain Velot had wanted to retrieve after the death of his master and protector. Now she really had to tread carefully.

Connie left the cabin, concealing the sock and its contents under her oilskin. A few steps down the gangway, she stopped dead in her tracks. Petrified, she stared at the spectacle. The moon had lit up a sea bristling with gleaming knives of ice. The gigantic shards seemed to reach into the sky. The huge pressure exerted by the ice cap was spawning icebergs no one could have imagined in their wildest dreams. Despite the risk of being found out, Connie remained rooted to the spot, both fascinated and appalled. As it died, Greenland was slicing into the sea and sky with blades of crystal such as the world had never seen before.

AVANNAA, 6:30 A.M.

Rudely jostled in the sled, John was beginning to regret that he had come. Sakaeunnguaq, the hermit of the Humboldt Gletsjer, was leading the way, driving the first dog team toward the Great Wound of the Wild Dog. They'd been on the trail for a good while. Saké raised his arm and gave the signal for a pause. John felt Qaalasoq's maneuver behind him as he drove the brakes into the snow. Even after an hour's run, the dogs' fury hadn't abated. Slowed down, then stopped in their headlong surge, they were steaming like gas flares. Several of them rolled on the ground, rubbing their backs on the ice, which was now flooded with their urine.

John got off the sled and took a few steps. Saké came to meet them. Qaalasoq's dogs calmed down as soon as they saw him. The last king of Thule had a sort of power over animals. John grabbed his thermos and swallowed a slug of tea before passing the cylinder to the two Inuits. After the barking and the noise of the sleds, the relative silence of the pack was like a balm. The transparent blue sky shone on a desert of ice marked in the distance by a few mist-covered mountains. Saké pointed southward.

"We're less than a mile from the Great Wound of the Wild Dog. You must watch out—it has been in flux lately. Since the collapse of Lauge Koch Kyst, we've intercepted messages saying that the scientists manning the international stations are leaving."

John listened in silence while noting that the hermit spent his time listening to the radio traffic on the ice sheet. Funny kind of shaman. Saké drank some more tea and exhaled a cloud of condensation that was immediately whipped away by the wind.

"We're going to head for Raphaelle, the closest Terre Noire station, which has probably been evacuated by now," their guide continued. "After that, we'll go on to the spot where Abraham Harper made his last call, all right?"

The two Inuits turned to John, seemingly awaiting his instructions. He pictured himself back at the Ritz with Geraldine. Five days earlier, he couldn't have imagined himself in a position of authority in such an alien land.

"Okay," he replied to his two companions' great satisfaction.

Qaalasoq gave the thermos back to him, and the convoy regrouped. They raced for twenty minutes over a trail that was almost smooth and finally approached the Great Wound. Suddenly, John felt as though he had happened upon another geologic era. Standing in the lead sled, Saké had slowed the first dog team. A crevasse a few yards deep and the width of a country road appeared on their right. John scanned the formation. Greenish striations scored the bottom and ran up the sides like huge varicose veins.

The sleds climbed a small rise. And then other rifts—each new one bigger than the last—appeared. Carving up the icy landscape, the fissures stretched far into the distance. The three men were moving across a plateau now, and they had the eerie sense that they were approaching some sort of void.

A few minutes later, they arrived at the edge of a vast basin. They cast their eyes over what looked like a sort of lunar crater dotted with little blue lakes that glistened in the sun. They moved down a broad trail and soon found themselves surrounded by what looked like the ridges they'd left behind. John had the awful sensation that he was at the bottom of an immense circular trap.

Suddenly, they heard the rotors of a helicopter. An enormous red and black Eurocopter rose from the horizon. It was flying at a low altitude. John saw that at the end of a cable it was carrying a mobile home characteristic of the scientific stations found in the Arctic and the Antarctic. Terre Noire was evacuating Raphaelle, just as Saké had said.

The sled thumped over a series of mounds and ruts. John spotted a burst of light just over a snowdrift less than a hundred yards away. Then he felt heat in his shoulder. In the sky, the helicopter hovered. The racket was deafening. Qaalasoq shouted at the dogs, and the team bounded ahead. Something must have happened that only the Inuit understood.

Fifteen minutes later, they reached Raphaelle. The base had half a dozen mobile homes painted in the red and black company colors. John could see the empty spot once occupied by the one dangling from the helicopter. The labs and dwellings surrounded a limpid blue pond. The presence of a body of water as vast as the ornamental lake in the Luxembourg Gardens in Paris gave the place an unreal aura. John felt as though he had arrived in another world, one that already was no longer Greenland.

Saké stopped the convoy near one of the houses sporting French and Danish flags. A few human figures, hooded and dressed in red bodysuits, were busy packing the premises up and ignored them. Everywhere, motorized machines attested to the orderly retreat. John got out of the sled, relieved that the jerky ride over the unforgiving terrain had ended.

It was at the edge of the water that the pain stabbed his shoulder. He felt under his anorak, and it was burning and wet. John quickly removed his outerwear to take a look. There was a bleeding graze where something had plowed along the muscle. John raced back to the sled and studied the place where he'd been sitting a few moments before. He didn't have to look long before he found the depression that the bullet meant for him had made.

Someone knew he was going to Raphaelle and had chosen that moment to bump him off.

"Something wrong?" asked Saké.

"Someone just tried to kill me."

"Hardly surprising!"

"I saw where the shot came from," Qaalasoq added.

He removed his sunglasses and pointed to the trail.

"The man was hidden behind a snowdrift. He fired the moment the big helicopter flew by, but he missed you. Greenland saved you."

"How's that?" John asked, looking skeptical as he put his outerwear back on.

"Because the trail is so contorted."

With his arms, Qaalasoq demonstrated how the sled had slipped into a deep rut at the moment of impact.

"If it hadn't been for that, the bullet would have hit your heart, not your shoulder. John scanned the landscape, searching for his assassin.

"The guy's still there. He'll try again. He has to be killed now."

"Let's not stay here," Qaalasoq said. "Let's take cover. You're with your compatriots here. That's a good thing."

"I hope so," John grumbled, telling himself his "compatriots" wouldn't necessarily be overjoyed to see him. Everyone on the shores of the Arctic knew that North Land had entrusted its image to a Frenchman—and an unscrupulous mercenary who had gotten the Harper women, mother and daughter, into his bed.

PARIS, QUAI D'ORSAY, THE FOREIGN OFFICE, 9:30 A.M.

Victoire hadn't seen Hélène Monties since they were at L'École Normale Supérieure on the Rue d'Ulm. Their careers had diverged, but they'd had occasion to correspond and send each other e-mails when Hélène was working in Cambodia. Back from Asia, the diplomat had joined the Foreign Office's Department of Economic Intelligence, a job she'd volunteered for.

She didn't make Victoire wait and offered her coffee and croissants. Nicknamed "First Light," Hélène had the reputation of being a work-aholic, up every morning at five and at work in the Foreign Office on the Quai d'Orsay by half past six.

"I hope I didn't disturb you, calling you so early," Victoire apologized.

"Darling, you never disturb me. I've gone over all your questions. You're working on something we're particularly interested in. I've even put a little dossier together for you. I haven't forgotten how you helped me understand Asia. Without you, I would have been taken for a ride in a rickshaw. I'm not too sure what you're up to, but I'm excited. I just hope it's not too serious."

Hélène looked at Victoire's bandaged hands.

"A clumsy maneuver with a can of Danish pet food."

"I have everything ready for you."

Victoire smiled despite the fatigue and the frazzled nerves from the previous night. She glanced at the red cardboard file on the table.

"Shall we begin?" Hélène suggested.

"Let's."

The diplomat put her coffee down and opened the file.

"All right. Christophe Maunay first: he joined Terre Noire right out of L'École des Mines. He spent a year at the Champs-Elysées headquarters, where he cut his teeth, and then he was transferred to Gabon. You know it's one of the places where Terre Noire has been prospecting for a long time. For France, they're a strategic partner. For Christophe Maunay, it should have been a launching pad."

"But it wasn't. Why not?"

Hélène Monties lowered her voice. "Because your dear little Maunay got caught with his pants down, if I may put it that way. He was said to be involved in a large pedophile ring active in France and Africa. He claimed he was innocent. According to our embassy, one Omar Al Selim stepped in and bailed him out."

"Who's he?"

"A rich Qatari businessman who puts money from Middle Eastern financiers into luxury apartment buildings in Europe, Africa, and now Greenland. He secretly fixed things for Maunay, who wound up back in Paris. Maunay became HR manager of Terre Noire after a stint in the personnel department in Le Havre. I heard that he was found butchered in a hotel room in Nuuk. Is that true?"

"It's true."

"An act of revenge by one of his victims?"

Victoire hadn't imagined this possibility. She'd gotten as far as a ritual slaying in the Far North. But now that Hélène had brought it up, she remembered that Maunay's genitals had been cut off. The photos came back to her, and she started feeling woozy. All those mutilated body parts made her nauseous and reminded her of Per Sorensen on the roof of Fermatown.

"You could be right."

"Shall I go on to the next one?" Hélène asked.

Victoire nodded. Her prodigious memory was recording all the details. But she was still feeling sick. Hélène tackled the second file.

"Connie Rasmussen is the great-granddaughter of the famous Knud Rasmussen. In 1933, a few months before he died, Knud Rasmussen, who was a Danish ambassador, defended his country at the International Court of Justice at the Hague against the Norwegian government. Norway had claimed sovereignty over the east coast of Greenland. History just keeps repeating itself."

"Who won the lawsuit?"

"Denmark. The Norwegians and the Danes have been rivals since the Middle Ages. In recent years, relations have been smoother, but faced with the planned end of oil-and-gas production in the North Sea, Norway is eager to strengthen its presence in Greenland. And it's not just about raw materials. With the melting of the ice, new shipping routes are going to open up on the Russian side, as well as on the Canadian side. Northern Greenland is becoming strategic. The Russians and the Norwegians have just formed an alliance to exploit the Siberian seaway together. The route will halve the cost of shipping between northern Europe, China, and Japan."

Victoire nodded. The stakes were enormous.

"What about the Harper family?" Victoire asked.

Hélène Monties turned a few pages and pulled out a brief history of the Canadian-American family.

"The mother and daughter finance Laura Al-lee-Ah's exhibitions and those of her Greenland friends. Since independence, that woman's star has risen. She's at all the international conferences. Having no official position in the government of Greenland has given her even more clout. She's a sort of conscience of the Arctic. We ourselves have asked for her help in our dispute with Canada over the continental shelf around Saint Pierre and Miquelon. France is the second-biggest world maritime power. Don't forget that our domain extends equally into the Pacific, the Southern Ocean, and the Indian Ocean, to say nothing of the Caribbean. That is, we have a lot of methane hydrate, a gas found at the bottom of the ocean. As you know, we think it could partly replace oil, in combination with solar energy."

"I see."

Victoire picked up her cup with both injured hands and brought it gently to her lips. As she'd expected, Hélène Monties knew the dossier through and through.

"And you," Hélène asked. "You're not too bored in the private sector?"

"No, the private sector is fine," Victoire replied.

In forcing her to kill the Dane on the roof of her house, the crisis in the Arctic had served as a form of therapy—or exorcism. She felt a lot better. It would be hard to explain that to Hélène.

"I feel like you're more relaxed than when you worked at Les Invalides."

"Maybe I am," Victoire replied.

ON BOARD THE BOUC-BEL-AIR, 7:50 A.M.

Connie Rasmussen opened her eyes and realized that she had fallen asleep fully clothed on the bunk in her cabin. She reached for the smartphone she'd discovered in Rox Oa's cabin. In the flickering light that was all the *Bouc* could produce, she started exploring the device. He hadn't input any telephone numbers or e-mail addresses. It contained a single encrypted folder titled "Le Guévenec." She got up to rummage in her sports bag for the decryption system that would allow her to decode the files about the captain of the *Bouc-Bel-Air*.

The decoding took a good quarter of an hour and allowed her to establish that the dossier was regularly updated. The phone hadn't been switched off since its owner's death. She recharged it and brought up the mailbox to get into the new documents. The last one dated from the day before and had been sent from an anonymizer no doubt tasked with protecting the identity of the sender.

She was finally able to open the first file, which consisted of a few notes in French and a series of photos. She recognized Isabelle Le Guévenec in the company of Romain Brissac in Le Havre, Paris, and Oslo, and then on the terrace of a chalet surrounded by fir trees. Other files contained bank statements for Loïc Le Guévenec at the Crédit du Nord bank. He was not very flush. Madame was spending her husband's money and that of the wildlife-protection foundation she headed.

The boatswain also had his boss's medical file and a list of prescription medications. A hip operation had been postponed because the *Bouc* had been rerouted to Greenland. The mysterious sender had even forwarded Le Guévenec's file to the personnel manager of Terre Noire at the Champs-Elysées headquarters.

Christophe Maunay had refused the captain of the *Bouc-Bel-Air* a loan of fifty thousand euros for the purchase of an apartment at La Rochelle. Connie couldn't get over the way the French treated their executives. Terre Noire's working environment was as bad as North Land's.

The last file really threw her. Apart from her penchant for Nobel laureates, Isabelle Le Guévenec had a thing for young men.

"The bastard!" she cried, recognizing Luc Martinet. "He jumped straight from my bed to hers!"

Sitting up in her bunk, she stared at Luc Martinet and Isabelle Le Guévenec making love. When her journalist had described "the key women in the Arctic" he was talking from hands-on experience.

Connie picked up her cell phone and called her favorite freelancer.

"Hi, Luc. It's Connie. I'm not disturbing you, am I?"

"Never, Connie."

"I really wanted to thank you for the article about Lanier being on the *Bouc-Bel-Air*. Your site is truly awesome. You must get lots of information."

"We have thousands of new hits a day."

"You also promised to put me in touch with Isabelle Le Guévenec. She's a passionate woman, going by what you write. It's obvious you know her well."

"Does she really interest you?"

"I'm thinking of asking her to Nuuk. She could give Inuit women an idea of what life's like in a company like Terre Noire. After the killing of the two bears and the murder of the HR guy, I thought her presence might help."

"Help what?" Luc asked.

"Help the image of the ship. It will be arriving in Nuuk, and the welcome won't exactly be wildly enthusiastic. It's bearing all the sins of global warming."

"I'm surprised the Congress is so interested in Terre Noire's image."

"The Northern Peoples don't want to put all their eggs in the one basket. North Land's also taking care of its image. They've even hired a playboy to do the job. Speaking of which, have you made any headway on Spencer Larivière?"

"I'm working on it, Connie."

"Could you give me Isabelle Le Guévenec's phone number?"

"Do you have a pen?"

Connie Rasmussen put the speakerphone on and added the number Luc Martinet gave her to her list of contacts. When she hung up, she got up to attack the most decisive day of her career. She took her clothes off and stood under the trickle of hot water that the *Bouc* could still provide its few passengers. She might as well make herself beautiful, if she was going to die on a French ship in distress. She had a free hand and now knew what she needed to do.

RAPHAELLE, 9:30 A.M.

John stared at the portrait of Romain Brissac that had been hung on one of the walls in the common room. A black mourning band ran across it.

The death of the Nobel laureate added to the gloomy ambience, but it was hostile, as well. The busy scientists turned their heads away when John and the two Intuits crossed paths with them. Everyone knew of John's affiliation with North Land and the obscure role he was playing. Rumors ran like wildfire on the ice sheet, but the atmosphere could not have been chillier. Who said the climate was warming?

The threat that had materialized with the attempt on John's life did not seem to stir the guy in charge of the move.

"There're only seven of us left on the base. I'll inform the others. If he gets too close, we'll spot him. Why does someone want to kill you?"

"I'm looking for Abraham Harper."

"He disappeared, too?"

"Yes," John replied.

"Well, you won't find him here."

Escorted to the mobile home that served as a common room, the three visitors had been told to look after themselves until Paul Gessen, Terre Noire's scientific director for the Arctic and one of Brissac's former students, got there. Qaalasoq and Saké had gone back outside for the luggage. John acquired three red bodysuits from one of the scientists, so they could blend in with everyone else and lessen their chances of being spotted by the sniper prowling around Raphaelle.

"How long can a shooter last out there?" John asked Saké.

"Weeks, if he has a tent, good equipment, and a good supply of food. If he's trained, that is."

John stepped outside to survey the horizon all around him. He found himself standing in the middle of a deserted landscape full of small hills and snowdrifts that offered an experienced hunter an abundance of hiding places. Fortunately, the area around the base was as flat as a board with a slight dip in the center, and any hunter could be spotted as soon as he ventured out of his hiding place. A few fundamental questions remained. Who knew that he was at Raphaelle? Who had given him away? Why did someone want to kill him?

Protected by his red bodysuit, John approached the pond. Bubbles were bursting on the surface and making a sinister gurgling sound. With one eye on the horizon and the other on this phenomenon, he walked all around the little lake. The wind let up a bit, and he inhaled something that smelled like rotten eggs.

"That water stinks," he said, rejoining Qaalasoq and Saké.

Qaalasoq replied that the phenomenon was identical to what they were finding at the North Land bases.

"They're outlets. The ice cap is rotting from below and, in some places, breaking down a layer of permafrost several thousand years old.

Methane is rising to the surface. The gas uses wells between the bottom and the top to come up in ponds like this one."

Saké lit a cigarette and threw it in the water. An orange flame over six and a half feet high shot into the air. The flame turned mauve and then blue before the icy water sucked it under. More than any long lecture, Saké's demonstration proved just how sick Greenland was.

"It's the same everywhere else," he said. "Sometimes worse."

John was beginning to see why the Lauge Koch Kyst region had broken away from the great island five days earlier.

The noise of rotors made them look to the north. The helicopter they'd passed was coming back toward them. Relieved of its load, it touched down a hundred yards or so from the base. The moving blades sent snow swirling into the air, producing a rainbow. The roar of the rotors gradually dwindled to a metallic meowing.

A man in a red anorak got out of the machine and walked over to a snowmobile. A few moments later, Paul Gressin was in front of them. The Raphaelle leader took off his tinted glasses. He was a tall, dark-haired man with a weathered face. He looked to be in his early fifties. John felt his piercing brown eyes studying him, as well as the two Inuits.

"Are you John Spencer Larivière?"

"I am," John answered, shaking the ungloved hand held out to him.

"You've come at a bad time. We're evacuating all our bases along the Great Wound. Come in. We'll get you warmed up."

Gressin led his visitors to the mobile home, which was now even more deserted than it was an hour earlier. Someone had taken down the portrait of Romain Brissac. The four men sat down at a table. Gressin didn't beat around the bush.

"I'm told Nicolas is on the *Bouc-Bel-Air*. It's been published online."

"It's true," John confirmed.

"How can journalists who aren't even here know that kind of thing?"

John looked evasive and said he had no idea.

"How is Nicolas?" Gressin asked.

"I have no way of knowing. I've never met the man."

"I believe you work for North Land," Paul Gressin suggested.

"Yes."

The scientific director nodded, though his look was impenetrable. Saké and Qaalasoq didn't say a word. They were happy to let the Frenchmen do the talking. Gressin looked at John again and went on.

"We're all traumatized by the collapse of Lauge Koch Kyst. Then there was Brissac's death, and now Maunay's murder in Nuuk. You've confirmed that Nicolas Lanier is on the boat, yet I haven't managed to get hold of him since last Sunday. I absolutely cannot understand his attitude. It's unbelievable!"

Gressin counted on his fingers. "It's five days since he answered his phone. What's going on?"

"I don't have any specific information about your boss," John replied. "But his disappearance has to be connected in some way with the disappearance of Abraham Harper. I've been hired by his wife to find him. The two men with me are also looking for him. Do you have any idea where he is?"

Gressin gave John and then the two Intuits a long, hard look. He couldn't conceal a sort of hesitation that didn't sit well with him. By nature, he was a self-assured leader. He decided to jump right in and get it off his chest.

"He set down here last Saturday on a company Eurocopter with Nicolas Lanier. They had both come from the American base in Thule. It was the first time I'd seen Abraham Harper and Nicolas together. I got the impression that they were cooking something up. There was an odd complicity between them."

"What did they do?" John asked.

"They spent the night here in one of the mobile homes and left at dawn the next day for Josephine."

"Where's that?"

Paul Gressin got up and removed a map of Avannaa from the wall. He laid it on the table and pointed at an area with a red ring around it.

"That's our second base in Avannaa. It's fully automated. The area's dangerous. It's on the slopes of Haffner Bjerg, a mountain that's 4,865 feet above the ice cap. We use the granite slope to go under the ice layer and take samples very deep down. Lanier must have wanted to show Harper something."

"How did they leave?" asked Saké.

"By helicopter," Gressin said.

"The kennel's empty. Where are Utunak's dogs?" Saké asked.

Gressin looked at the Inuit, and John realized that the two men knew each other. It was hard to tell whether they trusted each other or not.

"Half an hour after the helicopter took off, Utunak, the base's dog handler, got a call from Lanier asking him to join them at altitude 112—that is, halfway between here and Josephine."

Gressin pointed at a spot on the map.

"Why didn't they go all the way to Josephine by helicopter?"

"Too dangerous. Ten days ago, an American helicopter from the base in Thule was flying over the region. It burst into flames when it passed over methane emissions from the Great Wound of the Wild Dog.

The engine nozzles ignited the gas, and the machine didn't have time to land. It blew up in flight."

John thought back to the cigarette Saké had flicked into the pond. A lot of frightening things were happening on the ice cap. He wondered what could possibly have motivated the meeting of the two world rivals.

"Have you made any startling discoveries lately?" John asked.

"Yes," Gressin replied. "Romain Brissac had a unique theory about the end of Greenland that some people didn't like."

"What theory?"

"According to him, it was going to implode, rather than explode."

Gressin cast a suspicious eye on the two Inuits, who were silent and still. He switched from English to French. He, too, seemed to know a thing or two about the subterranean rivalries of the Arctic.

"The theory of explosion and ensuing tidal waves promotes speculation in real estate and finance," he went on. "You'll see next week. Whole neighborhoods in US and European coastal towns will change hands because of the exaggerated flooding risk. Some people will be ruined, and others will wind up making a fortune. Brissac and Lanier talked about the inevitable manipulation of real estate values."

"The movement of Lauge Koch Kyst would seem to support the explosion theory," John said.

Gressin responded, "There will be phenomena of the kind, but they will be the exception that proves the rule. According to our calculations, Greenland will dissolve from the inside—it will melt—without causing a cataclysm. And I should remind you that the flooding in New York was much less serious than anticipated."

John thought about it.

"You think that Brissac's theory might embarrass someone?"

Gressin nodded in agreement.

"Both Terre Noire and North Land work for groups invested in clean energies like solar, as well as those with real-estate interests, so there are financial stakes involved. The two companies needed to agree on a strategy to stop real-estate speculation in coastal areas, especially after recent violent storms. They were aware that some people would speculate on climate upheaval the same way people have always speculated on financial upheaval."

"Do you have a particular group in mind?" asked John.

"I'm just a scientist, but I assume Lanier and Harper have a pretty good idea."

John was getting a glimpse of the hidden face of atmospheric warming.

"That might explain last Saturday's meeting. Did Lanier warn the French authorities that a huge number of coastal holdings could change hands?"

Gressin looked skeptical. He spread his hands on the table and leaned toward John. "I'm not sure. It all seems so outrageous," he said. "And there's something else."

"What?"

"The warming will probably be preceded by a sudden cooling, though not enough to stop Greenland's melting. The drop in temperature will collide head-on with the tax policies put in place by various governments to limit CO_2 emissions. With energy-related interest groups claiming that global warming is a hoax, there will be enormous pressure to reverse those policies. We risk political chaos. Romain had predicted this cooling amid the warming. He didn't die by chance."

"What's going to happen now?" John asked.

"The spot we're sitting on is collapsing because the ice cap is melting sixty-five hundred feet below us. The ice basin where we established Raphaelle was ten feet deep six months ago. Today, it's sixty-eight feet deep. Since Sunday, we've been losing eight inches a day. We're like rubber ducks bobbing on top of water that's draining out of the tub."

No doubt about it, Gressin knew how to scare a person.

"How many days do we have left?" John asked.

"We don't know for sure."

Gressin changed his tone and the subject.

"I was told that someone tried to shoot you," he said.

"He missed because of a dip in the trail. But he's still out there."

"Do you know how to use a gun?" Gressin asked.

"Yes," John answered, seeing no need to disclose his service in the military. Gressin stood up and disappeared behind a door. He returned a few minutes later with a rifle and a box of ammunition.

"It's not state-of-the-art, but it could come in handy."

"Thank you."

John took the rifle as the two Inuits looked on with some interest.

"Come outside with me, and try it."

Gressin took his guest outside the mobile home and walked about fifty yards beyond the station's perimeter. John loaded the rifle and positioned it against his right shoulder. He looked for the silhouette of the sniper. Failing to spot him, he aimed at an abandoned snowplow. The two shots shattered what was left of the plexiglass windshield.

Gressin looked worried. "I wanted to talk to you away from the two Inuits."

John sensed that he had even more trouble on his hands. He turned to the chief scientific officer.

"You don't trust Qaalasoq or Saké?"

"I don't trust anybody, not even on the base. I wanted to tell you something in private."

John thought back to his ominous conversation with Christophe Maunay. Private conversations with the executives of Terre Noire generally didn't augur well.

"I'm listening."

"Yesterday, we moved our computers, and I saw that mine had been hacked into."

"Someone stole scientific data from you?"

"Yes, but they also went through the e-mails I exchanged with Nicolas Lanier and Abraham Harper that laid the groundwork for their secret meeting last Saturday."

"Did you tell Lanier?"

"He's not answering his phone."

"What about Geraldine Harper?"

"I was counting on you, because in an e-mail dated Friday, Nicolas Lanier advised Abraham Harper to hire a certain John Spencer Larivière to handle security for his daughter, Mary. I thought that might interest you."

John thought back to what Victoire had just e-mailed: Per Sorensen, the Danish killer, had photographed their house even before he'd met Geraldine Harper at the Ritz. So the leak obviously had to come from Greenland.

"Thank you. Who do you suspect?"

"The hacker could be here or at Terre Noire headquarters in Paris, North Land, or the American base in Thule. They intercept everything. It could also be an intelligence service in Greenland, Denmark, or Norway. I think you're in a better position than I am to find out. That's sort of what you're here for, isn't it?"

John nodded. Once again failing to find his assassin in his line of sight, he blew out the windshield of a second snowplow, which was slumped against a snowdrift over three hundred and thirty yards away.

"Bravo! I see that Lanier wasn't wrong to have you brought up here."

John smiled. His hands and his reflexes were doing the thinking for him. He had, in fact, been programmed by Abraham Harper and Lanier to confront another sniper here. Who and why remained to be seen.

Luc rode through the village of Dun-les-Places in the heart of the Morvan. The motorcycle's headlight lit a misty landscape dotted with stone houses and steeped in the scent of wet ferns. He had covered a good mile before finding the sign indicating L'Huis-Laurent. The muddy forest road forced him to slow down. After skidding a couple of times, he crossed a rotting wooden bridge. The forest was feeling increasingly dense and oppressive the farther he went. The chalet finally appeared, surrounded by fir trees, just as it was in the photo. Straight ahead, at the end of the road, was the place Mary Harper had called several times since her father had vanished.

There was nothing extraordinary about the house, apart from the wild and grandiose setting. The Morvan provided Europe with its Christmas trees and wreaths, and the hills around the house had a thick growth of firs. Luc parked the motorcycle some two hundred yards away and took off his helmet. Smoke was coming out of the chimney, but the harsh north wind was forcing it toward the ground instead of toward the sky. He positioned himself behind a tree and pulled out his binoculars.

Luc could see a light in one of the windows. He could also make out a fire in the fireplace. His phone vibrated. He answered and recognized Isabelle Le Guévenec's voice.

"Luc, I'm calling about Romain Brissac. Someone said he died on the *Bouc-Bel-Air* and someone else said it was on a helicopter. Do you know what happened?"

There was something suspicious about Isabelle Le Guévenec's call. Luc suspected that the captain's wife had checked with Terre Noire and learned that he had never been a company employee. He decided to catch her at her own game.

"Have you called the Champs-Elysées?"

He sensed a hesitation at the other end of the call. Isabelle had obviously called headquarters. Why was she playacting with him?

"I've never trusted headquarters. Besides, I don't know anyone there. And what I've just learned isn't about to make me want to call them. It seems the HR manager was murdered in Greenland. My husband hated him, reckoned he was a pedophile. And Maunay refused to give him a loan for a house."

Sly creature, Luc thought, ducking under the branches of a big conifer to stay out of the rain that had begun falling.

"Listen, Isabelle, I don't have time to get back to Le Havre at the moment. We have to take charge of the wounded from the *Bouc-Bel-Air* who are arriving at Roissy Airport sometime today. We also have to make arrangements for Romain Brissac's body. He died on a helicopter that was taking off from the *Bouc-Bel-Air*. It was an accident."

"No, Little Luc, it was no accident. It was murder."

Luc looked at his cell phone. Isabelle Le Guévenec had suddenly dropped the bantering tone and was trying complicity. Intrigued, he took the bait.

"What are you saying, Isabelle?"

"I'm saying that a well-brought-up young man like you deserves to make it to the top of Terre Noire. Now that that ghastly Maunay's dead, there's an empty position ready and waiting. But only if you don't die an idiot like he did. You know what really happened on the *Bouc-Bel-Air*. I might remind you that I know someone on board. I don't think you'd be wasting your time if you came to see me."

Luc told himself that he could try his luck, and if he was as cunning as a snake, he might get something. But first he had to clear up the mystery of those phone calls Mary Harper made to the chalet here in the Morvan. After that, he'd leave for Le Havre.

"All right, Isabelle, I'll finish making arrangements for the wounded and come to see you as soon as I'm done."

"You won't regret it. Speaking of which, Luc, there's just one small thing."

"Yes?"

"I'm not in Le Havre. I'm at my holiday house."

"Where's that, Isabelle?"

"In the Morvan, at Dun-les-Places. Go past the church, and take the forest road toward L'Huis-Laurent. The chalet's just a mile beyond that. You can't miss it. It's a bit wet, but I have a fire going."

Caught off-guard by this most unexpected news, he almost dropped the phone.

"Right, Isabelle, I'll let you know when I get to the Morvan."

Luc ended the phone call and leaned against the trunk of the fir tree. Less than a hundred yards away, Loïc Le Guévenec's wife was fanning a fire in a chalet where Mary Harper, heiress to the North Land empire, was desperately trying to get hold of someone important. Unbelievable.

Icy rain and fog soon replaced the mist. Luc gave himself some time to think and ducked farther into the forest to go around to the back of the house. The idea that there could be such a close connection between the two women completely threw him.

DUN-LES-PLACES, L'HUIS-LAURENT CHALET, 12:15 P.M.

Isabelle Le Guévenec put another log on the fire and called Connie Rasmussen. It had taken her awhile to digest what the legal advocate for the Northern Peoples Congress had sent her. She had occasionally run into the Danish woman in Le Havre and Oslo. The two women had hit it off without actually becoming friends. They really didn't have much in common, but Isabelle had no reason to dislike her. Once her anger had died down, Isabelle gathered her wits and thought long and hard, studying the information Connie had retrieved from the boatswain's phone.

Someone had gone through her private life with a fine-tooth comb. She'd been photographed in Oslo, Paris, and Le Havre in the company of Romain Brissac, her lover. Even her fling with that sly dog Luc Martinet had been photographed. Nicolas Lanier had asked her to leave Le Havre and go to this chalet, where she could lure Little Luc to see what he was made of. She speed-dialed the Danish woman's number.

"It's me, Connie. I've just read the file you sent. I'm alarmed. Why did Rox Oa have all that information?"

"He was keeping the documents in reserve to put pressure on the captain."

"Put pressure on him for what?" Isabelle asked.

"I don't know yet. The *Bouc-Bel-Air* is carrying the archives of the past in its womb, which means the future, in climate terms. The documents are a sort of club to hold over the captain."

Isabelle looked at the flames rising higher and higher. She didn't know what attitude to adopt with Connie Rasmussen.

"But why did you send them to me?"

"So you'll speak to your husband when the time comes and because I'd like to invite you to the Nuuk Cultural Center."

"But why on earth would you want to do that?"

"I think Terre Noire's image is suffering badly in Greenland. I think you could do some good by coming here and speaking on behalf of your foundation. I read Luc Martinet's article on the future-probe.com website."

"Luc Martinet?"

Something came together in Isabelle Le Guévenec's overheated mind. The fake member of Terre Noire's employee health and safety team could be a very real journalist.

"You haven't read the article he wrote about the two of us?" Connie asked.

"Of course I have. What's he like, this Luc whatever?"

"Tall, dark-haired, on the slim side, a bit moody. Pretty seductive. He's very interested in the Inuits and the *Bouc-Bel-Air*."

"And he has a butterfly tattoo on his stomach," Isabelle stopped herself from adding. What Connie Rasmussen had just told her was reassuring and alarming at the same time. She quickly ended the call, telling Connie that she would be happy to go to Nuuk and talk about her work defending blue whales and polar bears.

Standing at a window overlooking the sodden forest, she slowly gathered her wits. Then she called Nicolas Lanier. She took more than a bit of pleasure in knowing that she was one of the few people on earth who had direct access to the man whose advice many governments were ready to pay a fortune for. She didn't have to wait for it to ring twice before hearing his voice.

"It's Isabelle."

"Well?"

"I'm at the chalet. The young man who came to see me in Le Havre and passed himself off as one of your employees is named Luc Martinet. He's a freelance journalist with future-probe.com. He's making believe that he's in Roissy collecting Romain's remains. He'll be here shortly."

"Thanks, Isabelle. You're amazing. Entertain him, and get him talking. We've got to find out who he's really working for. Trap him."

Isabelle Le Guévenec watched the rain fall. Romain's death had taken her to a very dark and lonely place. She patted the USB flash drive on which the Nobel laureate had safeguarded the latest data on global warming and its consequences. She was the only person Romain had trusted. Since receiving the flash drive, she had carried it inside her bra. An exploding pinecone on the fire made her jump. The chalet in the forest was beginning to feel just a bit threatening.

INDIANA CLUB, MONTPARNASSE

Victoire looked up at her ex-colleague. Sébastien Le Gall was grinning from ear to ear. The noise and gesticulations of the players around the pool table were the best guarantee against fixed and directional listening devices. Sébastien Le Gall, an experienced analyst with Hubert de Méricourt's agency, had ducked out of Les Invalides to answer his old colleague's questions. Over the years, he'd acquired a solid reputation as an expert in the field of energy. Le Gall drew up scenarios and theories at Les Invalides, which everyone did their best to promptly ignore, because they were so disturbing. Like many other members of the service, he had been sad to see Victoire and John leave. After reminiscing for a moment, he came straight to the point.

"What do you want to know?"

"Terre Noire and North Land. What do you know about them?"

"Terre Noire owns all the scenarios having anything to do with the Anthropocene."

"What is the Anthropocene?" Victoire asked.

"The new climate era, ushered in by man-made pollution, specifically carbon emissions. At least, that's the dominant view. Terre Noire's at the center of current studies regarding oil and other energies, thanks to Gaia, their software for studying geological nappes."

"What does that mean?"

"Lanier knows exactly when the oil wells will start drying up, and when that happens, there will be great demand for any oil, wherever it can be found. Mind you, oil reserves are enormous, but the cost of extracting the stuff can also be enormous. But once there's a shortage, all the work that Terre Noire and North Land have been putting into energies will take on colossal value. The two companies stand to make a fortune that's far greater than what they've amassed so far. In fact, they could be the world's chief power brokers. North Land isn't as well tooled in this domain. On the other hand, they're unbeatable in tar sands and shale gas."

"So you could say that the two firms are at the center of the strategic stakes?"

"Yes, you could even say that Lanier and the Harpers hold the key to all the transactions of the coming energy crisis—and the related crises in finance, real estate, and politics."

"People would kill for that?"

"Millions of people."

"Have you written anything about this?"

Despite the racket they were using as cover, Sébastien lowered his voice.

"I'm retiring in six months. I want to live in peace. In any event, there'd be no point. We never met, and this conversation never happened."

"I know how it goes. Thank you anyway. It's been lovely to see you again."

"Give John a hug for me. Tell him we miss him."

"Thanks."

Victoire planted a kiss on her former colleague's cheek. She left the club and headed toward Fermatown, taking the Rue Froidevaux along the Montparnasse Cemetary. It would be a five-minute walk. John's absence was tying her stomach in knots. Familiar places were feeling foreign. She turned around several times, thinking someone might be behind her. She'd never seen the clouds so low. The weather was bizarre. No doubt it was the start of the Anthropocene. Arriving at Fermatown, she climbed the stairs to the media room and stood at the touch wall.

During her interlude at the Indiana Club, the search engine had paved the way for her. The system had gone through all the media sites and real-estate registries on both sides of the Atlantic. Omar Al Selim, Christophe Maunay's protector, was a specialist in making property investments for Saudi princes, African heads of state, and oil magnates in the Persian Gulf. She scrolled down the list of luxury hotels and historic buildings he'd played a part in buying. As a director of Equinoxe, he'd bought the Hôtel Louxor in Paris three years earlier. That pivotal place was less than two hundred yards from the Greenland House. Victoire took a deep breath and sat at the oak table to think. Omar Al Selim owned the Paris hotel where the man who had tried to saw her to pieces had stayed. Despite her disgust, she once again brought up the images of the mutilated body in Greenland. For the moment, the Qatari businessman was the sole link between the murder attempt in Paris and the slaying in Nuuk.

She logged onto the database run by the European Bureau of Civil and Commercial Information in Décines, near Lyon. It was the ultimate in economic information. The bureau's megaengine hummed for a few seconds after she entered the name of Omar Al Selim's company. Then it provided the answer: Equinoxe, a Norwegian real-estate development company, was headquartered in Oslo.

It was what followed that floored Victoire. The sovereign wealth funds of Qatar owned forty-nine percent of the company. Fifty-one percent was owned by Arctoil, the Norwegian oil company that had commissioned Terre Noire, along with the Russians, to examine the gigantic oil deposits in the Barents Sea.

Victoire logged back onto the bureau's database and tried to find out who represented Arctoil on Equinoxe's board of directors. A name popped up immediately: Thor Johannsen. The man who had tried to kill her had come from a hotel in Paris owned by the biggest oil company in Europe.

Victoire called Luc to press him to get information out of his Dane.

"You have to keep asking Rasmussen about Thor Johannsen."

"Why?"

"Because he's on the board of the company that owns the Louxor."

"I knew there was a connection. Send me photos."

"How's it going in the Morvan?" Victoire asked anxiously.

"Le Guévenec's wife is in the chalet that Mary Harper has been calling. It's completely screwy. I'm scared."

"Me too."

RAPHAELLE, 4:30 P.M.

John raised his arm and gave the stop command. The two dog teams, which were barreling ahead side-by-side, did as they were told. Saké got off the sled and joined them. John pointed to the snowdrift where he'd seen the blast from the gun.

"The sniper was over there, less than three hundred and fifty yards away."

"That's right," Saké said.

The Humboldt Gletsjer shaman returned to his dogs and untied the leader of the pack. He whispered something in his ear and took him to the edge of the trail. Kneeling close to his animal, Saké rubbed the dog's back while the others rolled in the snow. He pointed out the snowdrift, and the leader of the pack bounded ahead. Saké returned to his team and untied the other dogs, which raced off behind the leader.

"If the killer's still there, he's a dead man."

Jealous and yapping, Qaalasoq's dogs watched Saké's pack running over the snow. The shaman asked Qaalasoq to tow his sled. The two men worked in silence, economizing their movements according to the age-old rites of their people. The operation took less than five minutes.

"Let's go."

Qaalasoq, driving the sled with John in it and towing Saké's sled, raced after the freed dogs. John cocked the rifle Gressin had given him. They were approaching the snowdrift at a dizzying speed. They skirted the drift and found the dogs distressed and confused.

No one. The sniper hadn't waited for them, naturally. Qaalasoq got off the sled and examined the traces left on the ice.

"He has a Canadian snowmobile."

"Who uses that kind of snowmobile?" John asked.

"Everyone," answered Qaalasoq.

Saké indicated an invisible point above the horizon.

"Our man left that way. He was heading south, toward Haffner Berg. He must be waiting for us somewhere between Raphaelle and Josephine."

Saké took the leader of his team to the crest of the snowdrift. The dog sniffed and then retraced his steps. With his fur steaming and his tongue hanging out, he studied the snow, looking for a clue. He circled around the traces left by the snowmobile's tracks. All of a sudden, he dashed southward, and the others ran off behind him.

Saké rejoined John and Qaalasoq, and the dog team resumed its course. High in the sky, they saw a helicopter transporting yet another mobile home. They finally caught up to the freed pack and after half an hour's run came across a spectacle that threw them completely off.

The traces of the snowmobile's tracks in the snow had disappeared beneath a sheet of water that stretched far into the horizon. They were at the edge of a vast tipped basin. On one side of the basin, the water was relatively shallow. On the other side, beneath a wall-like incline, it was much deeper. The blue sky and clouds reflected in the water gave the impression of a formidable depth.

Qaalasoq untied the harpoon attached to his sled. He drew closer to the edge of the unforeseen lake that five hours earlier hadn't been on any map of the Avanaarsua. The Inuit stretched his arm back and hurled the harpoon with all his might. John saw the hasp and its steel point rise into the transparent sky before it curved out over the water and fell down vertically into the lake. The black line sank and disappeared.

They then measured the incredible depth of the water that separated them from the killer. John did a quick calculation. It had taken only a few hours for a lake to form and halt their pursuit of the enemy. The bastard who'd tried to kill him was profiting from Greenland's final agony.

Saké ran his eagle eyes over the ominous bank. The water stretched for miles to the right and the left, serving as an insurmountable barrier. The most horrible part was the silence of the dogs, which were lying on the snow with their ears pricked, listening.

"What will we do?" Qaalasoq asked.

"We'll have to go back to the base and use the inflatables, if it's not too late," John replied.

Saké took out his phone and rang a number before passing the device to John, who recognized Gressin's voice.

"There's a lake blocking our way. We need two inflatables. Do you have any?"

"You'll find them behind the last hut. I'll leave you a computer and a generator next to the mobile home we spoke in. Good luck."

The return of the two teams to Raphaelle was marked by a feeling of failure and growing fear. Far in the west, dark clouds weighed down the air. It wouldn't be long before the sky came down on their heads. And under their feet, the world was caving in.

DUN-LES-PLACES, YORÉVÉ DOLMEN, 12:50 P.M.

Luc had found refuge under a rock formation. The heavy cold rain fell without letting up, sending down streams of pine needles and slivers of wood. The weather was all out of whack. Luc hugged himself to stay warm. A few hundred yards away, the chalet was exhaling blue smoke that was immediately pelted by the downpour.

The situation was becoming as tumultuous as the weather. By giving Isabelle Le Guévenec's number to Connie Rasmussen, he had put his two one-night stands in touch with each other—one of them a passenger on the *Bouc-Bel-Air*, the other, the captain's wife. He was clearly walking on a basket of crabs. Was he a genius, or had he just done something really stupid? A violent clap of thunder made him jump before it rolled away over the hills.

He took out his phone, wondering if the ambient electricity would interfere with his call. The little jewel was working. He brought up the photos of Thor Johannsen, the Norwegian from Arctoil who also presided over the Hôtel Louxor. It was time to find out a bit more about him. Luc pressed the little green icon.

"Hi, Connie, it's Luc. How are you doing?"

"We're having crappy weather. I'm wondering if we aren't going to sink."

"It's lousy weather here, too. Were you able to get in touch with Isabelle Le Guévenec?"

"Yes, thank you."

"Do you remember I asked you about Thor Johannsen?"

It was quiet on the other side. Had his question embarrassed the lawyer?

"I'm sending you some pictures. What can you tell me about him?"

Luc sent the shots that Victoire had taken from the annual reports of Arctoil and Equinoxe. There was another silence at the other end, and he told himself he'd no doubt put his wet feet in it yet again.

"How did you get these photos?" Connie Rasmussen asked. Her voice was shrill with fear.

"From my editors at future-probe.com. Thor Johannsen does live in Paris, at the Hôtel Louxor, doesn't he?"

Still another pause at the other end, then forced joviality.

"Little Luc, you've hit a home run."

"Why do you say that?"

"Because Thor Johannsen is none other than Laura Al-lee-Ah's husband. Didn't you know that?"

"Your boss's husband?"

A shorter pause than the previous ones.

"Yes, Luc. Johannsen moves between Paris, Copenhagen, and Oslo. He has a suite in a hotel next to the Greenland House, but you didn't hear that from me, right?"

"Of course not."

Luc ducked when he heard the smack of thunder accompanying a nearby lightning strike. Certainly Connie had heard it too.

"Where are you, really?"

"In a storm in the Morvan," Luc answered, immediately biting his lip.

This time, he really had said something stupid, revealing his whereabouts in Dun-les-Places.

He ended his call with the Dane and sat down on the pine needles. As the water flowed over the granite of the Morvan, the realization seeped into Luc's brain. Thor Johannsen was connected to Greenland through his wife and to Terre Noire through Christophe Maunay, whom his friend Selim had rescued in Gabon. It was an extraordinary network of influence.

Arctoil's Norwegian board member was the hidden center of gravity in this whole affair. He alone linked the economic, political, humanitarian, and ecological aspects related to the end of the world. Luc called Aimé Toussaint, the lifeguard to whom he'd entrusted the mission of identifying Per Sorensen's contact at the swimming pool of the Saint-James.

"Hi, Aimé, it's Luc."

"I was going to call you. Tonight I'll be seeing the waiter who was at the Saint-James when that meeting took place. I'll show him the photos you sent me."

"Look at your cell phone. I'm sending you a photo of a Norwegian guy by the name of Thor Johannsen. I'll double the stakes if you get me any additional information on this Viking."

Aimé Toussaint burst out laughing.

"It's a pleasure doing business with you! I'll call you this evening."

Luc looked at his watch. It was still too early to turn up at the chalet.

He took advantage of a temporary letup in the rain and decided to survey the surroundings. He cut through a clearing about half a mile above the chalet. A vast boggy area full of ferns stretched out before him. All of a sudden, the dirt track he was walking on widened into a major road. Surprising.

A few hundred yards away, on his right, the trees parted, hinting at a gap in the forest. A sort of empty space over which a solitary black buzzard was soaring. On a tree charred by lightning he saw a rusty metal sign: "Terres Noires–Black Lands."

Driven by curiosity, he took the direction indicated by the sign and set out for the Black Lands. His temples started throbbing when, a bit farther along, he encountered an entirely different climate zone.

On the other side of a fence topped with barbed wire, Luc gazed at a vast expanse of black dirt that looked like a dried-out sponge. Stunted bushes of broom grew here and there. The impression of dryness in the middle of the ambient wetness made Luc almost dizzy. He had never before seen anything like it. He stepped closer to the fence that divided the two worlds and read another sign: "Terres Noires–Black Lands, Private Property, Danger of Death."

A nudge of the shoulder got the better of the rusty iron gate, and he slipped through to the other side. Fear was now merging with curiosity. He took out his phone and called Victoire.

"Could you see if the Black Lands of the Morvan played any role in the history of Terre Noire? After all, the name's the same."

"I'll have a look," Victoire replied. "Did you manage to get hold of Connie Rasmussen?"

"Yes. Thor Johannsen is Laura Al-lee-Ah's husband. He's Norway's oil man and the Russians' partner in the Barents Sea. He's the one who sent the killer from the Saint-James's swimming pool to the Rue the Deparcieux to kill us. I'm sure of it. The agency has to send someone around to protect you inside the house."

"I'll have to clean up a bit more first."

"Don't play the heroine. You should have called Guerot by now. I don't know how long I'll be stuck in this godforsaken hole."

Luc ended the call. He was working with two crackpots. He smiled, telling himself that he was just like them. In any event, the world as they knew it was about to end. Might as well have some fun before the final chaos set in.

THE GREAT WOUND OF THE WILD DOG, 10:10 A.M.

John saw the helicopter hauling away the last of Raphelle's mobile laboratories. The sky had suddenly turned black, and Terre Noire's scientific team hadn't wasted any time getting out of the Great Wound of the Wild Dog. John and his companions were now on their own. The dogs were running in silence. Their tails were down, as if they sensed an unfamiliar danger.

All that remained of the station were the two mobile homes. The rest had been taken away. On the snow, John could still see where everything had stood. The circular pond, an unreal blue under the black sky, seemed to be glowing from within. John got off the sled and headed toward the hut. He found the two boxes, each of which held an inflatable Zodiac H308 with an automated inflation system and all the accessories. Made of extremely heavy-duty material, the Zodiac could carry a snowplow or a van. It was exactly what they would need. Four cans of gasoline were off to the side. Faced with the deterioration of the Great Wound, all the stations in Avannaa were equipping themselves with Zodiacs or kayaks to explore the new inland seas of the terminally ill country.

After checking the state of the buoyancy tubes, as well as the motors, he retraced his steps and examined the surface of the pond, which, like an eye, was staring up at the sky. His feet, fitted with fur-lined boots, promptly sank when he was a few feet from the edge. Horrified, he had enough strength in his lower back to leap back before being sucked down. Enormous bubbles of gas were bursting at the surface of the immense pupil, giving off a pestilential odor. John felt a presence behind him and swiveled around. Qaalasoq and Saké were weeping.

Embarrassed, he left them alone to deal with their pain and went back to the sled. He picked up his luggage and walked up the steps to the common room. Everything had been taken away and cleaned up. All that remained was the map of Avannaa pinned to the wall with a sticky note in the middle. "Good luck!" read the message from Paul Gressin.

John took out his phone and familiarized himself with the information gathered by Fermatown. After the Per Sorensen incident, Luc had the bright idea of suggesting security inside the house too. John was annoyed with himself for not thinking of it earlier. How had Victoire gotten rid of the killer? He didn't want to ask for details, even though he was sure their exchanges were leak-proof. John was proud of Victoire and grateful that he could call her his own. She was a fabulous woman, the right woman for him. They probably wouldn't grow all that old together because of their jobs, but they really were made for each other.

Luc had just made an amazing discovery. As soon as the Lauge Koch Kyst catastrophe had made the news, Mary Harper had called the landline at a chalet in the Morvan where Isabelle Le Guévenec was staying. That the heiress to the North Land empire might have a relationship with the wife of the captain of the *Bouc-Bel-Air* seemed less surprising now that John was aware of the meeting between Abraham Harper and Nicolas Lanier.

Thor Johannsen's involvement in his being tailed from the Ritz and the attempted murder in Fermatown were beginning to make more sense. This could explain why Gressin's computer in Raphaelle had been hacked into. The big oil companies were known for the efficiency of their private espionage. North Land or Terre Noire—or both of them together—could undermine the joint interests of the Norwegian Arctoil and the Russian Gazprom.

John leaped to his feet and went to the window of the mobile home. Yes, the two companies could get in their way, separately or together. Why hadn't he thought of that earlier? From the very beginning of this affair, he'd felt torn between Terre Noire and North Land. Yet there was no evidence of any hostility between Abraham Harper and Nicolas Lanier.

How, on the other hand, could you explain Christophe Maunay's desire to defect from Terre Noire and join North Land? Maunay didn't hold a crucial scientific position at Terre Noire. As the HR man, though, he would have known certain things.

John sat down again to send a message to Victoire. He wanted her to get more information as quickly as she could. Why had Maunay been killed?

Back at the window, he watched the Inuits take care of the dogs and shut the kennel. Then he became aware of something that until that moment had been unthinkable. Drops of water were sliding down the pane of glass. It was raining.

Saké and Qaalasoq came back at the same time. They looked somber and outraged.

"It's raining!" cried Saké.

"Wasn't it supposed to snow?" John asked.

"At this hour and in this season, it never rains," replied Qaalasoq.

The two Inuits collapsed on the bench seats. There was no point in quizzing them about what they were feeling. John could plainly see in their eyes how powerless they felt in the face of the forces of nature that had been unleashed. He gave them the silence they needed and watched the rain fall. The drops let up and then stopped. Snowflakes finally appeared.

Driven by hunger, John went behind the counter to see what was left in the fridge. He pulled out an enormous rabbit terrine and one of three bottles of champagne that had been left for them. As a commando leader, he'd led his men into combat in conditions that were tougher but not as scary. Maybe he didn't know how to talk to women, but he did know how to deal with men. He poured the bubbly into three plastic cups. The first bubbles had trouble going down their demoralized gullets. By the second bottle, the out-of-whack climate looked a bit more bearable, if only temporarily. Tongues loosened under the effects of the alcohol. Half an hour later, John took the tupilaq out of his bag and placed the horrible polished-stone monster on the table.

"Now you can tell me how this hideous beast is going to help us."

Saké took the statuette in his hands and looked at John before he spoke.

"The tupilaq is a monster made of human and animal flesh stitched together. On its master's command, it hurls itself into the frozen immensity to find and kill the enemy. Then it comes home."

"That's scary."

"It gets even scarier when it encounters an enemy who's stronger than it is. That enemy becomes the new master," Saké said somberly.

John grabbed the statuette and guessed the rest. "And the tupilaq comes home to kill its former boss."

"Right," said Qaalasoq.

"And me, in all that, I'm the tupilaq, aren't I?" John concluded, thinking of the way he had been stitched together with skin grafts.

"Maybe," Saké said. Qaalasoq nodded in agreement.

A strange commonality linked him to this Greenland myth. By the third bottle of champagne, John was actually feeling sorry for the tupilaq staring at him with dilated pupils. Four human arms, ending in bear claws, were stuck on the body of a dog.

John tried summing up. "If I'm playing the role of a tupilaq, the problem is knowing who sent me, and who the enemy is."

"That's exactly it," Saké confirmed.

"The woman who sent me is named Geraldine Harper. She's your boss."

"It's not her," Qaalasoq said, emptying his cup.

"Well, then it's her husband, the man we're looking for. You told me so the other day."

"He doesn't know you. He's only a bridge between the sender and the sent," Saké said.

John thought of Lanier, but if that were the case, who had given his name to the Terre Noire boss?

"Then who sent me?"

Qaalasoq put his cup down and replied. "You're the one who'll tell us by devouring your enemy, by tearing him apart with your claws. Like the tupilaq."

"This thing of yours is weird. I can tell you don't drink champagne very often."

John put the statuette back in the bag. It was up to him to take charge.

"We'll sleep for a bit before getting back to the lake and setting off on the water. I'll pilot the Zodiacs."

The three men found places in the mobile home to spread out their sleeping bags. Lying across the doorway, John took out Geraldine Harper's phone and listened to Mary's latest calls. A conversation between the mother and daughter interested him the most. Mary was recounting her meeting with Laura Al-lee-Ah.

"Laura has all the police reports. But she thinks they're useless. She wants me to ask Spencer Larivière about his conversation with Christophe Maunay. Don't forget, they're both French. Laura thinks that before he was killed in the Hans Egede, Maunay told my babysitter things that would interest Greenland security. She wants to know what he said. She's on tenterhooks and following everything very closely. She'll probably have him arrested before he finds Dad. What do I do?"

The mother gave her a clear and succinct answer. "Stay out of it! Above all, don't disturb Spencer Larivière. Your babysitter wasn't asked to work for Terre Noire. Leave him alone. If he learns things of interest to Greenland security, I can assure you, he'll inform me immediately—and first. He knows it!"

Geraldine's instructions were clearly meant for him. She knew he'd be listening in, as per his job. John closed his eyes. Outside, the wind was becoming increasingly violent, causing the odds and ends of sheet metal that hadn't been well secured to bang around.

ON BOARD THE BOUC-BEL-AIR, *11:10 A.M.*

Connie Rasmussen studied the surreal horizon. Orangish clouds lit up a metallic sea filled with icebergs in shapes that had never before been seen. It was an unbelievably beautiful and rattling spectacle. The ship groaned under the ocean's onslaught as it tried to avoid the mountains of ice. In the distance, the distress signals from the shipwrecked sailors of the *Narvik* and its flotilla illuminated the sky.

The most disturbing thing in all this was the piecemeal entry of the French in this Arctic game. Luc Martinet was steaming full-speed ahead. That hunk was moving too fast.

The answer to her question was not long in coming. "Luc Masseron, aka Luc Martinet, is a former hacker who works for Fermatown, a little private espionage outfit run by John Spencer Larivière, a former member of the French intelligence agency."

The French were sticking their mitts in the cookie jar, causing trouble. Their presence was more disturbing than global warming. It absolutely guaranteed chaos. That's all they needed. Connie thought about Luc and John. Then about the rest. A violent wave forced her to worry about more immediate things.

On the captain's orders, the *Bouc-Bel-Air* was about to give the ship-wrecked sailors a hand. There would be confusion at sea, as well as on board. The remaining able-bodied men on the *Bouc* were gearing up for rescue maneuvers. But many of them feared they would need to be rescued themselves. The captain was far more courageous than most of his crew.

Connie came out of her lair to return to Sylvain Velot's cabin. She'd only just made it to the corridor when she bumped into the Inuit body-guard made available to her at Laura Al-lee-Ah's instructions. The man had never sailed before and was terrorized by the heavy weather and the dull thuds rising from the bowels of the boat. Connie overcame the smell of the vomit splattered on the floor and told her bodyguard to go rest.

"Are we going to sink?" he asked.

"Maybe."

The man disappeared immediately. Connie knocked loudly to make herself heard above the din.

"Who is it?" the bear killer yelled.

"Connie Rasmussen."

The sailor cracked the door open cautiously and looked behind Connie with suspicion in his eyes.

"I've got your key," Connie said, showing the object and then slipping it into the pocket of her red oilskin.

"I'd given up expecting you," Velot declared.

"Le Guévenec wasn't easy to convince. He's very busy with the storm and the rescue of the *Narvik*."

"It'll be rescuing us."

The sailor opened the door wide and let Connie in. Through the portholes, she could see the ailing *Narvik* and, a stone's throw away, the *Copenhagen*. Fighting to keep his balance, Sylvain Velot pulled on a wool sweater. The inclination of the ship was becoming alarming and the cold unbearable. The *Bouc*'s heater had just gone on the blink yet again.

"Let's go," he said.

Connie followed the man toward the gangways that led to the upper deck. They struggled up the steps and came out on a deserted corridor. Velot made a gesture that confirmed it was, indeed, here that Nicolas Lanier had gone into hiding. Walking along the gangways was beginning to require the skill of an acrobat. But they finally made it to the boatswain's cabin. Connie put the key in the lock, and when the door resisted, she invited the French sailor to take over.

Sylvain Velot got the better of the problem with a simple shoulder butt, and they both found themselves inside the cabin. The sailor closed the door and carefully examined the room where the seaman had bunked before getting himself skinned alive. Connie had the phone containing the report on Isabelle Le Guévenec and her husband hidden in the pocket of her oilskin. Velot would, without fail, head for the closet to retrieve his accomplice's weapon. She dreaded his reaction.

But to her surprise, he dashed into the shower room. He opened the glass door and, with the aid of a screwdriver, removed the bolts that held the shower in place. What on earth could he be looking for under the stainless-steel floor? The scenario she'd imagined went down the toilet. In this affair, nothing was going according to plan. She looked on, her heart beating hard and her forehead breaking out in sweat.

Velot picked up the metal shower base and asked her to get it out of the way. She swung it behind her. From out of the cavity underneath the shower, the Frenchman took two round metal discs as thick as the Breton custard tarts known as *fars*.

"Be careful. They're heavy," he said.

Connie seized the first one by the handle and felt her arm sag under the weight. She put it down in the cabin and came back for the second one. Velot had just taken two timebombs out of their hiding place. Connie realized that he intended to sink the *Bouc-Bel-Air*. No one had envisaged this kind of situation. She'd have to improvise, and fast.

"What are these?" she asked innocently.

"Scuttling cartridges. They fit into the circular slots in the hull in the engine room. We're going to sink this wreck and Lanier with it."

Connie just nodded. Sylvain Velot had received instructions to finish the dead boatswain's mission. She now had to find irrefutable proof. Once out of the boatswain's cabin, she let Velot get ahead of her before calling Laura Al-lee-Ah and recording their conversation.

"Hello, Laura, it's Connie. We're out of the cabin. It's done."

"Thank you. When you've disembarked in Nuuk, you'll give me back the phone. I assume you saw what was on it?"

"Yes," Connie replied, dreading what would follow.

"There's no point in the French getting their hands on that report. I wasn't in favor of it. I detest these things. But, well, Greenland's a small country, and we have to be well-informed to keep from getting gobbled up."

"There was also a revolver," Connie added.

"Put it back where you found it. We're not interested in weapons."

Curious reaction, thought Connie. She might not be interested in weapons, but that hadn't stopped her from giving Velot the order to send the *Bouc-Bel-Air* to the bottom, along with Lanier and the rest of the crew.

"What about the two cartridges Velot found in the bathroom?" Connie asked, referring to the bombs.

"Throw them into the sea. I'll call you again when the *Bouc-Bel-Air*'s docked."

Laura ended the conversation. Connie had just accomplished the first part of her mission. She knew that Laura Al-lee-Ah had hired Velot and Rox Oa to spy on the *Bouc-Bel-Air* and its captain, but definitely not to sink the ship and probably not to kill Brissac. The phone contained that irrefutable proof. The Greenlanders had been outwitted by powers smarter than they were. She immediately thought of Thor Johannsen, who had married the conscience of the Arctic. Norway was once again trying to expel Denmark from Greenland. There was nothing new under the sun—except that today, the Norwegians were using French sailors.

She went to the sailor's cabin, where he'd just placed the two bombs on a table. Velot turned to her.

"Now I need the plans for the engine room so I know where the scuttling slots are. Do whatever you have to to get them from Le Guévenec."

"I'll go and see him right away," Connie said.

"That's it. Go and talk to the silly old fool."

RAPHAELLE, 12:35 P.M.

The barking of the dogs awakened John and the two Inuits. He rushed to the front steps of the mobile home and understood. The station was covered with water. A lunar sun surrounded by a black halo was reflected in the lake like a threat. It was a scene from hell. He went down the steps and stuck his hand in the icy water. The snow had turned to sludge and dissolved between his fingers a couple of inches below the surface. The main thing was not to panic, even though they were about to be swallowed alive.

Saké put his boots on and ran to the kennel, driving icy sprays of water before him to get to his dogs and free them. Alert and terrorized, the animals stopped barking and started to whine.

John turned to Qaalasoq, who was also gearing up, and told him what to do. "Gather all the material we'll need. I'll go and get the Zodiacs and bring them around to the front of the house."

John slipped on his boots and circled around the building. With his feet submerged in the water, he pulled out the first inflatable. The pressurizing system was automatically triggered, and the first H308 inflated in a matter of seconds. He fixed the motor to the back on its steel mounting plate. Then he threw the ropes and all the navigation aids between the tubes. The bottom was still too high to allow the engine to float, and it took a superhuman effort to get the Zodiac to the front of the mobile home. Saké came to meet him with the dogs from the first team. With Qaalasoq's help, they attempted to get the first sled onto the Zodiac. But their feet sank in the muck, sabotaging their efforts. The situation was dire. John remembered his training stint in the 501st tank regiment and signaled to Qaalasoq to follow him inside the house. He grabbed the fire ax, which was still hooked to the wall, and started smashing the benches and demolishing the walls. After a few minutes, they had enough debris to extend the load-bearing surface under their feet and slide the sled onto the Zodiac.

John raced back behind the house. The water was rising. He triggered the automatic inflation of the second Zodiac. But his legs gave way under him, and he found himself with the tube opposite him at chest level. He clung to the ropes and hauled himself into the dinghy, using the strength of his arms alone. Sitting up, he saw that the house was sinking a bit more every second. He seized the oars and rowed around to the front.

By the time Qaalasoq emerged from the building, the water was up to his waist. He threw all the material he had been able to retrieve into the inflatable. John had to use all his strength to pull him on board. Out of breath, they turned around, only to see Saké disappear before their eyes. The second sled was pulling him under, along with his team of dogs.

Saké raised his arms above the water. Armed with a knife, the old man cut the last leather towline holding the dogs and then smiled before letting himself sink below the water. The dogs, though freed, were terror-stricken. They swam to John and Qaalasoq, who saved them all, one after the other. Only the leader of the pack returned to his master and went down with him. The water bubbled for a few seconds and then that was that. The dogs on the Zodiac barked and then howled, like wolves baying at the moon.

"Take your clothes off, dry yourself off, and put on some dry clothes."

John did as he was told, watching the demise of Rapaelle all the while. Every trace of the base had vanished. It was as if nothing had ever been there but an immense sheet of water. John would never be able to forget Saké's peaceful, almost complicit face as he went down, like a god of Greenland meeting his fate. Beside him, Qaalasoq spread rugs and dry clothes around them. John put on new garments and helped the Inuit rub down the dogs. An hour later, the starry vacuum of space didn't look like anything they'd ever known. The lake lit up the sky. John was sailing across a mirror dividing two realms of hell.

He took binoculars out of their case and began studying the white barrier far away that split the universe in two. His eyes lingered on something on the shore of the inland sea that had risen up beneath them. A rocky outlet with a tongue of ice that descended into the water would serve as a landing beach. He studied the expanse around them, looking for possible methane emissions that would rule out starting the motor on the front Zodiac in which they'd taken their places, along with the dogs.

"Do you think we can get there?" John asked.

Qaalasoq studied the water for a long while, searching for the slightest bubbling that would reveal the deadly fumes. Starting the gasoline-fueled motor could turn the inflatables into a fireship. The dogs scented danger and yelped like frightened puppies. After a few minutes, they calmed down and lay on their stomachs. Qaalasoq finally took his eyes off the depths. The Inuit smiled as if he'd come back from some other world. John knew he'd been communing with Saké. Qaalasoq realized John understood and grinned.

"We're okay," he said. "You can fire up the engine. The methane's no longer evaporating."

John picked up the first can of gasoline and started pouring the contents into the tank. He immediately stopped. Someone had replaced the gasoline with water. They were prisoners of the new waters of the Great Wound of the Wild Dog. To be sure, he checked the other cans. They didn't have the tiniest drop of gasoline either.

"Someone sabotaged the reserves."

PARIS, 18 RUE DEPARCIEUX, 4:40 P.M.

Victoire was looking for the cat. Caresse had vanished yet again. She called and felt her heart throbbing all the way to her fingertips. Per Sorensen's execution had drained her, and the aftershock was only now making itself felt. The slightest thing made her jump. The Persian reappeared, leaving wet paw prints behind her. Victoire felt calmer.

"There you are at last!"

Reassured, she resumed her investigation. The touch wall displayed one part of the puzzle. Thor Johannsen was prominently featured in the center. The Norwegian controlled not only Equinoxe, the real-estate company that owned the Louxor, but also thirty-three percent of Dan Energy, a Danish geological prospecting company that specialized in renewable energies and held forty-seven percent of Terre Noire. That was enough to give him right of scrutiny over Terre Noire, even if he wasn't an official part of the day-to-day operations.

Victoire brought up a breakdown of Terre Noire's shareholders' agreement: Nicolas Lanier, single, no children, twenty-eight percent; Romain Brissac, divorced, two children, twenty-five percent; Dan Energy, forty-seven percent. Thor Johannsen, as the biggest shareholder in Dan Energy, sat on the board of directors, along with the Danes and the Frenchmen, Lanier and Brissac.

Victoire could understand why Johannsen might have wanted to kill John, via Per Sorensen. John was working for his rival, North Land. But why butcher Terre Noire's HR manager, who was one of his own employees? Christophe Maunay and Thor Johannsen must have crossed paths several times. If it wasn't in Oslo or Copenhagen, maybe it was at the Louxor with Omar Al Selim. The protagonists in this case were coming out of the shadows.

The past could often shed light on the present, John liked to say in his more philosophical moments. Victoire, intrigued by Luc's discovery in Dun-les-Places, reread the story of Terre Noire's origins.

At the end of the nineteenth century, Mathurin Lanier, a blacksmith in Dun-les-Places, was intrigued by the radioactive properties of a certain mineral, autunite. Rocks containing this mineral were abundant in the region. When the disappearance of a number of local sheep and a handful of visitors to the Terres noires, or Black Lands, area aroused concerns, he explained that a geological accident several million years earlier had resulted in the development of quicksand that had swallowed the humans and the animals. His fame spread. Lanier's forge gradually became a mining and geological-exploration business. It grew rapidly in the twentieth century. Mathurin Lanier's sons bought more property in the Black Lands, with the aid of the Brissacs, who were prosperous bankers from Dijon. After that, successive generations of the two families would guide the fortunes of the business, which became Terre Noire. In the nineteen twenties, the company diversified into oil and then gas exploration.

Terre Noire experienced serious financial difficulties in 2008, because of the sudden drop in oil prices. Major companies all over the world froze their exploration operations. Lanier and Brissac joined forces with Dan Energy, a Danish company specializing in offshore wind farms and the processing of methane hydrates found in the ocean floor. Terre Noire was saved and became a key European operation, thanks to the Danes.

Victoire shivered. They had tried to kill her to stop her from seeing what was right in front of her. She grabbed her phone and called Guerot at Les Invalides.

"I'd like to see you, François."

"What about?"

"I'm anxious about my security, but more than that, I have things to tell you."

"I'll be right there, but don't be afraid. We're protecting you."

THE GREAT WOUND OF THE WILD DOG, 1:10 P.M.

John had been rowing for a good hour in the front Zodiac. At his feet, the prostrate dogs exhaled clouds of condensation that immediately dissolved in the air. The second Zodiac, tethered to the first by a rope, was making slow headway. It carried Qaalasoq, the rest of the dogs, and the sled they had rescued from Raphaelle. Stroke by stroke, the oars broke the surface, which was as smooth as an ice rink. Losing the gas reserves had slowed them, but they'd found a rhythm. The two boats were going faster than John had thought they would. From time to time, they passed bubbling methane that wafted the smell of rotten eggs.

The orphaned dogs pricked their ears, hearing the voice of Saké calling to them from the depths. From time to time, one of them barked in the direction of that unknown world. At any moment, they could all be joining him there, men and dogs.

John felt his arms tiring and asked Qaalasoq to take over. They managed the transfer from one Zodiac to the other without difficulty. The Inuit occupied the rower's seat at the front and got to work, smiling sadly. Qaalasoq was in constant touch with Geraldine Harper and regularly informed her of their progress without going into too much detail. He, too, had learned to live with the constant risk of phone tapping.

The hope of finding Abraham Harper alive had yielded to the desire to understand what had happened. No one at the heart of North Land was really under any illusion that their founder was still alive.

John stroked one of the dogs, which seemed to be dying from the methane, and then stretched out on the sled while Qaalasoq led the convoy to its destination.

He took out his smartphone to look at the latest news from Fermatown and was relieved to learn that Guerot was seeing to it that the woman he loved was properly protected. The idea that Thor Johannsen was the linchpin of the attempts to kill them from the very beginning seemed increasingly credible. Russia, Norway, and Iceland were pitted against Denmark and France, partners in Terre Noire. Canada was clashing with the United States at the very heart of North Land. The geopolitical situation was starting to yield certain keys. The role played by Connie Rasmussen, caught between Denmark and Greenland, was still unclear, but the game among the nations seemed obvious.

John was impatient for Luc to verify that the man who'd met Per Sorensen in the bar of the Saint-James swimming pool was, in fact, the Norwegian, in which case, a lot of things would start to be readable. An alliance between Norway and Greenland embodied by Thor Johannsen and Laura Al-lee-Ah opened up new horizons. John now believed in the role he'd been assigned. He received confirmation from Victoire that the warrant for his arrest had been signed and that a team of Greenland police was coming by helicopter to take him into custody. Norway and Greenland most likely did not want the world to know what had happened to Abraham Harper and what Christophe Maunay had almost revealed.

He shut off his phone and stared at the vast space around him. The staccato sound of the oars plunging into the cold water seemed to energize Qaalasoq as he followed the traces of Abraham Harper. The dogs appeared to be lying in wait, watching like hawks, as if some monstrosity was about to surge out of the water. John tried not to think too hard about what was happening sixty-five hundred feet below. But more foul-smelling bubbles were bursting on the surface and releasing multicolored entrails. The bottom of the ice cap was being subjected to some large-scale torture caused by colossal forces. Now appalling sounds were coming up from that icy hell, causing circular shockwaves here and there that shook both the Zodiacs. The phenomenon seemed to be intensifying.

John counted the minutes separating them from their landing spot. He sensed that at any second they could be swallowed up. He saw one of the dogs lean over the water to drink and pulled him back.

To keep himself from going crazy with worry, John pulled out Geraldine's phone and listened to the latest of the heiress's conversations.

The most surprising one was the call she had made to Isabelle Le Guévenec. The two women knew each other, having met several times at social functions and scientific gatherings.

She opened the conversation by telling Isabelle that her husband was a true hero who would be remembered with honor, despite the flak he was taking now. According to Mary Harper, Terre Noire and North Land were caught in the same storm. They would have to pull together.

She apologized for disturbing her in Le Havre, which Isabelle didn't bother to correct, even though she was a long way from her apartment. Mary Harper wanted more information about Christophe Maunay.

"What did your husband think of him, Isabelle?"

"Loïc has always thought he was a creep, and Lanier was wrong to keep him on."

"Do you know a John Spencer Larivière?"

"The name doesn't ring a bell," Isabelle Le Guévenec replied.

"Maunay wanted to reveal something sensational to that guy. Do you have any idea what he wanted to tell him?"

"None."

Mary Harper wasn't following her mother's orders to be careful. Isabelle Le Guévenec and Mary promised to keep each other informed. A lot of people were interested in the secrets Maunay had almost divulged to John. And some of them wouldn't be long in concluding that John had actually heard those confidences.

John heard a familiar flapping sound and sat up. Qaalasoq, with the help of the plastic their reserves of food and water were wrapped in, had just hoisted a makeshift sail above the front Zodiac.

PARIS, 18 RUE DEPARCIEUX, 6 P.M.

Victoire jumped when she heard the doorbell ring and raced to the window. She was relieved when she recognized Guerot.

"What's going on?" he asked, looking around.

"Come in. I'll explain."

The deputy director was carrying a sports bag. They went through the garage, heading toward the stairs. Victoire saw Guerot glance at the damaged tarpaulins covering Fermatown's cars. She shuddered at the idea that he might find some trace of Per Sorensen's execution.

She used her warmest voice. "François, up here, please. I've got news that'll be of interest to you."

Victoire showed Guerot the stairs and took him to the salon. "Let's sit in the confessional."

"The confessional?"

She bit her lip and could have kicked herself. Only the team called the salon where they met clients the confessional. John would have been annoyed with her. He didn't think much of Guerot, who was cold and uptight, ready to do anything to please whoever was in power. The errand boy, as Luc had nicknamed him.

"That's just a name we call it among ourselves. And you're part of the family, François."

The deputy director sat down in the same armchair that he'd taken on his last visit and narrowed his eyes on Victoire.

"You've hurt yourself."

Victoire forced a smile.

"I tried to put a dish in the oven, forgetting that I'd just taken it out five minutes earlier."

"What were you making?" Guerot asked, suddenly interested in the culinary talents of the young woman sitting opposite him.

Victoire was stumped for a second. The question had caught her off guard. "A *gratin dauphinois*," she replied. I dropped it on the floor and had to throw it out."

"That's a shame," Guerot replied. "In any case, we've had security officers here since Tuesday, as we said we would. They're on the Rue Fermat and the Rue Deparcieux. It's a discreet team. They haven't noticed anything out of the ordinary."

Victoire smiled her thanks. Per Sorensen had no doubt expected this, and that's why he had used the rooftop.

"Has John been able to get anything new on Christophe Maunay?"

Victoire leaned toward him and said in a confidential tone, "Believe it or not, just before he was killed in his hotel room, Maunay told John that he wanted to defect to North Land, lock, stock, and barrel."

Guerot went white, and Victoire took malicious pleasure in dragging out the suspense. She recounted Christophe Maunay's offer to help John. Guerot stopped looking at her hands and listened carefully. The defection plan was obviously fascinating him. This was a way to transfer intelligence that couldn't be prosecuted as corporate espionage.

"And that's not all, François."

"What else is there?"

"Maunay wanted to flee France. He promised John that he'd reveal terrible secrets about Terre Noire if Geraldine Harper could get him a new identity and a Canadian passport."

"What terrible secrets?" Guerot asked, looking stricken.

Victoire took a deep breath and caught a whiff of chlorine. Caresse had most likely knocked over a bottle of bleach in the kitchen. She continued her story.

"He didn't have time to say. They were interrupted by Qaalasoq, one of the Inuits with John. Maunay died that night, butchered."

Victoire closed her eyes momentarily, remembering the Dane she had decapitated. Guerot was looking at her as though she had just fallen to earth. Maunay's defection would have been a great blow to him. Guerot surely had given the Terre Noire HR manager a secret defense clearance, considering the strategic stakes and the major intellectual property the company dealt in. Guerot was going to be in hot water down at Les Invalides. He'd backed the wrong horse, big time. Victoire could already see the smirking faces of his colleagues.

For a few moments, they sat in silence. The deputy director conceded in a barely audible voice, "That's frightening."

Victoire nodded in agreement. "I learned that a Qatari, Omar Al Selim, who's a grand officer of the Legion of Honor, got Maunay out of trouble once. Al Selim turns up in a lot of real-estate deals in Paris. Do you know anything about him, François?"

Guerot was staring grimly into space. Victoire had the feeling that he was no longer there. She tried to bring him back to earth.

"If you want to know more about Maunay, you should contact this Omar Al Selim."

"We know him well, but I don't think that would be a good idea," Guerot replied. "Why don't you go see him? I have so few good people left who can do the type of intelligence gathering that's required in this kind of situation. We've got good cops and good engineers, but when it comes to politics and world strategics, it's beyond our capabilities these days. A formidable guy like Al Selim needs to be handled by someone sharp and intelligent."

Victoire appreciated the compliment and smiled.

"Tell him that you work for North Land. You're investigating the murder of an executive in a hotel in Nuuk. You've learned that he knew him. That'll sound credible for starters. Al Selim is used to talking with top-tier investigators. He's worked with us in the past as a go-between in financial and political matters. I can't tell you any more than that. We need him, and he needs us."

Victoire was seduced by the idea, but showed him her bandaged hands.

"Forgive me," he said. "I was forgetting that you can't drive because of your hands. I'll send an unmarked car to take you to Deauville, where Al Selim rents a suite year-round at the Hotel Normandy. The officer can take care of your security at the same time. After you come back, you can tell me what he knows about Maunay. We'll finally find out what he wanted to reveal."

Victoire smiled.

"You think Al Selim will agree to talk to me?"

"We'll see to it that he does," Guerot replied. "Speaking of which, how's John?"

"Good, but someone tried to kill him."

"No!" Guerot exclaimed.

Victoire told him about the bullet that grazed John's shoulder shortly before they arrived at Raphaelle. Guerot asked for details, but she couldn't provide them. John hadn't told her.

"What about your Little Luc?" the deputy director asked, watching the cat that was ignoring him as she sauntered past. "Where is he?"

"In the Morvan," Victoire replied. "You won't believe it, but Mary Harper from North Land has made several calls to a chalet there that belongs to Terre Noire!"

"Really?" Guerot asked, moving forward in his seat.

"Yes," Victoire said, taking pleasure in his reaction. "Mary Harper was no doubt trying to get in touch with Lanier after the collapse of Greenland."

"Why?" Guerot asked, disconcerted.

"We think that after that catastrophe, North Land wanted to get Terre Noire's advice on the causes and consequences of the cataclysm," Victoire replied.

"You think?"

"Of course!" she declared. "Now Mary Harper knows that Lanier's on the *Bouc-Bel-Air*."

"Are you sure about that?"

"We have confirmation," Victoire replied.

"From whom?"

"Connie Rasmussen, the legal advisor for the Northern Peoples Congress."

Guerot tapped his fingertips together, looking thoughtful.

"The Luc Martinet who published the article that mentioned Lanier—he's your Luc, isn't he?"

"Yes," Victoire admitted, hoping to be forgiven that little secret. She immediately added, "Connie Rasmussen really insisted that he publish it, and John got the green light from North Land."

"And you agreed?" Guerot said with a hint of a reproach.

"You'd like information about Lanier, wouldn't you? Connie happens to be on the same ship. She promised to keep us informed in exchange for publishing the article. You know better than I do how it works."

Guerot nodded as an affirmation. Intelligence was an ecosystem in which nothing was traded without something in return.

"What exactly is she looking for, this Danish woman?" he asked.

"We don't know."

Guerot observed the cat at Victoire's ankles. He roused himself from his thoughts and posed the awkward question she'd been waiting for.

"What's John doing on the ice cap twelve and a half miles from Haffner Bjerg? Why is he in that part of Greenland?"

Victoire noted the precision and remembered that John had given Guerot the means of tracking him all over the planet, thanks to the three little balls he'd had grafted onto his ear.

"He's looking for Abraham Harper, North Land's CEO."

"I don't get it anymore," Guerot replied sharply. "He spoke to me about protecting the daughter, not the father. Is this new?"

Victoire sensed that Guerot didn't appreciate being kept out of the loop. She replied, trying not to lie too much.

"He was hired to protect the daughter first, and then he was asked to find the father. One thing led to another. We hadn't expected the second assignment."

"And the father, where's he?"

"Somewhere in the Great Wound of the Wild Dog."

"Tell John that I'd like to hear from him more often. Just because he left Les Invalides, that doesn't mean he should be hiding things from us. His safety depends on it. I really don't want to have to come back here to find out what's going on."

"I'll get on him," Victoire replied, trying to smile as persuasively as possible.

Guerot got to his feet and picked up his sports bag.

"Thanks for the security," Victoire said. "And for the driver."

She showed him out.

"An officer will call you on my behalf. He's one of our most trust-worthy men. Your case is starting to cost us dearly, but I sense we're about to discover some interesting things. We'll cover expenses, but you'll give me the receipts, right?"

"Of course, François."

Luc put the phone away after his conversation with John. It was time to leave the Black Lands behind and get closer to the chalet where Isabelle Le Guévenec had taken refuge. The wind had blown away the mist, revealing patches of wet vegetation. He retraced his steps, taking care not to get lost, and went back to the dirt track.

Before staging his fake arrival, Luc followed John's advice: "Whenever you enter a new place, locate the exits first." John had taught him everything—how to spot the hidden hands, how to pick up smells in the air, how to look for cameras and bugging devices, how to determine shooting angles, and how to spot killers behind a secluded window. Moving upwind, he approached the chalet on tiptoe. He circled the house and located the kitchen. He studied all the windows. The attic overlooked a rotting haystack. A shed next to the chalet housed an old tractor.

He silently returned to his motorcycle. To give Isabelle Le Guévenec the impression that he'd only just arrived, he ran with the cycle for a few hundred yards before kickstarting the engine. He accelerated when he saw the chalet and pulled up at the front steps. Isabelle Le Guévenec opened the door and came out on the veranda.

"I wasn't expecting you so early, Little Luc."

"It didn't take as long as I thought it would to transfer the wounded *Bouc-Bel-Air* mates. The whole crew was fantastic. And I drove fast."

Isabelle Le Guévenec seemed more distant than in Le Havre. He went up the steps and contented himself with a peck on each cheek. The atmosphere had changed.

"Have a seat."

He sat down in a rocking chair opposite the fireplace where the fire he'd seen from outside was burning. The main room served as both a living room and a dining room and was furnished in a rustic style in keeping with the rugged region. On the sideboard, photos in leather frames had been turned around to face the wall. Isabelle didn't want him to see her family mementos. He was just a passing fancy, a breath of fresh air in a very full life.

"I've got some tea in the kitchen. Can I tempt you?"

Luc nodded and waited. Isabelle came back with the cups and a pitcher of milk. She put the tray on the coffee table in front of the fireplace and got straight to the point.

"Why didn't you tell me the truth in Le Havre?"

"What truth?" Luc replied innocently, wondering what particular lie he would have to wriggle out of.

"You've never worked for Terre Noire. You used a false identity to come and interview me. Why didn't you tell me you were the Luc Martinet who writes for future-probe.com?"

"Because you wouldn't have been yourself, Isabelle. I needed the truth."

"You've got some nerve, talking to me about truth!"

"Didn't you like my article about the two women of the Arctic?"

"It's very good, but you gave us a fright. With all that's going on, my husband's worried. Nicolas Lanier asked me to get out of Le Havre because of you and take refuge here. You're a monster."

"What is here, exactly?" asked Luc, as though he was starting another interview.

Isabelle Le Guévenec served the tea and put another log on the fire before she answered.

"Here is the Terres Noires, the Black Lands. This is where it all began at the turn of the twentieth century, when the Lanier and Brissac families discovered and explained a geological phenomenon that still amazes newcomers. There's a huge patch of quicksand a mile away. I don't know much about it, but I do know that the solid ground has yellow broom growing on it, and the quicksand has dark broom. Don't ask me why."

Luc didn't give a damn about the plants. What he had in mind was John's question about the revelations Christophe Maunay had very nearly made before he died.

"Isabelle, I'd like to do a story on your husband for future-probe. com. That guy is incredible."

"Really, writing profiles is an obsession with you!"

"Le Guévenec is a one-off. The Arctic falls on his head. He loses half of his crew. Then the bears attack the survivors. Lanier comes aboard—no one knows how. A helicopter crashes on his ship, killing Romain Brissac. Now he's off rescuing the shipwrecked victims of the *Narvik* under the hostile gaze of the legal adviser to the Northern Peoples Congress. You've got to admit, that's a lot for one man!"

Isabelle began to sob. Luc had just put both feet right in it.

"You can cry, Isabelle. Your husband's a fantastic guy."

"I was thinking of the helicopter. Of Romain."

"Ah, him too, obviously."

Luc had forgotten about Isabelle's liaison with the Nobel laureate and felt like a dolt. He spotted a box of tissues and handed her one. Then he tried clutching at straws. "Romain Brissac had some specific theories about the end of the Arctic and Greenland," Luc ventured cautiously. "His death might have been quite convenient for some people."

Isabelle looked up at him, the tears streaming down her face, and her hands clasped together on her knees. Luc felt that the moment had come.

"I'm sure Brissac's death is related to Maunay's," he declared earnestly.

Isabelle Le Guévenec walked over to the window and stared at the rain, which had started falling again. Then she spun around.

"You mean that creep Maunay might have sabotaged the helicopter that was supposed to evacuate Romain to the American base in Thule?"

"I'm afraid so," Luc confirmed. "The guy was a sleaze. From what I hear, he had to be hustled out of Gabon because of something he had gotten himself into. I think Maunay had his own men on the *Bouc-Bel-Air* and in Raphaelle. You have to ask your husband for the names of crew members who were in direct or indirect contact with him."

"Loïc would never give me such a list. He has never kept me abreast of his affairs," Isabelle confessed with bitter regret in her voice. "He's always taken me for a half-wit."

Luc took Isabelle's hands in his own.

"The person who murdered Romain is on the *Bouc-Bel-Air*."

"Do you really think so?"

"We ought to do it for Romain, for his memory."

Isabelle let another tear escape. It was followed by a sob.

"All right, I'll call Loïc. But I can't talk to him in the state I'm in. Have some cake. I'm going to freshen up."

Luc turned away. Outside, the weather wasn't getting any better. Forecasters had just placed the whole northern half of France on red alert.

ON BOARD THE *BOUC-BEL-AIR*, 2:50 P.M.

Loïc Le Guévenec felt a shooting pain in his lower back when he turned around to make sure no one was following him. Stuffed with analgesics and morphine to relieve the pain that just wouldn't go away, he was starting to lose all sense of time and space. He knocked the agreed number of times and waited. Nicolas Lanier finally cracked open the door.

The stench in the Terre Noire chairman's cabin was unbearable. Le Guévenec didn't know if he'd be able to carry on a conversation. What foul play was forcing Lanier to stay holed up in his cabin when the whole world knew he was on board? Ever the loyal captain, Le Guévenec avoided asking. Only one thing obsessed him: to take the *Bouc* back to Nuuk and then to Le Havre.

"So, Captain, where are we?" Lanier asked, motioning to the chair where he could sit.

"Not far from the shipwreck. But the sea's too strong. We're pitching too much to be effective."

"Still, it's good we could drag ourselves this far."

"I'd like to set a course for Nuuk."

"Go ahead, Captain," Lanier said, sounding exhausted.

"There's something else," Le Guévenec said.

He wasn't in the habit of mixing private matters with his official duties. Telling Lanier about the conversation he had just had made him very uncomfortable. But because Isabelle was in his boss's country house, he had to overcome his embarrassment.

"My wife just called. She'd like me to send her the names of the crew members who were connected in any way with the boatswain and Christophe Maunay. I know that might seem odd."

Le Guévenec registered Nicolas Lanier's surprised silence. Looking agitated, the head of Terre Noire stood up and went to the porthole. Then he turned around. "Do you have the list?" Lanier asked.

"After the boatswain's death, I went to retrieve his papers. I found a notebook with phone numbers and e-mail addresses. Some of them belonged to sailors on the *Bouc* and the *Marcq-en-Barœul*, such as Velot. There were also the names of other people, addresses, plans, and numbers."

"You never told me about this notebook."

"I only made the connection between Maunay, the boatswain, and Velot after the helicopter carrying Brissac was sabotaged. There was also a smartphone in the head seaman's cabin with a report about me and my wife. I put it back in its place to see whether someone else would come and get it."

"And someone else was interested in it?"

"Yes. Connie Rasmussen. She stole it. So she has to be linked to the boatswain in some way. I've unmasked her. I wanted to talk to you about that."

"What have you done?"

"Nothing for the moment. I wanted to see you before I did anything. We've got her for theft. I can arrest her without further ado and put her in irons. I'm awaiting your instructions."

Looking at the boss of the *Bouc* with admiration, Lanier stroked his beard. The old sea dog was obviously wilier than he looked. He had underestimated him.

"Don't do anything about Connie Rasmussen for the moment, and send a copy of the notebook to your wife."

Le Guévenec struggled to get up. His hip would have been operated on by now if Lanier hadn't sent them to Greenland. The idea that Isabelle might know more about this than he thought forced him to sit down again. He was short of breath.

"You don't trust your wife?" Lanier asked.

"Of course I do. But, well, I don't get it. How could she know?"

"Do what I tell you."

"What about the Danish woman?"

"Don't put her in irons. She could be useful."

For some days now, Le Guévenec had felt all of his certainties shatter, one by one. That the chairman of Terre Noire could provide Isabelle with ultraconfidential documents and forbid him to arrest Connie Rasmussen for stealing those same documents was throwing him completely.

When the time came, he'd vent his bitterness over the loan that Terre Noire had refused him for the purchase of the apartment in La Rochelle.

"I know that appearances can be misleading, but I'm like you, Captain. I'm steering Terre Noire through troubled waters. I'm skirting icebergs. Only I can't see the tips of mine. And as for radar, I'm forced to tinker. Maunay was supposed to be my radar. That's why I'm still lying low here like an animal. As long as I haven't identified the iceberg that's going to sink Terre Noire, I'll be your passenger. I can eat pasta and rice every day for as long as it takes. Don't fret about that. I have total confidence in your wife. She's a good person."

Le Guévenec nodded. Lanier was talking about a world he hadn't really mastered. Now he had to bring up one more disagreeable request.

"Connie Rasmussen has asked for the ship's plans. She wants to inspect the ship with Velot, the one who killed the bears. I've categorically opposed it, but like Isabelle, she knows you're here and has asked me to talk to you. You'd think they'd agreed on it together. What's more, there's a story on them on the Internet: 'The women of the Arctic.' Can you imagine?"

Nicolas Lanier ran a grubby hand through his hair. The captain's physical and mental state worried him. He was beginning to look like a bogeyman who'd been pulled out of Alberta's tar sands. "You handle ice better than women, Le Guévenec," he replied after a few seconds of silence.

"That's true," the seaman agreed, trying to smile.

"Give Connie Rasmussen the plans. In any case, we can't do anything else. Greenland is standing behind this lawyer. Maybe there's something else standing behind her, as well," Lanier added with a strange look.

"But, for heaven's sake, you're handing secrets over to the enemy!"

"Greenland isn't an enemy, Captain. It's a client. As for secrets, they're in the samples of ice this ship is carrying. Never has a ship carried knowledge so vital for humankind."

Le Guévenec made a painful effort to get up and walk to the door. He was clutching his back. Lanier stopped him just as he was leaving.

"Don't worry about your loan. I've issued instructions. You can buy whatever you like in La Rochelle, Loïc."

"Thank you...Nicolas."

THE GREAT WOUND OF THE WILD DOG, 3:15 P.M.

John stopped rowing a hundred yards from their landing spot. They hadn't sunk, and the lake hadn't opened and pulled them to the bottom. But the invisible menace was still there. The smell of gas was coming off the water again and making their heads spin. Two of the dogs were lying on their sides, panting and vomiting. And the methane emissions were beginning to make the other dogs sick, as well. Qaalasoq didn't say anything, but he was already the color of a corpse. John knew they couldn't stay on this deadly lake much longer.

What they were about to confront was just as unforeseeable as the dying of Greenland. The killer was probably waiting for them behind one of the snowcapped hills overlooking the ice they were going to land on. He would have no trouble picking them off one by one, like the tin ducks in a carnival shooting game.

With the help of his binoculars, John assessed the enemy's possible shooting positions. The bastard would kill them just before they landed, when they were still grouped together and vulnerable. That's what he, as a sharpshooter, would have done: destroy the enemy on his landing craft. Plan B was not landing in this place, but choosing a higher spot to the left or the right that would shield them from view. Then they'd have to do some climbing and take the enemy from the rear. Risky with just two exhausted men, sick dogs, and a sled they'd be forced to leave behind.

John analyzed his options: death by gas or death by gunfire.

"Can the dogs serve as infantry like they did in Raphaelle and attack first to flush out the enemy?" John asked Qaalasoq, who was lying on his stomach beside him.

"I think it's possible. With a bit of luck. But we can't stay here any longer. They'll die one by one. And we will too."

John realized that the sniper was most likely thinking the same thing.

"If I were in his place, I wouldn't let us land with the dogs ahead of us. I'd shoot now."

Qaalasoq reflected for a few seconds.

"He didn't see the dogs race off in pursuit at Raphaelle. I don't think he's an Inuit. I don't think he'd be expecting the dogs to attack."

"Let's go," John commanded.

Lying next to Qaalasoq, he took the old Remington that the Raphaelle leader, Gressin, had given him, and aimed it at the coast. The Inuit took the oars and paddled through the water at a clipped pace. Around them, the dogs that were still fit sat alert, like marine commandos ready to leap onto the beach and grab the enemy by the throat.

With his hand tight on the butt, John watched as the coast swiftly loomed closer. His heightened senses picked up the imminent danger. But it wasn't the one he had expected, and it was too late to change the plan and backpaddle. The first Zodiac ran aground on the tongue of ice, followed by the second. John and the dogs charged ahead, running to a sort of escarpment in the form of a snowdrift.

He realized too late that he'd landed in a trap as deadly as the gas chamber they'd just left behind. The sea of ice, weighed down with rocks, was hurtling into the lake at frightening speed. The ground under his feet was taking him back to the place where he'd landed. The killer hadn't run the risk of sitting in a defensive position on such shifting terrain. Hidden on the granite peaks of Haffner Bjerg, he was waiting for nature to do the job for him. John ran to Qaalasoq and helped him pull the sled off the Zodiac with the help of the dogs that were still able. Men and dogs pulled the load. John felt like they were going up a down escalator.

They managed to move ahead, leaving the sick animals behind. But exhausted by the crossing and the gas emissions, John knew they wouldn't be able to hold out much longer. In a few minutes, they'd be swallowed up on the very spot where they had landed. To the left and the right, unmoving rocky slopes framed the enormous escalator that was taking them back to the lake. Salvation lay there. The enemy lay there, as well. Six hundred and fifty yards of moving ice divided the two walls. The killer was on one of them. John didn't want to get it wrong.

While pulling on the rope like a maniac, John assessed the enemy's strategy. If he'd been the sniper, he'd have made sure he had the sun at his back. So the killer was on the left, between them and the dying light of the sun. He chose to go right and get out of the firing line, praying he was making the right choice.

"This way!" he yelled to Qaalasoq.

Men and beasts managed to reach a patch of ground on the side of the enormous tongue that wasn't moving as quickly as the middle. They made enough progress to get away from the lake and finally reach ice that seemed to be stable.

"One more effort," John said.

They hoisted the sled and its load over a gigantic granite ridge. On the other side, they were shielded from the line of fire. Exhausted, they stretched out with the dogs on a rock formation that was warmed by the sun. Slowly, they stopped panting. And then they felt it: the ground beneath their shoulder blades and their shattered backs was shaking.

Behind them, the glacier shrieked as it hurled itself into the lake. The sound of rocks being ground and ice being crushed accompanied the roar of the vast bloodletting that was putting Haffner Bjerg to death. Even in Afghanistan, John had never heard the mountains cry out.

ON THE BRIDGE OF THE BOUC-BEL-AIR, *3:35 P.M.*

Connie Rasmussen made headway by clutching the handrails. Through his binoculars, the stooped captain was watching the rescue operations on the ships in the *Narvik*'s flotilla. The wind was blowing across the patched-up bridge. The roiling sea was making the ship pitch. In the distance, low clouds were flowing over the water. Le Guévenec turned around, grimacing with pain.

"Madame Rasmussen, you didn't tell me the Northern Peoples Congress had chartered Norwegian ships."

"I didn't know, Captain. I'm just a lawyer, and maritime chartering isn't my responsibility."

Le Guévenec stopped watching the rescue operation for a second and turned to the Valkyrie disguised as the Little Red Riding Hood of the Arctic.

"What's your game, Madame Rasmussen?"

"A dangerous one, Captain."

"I'm sure."

Connie held on tight. The *Bouc* had just taken a breaker on the starboard side. Big waves came crashing down on the foredeck. Le Guévenec, imperturbable, looked at the stern once more.

"We won't be taking part in the rescue," he said with a hint of regret. "Your friends are taking care of it. We're in too bad a shape. I'm setting a course for Nuuk."

"Do you have the plans I asked you for, Captain?"

Le Guévenec brought his hand down to a built-in drawer and took out a blue plastic pouch, which he held out to Connie without letting go.

"If it were just up to me, I wouldn't give you these."

"I know. But you've spoken to Lanier, and he ordered you to. Those around you think very highly of you, Captain. You're one in a million."

The captain of the *Bouc-Bel-Air*, troubled and exhausted, felt himself go weak. He replied in an almost inaudible voice, "Why do you need the plans?"

"So as not to get lost on board. I'm sailing in troubled waters. I'm like you."

Le Guévenec pulled up the collar of his battered pea jacket. They could talk about global warming all they liked, but here the air was getting colder. This was yet another mystery he couldn't fathom. Connie Rasmussen took the pouch containing the ship's plans and planted a kiss on the captain's cheek. She left the bridge before Le Guévenec, scuppered by her lipstick, could change his mind and take them back.

She found Velot in his cabin and gave him the plastic pouch. The Frenchman took out the plans and hastily unfolded them over the bunk. He turned the sheets over, one by one, until he located the ones for the engine room.

"Here are the slots for the scuttling devices."

Connie leaned over the drawing and saw, under the sailor's filthy finger, the two circles in the hull on each side of the drive shaft where the explosives would go.

"How long till we've left the rescue zone?" Velot asked the lawyer.

"Half an hour," Connie replied.

"This stinking tub will go down before that," the Frenchman said with a nasty smile. "It's going to take Lanier and that old goat Le Guévenec on a voyage to the bottom of the ocean. There's a Zodiac in the shed on the foredeck. That'll do for the two of us and your Inuit bodyguard."

Things were taking a nasty turn. Velot folded up the engine room plans again and put them back in the pouch. Then he addressed Connie.

"Is your bodyguard armed?" he asked.

"I have no idea. Why do you ask?"

"There's still an engineer in the engine room. We'll be forced to get rid of him. I can do it with my bare hands, but a weapon would be better."

"Indeed," Connie.

Velot straightened and went to the porthole to watch the launches from the *Copenhagen* that were assisting the shipwrecked *Narvik*. Then he turned around.

"I know where there's a weapon."

"Where?" asked Connie.

"In the boatswain's cabin."

"Where in the cabin?" she asked, her heart beating like the damaged boiler of the *Bouc-Bel-Air*.

"In one of the closets. Maybe with the underwear. Let's go."

Connie nodded and spun on her heels. She'd go whole hog to gain control of the situation.

Dun-les-Places, L'Huis-Laurent Chalet, 7:55 p.m.

Luc couldn't believe his eyes as he copied the message Isabelle had received on her phone. What Le Guévenec had found when he went through the boatswain's things was extremely interesting. The list of addresses in Oslo, Copenhagen, Nuuk, Paris, and Le Havre attested to powerful logistics. He recognized the numbers for the Hôtel Louxor and the bar of the Saint-James swimming pool. The numbers in Nuuk had to correspond to places John had visited. Per Sorensen, Rox Oa, and Sylvain Velot were just the tip of the iceberg. Luc had no way of knowing who the other numbers belonged to. He checked to see if the number of the chalet in the Morvan was on the list and was relieved when he didn't find it. Fermatown had just put its finger on a powerful international network of swift and dirty killers.

"This is fascinating," Luc said.

Isabelle Le Guévenec looked at him with a strange smile. It was a look he hadn't seen on her before.

"I suppose you're going to ask me about the connection between Terre Noire, which owns this chalet, and Mary Harper, who tried to get hold of someone here. Because you haven't come all this way just to see me, have you?"

Luc was about to answer when the door handle moved slightly. A shadow passed in front of the window. Isabelle stiffened in fear. Luc quickly signaled the plan.

"The attic!"

He took her by the hand and pulled her toward the stairs that led to the top of the chalet. They'd just reached the last step when the thunder of automatic rifles split their eardrums and shattered doors and windows. Luc secured the hatch.

He gestured to the opening and pointed to the black plastic tarpaulin covering the haystack. They held hands and jumped. After running across the wet grass, they penetrated the forest, heading in the direction of the Yórévé dolmen. It was impossible to retrieve the motorcycle. The enemy had blocked off the road to Dun-les-Places. Leaping over ferns and bushes. Luc told himself that Isabelle was hiding something important, all the same, something that might explain why they'd come to kill him.

Who knew he was in the Morvan? He quickly went through the possibilities while he was running. Then he had to stop and catch his breath. The weapons had gone silent. Exhausted and bathed in sweat, Luc asked Isabelle if she was all right. She nodded. She, too, had to be asking herself a whole heap of questions. What if the killers had come for her? What secret was this woman carting around? No longer winded, they ran another hundred feet or so before diving into the trees again.

It was Isabelle who now guided their escape. They crossed a clearing and soon came within sight of the Yórévé dolmen. No one seemed to be chasing them. When they were only a few dozen yards from the dolmen, Isabelle stopped and cocked her ear. Nothing.

A minute later, they were sitting side by side under the huge stone table. The rain had started falling again. He wrapped his arms around her and scanned the forest. Like an imbecile, he'd left his gun in the motorcycle. The killers had burst in just when she was about to tell him something that John absolutely had to know. He pulled her closer and whispered in her ear, "You were going to tell me about Terre Noire and Mary Harper."

"Abraham Harper is Nicolas Lanier's father. Mary is Nicolas's half sister."

"You're joking! How do you know?"

"Lanier told Romain Brissac, and he told me. Nicolas and Romain had no secrets from each other."

"And Abraham's paternity makes the situation tricky?"

"The trouble started when Mary Harper learned at L'École des Mines that the man she'd fallen in love with was her half brother."

"Geraldine Harper knew?"

"She'd known for a long time. Abraham used to go to a lot of international conferences on scientific prospecting, like the one today in Nuuk.

He met Emmanuelle Lanier at one of them. One thing led to another, and soon enough, he had fathered a child with her. I've always wondered if it was out of love or if it wasn't a kind of investment. Abraham's a funny coot. He's a hard man, but also a visionary who's always been twenty years ahead of everyone else. You've never met him?"

"I've only seen him in photos," Luc replied.

"Harold, the Harpers' son, has a degenerative brain disease that means he won't be taking over for his father at the helm of North Land. I think Abraham found that very painful, and he decided to form an alliance with Terre Noire before one actually existed by making a son at the company he didn't have the means to buy out. It was sort of an investment in the future."

"Why do you say an alliance before it actually existed?"

"Because North Land and Terre Noire were supposed to announce their merger at the meeting on global warming in Nuuk."

"Romain Brissac was for it?"

"Romain and Nicolas have always done everything together. They both supported the merger."

"Why are they trying to kill us?"

"Together, the two companies hold such a reserve of knowledge, they're close to becoming the planet's most formidable decision makers. Not everyone's happy about the merger."

"Notably the Norwegian, Thor Johannsen, and his Russian and Icelandic allies, right? They don't want France, Denmark, and Canada to have a monopoly," Luc said, proud of his political science.

Isabelle gave him an admiring look.

"You understand almost everything, Little Luc."

"Why do you say almost?"

"There's also the thing Maunay wanted to talk about—that's why Lanier's still hiding on the *Bouc* with Loïc. How are we going to escape this trap?"

"I'll just get out the Yellow Pages."

THE GREAT WOUND OF THE WILD DOG, 4:10 P.M.

John advised Luc to call the police. Honestly, you had to explain everything to these young people. Then he turned to Qaalasoq, who was lying at his side on the rocky slope. The Inuit looked as far away as the sky above their heads. Behind the ridge that was shielding them from the killer, the ice kept plummeting into the lake, making the mountain tremble. A hundred and twenty feet below, the alarming surface of the new Dead Sea stretched to infinity.

John had to shout to make himself heard. "Did you know Abraham Harper was Nicolas Lanier's father?"

Yes," Qaalasoq replied without moving an inch.

"Does that pose a problem?"

"It has posed a problem ever since Mary found out that Lanier is her half brother. She found out a month ago."

John saw himself at the Ritz with Geraldine, who seemed strangely satisfied with his looks and his bearing even before he'd uttered a word. Mary's words at L'École des Mines came back to him. "My mother chose you so I'd sleep with you, but there's no chance of that."

"Basically, Geraldine Harper chose me so Mary would get interested in someone other than her brother! I'm a way of taking her mind off things. I'm the rabbit they pulled out of the hat to keep the little one amused."

Qaalasoq sat up and smiled.

"Don't be annoyed."

"I think you've spent a lot of time and money for me to come up here and risk my neck just to distract a kid who spends her time avoiding me like the plague. It's pretty dumb, your little ploy, even if it pays well."

Qaalasoq cautiously climbed to the top of the ridge to see if the killer was attempting a crossing. Reassured, he turned to John.

"You're not here just to play babysitter or Romeo. There are more serious things awaiting you. I think you've figured that out."

"Yes," John replied grumpily.

The noise of an engine made them lift their heads. A helicopter had emerged from behind a cloud on the horizon and was heading toward them. John tightened his grip on the rifle and watched closely, ready to fight for dear life. He was scarcely reassured when Qaalasoq shouted, "It's one of ours."

John recognized the national colors of Greenland on the fuselage. The machine stabilized, hovering six hundred feet above them. Then it launched a missile straight at them. The object, as big as a football, bounced several times on the slope of Haffner Bjerg before stopping a few yards from their position. It exploded like a grenade, releasing a stream of red smoke into the air.

"They're marking us," John shouted. "They're measuring the direction and the speed of the wind. It's the police. They've come to arrest us for the murder of Christophe Maunay. We'll never know what happened to Abraham Harper."

John was frustrated but also relieved. They would escape the killer and the deadly geological traps of this country. Long live the police, he told himself. The Sikorski was too heavy to touch down on the steep slope. It descended and then hovered about forty feet above an area of gravelly rock. A man in uniform appeared at the door and signaled to them to climb toward a sloping ledge that was out of sight less than a mile away.

"He wants us to go up," John shouted. "He can't put down here. The slope is too steep."

Qaalasoq nodded to indicate that he understood and started to climb. With the help of the dogs, they pulled the sled over the rocks. John realized there was no point now in wearing themselves out with the sled. He signaled to Qaalasoq to abandon it and its load. The Inuit started waving his arms and shouting in the direction of the helicopter. John immediately understood and started shouting with him. The Sikorski started to bank over the lake.

"No! No!" they shouted.

John tried desperately to get the pilot to understand that he was heading straight for death. The machine had already executed half an elegant turn over the water when yellow and bluish sparks escaped from the jet pipe. Oblivious to the danger, the pilot calmly began circling back.

The methane in the lake burst into flames in one big whoosh. John and Qaalasoq watched as the pilot tried to gain speed to escape disaster. It was a fatal mistake. The acceleration of the turbines only spiked the heat. A blue-tinged halo surrounded the Sikorski. It was like a pot on the burner of a malfunctioning stove. A fireball lit up the interior of the cabin, imprinting the blackened silhouettes of the pilot and co-pilot against an orange background. Then came the explosion and the crash. The impact only intensified the blaze. John and Qaalasoq took in the scene. The fire was setting mile after mile of water ablaze.

A gigantic flare rose into the sky, blocking the horizon in a wall of fire. Very quickly, it seemed to suck up all the air. They had to climb to the peak of the crest to breathe. Stumbling over the rocks, they got themselves and the dogs to the sloping ledge that the crew of the Sikorski had signaled them to go to. Drained and sweaty and their skin burning, they dropped to the ground and lay with their faces against the rock. The biggest firewall the world had ever known slowly settled down and finally went out.

And finally, they dared to raise their heads and get to their feet. What they saw terrified them more than ever.

The lake had dropped a good hundred or so yards in a few minutes, boring an immense circular crater. The void that the fire had left was a vision of horror. Behind the ridge, the sea of ice had turned into a roaring waterfall. They were standing above an unimaginable underworld. John sat down again and placed his gloveless hands on the burning-hot rocks. It was the dogs that understood first. Leaping and whining, they warned the men of the new danger.

John felt a dampness and then water running under his fingers. The thin trickle became heavier, as though a stream was springing up beneath their feet. John and Qaalasoq turned around at the same time to look at the mountain peak. A wall of mud was coming down the slopes of Haffner Bjerg toward the lake. The hideous mass, the khaki-brown of an Alpine hunter's outfit, was sending rocks in all directions.

They abandoned everything and raced with the dogs to the ridge that divided the sea of ice from the river of mud hurtling toward them. With undreamed-of strength, they managed to climb the few dozen yards to the top of the ridge. John turned around and couldn't believe his eyes. The mudslide, as wide as a river in the tropics and about twenty feet high, now covered the spot where they'd been only a few seconds before. A dog that had injured its leg had stayed behind. He looked up at John. Too late. The terror he read in the dog's eyes was too much to bear. John looked away. The mud swept everything away in a frightening din. He saw the sled, crushed like a wisp of straw, disappear, along with their equipment.

Clinging to the ground with the surviving dogs, they lay motionless and mute, beyond thought.

PARIS, 18 RUE DEPARCIEUX, 8:35 P.M.

Despite her bandaged hands, Victoire was back to brushing Caresse. The familiar chore was a balm for her nerves.

"Don't worry, baby, the brutes are busy elsewhere."

She finally released the Persian and went back to analyzing the boatswain's notebook. The extracted data was displayed on the wall. In less than ten seconds, the software that connected them to another database had drawn up a logistical map of the network that was seeking to wipe them out.

The targets and potential meeting places appeared on GPS surveys and geographic maps. Victoire immediately recognized the square formed by the streets around them—Deparcieux, Fermat, Daguerre, and Froidevaux—and felt acute fear at her fingertips. Thanks to the program, she identified Isabelle Le Guévenec's apartment in Le Havre, the chalet in the Morvan, the Hôtel Louxor and the Saint-James Club in Paris, an isolated house on the edge of a fjord in Nuuk, Connie Rasmussen's cottage on the coast of Denmark, Terre Noire's headquarters on the Champs-Elysées, and North Land's base in Montreal. And last, Mary Harper's student digs, on the Boulevard Saint-Michel. The bastards were also interested in the North Land heiress.

Rox Oa must have shared with the other members of the network a series of objectives that covered targets to be eliminated or hideouts to lie low in. Half a dozen maps resisted her efforts to identify them. Too many possibilities. Nothing looked more like a fashionably leafy Australian suburb than a housing development in Montigny-le-Bretonneux.

She tried one last time and relaunched the program. Her eyes nearly popped out of her head when she saw the photo identifying one particular address. The touch wall brought up the façade of a glass building that was all too familiar. She recognized the Hôpital Léopold-Bellan at 21 Rue Jean-Zay in the fourteenth arrondissement. What connection could there possibly be between these assholes and that establishment, less than five minutes from her door? Driven by fear and curiosity, she left the house, coming out at 9 Rue Fermat. After crossing the Avenue du Maine, she found herself outside the hospital entrance. She strode confidently inside.

The smiling authority, which she used to cover massive fear, worked like a charm, as usual. The young woman at the reception desk responded to her smile. Victoire pushed one of the doors open with her elbow and found herself in a corridor enveloped in semidarkness. Without knowing exactly where she was going, she strode on purposefully. Passing a laundry room, she grabbed a pink patient's gown and slipped it over her clothes. She then saw that it was her bandages, not her assumed authority, that made the task easy. She felt a bit annoyed about that, but only briefly. Her killer had done her a favor by forcing her to walk around with wrapped hands.

With its discreet architecture, the Léopold-Bellan hospital was in a neighborhood of modern buildings between the Place de Catalogne and the Gare Montparnasse. Victoire had walked past it several times without realizing what it was. She stopped in front of a map beside the elevator and examined it. For want of knowing what she was actually looking for, she decided to go to the top of the building and come down again, inspecting each floor along the way. When she reached the sixth floor, she completed her disguise by slipping her arm into a sling plucked from a storage room. She quietly opened the door of the first room and apologized to the woman, who was half asleep.

Going from room to room, she realized that the sixth floor was reserved for women. When she got to the fifth floor, Victoire came upon a door code that barred access to a security wing. She took out her smartphone, activated the touch-wear detection app, and directed the camera to the keypad. In less than ten seconds, the software suggested six codes in order of diminishing probability. The second attempt was a success. Victoire pushed the door, looking at the floor to avoid leaving her portrait in the security camera's field. She had no choice, anyway. She had to clear up any doubt about the threat lurking less than five hundred and fifty yards from Fermatown.

In the middle of the corridor, two rooms with walls of glass faced each other. Victoire immediately thought of the isolation wards for patients with serious infections. She advanced cautiously and saw that the room on the right was occupied. An old man in pajamas was lying in bed with an oxygen mask over his face. Sitting next to him, another man wearing a surgeon's mask seemed alert and on guard. Victoire stood on tiptoe and saw that he had both hands in a plastic bag. No prizes for guessing he was a bodyguard hiding a weapon in the biodegradable bag from the local bookstore.

Her cell phone vibrated in her pocket. She stepped back down the hall and took the call.

"It's Thomas," the caller announced.

"Thomas?"

"I'm down below at your place. François Guerot sent me."

Victoire suddenly remembered the driver who was supposed to take her to Deauville to grill Al Selim.

"I'm coming right away," she replied.

She was sure, though, that she had buried an image or a memory of the Léopold-Bellan somewhere in her brain. Fear and fatigue were dulling her faculties—even her limbs. Her legs could hardly carry her. Victoire dumped the patient's robe and sling in a laundry cart and went down the stairs. She reached the bottom floor and left the building. Outside she waited for the light to change and crossed the Avenue du Maine.

Dun-les-Places, Yorévé dolmen, 8:50 p.m.

Luc called the Château-Chinon police again to find out where they were. The officer on duty told him that the patrol car had gotten stuck on a forest road and then had blown out two tires on the dilapidated wooden bridge that crossed the torrent.

"We can't possibly send a helicopter in this weather. We'll see what we can do, but the weather's only getting worse."

Luc and Isabelle were caught between forbidding topography and weather and killers who'd stop at nothing. He realized that he should never have used his phone. John had taught him that any smartphone, even when switched off, could be used to locate the user. Ever-cheaper software enabling this sleight of hand was available on the Internet. They might not be able to decode his conversation, but they could find him. Suddenly, yellow light pierced the darkness between the bushes. The big flat stone over their heads blew apart under a burst of semi-automatic fire. Petrified, her face covered in blood, Isabelle huddled against him. He grabbed her by the arm and started running headlong into the darkness.

Ferns as sharp as knives cut into their skin. They nearly slipped several times on the moss and the thick carpet of wet pine needles. All Luc knew was that they were going down a slope. Isabelle took over.

"This way."

He let himself be guided, lungs on fire, to a sort of path surrounded by menacing shadows that suddenly loomed taller. They were going down, toward the edge of a shoulder. As Isabelle instructed, they leaped into a void and fell on top of each other. They were on the forest road.

"Over there," Isabelle pointed.

They reached a boggy area, and Luc recognized the barbed-wire fence. Fully exposed, they followed the rusty enclosure and came under another burst of semiautomatic fire just as they were stepping inside the gate. The enemy had spotted them but was still a way off and was aiming badly. The wire fence whined and shook as the bullets hit it. Isabelle ripped up the "Danger of Death" sign, and they kept going.

"Follow my footsteps exactly."

Luc did so without protest. Isabelle was racing ahead on a kind of natural checkerboard full of broom. In the moonlight, he noticed the differences in the color of the bushes. It came back to him. Certain bushes spelled death, and others salvation. His heart stopped beating when Isabelle hesitated between two paths in the middle of the Terres Noires.

"If I get stuck, you step back right away."

Luc's body ached from the tension. They crouched with the third burst of gunfire. The bullets hit the moss not far from their feet and made sucking and gurgling noises as they sank into the ground. Isabelle set off again. They reached an embankment and began to climb it, with Isabelle in the lead. Then came the fourth burst of fire.

"Over..."

Luc saw the blood spurt from Isabelle's back before she crumpled to the ground. He gathered her up and finished the climb to the top of the embankment, where he gently laid her on the ground. Isabelle Le Guévenec was smiling, amazed and at rest. He hugged her body and cried. She had gone without a word, like a cut flower. When he raised his head over the ridge again, he saw the men running toward him. He'd fight with his bare hands and die, too, like a soldier. John would be proud of him. The two killers bounded forward to attack the hundred or so yards between them and the slope.

Suddenly they were sinking between two clumps of broom. They looked at each other in shock and disbelief, as though it was some kind of joke. But for a million years, the Terres Noires of the Morvan had been no laughing matter. The two men didn't really grasp what was happening until their legs had completely disappeared in the mossy muck. Desperate, they grabbed what they could to save themselves. All they found was lichen.

Luc watched in the cold moonlight from the top of the embankment as the two men frantically tried to hoist themselves out of the abyss that was sucking them down faster and faster. Soon all that remained were their two panic-stricken faces. Then they disappeared in a gurgling of mud bombarded by the rain, which was coming down harder. Soaked to the bone, Luc returned to Isabelle, who was waiting for him on the other side, in a new world.

All of a sudden, he heard the improbable sound of a harpsichord and leaned over her body. He took the phone out of the last dress Isabelle Le Guévenec would ever wear, and the screen lit up with a message: "I've just got my loan for La Rochelle. Now that Romain has gone, I'm wondering if we might not be able to start fresh. Your Loïc."

Luc switched the thing off and closed Isabelle's eyes with infinite tenderness. The rain was coming down harder still. He wept like a child.

Josephine, 5:55 p.m.

John and Qaalasoq were now within sight of Josephine, after an exhausting trek over the slopes of Haffner Bjerg. They stopped a hundred yards from a pyramid made of plastic, reinforced along the ribs with steel plates. A greenish light coming from the depths lit up the mouth, which was ten feet high and as wide as a road. Around it, the deformed icy landscape resembled the canyons of Colorado.

"What's the green light coming out of that hole?" John asked.

"Algae."

John nodded and studied the area. To their left, the summit of Haffner Bjerg was lost in the mist. Behind them, the ice cap was now just a jumble of drift ice and methane eruptions. Rifle in hand, he studied every detail of the terrain for a long while. The killer was waiting for them behind the misty mountain slopes or in the bowels of the ice, behind the opening. Qaalasoq crouched and stroked the rocks. He stood up and delivered the verdict.

"There was still ice here two hours ago."

"What does that mean?"

"The land is changing from minute to minute."

"Is this really where Abraham Harper made his last phone call?" John asked, trying to guess where the attack would come from.

Qaalasoq pointed to the way they had just come. "Abraham made his last call from the sled a mile before he got here. That was last week. There was still ice here then, and snow."

"He was heading here, wasn't he?"

"Of course."

Qaalasoq lowered his eyes and observed the scrawny dogs lying on the snowless rocks. He finally lifted his head and said in a low voice, "I have faith in you."

"It's not going to be easy."

John couldn't take his eyes off this portal that opened into the world below. He knew he wouldn't escape and felt something like rage. They couldn't go back. They'd come to the end of the road.

"I assume Abraham went in. Do you think he's still alive?"

"An Inuit hunter could last a week without eating in those depths. Abraham Harper, despite his age, is a force of nature. He could still be alive and waiting for us."

"Have you been here before?"

"Yes. There's a tunnel that slopes gently down to two thousand feet. The station's fully automated. Down there is where Terre Noire gets its ice core samples measuring tens of thousands of years of cooling and warming."

John was a soldier by training, but courage had its limits. The idea of taking a bullet to the head with his first few steps inside didn't really thrill him.

"Send out a dog as a scout," he suggested.

Qaalasoq untied the fittest of his faithful huskies and spoke in his ear. The dog ran over the rocks and disappeared into the green glow that marked the entrance to Terre Noire's last subglacial base. The seconds passed, then minutes. Then the wait became unbearable. Around them, the surviving dogs growled and bared their fangs, eyes glued to the entrance.

"They can smell something," Qaalasoq said.

"Me too."

The dog reappeared at the entrance and ran back to them, throwing panic-stricken glances all around. He went to his master and lay at his feet, whimpering. Qaalasoq bent down and gently lifted his head. John saw terror in his eyes. Then the dog raised himself to the attack position.

"Get the dogs in formation, and keep your distance from me. If you hear shots, get down. Wait for orders. Don't be a hero."

All it takes is one idiot, John thought.

As if they'd understood the maneuver, the dogs lined up between the two men. At the signal, they all advanced in orderly fashion toward the plastic pyramid. Chests and muzzles gave off curls of condensation. No barrage of artillery interrupted their march over the loose stones. The closer they got, the more unbearable the atmosphere became. They were thirty yards from the door. The moment to close ranks was approaching. But grouped together, they'd be more vulnerable. John decided to compensate for that weakness by acting quickly and ordered the assault. Man and beast hurtled forward, and together, they dove into the tunnel.

The tunnel was big enough to accommodate two trucks side-by-side. They raced ahead, ready to fight, then stopped, mesmerized by the spectacle. Green algae was clinging to the ice. Much of it was dead on the ground, giving off a stench that recalled the gas emissions they'd breathed earlier. Facing them, a transparent cabinet six and a half feet tall and twenty inches deep housed a whole high-tech system in working order. Computers and screens blinked behind dark bulletproof glass. Cables of every color ran out of the cabinet and into the ground and the ceiling. Humidity sensors, seismographs, and barometers sat cheek by jowl with tape recorders and supercomputers.

"This is where your compatriots study the causes and effects of the Anthropocene," Qaalasoq said.

John decided to put off till later any explanations regarding the latest climate age of humanity. None of what he could see could have frightened the scout dog so dramatically. The tunnel extended beyond the cabinet. On either side, a thin trickle of water ran down toward

Greenland's sick insides. They advanced cautiously and, after a hundred-yard bend, came upon the unthinkable.

John saw the two human heads first, blackened by cold and death. The two pairs of eyes were watching a camera mounted on a tripod three yards from the monstrous assemblage. The murderer had filmed the scene and left a sentinel behind. There were dogs, too. The severed limbs of the men and the dogs formed the eight legs of this hideous montage that pushed the limits of barbarity way beyond madness. Around them, the frightened dogs barked and fled, abandoning them to their fate.

The tortured faces were unrecognizable. White stones had been stuck in the eye sockets, replacing the victims' ripped-out eyes. It was impossible to know whether they were Abraham Harper and his guide.

Feeling sick, John thought back to the tupilaq Qaalasoq had given him.

"Is it them?"

Qaalasoq had fallen to his knees.

"So this is a real tupilaq?"

Qaalasoq turned to him.

"The tupilaq is a myth. There has never been such savagery in Greenland. That was actually why we got you up here. Only a foreigner could understand. A barbarian."

The click made them jump. The camera had just done a half circle on its tripod and was filming them. Someone, maybe on the other side of the planet, was fabricating a story after having dreamed up a monster. They were trapped. John turned toward the entrance of the tunnel and knew he hadn't gotten it wrong. One of the dogs came back to them, breathless and bleeding from the mouth.

"The bastard's killing the dogs. He's poisoning them!"

Mad with rage, Qaalasoq rushed toward the mouth of the tunnel to save his dogs. "No!" John yelled. "That's exactly what he's waiting for!"

It was too late. The force of the bullet spun the Inuit around. The second shot went through his head and took off the back of his skull. Blood and brains spilled over the curved ice walls. There was nothing left to do now but try to survive.

John crouched behind the glass cabinet and pointed his rifle at the exit. He was on his own now on the dying ice cap, with only a child's toy to defend himself against his enemy's powerful weaponry. The echoing shots had blasted open a technical data file at the back of his brain. The demonic piece of shit waiting for him on the other side was armed with an FR F2 precision rifle that fired 7.62-caliber bullets that were no doubt grooved to increase the damage. It was a French weapon the Taliban had gotten hold of, thanks to oil money.

Lying on his back, eyes wide open, Qaalasoq smiled, finally at rest.

ON BOARD THE BOUC-BEL-AIR, 6:40 P.M.

Connie Rasmussen took her courage in both hands and knocked on the door. Sylvain Velot appeared. The Inuit bodyguard was standing behind the sailor.

"Well?" the Frenchman asked.

"I went through everything, but I didn't find anything. Le Guévenec must have cleaned up and confiscated the gun."

She tried to smile stupidly, overcoming the fear that was gnawing her guts. She could feel the steel revolver against the small of her back, where she'd slipped it between her shirt and the belt of her pants. Velot and the bodyguard looked worried. The time had come to pose the question that most interested the Danish government.

"I'm not sure that Laura Al-lee-Ah is okay with this sabotage."

"Laura's not the one who gives the orders. It's her husband."

At last Connie had the answer, duly noted on the recorder she was carrying in one of her pockets. She followed them closely and saw that they were armed with iron bars. Knowing what they intended to do was making her sick.

It seemed like every piece of metal in the *Bouc-Bel-Air* was groaning as the vessel braved the increasingly heavy waves. The vessel was also shaking badly. Suddenly Connie knew. They were going to sink the ship off the coast of Sondre Stromfjord, a chasm over sixty-five hundred feet deep.

They didn't see anyone. The few members of the crew who were still able-bodied were with the captain or in the hold, trying to secure a snowplow that had broken its moorings in the rough sea. It was rocking back and forth like a battering ram with each rise and fall of the ship and would surely punch a hole in the hold if it continued. Given everything that was happening, maybe Velot wouldn't need the scuttling cartridges. Three years before, during a secret briefing at the Kastellet fortress in Copenhagen, Hanne Jorth, the charismatic head of the Danish Defense Intelligence Service, had been very clear. "Connie, I want you to infiltrate Greenland's inner circle and find out what the new government is up to. I expect the same kind of excellent work that you did when you penetrated that neo-Nazi cell, Club 88. This time, it's more serious and more dangerous."

Thanks to her cover as a legal adviser and to her great-grandfather's prestige, she hadn't had any trouble winning Laura Al-lee-Ah's trust. Also, the new government was aware of its vulnerability and didn't want to burn its bridges with the country that had bestowed such lavish subsidies on the new republic.

With the financial crisis and the consequences of global warming, things had taken an unforeseen turn. The Norwegians, who were allies of the Russians and the Icelanders, had gained the upper hand over the supporters of Denmark and Canada. Laura Al-lee-Ah and Thor Johannsen had largely contributed to this development, even if the couple had come apart at the seams. Had she contributed to that by chasing Thor Johannsen, even though nothing had happened between them?

For a few months now, Denmark's economic and political interests had been melting as fast as the ice sheets of Siberia and Greenland. The French couldn't be trusted, even though there were allies within Terre Noire. According to Hanne Jorth, the French just weren't reliable, prone as they were to internal disagreements that made relations with Paris fraught. At Kastellet, contact with Hubert de Méricourt's agency was Hanne Jorth's responsibility.

As she moved past the kitchens, Connie slipped on garbage that had been knocked over, and she almost fell. She tried to grab whatever she could for support. Then a wave hit the ship, and she was thrown against a wall. Connie felt the gun ram her spine and knew she would have a bruise. The descent into the bowels of the *Bouc* was interminable, but finally they made it to the last gangway. Velot punched the code and opened the door of the airlock. All three went in. The sailor closed the door behind them before unlocking and opening the second door giving access to the platform. They were now thirteen feet above the engine room.

"I'll go down first," Velot said.

Ever since he had killed the two bears, Velot had become popular with the crew. Of course, shooting the animals had been premeditated. It was meant to weaken Terre Noire's image and foil the merger with North Land. Good manners among the economic and political players in the Arctic Circle were a thing of the past.

Connie followed the two men down the ladder and onto the waterlogged floor of the engine room. They were heading toward the man in blue overalls, the chief engineer, who was watching over the only engine in working order. He glanced at the three visitors, his face smeared with oil and grease. Connie thought she detected a vague smile on his lips. She didn't have time to do anything.

The two iron bars came crashing down. Blood spurted over the tubes and apparatuses that measured fluids and pressure. The chief engineer's face was soon no more than a bloody pulp. Connie watched as he collapsed at the foot of his machine. His legs stirred and then stopped after one last convulsion. Connie was stunned and petrified by the speed and brutality of the attack. She could not force herself to use the gun. When would she have the courage to shoot the two agents from the Russian-Norwegian alliance? All of Denmark was behind her.

Velot and the Inuit bodyguard had moved closer to the hull. Thanks to the plans, the Frenchman had located the first circular slot. She watched as Velot put the explosive device into the cavity and fiddled with the detonator. She absolutely had to gather her wits and keep these bastards from sending the *Bouc* to the bottom of the sea. She managed to take her eyes off the victim and rejoined the two men as they were installing the second device on the starboard side.

"How long?" she asked, trying to hide her rising panic.

"Half an hour," Velot replied. "That'll give us plenty of time to go back down and put the Zodiac out to sea."

Connie nodded, trying to look pleased and keep them off guard. She intended to act with the same brutality that they had shown and blow them away without pity. The unconscionable murder of the engineer had finally wiped away any of her remaining qualms. She was on her own, and she had free rein as the custodian of Denmark's interests. She'd kill them on the gangway between the aftercastle and the forecastle. That was the best place, because the gangway was long. The main thing was to follow behind them. She'd shoot the guy in front of her, and, right after that, she'd take aim at the other one. Then she'd alert Le Guévenec and have a conversation with Lanier, which would certainly be stimulating.

"You coming?" Velot asked, giving her a look she didn't like one bit.

"Let's go."

Sweat broke out on her forehead when the two assassins planted themselves in front of her. These two bastards were going to make her go out first. Maybe they'd guessed what she was cooking up. Velot probably suspected that she had the revolver. A thundering bang made them look up. It was followed by a horrible cry, which was swiftly drowned out by the noise of the storm. The wild snowplow had most likely killed one of the last sailors of the *Bouc-Bel-Air*.

Connie saw the panicked look on the face of the Inuit, who had begun climbing up the ladder. She sensed that Velot feared his acolyte would do something stupid. He trailed behind him. She took up the rear. When he reached the platform, the Inuit stepped aside to let the Frenchman unlock the door. She let the two men pass in front of her. Velot turned around to close the door behind them and then went to open the next door. Why was the piece of shit grinning? Connie had a bad feeling and let the two men exit the airlock in front of her so that they could get well ahead. Which they did without any fuss.

When the hatch promptly shut again, she realized, too late, that she'd just allowed herself to be trapped in the airlock without any hope of escape. She heard the sound of the bolts shooting home in the steel and started screaming like one of the damned and banging on the metal wall. She was caught like a rat in a trap on a ship that was about to be wrecked.

AUTOROUTE A6, 10:55 P.M.

Crouched on his Harley, Luc was driving through the wind and icy rain toward Paris. Speed put distance between him and the bloody images he was bringing home with him. It forced him to focus on the road. He would never erase Isabelle Le Guévenec's eyes as she lay beside him, dead. The captain's wife had given up her secrets with grace. Luc felt even more enraged at the bastards, who had deserved a death more horrible than the one they had met in the Terres Noires of the Morvan.

He slowed down only when he saw the Porte d'Orléans and was amazed that he hadn't gotten a ticket. He still had a driver's license more because of his talents as a hacker than because of his respect for speed limits.

Obsessed with Thor Johannsen, Luc drove along the Avenue du Maine to Montparnasse and then crossed the Seine at the Pont Alexandre III before heading to the Faubourg Saint-Honoré. He parked his motorcycle on a deserted street and joined Aimé Toussaint at the bar. He couldn't wait to nail the Norwegian. The more he thought about it, the more Laura Al-lee-Ah's husband looked like the guy who'd met Per Sorensen at the poolside bar.

"Well?" he asked the tall black lifeguard built like a breaststroke champion.

"Come on. He's waiting for us."

Luc tucked his helmet under his arm and followed Toussaint. They crossed the street and entered one of the most fashionable and stylish dives in the capital. The contrast with the Morvan was striking. Toussaint was a regular visitor and led him over the carpet and then

up the marble stairs to the elevator that would take them to the subterranean swimming pool. Everything in this hushed palace exuded luxury and tastefulness. They walked past fitness rooms and met figures
cloaked in white bathrobes discreetly embroidered with the club's logo.

"Here, people eat and swim any hour of the day, all year round. But
even here, business never sleeps."

"So I see."

They passed a table where an overfed Middle Easterner was sweating at a computer. Luc thought of Omar Al Selim. The man looked up
and gave Luc a unequivocal wink. Too fat, Luc thought, noting that
he couldn't be the Qatari.

Aimé Toussaint took them to a cloakroom that smelled like tropical
flowers laced heavily with chlorine.

"Follow my example."

Luc hung up his leather jacket and stowed his helmet in one of the
lockers. He slipped a pair of disposable plastic shoe covers over his feet
and draped a bathrobe over his arm.

"Let's go."

Aimé opened another door, and they were standing on the tile floor
of one of the most luxurious swimming pools Luc had ever had the
good fortune to see in his short life. The reflections of Roman columns
and marble statues quivered on the surface of the pool, where a couple
was swimming. A tray holding two flutes of champagne awaited the
happy pair. Feeling like a fool in his plastic booties, Luc followed Aimé
to the bar, which was shimmering under invisible spotlights. Then he
laid eyes on the most irresistible barman he'd ever seen, dressed in
white and as handsome as a newly minted god.

"Let me introduce you to Gabriel," Aimé said in a voice dripping
with innuendo.

Luc remained speechless and confused.

"Gabriel was here the day Per Sorensen met the man you're interested in. He's seen all the photos."

Gabriel glanced at the pool and took out the packet of photos.

"Well?" Luc asked, trying to concentrate.

The archangel Gabriel spread the full set of pictures over the mar-
ble-topped bar and smiled apologetically.

"The man I saw with Per Sorensen is not in any of these photos."

"But that's not possible!"

Luc moved the photos around, looking for shots of Thor Johannsen.
He stuck the face of the Norwegian oilman married to Laura Al-lee-
Ah under the barman's nose.

"What about this one?"

"Your man was younger and darker. He comes here from time to time."

"What's his name?" Luc asked, crestfallen.

"I have no idea. I've only been here six months, and I don't have access to the client files."

"What does he look like?"

"I'd say he's discreet. Just about fifty or so. Maybe less. Medium height and a good swimmer."

Luc was devastated, gutted, lost. All his certainties about the role of the Norwegian and Arctoil were melting like the ice shelf in the sun's rays. He turned around to contemplate this display of wealth and told himself that, from the very beginning, they'd all missed something crucial. They were being taken for a ride. The angel, too, seemed sorry.

"Can you do me a favor?" Luc asked Gabriel.

"Sure."

"I'll send you a software program that lets you sketch a picture of the guy. Aimé will help you. I've got to go."

Luc thanked them and headed for the exit, leaving the two men behind at the bar. All that was left for him to do was go home and hack into the Saint-James database to identify Per Sorensen's Paris contact. He cursed the time lost, retrieved his helmet and his leather jacket in the cloakroom, and found himself out on the Rue du Faubourg-Saint-Honoré. His phone vibrated just as he was about to start his Harley. He recognized Connie Rasmussen, though her voice was breaking up.

He thought he made out that the *Bouc-Bel-Air* was in trouble and that something had happened in the engine room. She was calling for help. Then the conversation was cut off. On the off-chance, he called Terre Noire headquarters on the Champs-Elysées and tried to get put through to the crisis unit.

"We don't have such a thing, monsieur."

"I'm calling about the *Bouc-Bel-Air*. Get me someone in charge!"

"There's no one here at this hour."

"You've got a ship that's sinking. The entire world is watching you, and you can't even be fucked to put a crisis unit together."

"I haven't been given any orders. I'm just on night duty."

"Get hold of Le Guévenec, the captain of the *Bouc-Bel-Air*. It's a matter life and death, and tell him there's a problem in the engine room and that someone's calling for help."

"Yes, monsieur."

Furious, Luc ended the call. He straddled his motorcycle and headed for Fermatown.

Lying on his stomach behind the glass cabinet, John was watching the tunnel entrance. With the small amount of energy remaining in his phone battery, he tried to text message Geraldine Harper to tell her the desperate situation he was in. He composed a text message and pressed the key. The answer came instantly: no service. Trapped in the disintegrating bowels of Greenland, he was dogless, friendless, and now disconnected.

The cold was beginning to stiffen Qaalasoq's body as he lay on the ground, his face looking up at the archway. One hand was open against the icy floor. Behind him, the horrible assemblage of sawn-up bodies guarded the entrance to a postglacial world like some demonic multiheaded Cerberus. An endless moan was rising from the bowels of the ice cap. A closer, more familiar sound made him lift his head. Drops of water were falling from the ceiling and bouncing onto the Inuit's cupped hand.

His false refuge was rapidly melting. And the camera was filming the scene. The piece of shit had only to wait on the slopes of Haffner Bjerg in front of his screen. The enemy was both in front and at the rear, watching his every move. It was hard to imagine a more cata-strophic situation.

The computers and measuring tools were blinking away, safely protected in the glass cabinet. The system that sounded the ice cap had to be connected to one of Terre Noire's seaborne or land-based sites. He was looking at a source of energy. If he could just tap into it, he could possibly recharge his phone and contact the company's scientists. But the damp and insidious cold were acting like a sleeping pill. He had already lost feeling in his lower limbs. Time was running out.

He used what strength he had left to crawl back to the tripod supporting the camera and knocked it to the ground. Rid of the intrusive eye, he rushed to one of the cases of equipment and lifted the lid. Nothing of any use there. He crossed the tunnel to a metal trunk. Instead of the ax he was hoping for, he found an old American shovel. He went back to the cabinet to break the glass. The first blow scarcely made a dent in the bulletproof glass. He was about to strike a second time when one of the lights went out at the same time as the soft humming of the computers. He found himself standing between the dead cabinet and the rotting tupilaq, which reeked like an anal cavity. Abraham Harper, assuming it was he, was no more now than a decaying carcass.

It was the silence that alerted him to the danger. Someone was walking in his direction. His instinct told him to flee. Despite the lack of sensation in his feet, he managed to hurl himself toward the bend. When he looked back, he saw the archway crash down over the very spot where he'd been lying just seconds earlier. The roar was like an explosion of dynamite. The blast split his eardrums and dashed him against the curved wall before sucking him down.

But instead of winding up in the darkest depths, he found himself on his haunches in the middle of a fissure. In caving in on itself, the ice cap had destroyed the tunnel. He was in one of the horrible cracks they'd seen around the entrance to the underworld when they'd gotten to the base. As Qaalasoq had foreseen, the landscape was evolving at distressing speed. The dynamite had just sped up the process.

He reached for the rifle and was appalled to realize that he'd lost it in the explosion. Panic replaced the numbness. He was without a phone, a weapon, or provisions at the bottom of an unworldly abyss. Then the sky above him suddenly lit up in gigantic waves of color that passed at dizzying speed. Intense greens gave way to oranges, pinks, and purples. A storm of lights that had escaped from an invisible sun nailed him to the spot. Terror gave way to a sort of pernicious enchantment. John's first aurora borealis couldn't have come at a worse time.

Pain wrenched him away from the light show. When he was blasted out of the tunnel, he'd torn something between his shoulder blades. John knew the other guy would not be long in surging, and he had to act fast. Lit up by the fireworks setting the sky ablaze, he dragged himself along the bottom of the fissure and discovered, on his right, the entrance to another seam that was at a ninety-degree angle to the one he was in but not as wide. He turned into it before falling upon another fissure, which was a few yards in and parallel to the first.

He was in the middle of a vast labyrinth of crisscrossing crevasses that looked like giant claw marks. He looked up and saw the black tip of Haffner Bjerg caught in a silent storm of lush colors that had descended from another world. The mountain had grown even taller.

In the midst of all this, his thoughts turned to Victoire.

PARIS, 18 RUE DEPARCIEUX, 11:55 P.M.

Back in the Daguerre village, Luc parked his Harley on the sidewalk between Fermatown and La Bélière. The rain had turned from glacial to tropical. These days, the weather could go from winter to monsoon season in a few hours. Luc felt a sudden foreboding and looked up at the windows. On the third floor, the lights in the kitchen were on, and he made out the shadow of a tall man. Luc took off his helmet and decided to approach the house via the Rue Fermat.

The blood in his veins turned to liquid air. He pushed open the gate to 9 Rue Fermat and ran along the waterlogged garden path before entering the vast garage. He took off his shoes and raced up the stairs in his socks, his muscles tensed. On the second floor, he crossed the hall that separated the confessional from the room with the touch wall. A glow from the kitchen on the third floor spilled downstairs. Victoire's high-pitched laugh startled him. His nerves really were in a bad state.

Luc pushed open the door and found a tall guy standing by the window. He had frizzy ginger-colored hair and hazel eyes. And he was drinking milk from Luc's favorite cup. Luc was seized with a fit of jealousy. Victoire did the introductions. "This is Thomas Curvien, who works with our friend François Guerot. He's keeping an eye on me."

Luc nodded and held out his hand to the colossus, who promptly crushed his fingers.

"Hi, pleased to meet you. Victoire has told me great things about you. It seems you've just come back from the Morvan. Beautiful place, isn't it?"

"Yes," Luc replied, his eyes fixed on his prized porcelain cup. He was in the grip of a feeling he couldn't quite hide. It was bringing out the boy in him, envious of the stranger who was trying to bed his mother. He really hated the "old guys" in the agency.

"I've got to talk to Victoire."

The bodyguard threw a look at the mistress of the house, who smilingly let him know she welcomed a tête-à-tête with Luc.

"I'll be down on the street," the bodyguard said. "I'll get the car ready."

He put Luc's cup on the oilskin tablecloth and headed downstairs. Luc closed the kitchen door and turned to Victoire. They were alone at last.

"Where are you going with this guy?"

"To Deauville to meet Omar Al Selim. Don't look at me like that!"

"Are you mad?"

"I've been mad with anxiety ever since I lost contact with John. I have to do something. I can't just sit here anymore. The agency knows this Omar Al Selim. I'm going to talk to him about Christophe Maunay. Maybe he'll tell us what Maunay wanted to reveal to John before he was murdered. He's definitely got things to tell us about Thor Johannsen."

Victoire recounted her visit to the Léopold-Bellan hospital.

"There's a guy there who could turn out to be Abraham Harper or Thor Johannsen, which would undermine a lot of our assumptions, again."

"What makes you say that?"

"I saw white hair and a bodyguard. Bellan is known for respiratory diseases. According to what I've read, both Harper and Johannsen are smokers. I've got a bad feeling we've been taken for a ride since the very beginning."

"I'll look into it," Luc replied.

"How did it go in the Morvan?"

"Badly."

Luc told her about Isabelle Le Guévenec's death and the fitting demise of the two killers in the quicksands of the Terres Noires. He also explained his disappointment that Thor Johannsen was not the guy who'd been seen at the swimming pool at the Saint-James.

"Yet I was *sure* the Norwegian sent Per Sorensen after you, just as he sent the guys who shot Isabelle and the one who tried to kill John on the ice shelf."

"There's something we're still not seeing," Victoire replied. "But I'm sure that the people who killed Christophe Maunay tried to kill us for the same reasons. Maunay knew things that we're on the brink of finding out. There's something wrong with the way we're looking at the problem. That's why I want to meet Omar Al Selim."

"What does Guerot think?"

"He agrees, as long as I don't go on my own. That's why he assigned me the bodyguard down below. Don't be jealous. Please, try to reach John."

"I promise I will."

Luc watched Victoire go downstairs. Outside, the slamming of the car doors made him jump. He saw Isabelle's face again in the rain and rushed to the window to make sure Victoire had reached the car safely. He verified that she was okay and noticed that she was about to leave town in a Mercedes. For once, the agency wasn't skimping. He crossed the hall to the other room to review the boatswain's notebook. The notion that Abraham Harper, whom everyone was looking for at the North Pole, might actually be lying a few yards from their place intrigued him. But why would Geraldine and Mary Harper have played along with such a stupid masquerade? Why would the people who killed Brissac and Isabelle Le Guévenec be carrying around the address of the hospital harboring Abraham Harper? This mystery had to be solved.

Standing in front of the touch wall, he ran his hacking program to break into the hospital and encountered a highly effective security system. All his Trojan Horses, worms, and other spyware were detected and rebuffed in a matter of seconds. It was light-years ahead of government-style security. The discreet hospital was as well protected as the Jupiter PC of the Elysée Palace, where the French president lived.

Luc peered at the touch screen. The more progress they made, the more they were led back to their own neighborhood. The invisible enemy had just successfully rejected his assault. And no doubt he'd been spotted in spite of all his precautions and his network of anonymizing sites. This kind of resistance spelled deep pockets. He was anticipating a devastating reply. Luc went to the window and scrutinized the Rue Deparcieux, expecting to see killers loom. All he saw was the unmarked car of the agency surveillance team, and he felt reassured.

He left the house, started his motorcycle, and headed toward the Montparnasse Cemetery. In less than five minutes, he was outside the hospital, intending to physically break down the digital wall that had just resisted him. Who was in the isolation ward on the fifth floor?

7

SATURDAY

Reassured by Thomas's presence beside her, Victoire watched the countryside flash past. The bodyguard François Guerot had sent her was showing zeal and discretion. Unable to take the wheel because of her injuries, she was churning over everything they'd been through for the past week.

"Do you know if François was able to locate John?" she asked her driver.

"François?"

"François Guerot, you know."

The driver was silent for a moment. His hands tightened on the wheel.

"I'm not involved in investigations. I drive and provide security. That's all."

"We'll see when we get to Deauville."

Victoire thought back to what she'd seen at the hospital. The man with the white hair could well be at the center of this deadly enigma. Isabelle Le Guévenec's murder reminded her of the one she'd committed. Per Sorensen and the killers in the Morvan belonged to the same organization. The trail leading to the Norwegian had proven to be wrong. And Luc had drawn a blank at the Saint-James. She put in her earphone so as not to disturb the driver and once again tried to call John. She got the same message: unreachable.

Victoire went back over the maps and phone numbers from the *Bouc-Bel-Air* boatswain's notebook. She opened the file she'd transferred to her phone and called the first of the numbers they hadn't yet identified. After a few rings, someone answered without saying a word. What she heard amazed and spooked her. The noise of the wind soon overwhelmed the heavy panting of the person who answered. He ended the call, apparently having caught on. Her instinct told her that she had just been in touch with one of the killers sent after John on the ice cap.

If she called Guerot, maybe she could get the Greenland police to locate the man and keep John safe.

"Stop wherever you can. I've got to call François."

"Yes, madame."

She went through the other numbers and called the second one. No answer. She called the third number and received was aghast when the opening notes of Ravel's *Boléro* rang out in the driver's bag behind her seat.

"Let it ring. It's not urgent."

Victoire complied. Her lungs on fire, she stared at the road and tried not to scream. Terror was devouring her insides. Her executioner was sitting right beside her. Then she remembered that he hadn't recognized Guerot's first name. Preoccupied with John's precarious situation, she hadn't really registered the anomaly. Guerot had told her that he would send one of his most loyal employees. How could one of the agency's most loyal employees not know his boss's name? The answer was obvious. He wasn't with the agency at all.

Someone had wiretapped Fermatown and was eavesdropping. The other side had overheard her request for protection and sent one of theirs instead of the man who was supposed to come. They hadn't yet reached their destination. Her only chance of survival was not to let him know that she was the one who'd made the phone call. She clung desperately to the idea that it could be a coincidence. She had to be sure before attempting the impossible.

"It's really a shame, what's happening to François, with this transfer to Toulouse. He must be pretty upset, no?"

"Yes, he's upset."

Victoire couldn't utter another word. François was not being sent to Toulouse. So she was, indeed, sitting next to a henchman who had never set foot in the agency. The tears sprang to her eyes without warning. Her hand slid toward the door: it was locked. They drove past a service station without stopping. Terrorized and handicapped, she didn't dare say anything. In any case, she was incapable of speaking. She saw his knuckles, white on the wheel. Her eyes scanned the darkness—pitch-black, shot through with flashes of lightning. For a few weeks, they'd been forecasting a weather phenomenon no one had had the time to name. It was a kind of tornado, they said. But the alert didn't come in the form of heavy gray thunderclouds. The warning sign was a raspberry-colored glow in the sky.

Luc parked the Harley on the Rue Vercingétorix and covered the rest of the ground on foot. Thor Johannsen, the man behind the Russian-Norwegian alliance, hadn't gone to the Saint-James swimming pool to meet Per Sorensen, because he was hospitalized at the Bellan. The white hair Victoire had seen had to belong to the Norwegian—Luc could still see his mane in the press photos. The hospital had become the Paris headquarters of the Blues, who wanted to drive the Canadians out of Greenland.

How to get in? Luc decided to go for the bold approach, same as at the Louxor. Without makeup and high-heels, and carrying a helmet, he'd have more trouble than Victoire, whose native elegance opened all doors. He was about to cross the street when the sound of another motorcycle made him turn toward the Avenue du Maine. A biker dressed in similar gear slowed down outside the hospital.

Intrigued, Luc disappeared into the shadow of an apartment building. The man parked his cycle and got off. Luc saw him remove his helmet and take an envelope from the top box. The motorcyclist then walked unimpeded through to the lobby, as though he were right at home.

Such an opportunity was not going to turn up twice.

Luc crossed the street, walked up the few steps, and went inside, his helmet in his left hand and a USB key in his right, which he raised above his head.

"That idiot forgot this," he said to the young woman at the security desk. She smiled back at him.

Luc followed Victoire's directions and dived into the corridor facing him, being very careful not to catch up to the biker. He saw the elevator door close and took the stairs to the fifth floor. He was just opening the stairwell door when he saw a stretcher coming. He quickly stepped back and watched through the window in the door as a male nurse wheeled the white-haired man by. With him were the bodyguard and the motorcyclist. The entourage got into the elevator.

Luc rushed down a half flight to look out the window in the landing. He saw the three men push the stretcher to an ambulance that had just arrived. At night, it was impossible to see the patient's face. He pulled out his phone and took as many photos as he could. Mad with rage, he went back up the stairs and out into the corridor. He punched in the security code to the isolation ward, which Victoire had given him, and went to the room she had described. A female nurse was changing the sheets.

"Did you forget something, young man?"

"Monsieur Johannsen said he left his watch on the night table."

"Who's Monsieur Johannsen?" the nurse asked, surprised.

Luc felt like a fool. He said the first thing that came into his head. "A visitor."

The nurse slid the drawer out of the night table. It was empty. She stared suspiciously at Luc.

"You can report it missing at the security desk."

Luc recovered and seized the opportunity.

"Thank you," he replied, giving her his most winning smile.

Back on the ground floor, he approached the young woman at the desk and said he wanted to report that a watch was missing from the room on the fifth floor.

"The patient who just left?"

"Yes," Luc replied.

Pen in hand, he started writing on a sticky note.

"I'll give you his contact information in case you find it. Too bad he just left in the ambulance. Um, I never know where to put the 'h' in his name."

"There's no 'h' in Omar Al Selim," she replied.

Luc took the news in stride and scrawled something on the little square of yellow paper. He suddenly remembered that Victoire was on her way to Deauville. She was supposed to be meeting the man who had just been released from the hospital with an oxygen tank.

"Omar Al Selim *is* going back to Deauville, isn't he?"

"Monsieur Al Selim is going back to Qatar to die. We'll all miss him. He was a charming man. He had a big heart."

"What's his address in Deauville?"

"I don't know."

Luc glanced at the screen of a small television, which was relentlessly relaying images of Greenland in its death throes.

"Do you really think it's the end of the world?" she asked.

"Yes," Luc replied as he left the Léopold-Bellan. His legs had turned to water, and there were tears in his eyes.

Omar Al Selim was taking his last journey home. So who was Victoire going to meet in Deauville? If Thor Johannsen wasn't the man at the Saint-James, who had sent the killers after them? Thrown by the collapse of all his theories, Luc nearly got himself hit by a car as he crossed the street. It took him another few seconds to compute that Victoire was heading for certain death. He called her cell phone and recognized the sound of her breathing.

"Only answer 'yes' or 'no.' I know you're in danger, and you're heading for Deauville."

"Yes."

"I think the agency was outsmarted, and the guy driving infiltrated the apparatus."

"Yes."

"I'm going to alert Guerot so he can send backup."

"Yes."

"Now, say something stupid to reassure the guy in the driver's seat."

"You should never have switched Caresse to that low-fat cat food. She hates it, and she hates you for doing it!"

"Good job. I'll see to everything."

One minute later, Luc had Guerot on the line.

"Don't worry, Luc. I'll get a team on it. I'll alert the police at Pont-l'Evèque. Try to catch up with the Mercedes on the Deauville road, and call me as soon as you see them."

"Thanks."

HAFFNER BJERG, 9 P.M.

John lay on his back and let himself be bewitched by the sky over the chasm that was about to engulf him. The pinks, reds, purples, blues, and greens were performing a gargantuan ballet in the heavens. Death had become a promise. Taken out of his own body by the beauty of the spectacle, he rushed to meet unknown worlds.

The dull rumbling of the ice cap brought him back to reality. He snapped out of his trance and shook off the desire to leave this world for the great beyond. The hands at the end of his arms seemed such vulgar, incongruous things. He tried moving them, along with his legs, and was amazed to see that he still functioned. He decided to see if he could get himself out of the cleft and managed to climb up, planting each foothold with great care. When he got to the top, he surveyed the landscape of fissures and frozen crests that was holding him captive.

The desire to see Victoire again and hold her in his arms gave him the strength he needed to think. Hate suddenly spurted through his veins like a hot tonic. A survival instinct told him not to stay where he was. The other guy was armed, mobile, and dangerous. He left his lair and started walking in the direction of the black mountain. The granite of Haffner Bjerg felt like a lifeline, a safe haven. He absolutely had to get out of this decomposing world if he didn't want to end with it.

The enemy, his cheek pressed against the butt of his gun, was waiting for him on the home stretch, he knew. He forced himself to keep going. Instead of heading straight for the top, he decided to make a wide curve to the right to have the sun at his back. He scaled cavities and craters. After an exhausting half hour of climbing up rock faces and racing down them, his eye caught a moving splotch lit up by the colors of the aurora borealis. The sniper had just taken up a new firing position.

Something wasn't right. Lying on top of a snowdrift, he watched. According to the plan he had devised, he should have skirted around his adversary. But the guy was a hundred yards in front of him. The bastard had guessed his maneuver! How had he known?

The part of his brain that wasn't paralyzed by the cold began a logical process of deduction. He quickly found himself at the edge of an abyss more fearsome than all those he had already experienced. The enemy had tracked him, thanks to the radio frequency identification chips camouflaged in the steel balls he'd had attached to his ear by Patrick on the Rue Sarrette before taking off for Greenland. The killer was using the GPS apparatus that linked him to the west wing of Les Invalides.

Galvanized by rage, he brought his hand to his ear and ripped out the three balls in one fell swoop. Blood spurted over the ice. The intense pain forced him to drive his head into the snow to numb his earlobe and stifle his urge to scream. He remained prostrate and waited for the pain to subside. Then he looked at the three balls and the red flesh in his hand. Ideas promptly came together in his mind like white-hot knives. Don't let the blood give you away. Strike first. Kill.

He turned back and looked at the ridge. Twenty yards to the right there was a dip in the ice. He dropped down the length of the slope. With his hand over the wound so as not to leave a red trail behind him, he moved to a cavity. Having reached what looked like a refuge big enough to hide a man, he moved to the bottom and thrust his arm into the mix of sand and decomposing ice. When he pulled his hand out again, his hand was empty. He lay on the ground and crawled forward twenty yards or so, taking care to erase his traces. He would survive by thinking what his predator thought and seeing what he saw.

Satisfied, he stood up and climbed to the top of the crest and dropped to the other side. He turned to the left and positioned himself three yards above the spot where he'd hidden the balls.

He didn't have to wait ten minutes. The racket of the automatic rifle split his eardrums. The bastard was spraying the cavity just below where he had buried the balls just below him. Thirty or so rounds had been fired at the target. John rolled up his pants and grabbed the screwdriver that he'd bought in the Nuuk mall and brought with him all the way to the top of the world.

He quietly climbed back up to the ridgeline and finally spotted him. The man was wearing alpine hunter's gear and a balaclava ski mask. The infrared scope of his rifle was plastered over one eye. As a soldier used to close combat, John saw in his enemy's movement the ease of a hunter who always got his prey. He had the assurance of a winner. John ducked again, not wanting to take any risk, and counted the seconds that would bring the other man to the point just below him. Four, five, six... The image was burned on the screen of his feverish brain. The still-smiling predator scanned the face of the crest. Seven, eight.... In a second or two, that smile would disappear. Nine. It was now or never.

John tensed. The other man raised his head and started to aim his rifle at the threatening shadow. One second too late. John's powerful kick diverted the burst of fire, which was lost in the abyss. John hurled his two hundred pounds of muscle, along with the weapon he was holding. He had to strike precisely. His fist, as rigid as steel, was accurate and fast. The outcome of the fight was no longer in doubt. He shrieked and twisted the screwdriver, which punctured the carotid artery. The enemy's viscous, burning-hot blood sprayed the snow and the clothes of both the tangled fighters.

Though injured and encumbered by his rifle and equipment, the killer fought on. But the surprise element had done the trick. John felt the other man flag. A final kick ripped the scope away and part of his face with it. The bottom of the crevasse was starting to look like the cold room of a butcher shop. John managed to free himself from his adversary's hold and raised a bloody hand over the man. The screwdriver dripped blood before puncturing the predator's face. John stopped striking just as the pink and green lights of the sky stopped flashing over the ice.

The sacrifice over and done, John went through the dead man's pockets. His felt a cell phone. He had to clean his hands in the snow before he could use it. This final chore felt as exhausting as putting to death the piece of shit who'd murdered Qaalasoq, Saké, their dogs, and probably Maunay, as well. His mind totally empty, he called Guerot to ask for help. When he could breathe more calmly, he got to the point.

"These bastards managed to get into the GPS system. I had to rip out my RFID chips. I feel sick, François."

"Where are you?"

"On the slopes of Haffner Bjerg."

"Still on the ice cap?"

"Yes."

"Get to solid ground. I'll send a helicopter."

John looked at the suddenly silent phone and told himself that he'd never have the strength to climb back up. It was too high. Besides, the mountain he was expected to climb was itself climbing toward the sky.

NORMANDY AUTOROUTE, 2:05 A.M.

Luc parked his Harley near the pump and filled the tank, wondering if he hadn't overtaken the car that Victoire was trapped in. The rain and the slippery road meant he hadn't gotten a good look at all the drivers he'd passed since Paris. The highway had become a veritable ice rink, lit up by pink and red flashes of lightning.

When he had filled the tank and paid for the gas, he ducked into the restroom and used his cell phone to launch the identification program for the access maps retrieved by Le Guévenec from his boatswain's notebook. The recognition software proposed a site in Oklahoma, a village in Bangladesh, and a town in the wilds of the Calvados in Normandy. Luc chose the latter and zoomed in on the priory of St. Thérèse, thanks to the data provided by the Institut Géographique National. The imposing building, planted at a hairpin bend, was a hundred yards from the railway line that linked Deauville and Lisieux. He grabbed his phone and called Victoire.

"The driver is taking you to the priory of St. Thérèse in Vieux-Bourg. It's close to Deauville."

"Yes, I know."

"You checked like I did, using..."

"Yes, Papa," Victoire replied.

"Good. I'll get there before you. I assume you haven't passed Pont-l'Evèque. There'll be a police roadblock. Guerot has alerted the cops."

"You know very well that Caresse does not like tuna packed in water."

"Hang in there."

Victoire really was an exceptional woman. Before straddling his motorcycle, Luc called Guerot.

"They're taking Victoire to the priory of St. Thérèse in Vieux-Bourg."

"That's a church?"

"It's a sort of manor. I'll get there ahead of them. Have you found John?"

"He's saved. You wouldn't believe it, but they managed to intercept the frequencies of the chips he had sewn into his ear. We'll need to look into that quack on the Rue Sarrette."

"You're right."

Guerot ended the call. Luc told himself that John had put his blind faith in a doctor who perhaps wasn't so squeaky clean. What's more, he could have been the one who'd gone to the Saint-James to tell the killer about the window in Fermatown's roof. Luc remembered that John had once invited his favorite doc over for a drink. That reminded him of the computer-software sketch the angel at the Saint-James had promised. He called Aimé Toussaint and asked if his protégé had completed the drawing.

"I'll send it to you."

One minute later, Luc brought up on his cell phone a sketch of a middle-aged man with brown hair and creases around his eyes shown in three-quarter profile. The face didn't closely resemble any of the protagonists in this affair. Yet again, everything he'd constructed was swept away. Luc thanked Toussaint and asked him to put pressure on his angel to come up with more.

Enraged nature obliged him to lift his head. A tree split in two by the storm had just ripped out the power lines, causing a succession of sparks a few yards from the gas station where he'd just filled up. The lights went out one after the other. It was worse than in the Morvan.

He straddled his motorcycle with a savage determination to make headway, even if he was the only one on the road. He himself was forced off the pavement several times because of the squalls, and he had terrible trouble getting to Vieux-Bourg. He drove past the priory without seeing it and had to retrace his route with the aid of his GPS. He parked a hundred yards or so from the main entrance and continued on foot in the pelting rain. A huge flash of lightning lit up rows of apple trees. A panic-stricken cow jumped a fence and started wandering over the road. Climate change was coming down from the pole at an amazing speed.

Thérèse's priory was a hybrid bit of masonry, a cross between Norman manor and fortified farmhouse. He saw a light in a window on the second floor, and after looking around, he slipped through the half-open gate. Not wanting to arrive the most direct way and get himself spotted, he skirted the orchard between the house and the road. As John had taught him, he went to the rear and found himself near a garage, which he entered to take cover and think.

How was he going to get in on his own? What sort of crew was he going to fall upon? He became aware of how reckless and alone he was. What the hell was Guerot doing? He took out his phone and called Guerot's number. The answer was immediate and threw him off his stride.

"I've been here for five minutes. My men are covering the road and the orchard. We wanted you to get here before we went in."

Luc turned and made out Guerot's silhouette in the darkness of the garage.

"Where's Victoire?" Guerot demanded.

"She's coming," Luc replied, disconcerted but reassured by the deputy director's presence.

Thunder shook the barn to its foundations. Luc instinctively tensed.

"One of my men has already been able to slip inside," Guerot said. "But there's something we don't understand."

Luc turned to his neighbor, who was putting a cartridge in the firing chamber of his gun.

"What don't you understand?" Luc asked.

"Come. You're going to explain to us."

Luc followed Guerot. The deputy director rushed to one of the ground-floor doors, which he opened without any trouble. A timeworn stone staircase rose in front of them. They climbed the steps in silence and headed toward a room where a lamp was lit. Guerot went in first, on tiptoe. Just as Luc was following him in, lightning flashed, and the lamp flickered. Guerot turned around, and the image burned into Luc's brain. Facing him was the barman's sketch. The man who had sent Per Sorensen to murder Victoire was none other than François Guerot. Luc immediately felt something metallic grip his right wrist and then his left. He was trapped.

NORMANDY AUTOROUTE, 2:25 P.M.

Sitting next to the man who intended to murder her, Victoire didn't dare ask him to stop at a service station again. The guy would be forced to kill her immediately if she did. The nonchalant way she was playing with her phone allowed her to add minutes to those she'd already stolen from death. At least that is what she hoped.

The weather was doing her a favor. After Rouen, the tropical atmosphere and drizzle had turned into heavy showers that forced the driver to take extra care. The highway was starting to look like a swamp and becoming dangerous. That gave her time to piece together her ideas and scattered images. At Pont l'Evèque, the police Guerot had promised were nowhere in sight. Smells and expressions she hadn't given any importance to came back to her. With the benefit of hindsight, recent memories took on a precise meaning on her inner touch wall, which, facilitated by fear, worked every bit as well as the one in Fermatown.

She saw once more Guerot's face riveted on her bandaged hands and thought back to his sudden pallor when she'd mentioned Christophe Maunay's intention to leave Terre Noire and go over to North Land. Victoire had put the obvious disappointment Guerot felt down to Maunay's defection from Terre Noire. Now she realized that Guerot was outraged because Maunay had betrayed him. She had been seriously naive to believe in Guerot's patriotism.

Guerot quaked at the thought that Maunay might tell John how he had served interests other than those of France once he had fallen into the grips of Thor Johannsen after the pedophilia scandal. Victoire once again smelled the odor of chlorine that Guerot trailed behind him. If neither Johannsen nor Omar Al Selim had gone to the bar at the Saint-James swimming pool, it had to be Guerot. And like an idiot, she'd told him about Luc's trip to the Morvan and unwittingly guided the killers to the Terre Noire chalet.

She saw the railway embankment through the windshield. They were approaching Vieux-Bourg. All she could do now was survive and count on Luc. The words stabbed her in the heart. Luc had said, "I'm going to alert Guerot so he can send backup." She gulped and thought she might well die before her driver had a chance to wrap his hands around her throat and throw her in the ditch, which had turned into a torrent. They had served themselves up to their enemies on a plate, bound and gagged. Doing her best to keep up her act, she tried to send Luc a text message to warn him but saw she had no bars.

She was about to try John when the driver swore.

"Shit!"

Victoire looked out the window and saw why. The narrow road running along the railway track had turned into a river of mud, and it was coming toward them at terrifying speed. The torrent was pushing a mass of detritus and branches ripped off trees. Worse yet, it was carrying the corpse of a cow that must have drowned somewhere along the way. It was all about to hit them head-on when the driver swerved the Mercedes across the road. Victoire opened the window on her side just before the car was swept away.

Water was flooding into the Mercedes. Victoire undid her seat belt and started hauling herself out the window. She was halfway out when she felt the monster grip an ankle. An old karate move allowed her to shatter something that felt like cartilage with her free foot. The man let go. Completely out, she went with the flow. Too big to imitate her and reeling from the blow he'd just received, her would-be executioner disappeared, along with the carcass of the cow and the Mercedes.

Carried like a wisp of straw toward Pont-l'Evèque, she managed to keep her head above the water long enough to snag a low-hanging tree limb. She clung to it and was finally able to get a toehold on the embankment. One last effort, and she climbed up and collapsed next to the tracks.

HAFFNER BJERG, 9:50 P.M.

John contemplated the distance he had covered. Through sheer will power, he had managed to get away from the ice cap in distress and to hoist himself onto the rocky slopes of Haffner Bjerg. Lying on his back, he had nothing more to do but wait for the help Guerot had promised.

He had never really analyzed the reasons he felt animosity for the man and was angry with himself for having given him the cold shoulder during his time at the agency. He suddenly thought about his change of position and the fact that the chips indicating his location were back there, three hundred and thirty yards below, on the ice. He was worried that the helicopter pilot hadn't gotten the message that he was on Haffner Bjerg, not the ice shelf, which was dangerous because of the methane emissions. He decided to call Guerot to tell him to advise the pilot to avoid the emissions at all cost. The background noise of a storm drowned out Guerot's voice. He tried to tell Guerot where he was anyway, not knowing if the man could hear.

He then tried to get in touch with Victoire and Luc, with no success. Nothing was working anymore. Gripped by sudden anguish, he called Geraldine Harper and gave her an account of what he had just been through.

"Are you sure it's my husband's body?"

"I'm not sure of anything. The bodies were horribly mutilated. Now they're sinking into the ice. In a few hours, there'll be no trace of the last Terre Noire station. I don't think you could have withstood the spectacle."

"Who's behind all this, John?" Geraldine asked.

"I still don't know."

She seemed resigned. She assured him that a North Land helicopter would be sent to pick him up. John thanked her and switched off the blood-stained cell phone. He lay down and thought that after all he had endured, sleep would come easily, even in this place. But all he did was doze. Ten minutes later, he registered the drone of an engine that could only belong to a helicopter. His burning lower back made it impossible to move any better than a wounded animal. He couldn't get up. A Sikorski flew toward him over the ice.

Relieved that he'd be leaving this hell behind, he watched as the machine grew bigger. He didn't recognize either Terre Noire's colors or those of North Land. A detail on the machine's insect legs attracted his attention—it looked odd. Suddenly, the helicopter went into a stationary position. Why was it stopping above the white expanse? John feared that Guerot hadn't gotten the message and advised the pilot. The helicopter was hovering above the spot indicated by the chips buried in the snow, along with a piece of his ear. They were going to try to touch down and look for him there at the risk of being set ablaze by the methane gas.

Despite the pain, John managed to get to his feet. He was just starting to wave his arms when the unthinkable happened. The machine rapidly gained altitude again. It climbed to six hundred feet. The maneuver was unbelievable. The helicopter dipped its nose toward the crack indicated by the RFID chips. Suddenly, an air-ground missile shot out and zoomed toward the ice, while the pilot, clearly warned about the effects of the gas, slipped away as fast as he could, the blades and the engine of the helicopter going full-bore.

The rocket exploded at the exact place where he had left the chips and the body of his enemy. An orange fireball shot out from the ice, sucking up the air around its incandescent heart. The sphere dissolved in a cloud of black smoke. But the match had been lit. Fissures and crevasses erupted in fire, sending blue flares into the night sky. Then the flames swept over the vast white expanse, burning thousands of cubic feet of methane.

Far away on the horizon, the helicopter was nothing more than a tiny, unscathed dot. Haffner Bjerg was a black island in the middle of an epic gas stove sending masses of noxious carbon into the atmosphere. John felt his clothes expelling warm water, which was running down his legs and puddling at his feet. A soothing warmth enveloped him, relieving his numbed limbs. He started spinning around with his arms out. He was part of a spectacle no human being before him had ever seen. But the euphoria didn't last long. The comforting warmth quickly became a heat wave.

Fifteen minutes after the pack ice was set alight, he was forced to take his clothes off and seek refuge among the rocks of Haffner Bjerg. Everywhere he looked, he could see only blue sparks with yellow tips running from one breach to the next. Like an immense Norwegian omelet, the ice sheet was folding in on itself. The mountain where he'd sought refuge was climbing up to the sky.

The heat finally dwindled, and the flames slowly died out. He found himself perched on top of a black and white desolation in the grip of a chilling feeling of loneliness. Qaalasoq and Saké had done the right thing, dying before him.

St. Thérèse's Priory, 3:10 a.m.

Luc took advantage of Guerot's absence to try to rip off the handcuffs that were keeping him attached to the radiator pipe. All that did was hurt his wrists. Guerot had cuffed him by stealth as soon as they'd stepped into the dining room. Facing a piss-yellow wall, he looked at his two hands, prisoners of a nonfunctioning central heating system. All it had taken was a simple click for him to find himself delivered up to and at the mercy of a counterespionage rat with an oversized ego.

He thought of something John had said about the piece of shit, a man he'd never really liked. "Guerot's a sick man who hates the whole world." The body search Guerot had thrown himself into had left nothing to chance. Luc was relieved of all his things—phone, keys, revolver. He heard footsteps behind him and turned his head around. Guerot had come back and looked worried. He walked over, making the floorboards creak.

"Where did you put Per Sorensen's body?"

"In Montparnasse."

"Where?"

"So it was *you* at the Saint-James swimming pool with Per Sorensen?"

"Yes."

Luc swallowed hard. The seconds he still had left could not be counted in the hundreds. Since the other man had gotten down to confessions, he figured he might as well not die an ignoramus.

"Who told you about John's meeting at the Ritz with Geraldine Harper?"

"Thor Johannsen. We infiltrated Raphaelle."

"So you're working for the Norwegians and the Russians."

"We work together. Thor knew Geraldine was coming to Paris to see her daughter, Mary, but also to see a private intelligence outfit. We wanted to know which one and why."

"Why did you decide to liquidate us, one after the other?"

"Because you'd become a danger without knowing it. You were on the verge of discovering the truth."

"What truth?" Luc asked, trying to slip his hands through the cuffs.

"The Norwegians, the Russians, my lot—we're never going to let a single company hold all the science and knowledge that shape the next thousand years. The merger of North Land and Terre Noire is an odious plan. I'd even say it's incestuous, because of Lanier and his half sister. We can't tolerate such a coupling."

"Whose side are you on?"

"The side of democracy, which can't accept such a concentration of knowledge—that is, of power."

Guerot had moved in close. Luc felt his breath on his shoulder, and then he heard the sadistic mewing. "Don't wear yourself out. I know your wrists are smaller than the average man's. That's why I brought some women's cuffs along."

The guy really was sick. As though nothing were out of the ordinary, his voice returned to normal. Trained to dissemble and keep a low profile in the world he was a product of, Guerot was as happy as a pig rolling in mud.

"Your little team was on the verge of figuring out that we would never let Terre Noire hand over its knowledge to North Land, meaning we would never let the Canadians and the Americans get their hands on it. The battle for the pole started a long time ago. It also involves Siberia. We couldn't accept a merger between the only two oil-and-gas companies capable of reading the Anthropocene."

"The Anthropocene?"

"The planet has entered a new age, a new climate, and a new economic era. The world is changing, as you may have noticed."

"You tried to kill Lanier, but you fluffed it. Your sniper got it wrong and killed Abraham Harper instead of his son on the sled that belonged to Terre Noire."

"I see you really are dangerous, Little Luc. Don't worry, I'll kill you nicely. You won't feel a thing. We'll even have a bit of fun beforehand. Look at this lousy weather! I'm going to suggest something nice and erotic. I know your dossier forward and backward. I'm the one who clears new recruits, after all."

Luc shuddered when he felt the hand caressing the back of his neck and playing with his curls.

"Why did you kill Maunay?" Luc asked, holding his breath.

"Maunay had his own man in Josephine who could hack into the databases of both Terre Noire camps on the Great Wound. When he realized we'd killed the father instead of the son, he lost it. He raced off to Nuuk to join his boss and spill the beans. Christophe always did have delicate nerves. We couldn't let him do that."

Luc felt Guerot's hands meet under his leather jacket and attack his belt buckle. The bastard was going to rape him up against the radiator.

"Were you the one who recruited Maunay in Gabon?"

"Christophe got himself caught playing with little boys. Very young little boys. We saved his ass. He owed us."

"Thanks to Omar Al Selim, your friend Thor Johannsen's pal."

"I see you're well-informed, sweetie. Let's see if you're well-hung."

Luc felt the two hands slide under his pants. He tried a kick, but the other man had pinned his legs to the wall with his knees. Luc thrashed wildly, fearing his final hour had come. The other man groaned at his back like an animal. The floor creaked louder, and Guerot cried out even before he'd done the job. The second scream was earsplitting and ended in a vile gurgling noise. The hands under the belt released their prey and slid to the floor with the rest of the body. Luc felt a splash of warm liquid.

He turned around and saw a half-naked Victoire holding a bloody ax high over Guerot's back, which had been cleaved in two. With dripping-wet hair, she was staring at the rent blazer gushing blood.

Their eyes met and then slowly, cautiously, Victoire moved in closer to the corpse.

"The handcuff keys are in the right pocket of his trousers."

Victoire bent over the body and pulled out the keys. After that they linked hands and fled the black lands of madness. Outside, the storm doubled in violence.

HAFFNER BJERG, 10:30 P.M.

John emerged from his sleep, shivering with cold. The phone call he'd made to Victoire had acted like a tranquilizer and had thrown him into a heavy sleep. He raised his head toward the noise and raced over the rocks, barefoot, trying not to break a leg. The enormous Sikorski in North Land colors was describing a huge circle.

At the foot of Haffner Bjerg, plains were reappearing in broad daylight after thousands of years of obscurity. Enormous chunks of ice, as big as cities, were carving up new spaces. Here and there, steam rose into a brand-new sky. The machine completed its loop and got into position fifty yards from where he was standing.

John waited in the icy wind for the machine to touch down and took a few steps in its direction, wondering who would emerge from the cabin. Victoire's reassuring words were not enough to extinguish his mistrust. The Far North had taught him to expect nasty surprises.

The door opened, and he saw the red anorak of Connie Rasmussen, who leaped to the ground and ran toward him before throwing herself into his arms.

"I'm alive."

"So I see."

Two bearded men, their hair flying in the wind of the rotor blades, came toward him, carefully navigating the rocks.

Connie Rasmussen did the introductions. "Messieurs, you have before you John Spencer Larivière, who did what he came to do and went as far as he could possibly go."

The two men bowed their heads as a sign of respect. John realized that these two had also overstepped the limits of everyday life.

"John, let me introduce you to Captain Loïc Le Guévenec, captain of the *Bouc-Bel-Air*, who just saved my life, and Nicolas Lanier, the head of Terre Noire."

The three men shook hands and, after all they'd been through, found they were at a loss for words.

"I've heard a lot about you."

"Same here," said Lanier and Le Guévenec.

"I'm sorry about your wife," John said, looking at the captain.

Le Guévenec looked down.

"And about your father," John said to Lanier. "I didn't get there in time."

"You couldn't have. I was the one targeted. I wanted to show Abraham the scientific data we'd gathered. When the Lauge Koch Kyst collapsed, I left him on his own to rejoin the *Bouc-Bel-Air* and its captain. I quickly realized they'd killed him, thinking they'd gotten me."

John was musing as he watched the shattered horizon that surrounded them.

"It seems it was your father who insisted on giving me this mission. Why me?" he asked Lanier, dreading the answer.

"Actually, it was Hubert de Méricourt, your old boss, who suggested you. I talked to Abraham about it. Méricourt didn't trust his own people. He knew he was harboring a traitor and didn't want to take the risk of intervening directly. We needed a developer. A bit like in chemistry. Someone who could reveal the enemy and go after him."

"A tupilaq, in a way."

"Yes."

"And Guerot?"

"He'd used Maunay to recruit a dodgy boatswain and smuggle drugs and alcohol onto the *Bouc-Bel-Air*. I'll show you a black box that contains pure cocaine. It comes from evidence storage at the county courthouse in Paris—Guerot knew the clerk."

As he walked toward the helicopter with the two men and Connie Rasmussen, John thought of Victoire and Luc. Over time, all this would become a memory. But how much time did they have left? High above their heads, a weird sun shone over day one of the Anthropocene Age.

CANADIAN EMBASSY, AVENUE MONTAIGNE, SIX MONTHS LATER

"Loïc Le Guévenec, by virtue of the powers invested in me, I hereby name you *chevalier* in the National Order of the Legion of Honor."

Thunderous applause followed Nicolas Lanier's words. Standing in the first row in a scarlet-red dress, Connie Rasmussen wiped away a tear. John and Victoire linked hands. Afterward, they joined Geraldine Harper over *petits-fours*. The buffet lunch put on by Terre Humaine, a company born of the merger of North Land and Terre Noire, was sumptuous and totally vegetarian. John could live with that.

Mary Harper, wearing the black and white colors of the new company, stood alongside Geraldine, who noticed Victoire's round stomach under her blue dress.

"When's the baby due?"

"Three months."

"Congratulations."

Lanier walked up to John and Victoire.

"I heard there were three of you."

"The third one's over there," John said, glancing at Luc, who stood a head taller than the other guests gathered around the descendant of the Great Rasmussen.

Outside, a storm raged over the Avenue Montaigne. The rain had turned to hail, and the temperature had dropped to freezing in just half an hour. Luc took advantage of a break in the conversation to join Connie Rasmussen. He took her by the arm.

"Connie, darling, what would you say to a game of pool in this lousy weather? Afterward, I can show you what I'm writing about this whole incredible business. Lots of people e-mail me at future-probe. com to ask me about you. You've become a heroine."

"Tell your readers I can't accept your offer."

"Why not?"

"I'm going back to Le Havre tonight. The *Bouc-Bel-Air*'s finished being repaired, and its captain is taking me on a cruise."

"You're kidding!"

Thank you for reading *The Greenland Breach*.

We invite you to share your thoughts and reactions on
on you favorite social network and retail platforms.

We appreciate it.

About the Author

Bernard Besson, who was born in Lyon, France, in 1949, is a former top-level chief of staff of the French intelligence services, an eminent specialist in economic intelligence, and honorary general controller of the French National Police. He was involved in dismantling Soviet spy rings in France and Western Europe when the USSR fell and has real inside knowledge from his work auditing intelligence services and the police. He has also written a number of prize-winning thrillers, his first in 1998, and several works of nonfiction. He currently lives in the fourteenth arrondissement of Paris, right down the street from his heroes.

ABOUT THE TRANSLATOR

Julie Rose is a prize-winning, world-renowned translator of major French thinkers, known for, among other works, her acclaimed translation of Victor Hugo's *Les Misérables*, which was published by Random House in 2008. She has translated twenty-eight books, including many French classics, and writes on the side. She lives in her hometown of Sydney, Australia, with her husband, dog, and two cats.

ABOUT LE FRENCH BOOK

Le French Book is a New York–based publisher specialized in great reads from France. As founder Anne Trager says, "I couldn't stand it anymore. There are just too many good books not reaching a broader audience. There is a very vibrant, creative culture in France that we want to share with readers."

www.lefrenchbook.com